Date with Malice

a Chapman is the pseudonym of Julia Stagg, who has five novels, the Fogas Chronicles set in the French enees, published by Hodder. *Date with Malice* is the ond in the Dales Detective series, following *Date with th*.

Praise for Date with Death

'Great fun' – Carol Drinkwater

classic whodunit featuring two very likeable characters . A satisfying read riddled with dry Yorkshire humour (and dry stone walls)' – Cath Staincliffe

'An engaging twist on the lonely hearts killer motif . . . should leave readers eager for the sequel' – *Publishers Weekly*

engaging cast of characters and a cleverly clued puzzle ve Chapman's debut to the top of the English village murder list' – *Kirkus*

Also by Julia Chapman

Date with Death

Julia Chapman

DATE WITH MALICE

PAN BOOKS

First published 2017 by Pan Books
an imprint of Pan Macmillan
20 New Wharf Road, London N1 9RR
Associated companies throughout the world
www.panmacmillan.com

ISBN 978-1-5098-2385-7

1 3 5 7 9 8 6 4 2

Visit **www.panmacmillan.com** to read more about all our books
and to buy them. You will also find features, author interviews and
news of any author events, and you can sign up for e-newsletters
so that you're always first to hear about our new releases.

In memory of Sandie George

A lady who loved books.

(I think you would have loved Bruncliffe, too, Sandie!)

1

'She's trying to kill me!'

Samson O'Brien resisted the urge to let his head drop into his hands in despair. Knuckles white with the effort, he tightened his grip on his biro and smiled at the elderly lady sitting opposite him.

'Mrs Shepherd . . .' he began, 'I really don't think—'

'She is. I know she is,' the old lady interrupted him. 'I saw her, you see. And now she wants me gone.'

He tried again. 'Mrs Shepherd, you can't just accuse someone like that without—'

'Proof!' Two frail hands flapped away his protestations. 'It's up to *you* to get the proof. That's why I want to hire you, young man.' She smiled, a gentle face under curly white hair, eyes faded behind her glasses, and leaned towards him. 'You come highly recommended. I heard all about the incident up at High Laithe. Such a dreadful thing. All those dead people. And the fire. Poor Lucy. Suffering all that after what she's been through. Oh, and I heard about you in your boxer shorts, too . . .' A dreamy look drifted across her features, her smile becoming even wider, and Samson felt his cheeks beginning to burn.

He doubted the day could get any worse.

*

What a morning. Could it be any better? Delilah Metcalfe reached the top of the fell, her breath coming in short gasps that punctuated the December air. Lungs burning, she paused, bent at the waist, hands on thighs as she drank in the view before her.

Malham Tarn sparkling blue as the sun crept above the horizon, the dark mass of Darnbrook Fell rising from the red-tinged moor in the distance and, arching over it all, a sharp sky that warned of colder weather to come.

A heavy warmth came to rest against her left leg.

'How you doing, old boy?' She reached down and patted the familiar grey head of her Weimaraner. 'Not too much for you?'

Tolpuddle leaned into her, panting slightly. He'd run well. Considering.

Considering that he'd been stabbed only a month ago.

She tried not to think about it. About the fire at her sister-in-law Lucy's caravan, the mad chase after a killer, the poor people who'd been murdered. Taking a deep breath, she focused once more on the tarn. It was over. And Tolpuddle was back running with her.

'We'll take it easy going home, eh?'

The dog regarded her solemnly, amber eyes bright, no signs of distress. Herriot, the vet, had pronounced him fit enough to accompany her once more, even though she'd not been sure. Not that she hadn't wanted Tolpuddle back out on the fells. It had been torture going off every morning without her companion, no large shadow stretching out in front of her and pulling her on.

Equally torturous had been returning from a run alone to her cottage at the top of the hill in Bruncliffe, her dog waiting anxiously inside. Usually with some cushion or shoe, or something she'd unwittingly left within paw-reach, torn to shreds beside him.

Separation anxiety. She had a Weimaraner riven with separation anxiety. As well as two businesses in debt, a bank manager on her back, an ex-husband, and a trouble-making tenant who shared her office building – all at the tender age of twenty-nine.

After the last month, none of that seemed to matter any more. She was simply glad that she and Tolpuddle were still alive.

'Come on then.' Delilah turned her back on the view with the confidence of a local, knowing it would be there, albeit different, when she ran the next day. And the day after that. And the day after that. As a native of the Yorkshire Dales, she felt part of this landscape, her family history sewn into the fabric of the hills and dales that surrounded her. She pitied any person who wasn't part of it too.

'Last one down buys breakfast,' she shouted, starting to run.

The dog barked and fell into place alongside her. It wasn't long before his loping stride was outpacing hers, pulling her faster and faster down the hillside towards home.

'. . . Little things – things no one would notice – they're going missing. My watch. Arty's cufflinks. Clarissa's head-scarf . . . Little things. But I notice. I see her. Prowling the corridors late at night—'

'Did you report your watch missing, Mrs Shepherd?' Samson asked, trying to rein in the woman's wandering flow of conversation.

'Why, no.' She gave him a fierce look. 'Why would I report it? It wasn't my watch that went missing.' She pulled back the sleeve of her coat to reveal a delicate gold timepiece on her frail wrist. 'It was Edith's.'

'But you just said . . .' Samson felt his spirit draining from him. Thirty minutes Mrs Shepherd had been in the office. He'd popped out to get milk for his breakfast and she'd been waiting on the doorstep when he returned at barely eight o'clock. It had been half an hour of his life that had sapped him of years to come.

Turning his focus to the window and the large initials D D A spanning the glass, he found himself praying that someone would barge in, asking him to fix their love life. It had happened a couple of times in the last few weeks, unsuspecting lonely hearts mistaking the newly formed Dales Detective Agency for the Dales Dating Agency – an easy misunderstanding when the two businesses were located in the same building and shared the same initials. But while it had irritated him before, right now it would be a welcome diversion from the befuddled waffling of the old lady opposite.

'Mrs Shepherd,' he said, deciding it was time to get firm. 'I'm confused as to why you are here—'

'Confused?' She laughed, a tinkle of sound, her eyes sparkling. 'That's what they all tell me. I'm confused. But I'm not. I know what I saw. And I know what she's up to. She's trying to kill me.'

Bruncliffe. A huddle of houses down below, the town fitted perfectly into the curve of the landscape, a limestone crag towering over the back of it, fells rising on three sides.

Standing guard to the north and the south were twin mill chimneys, both now defunct, and cutting through the middle were the direct line of the railway and the meandering path of the river.

It was home, that collection of slate roofs and stone buildings. The only place Delilah Metcalfe had ever lived. On a day like today when the sun was shining, that wasn't something she was in a hurry to change.

Taking the steps two at a time, she jogged down from Bruncliffe Crag onto Crag Lane, high above the back of the town. Tolpuddle was already heading off to the right towards the small cottage where they lived. But Delilah was looking at her watch.

It was gone eight-thirty. She might as well go straight to work and change there. Especially now it was no longer a secret that she was running again. Since the events the month before, the whole place knew that Bruncliffe's former champion fell-runner – the woman who'd turned her back on the sport years ago – was back in training. How could they not? She'd chased a killer across the hills. Something like that wasn't going to stay quiet for long.

'This way,' she called, beckoning the dog. 'Come on.'

Tolpuddle's ears picked up at the change in direction, he tilted his head sideways and started trotting, making for the steps that would take them down to the town. Like every morning for the past month and a half, he was eager to get to the office. To get to *him*.

She sighed. Was it worse to have an anxious dog or one that was besotted with the local black sheep? A black sheep with a mane of dark hair and a wicked smile . . . and the ability to turn an entire community upside down within a matter of hours on his return from a fourteen-year exile.

She jogged after her faithless hound. Tolpuddle wasn't the only one finding being at work a lot more appealing of late.

'So, will you do it?'

'Find out who's trying to kill you?' Samson asked, incredulous at the words coming out of his own mouth.

'No. You're not listening,' said Mrs Shepherd, her small fist thumping the desk. 'I told you. I know who's trying to kill me. I need you to catch her. Preferably before she succeeds.'

'But I—'

'And don't worry,' she continued, cutting across his excuses. 'I'll pay.' She delved into her bag, placing a compact mirror on the table along with a lipstick, a crumpled tissue, a half-eaten roll of Polo mints and an unusual pillbox with a rainbow of inlaid semi-precious stones across the lid. 'Here! How much will it be?' She held up a small black purse and opened the clasps, smiling at him expectantly as she shook coins out into her hand.

'I don't think—'

The door crashed open and a large figure loomed in the doorway. 'Ralph!' boomed a voice. 'He's gone missing!'

Outside the office window, down the narrow confines of Back Street, across the cobbled marketplace where the butcher was just raising the shop blinds and a young woman was opening the estate agent's, past Peaks Patisserie, which was already busy serving early morning coffees, turning right up Fell Lane with the police station on the corner and the library opposite, up the hill and through the entrance of Fellside Court retirement complex, up on the first floor in a small apartment overlooking the court-yard at the back, a hand was opening a bedroom door.

The shadow that fell across the thick pile of the carpet crossed to the bedside table, where the same hand placed a rainbow-coloured pillbox next to a photograph. With silent steps, the shadow shifted once more and the room was vacated, the door left open.

2

'I'm sorry,' Samson said, addressing the man who'd barged into the office, 'but we're in the middle of a meeting. I'm going to have to ask you to wait outside.'

Clearly, the man was stone-deaf, as he continued to enter the room regardless, tipping his cap briefly at Mrs Shepherd before perching his bulky frame on the edge of the chair next to the old lady. Samson caught the familiar perfume of farmyard.

Clive Knowles, from Mire End Farm up the dale towards Horton, a place notorious under the management of old Ralph Knowles for the ramshackle state of the yard and the neglect of the fields. Samson remembered his mother making his father laugh years ago when she'd pointed out that the Knowles' farm should be renamed Mire Start, given the state it was kept in.

Judging by the stale smell of beer and body odour issuing from across the desk, in the time Samson had been away from Bruncliffe the current generation hadn't had a sudden conversion to cleanliness – personal or otherwise.

'This can't wait,' the farmer said forcefully, pointing a thick, dirt-smeared finger in Samson's direction. 'Ralph's gone missing and I need you to find him.'

'As I've already explained, Mr Knowles—'

'It's okay, Samson dear,' said Alice Shepherd. 'I'm not

in a hurry to go home.' She smiled at the farmer, tiny beside his bulging jacket, and encouraged him to continue. 'Now, when did you last see Ralph, Mr Knowles?'

The farmer turned to the old lady. 'Yesterday evening. I checked he was all right before going to bed. He's been a bit under the weather, you know, a bit out of sorts.'

'And this morning?' she enquired.

'He wasn't there at breakfast.'

She tutted, shaking her head, a finger on her chin as though pondering this mystery.

'He won't cope out there on his own,' continued the farmer, a crease of concern across his florid forehead.

'Don't worry, dear.' Alice Shepherd patted his knee, releasing another waft of animal aroma. 'Samson will make us both a cup of tea and then we can get to the bottom of this.' She turned her pale blue eyes on the man behind the desk and smiled sweetly.

Samson was halfway up the stairs to the kitchen on the first floor before he realised the absurdity of the situation. It was so typical of Bruncliffe. Everyone involved in everyone else's business. And now he had a confused pensioner doing his job for him. He groaned. This was precisely the reason why he'd left his home town in the first place. The claustrophobia. The lack of privacy. The tea that could kill an ox.

He filled the kettle, throwing four teabags into the pot, and consoled himself that in April he would be moving on, hopefully returning to London and the police work he was currently suspended from. There'd be no more old ladies making wild accusations. No more smelly farmers. No more Bruncliffe, and no more being the black sheep.

The back door banged and a familiar voice called out, accompanied by a sharp bark. No more Delilah Metcalfe, either.

The intervening months couldn't go quickly enough.

'You don't know where he is?'

'No. I told you already.'

'That's why he needs Samson.'

'I don't need Samson. I need bloody Ralph back where he belongs. Time's running out—'

'Have you told the police?'

'Lot of good that'll do—'

'Oh, a cup of tea. Just what we need. Samson, you are a dear.'

Samson stood in the doorway of his own office, tray in hands, feeling like a tea boy intruding on the three-way conversation. Alice Shepherd and Clive Knowles were sitting in front of his desk; Delilah Metcalfe, in her running kit, was sitting behind it, notepad on her lap as she cross-examined his potential clients.

'Tea! Thanks, Samson,' said his landlady, reaching to take the third, and last, mug. 'Didn't you want one?'

He sighed, placed the empty tray on the floor and perched on the edge of his desk, Tolpuddle's head immediately coming to rest on his thigh. As an undercover police officer working within the country's premier law-enforcement agencies – the Serious Organised Crime Agency and its replacement, the National Crime Agency – Samson O'Brien had had his fair share of bizarre working environments. But nothing had prepared him for working life in Bruncliffe, where everyone had an opinion.

And, being Dalesmen and women, they felt the right to express those opinions forcefully. And often. The Metcalfes – Delilah and her five older brothers – were fine examples of this cultural trait, as Samson knew better than most.

He ran a hand over his chin, which had been on the receiving end of Delilah's infamous right hook the day he returned to town. The reasons hadn't been clear. Her frustration at the fact that Samson, the idol of her childhood, had left Bruncliffe in a moonlight flit and hadn't been heard of in the intervening fourteen years. Her anger at Samson's absence from the funeral of his best friend, her beloved brother Ryan, who'd been buried two years ago. But also her realisation that if she hadn't hit the returned black sheep, her oldest brother Will would have. And that, thought Samson wryly, would have been far more catastrophic. Although his reputation wouldn't have suffered quite so much. Being laid out cold by a woman, no matter how pretty she was, wasn't the beginning he'd envisioned for his new detective agency.

'So where were we . . . ?' Delilah's attention was back on the farmer. 'No police.'

'Why not?' asked Samson. 'Surely, in a case like this, you need to notify them as soon as possible? You don't want Ralph wandering around in this cold.'

'He's got a good coat, so the cold won't bother him,' muttered Mr Knowles. 'I'm more worried about him being run over.'

'Has he done this before? Wandered off?'

Mr Knowles nodded. 'Every chance he gets. We've got to keep an eye on him. Normally I'd know where to start looking. But this time . . .' He shrugged, the air seeming to thicken around him at the odour released from the creases of his clothes.

Samson looked out of the window. Despite having lived away from the Dales for more than a decade, he wasn't some tourist to be fooled by the blue skies above. It was almost freezing out there, and the clouds he'd seen gathering over the west side of town when he'd gone for milk had the ominous presence of snow in them.

An elderly person wouldn't last long out in this, good coat or not. And Ralph Knowles must be well into his eighties by now. Suffering from dementia too, given the way his son was talking about him.

'You need to call the police,' Samson insisted.

Mr Knowles shrugged. 'He's done this before. They won't want to know about it.'

'Don't be ridiculous!' Samson stood, shocked at the nonchalance of the reply. 'Of course they will. I'll call Danny at the station.' Fingers already scrolling for the number on his mobile, he didn't notice Delilah's surprised expression. 'The sooner they get looking, the better. There's snow coming—' He paused as the youthful voice of PC Danny Bradley came on the line.

'Samson?'

'Hi, Danny. We need to mobilise a search party. Ralph Knowles is missing. Last seen . . .' He glanced at the farmer.

'At Mire End Farm yesterday evening,' muttered Mr Knowles.

'Ralph Knowles?' asked the young constable as Samson passed on the information. 'Is that Clive Knowles' Ralph?'

'Yes.' Samson couldn't help but hear the weary sigh emitted at the other end of the phone.

'I'm not sure Sarge will agree to sending out men again.'

'Make him agree! We need to get people out looking. Ralph won't survive the weather that's coming, at his age.'

'Perhaps,' said Delilah, lips twitching, 'it would help if you had a description of Ralph when he disappeared?'

Samson nodded. 'Mr Knowles? Can you give a description?'

'A description?' The farmer scratched his head. 'Short. Stocky. But not fat, mind.'

Samson relayed the answers to the policeman before turning back to the farmer. 'What was Ralph wearing?'

The question was met with a frown from Clive Knowles and what sounded like a hiccup from Delilah, her hand flying to her mouth.

'Wearing?' asked the farmer, glaring out from under his cap.

'Yes. What did he look like?'

'The usual.'

'Which is?' Samson bit back his exasperation.

'White body, black face, white rings round his eyes. And,' he turned to the old lady next to him, 'excuse me, Mrs Shepherd, for saying so, but he's well hung.'

'Sorry?' Samson's eyebrows shot into his hairline. 'What did you say?'

The farmer shrugged. 'He's well hung. That's the most important bit about him. How else do you expect him to service all those yows?'

The laughter coming from the other end of the line was

audible not just to Samson, and he saw Delilah's lips curving into the smile she'd been suppressing.

'What?' asked Mr Knowles, indignant at the humour in the face of his predicament. 'What's so funny?'

'Ralph . . . I thought . . .' Samson stuttered, reassessing the entire conversation. 'Isn't Ralph your father?'

'*Father*? What the heck would I be talking about Father for? He died some ten years back. No, lad, this is far more important. Ralph's a Swaledale prize-winner. Paid seven grand for him, so I bloody need him found!'

'Ralph's a sheep?' Samson asked, as his image of a disorientated old man wandering the hills was shattered by laughter from Delilah, Mrs Shepherd and, with the strangled sounds coming down the line, Daniel and half the police station. 'A bloody *sheep*?'

Mr Knowles shot to his feet. 'A prize tup is what he is, missing right in the middle of mating season. And I want you to find him!'

Samson sank back onto the desk. Whatever he'd imagined when he'd decided to come home, it wasn't this.

'How was I to know it was a bloody tup he was talking about?' grumbled Samson as he carried the tray of empty mugs up to the first-floor kitchen, his prospective clients having finally left the building.

From the landing above, Delilah laughed. 'Everyone in Bruncliffe knows Ralph. Certainly most of the women, anyway, as he's all Clive Knowles talks about when he comes to the speed-dating events.'

Samson shuddered. He'd had first-hand experience of one of the Dales Dating Agency's speed-dating evenings, one of the businesses that Delilah ran from her upstairs office. While he hadn't been as scarred by the episode as he'd expected, it wasn't something he was in a hurry to repeat. And he pitied any woman who'd had to endure four minutes of Clive Knowles leaning across a table with his bad breath and farmyard aroma.

'Still,' continued Delilah, 'it's a job. He's hired you.'

Samson nodded wearily. It was a job and he badly needed the income. But looking for a missing ram in a landscape littered with sheep was a long way from the excitement of his former life. Suddenly he had a pang of nostalgia for London, with its anonymity and its vibrancy. As well as the danger.

'And what about Alice Shepherd? Are you going to follow up on what she said?'

'Are you serious?' Samson paused on the top step, eyebrow raised. 'She's clearly muddled. She couldn't even get her accusations straight, telling me one moment that her watch had been stolen and then that it hadn't.' He shook his head. 'I couldn't take money from her. It would be wrong.'

'Perhaps. But it wouldn't hurt for you to go up to Fellside Court and have a look around, would it?'

He glanced over at Delilah, her face the picture of innocence. 'And visit my father while I'm there?'

She shrugged. 'Why not? Kill two birds with one stone – if that's not too inappropriate, given Mrs Shepherd's fears. When did you last see him, anyway?'

'What's it to you?' he asked, the words sharper than he'd intended.

His relationship with his father was a sore point. It was

also a topic Bruncliffe could never get enough of. The O'Briens, father and son, left widowed and without a mother when Samson was only eight, the idyllic life they'd known on Twistleton Farm at the far end of isolated Thorpdale wiped out in the space of a couple of months. Then the drinking had started. By the time Samson was in his teens, he was skipping school to tend to the sheep and to his father, dragging him from the pub where every penny the farm brought in was spent on beer. Or whisky. Or anything Joseph O'Brien could get down his throat that would put him into an alcoholic stupor.

Growing up as Boozy O'Brien's son had marked Samson out as different; quick to defend his family name with fists if need be, he'd been a cynical child and a belligerent teenager, wary of everyone. Having an Irish father and a mother from a distant dale was a further stigma in a town filled with people who could count back generations within a radius of five miles. No wonder then that this lad, although born in the district, was forever branded an offcumden: a stranger, not of these parts. No surprise, either, that he was viewed as trouble.

That Samson had left the town in a blaze of disgrace when he was twenty only added to the saga of the O'Briens, latterly of Thorpdale, now of no fixed abode. It had been the year of foot-and-mouth, the area already stressed by the outbreak that was tearing farms apart and destroying livelihoods that had existed for centuries. In the midst of all that tension, Samson had snapped, and at the christening of Delilah's nephew Nathan, he'd got into a fight. With his father. As far as the local grapevine was concerned, by attacking his father and then tearing off into the night on a stolen motorbike, the young O'Brien had merely lived up to the reputation he'd been building for years.

But then the good people of Bruncliffe didn't know about the shotgun that had been pointing at him when he'd returned home that evening. Or about the argument that had caused father and son to fight in the first place. Samson wasn't about to enlighten them now.

Nor, after a mere seven weeks, was he about to place his trust in a man who'd done so little to earn it in the past. Even if his father did claim to be sober.

'Sorry,' he muttered, brushing past Delilah to reach the kitchen. 'Touchy subject.'

'So I gather,' she said. 'But Alice Shepherd was obviously worried enough to come down and see you. She even tried to hire you. The least you could do is call in and help put her mind at rest.'

Samson didn't reply. He knew she was right. He just didn't want to admit it.

'Well, if you change your mind, I've got at an appointment at Fellside Court tomorrow morning—'

'For the Dales Dating Agency?' Samson was grinning now. 'Are things getting that desperate?'

The punch came out of nowhere. A straight-arm jab into his right shoulder that almost made him drop the tray, his arm numb in its wake.

'That's for being so disrespectful! To me and to the pensioners of this town. They have a right to a love life too.'

'I'll take your word for it,' said Samson with another grin, making sure he stepped back beyond her reach.

'What are you organising? A not-so-speedy speed-dating session?'

She laughed. 'No. It's nothing to do with the dating agency. I'm in charge of the website and it needs a bit of upgrading, so I'm meeting the new manager to discuss some changes and to get her photo. She's been hard to pin down but I've finally got a meeting with her. And talking of websites . . .' She looked at him expectantly.

Delilah Metcalfe. He still couldn't get his head around the idea that the scrawny kid who'd followed him and Ryan everywhere had evolved into this multi-talented woman. Not only did she run a dating agency which seemed to be going from strength to strength – despite a rocky patch the last few months, thanks to a deranged killer – but she also operated a tech company, designing and maintaining websites. From what he'd heard, she was good at it too.

'Are you going to take me up on my offer?' she asked.

He turned away and busied himself with loading the mugs in the dishwasher. As he'd refused payment for his time helping her uncover the identity of the person murdering her clients, Delilah had volunteered to build him a website for his new business, the Dales Detective Agency. She was keen. Kept running ideas past him. And she couldn't understand why he kept stalling.

How to explain? That there was trouble coming in the next few months. Trouble from his past life in London which would mean his time in Bruncliffe would be over. Trouble that might see him spending time in jail.

'I'll think about it,' he muttered. Feeling the need for fresh air, he headed back down the stairs, grabbed his jacket and helmet and left through the rear porch, cursing as, not for the first time, he tripped over the trainers and hiking boots that were strewn across the floor. His father's scarlet-and-chrome Royal Enfield Bullet was waiting in the yard. It was the same one Samson had fled the town on fourteen years before. He was pretty confident he'd be fleeing on it again before long.

Alice Shepherd was afraid. She'd done her best to put on a brave face at young O'Brien's. Such a strong lad and just like his mother, with those sharp blue eyes and masses of dark hair. But would he be willing to help her? He'd said he'd let her know, but she'd sensed hesitation in him.

It was the confusion. She knew she'd made a mistake somewhere. Something she'd said to him had left that familiar look on his face. The sideways glance people gave her now, as though weighing up the merit of her words. As though she couldn't be trusted with the truth.

But she knew what she'd seen. That flash of blonde hair passing under the light in the corridor during the depths of night. There was no mistaking that. It hadn't been just the once, either. Trouble was, she couldn't remember exactly when it had happened. Had it really been the same days as the small disappearances – the cufflinks, the scarf, her watch? Even she didn't trust herself any more.

She walked slowly towards Fellside Court, the front of the two-storey building set at an angle from the road. Behind it, two wings protruded, forming a U-shaped cluster of flats. Or 'apartments designed to promote independence', as the developers preferred to call them.

They weren't supposed to promote fear.

Heartrate picking up, she passed the double doors of

the main entrance, choosing instead to walk down the side and around the back to enter through the courtyard. Enclosed on three sides by the building, with a scattering of benches, chairs and tables and a couple of young cherry trees, the space was a sheltered oasis for the residents. On a morning like today, it was a suntrap and one of the things that had attracted her to the complex.

That and the glass wall.

It towered above her, linking the two wings of the building in a sheet of brilliance, the blue skies and the fells reflecting back off it, making the views seem endless. Stretching from the ground all the way up to the roof, the seamless window allowed light to flood in along the corridors, turning even the dullest day a little brighter.

All that glass. Letting the sunshine in. Letting the secrets out.

A sharp rapping noise to her left pulled her attention to the residents' lounge, which ran the length of the ground floor on that side: more long windows looking out across the courtyard. It was already busy, people stretching and flexing ready for the morning aerobics class. Arty Robinson was inside, tapping his watch and beckoning her in.

Arty. Lovely Arty. A retired bookmaker, he still lived life as if it was one long gamble with the odds in his favour. She let her gaze drift up to the right to Arty's flat, tucked into the corner of the glass wall, his balcony protruding, the tips of his precious rose bush peeking over the edge. Did he see things, too? His apartment was directly opposite hers, one of six that overlooked the space below. Eric Bradley was next door to her, in a large two-bedroomed place; across the courtyard and next to Arty was a guest suite for overnight visitors; Rita Wilson was in the ground-floor flat below that; and next to her was the second of the guest apartments. Without the views of Bruncliffe the front of the building offered or the dramatic vistas of the fells the outer flats had, the two inner-courtyard apartments that Alice and Arty occupied had been a lot more affordable. Which had been the reason she'd chosen the one she had, above the residents' lounge. She suspected it was the same for Arty, the pair of them cloistered here because of finances.

Until recently it hadn't bothered her. She'd liked living in her small home above the courtyard, socialising with the other residents who'd become friends. And if she angled her chair just so in her lounge, she had a view up onto the fell that rose behind as good as that from Eric's.

But in retrospect, perhaps it had been unwise. She could see too much, right across to the other apartments and through the glass on the corridor that joined them.

That was the problem. That glass. And the flash of blonde hair at night.

Another rap on the window made her start. Arty, mouthing at her to hurry up. She entered the building, turned left along the corridor and headed for the lounge where Vicky Hudson, the care assistant, was already introducing the fitness session.

'Now, no overdoing it,' Vicky was warning with a smile, the ends of her dark bob catching the dimples in her cheeks. 'And if you don't feel up to a particular exercise, just sit and relax until the next one. So, if you're ready, let's begin with a gentle warm-up . . .'

Alice slipped through the throng at the back of the room to where Arty was waiting for her.

'You took your time!' he whispered. 'Here, stick your bag on that chair or they'll all be taken, and then nip up and change.'

'Thanks, Arty,' she said, passing him the bag, her room keys in her hand. 'I'll be down in a minute.'

She was smiling as she left, thinking about the word 'nip'. She wasn't sure she'd nipped anywhere in the last five years, a hip replacement having seen to that. But she was still able to use the stairs. She climbed them steadily, reaching the first floor slightly out of breath. Pausing at the top to calm her pulse, mindful of all that the doctor had said, she turned right down the corridor and entered her flat. The first thing she saw was the view of the courtyard and the slice of fellside behind the building opposite. The second thing she saw was the open bedroom door.

Had she left it like that? She tried to recollect her movements but a familiar haze of confusion veiled her mind, punctured by sharp slices of her youth. Herself on a bike out past Horton. The feel of her grandfather's hand holding hers. Memories from more than seventy years ago as clear as the present, yet the events of this morning remained shrouded in a deep fog.

Telling herself it didn't matter, she crossed the thick carpet to the wardrobe. Then she saw the stripes of colour on the bedside table. Her pillbox. How had that got there? Hadn't she put it in her handbag this morning, after she'd taken her medicine?

She couldn't remember. The irrefutable presence of it, here and now, seemed to taunt her failing wits.

Hand shaking, she picked it up, staring at the piece of yellow tiger's eye that designated Wednesday. She lifted the lid. Two tablets stared back at her from a space that should have been empty. A space she'd been sure she'd left empty this morning.

3

'That's where he was. Where he should be. But he's not. And I need him back, servicing this lot.' Clive Knowles flicked a grimy hand at the field filled with ewes, their white bodies merging with the limestone rocks scattered across the scraggy grass.

It was poor land, dropping down to the river on one side, rushes and tussocks in abundance. Samson could see how Mire End Farm had got its name. Even allowing for the winter weather, it was wet underfoot. Behind him, across the rough track that served the property, the fields climbed steeply, the unmistakable flat top of Pen-y-ghent rising above them. Not much better grazing up there, either. As for the farm itself . . .

About eight miles north of Bruncliffe, out past Horton off a narrow lane that twisted and bumped along the side of Pen-y-ghent, the Knowles' farm was a collection of buildings in various states of disrepair. Two barns stood sentry at the entrance, the roofs pockmarked with slipped slates, the doors rotten, the paint long since flaked off. At an angle to them was the farmhouse. Or what was left of it.

Once it had been an imposing home with three windows spanning the front, but neglect had taken its toll, allowing the elements to attack. The wind had been first, flipping up a loose slate or two or three, until the roof was pierced and the rain that battered the Dales in the winter months gained access. Seeping down through the rafters, the damp had got into the walls and eroded the mortar, loosening the stones and causing a large section to fall away below the level of the gutter, exposing the block-work of the inner wall. With some of its support removed, the top left window now slumped perilously in its frame, in danger of falling out. It wouldn't be long before the rest of the wall followed it.

Samson had deliberately parked his Royal Enfield at the opposite corner of the yard, the scarlet-and-chrome motorbike bright against the gloom cast by the barns. He'd found Clive Knowles round the back of the house in amongst a tangle of old cars, rusting machinery, a pile of discarded tyres and an abandoned trailer from an articulated lorry that was being used as a makeshift chicken coop. Hens picked futilely at the muddied yard and an ageing sheepdog lying on a bale of hay lifted his head to give a half-hearted bark at Samson's approach. The farmer had held out a grease-covered hand in greeting, and together they'd walked down to the site of Ralph's disappearance.

'I can't afford to lose him,' muttered the farmer, leaning on a rickety gate which was listing under his weight. 'I can't afford another bad year.'

Neither could the farm, thought Samson. Poor land or poor management? Surveying the fields, it was hard to tell which had caused the rundown condition of Mire End. And Samson O'Brien knew only too well how closely the two could be connected. There had been days working on

Twistleton Farm when he'd cursed his parents for buying it. Nestled between two streams at the head of Thorpdale, the O'Brien property had had its fair share of soggy land and the problems that brought with it. Not to mention an alcoholic owner drinking all the profits. But it was a pleasure to manage, compared to this. Or it had been.

'How long have you had Ralph?' he asked.

'Bought him at the end of October last year. More than I've ever paid for a tup.'

'He's a Swaledale?'

Clive Knowles nodded. 'Pure-bred. Worth a lot.'

Samson didn't doubt it. The hardy breed, with their distinctive black-and-white faces, had grown popular, known for an ability to withstand harsh winters on exposed land. He could remember auctions at Hawes where the top rams had fetched thirty grand or more.

'You said he's escaped before?'

'Several times, the bugger.' The farmer pointed at the far side of the field where an upsurge of rock beneath the soil raised the level of the ground. 'He gets up on top of that and leaps the wall. I put a length of barbed wire across the top of the stones, and that stopped him. But not this time, clearly.'

'He burst through the wire?'

'No. It's still there. He must have jumped over it.'

'That's pretty impressive,' said Samson, assessing the height of the distant wall. 'You don't think someone might have taken him?'

The farmer shrugged. 'That'd be a first. Someone bothering to come to Mire End to steal. Not much round here worth taking.'

Samson didn't contradict him. Even with the upsurge in sheep-rustling across the Dales, it would take some finding to arrive at Mire End Farm. And a lot of optimism, once arriving there, to think there was anything of value on it.

'Well, are you going to have a look around or what?' A glare accompanied the words. 'Like I said, I need him back. The farm's depending on it.'

'I can't promise anything,' said Samson, opening the gate and entering the field, the sheep looking up before resuming their relentless grazing.

'That's all right. I don't set much store by promises,' the farmer muttered. 'Been stung by them before. Make sure you take your time, mind. You might catch something I missed.'

With that, Clive Knowles wandered back towards the crumbling farmhouse, leaving Samson in a field full of sheep. Bizarrely, the former policeman turned private detective felt completely at home.

Trying to ignore the surge of nostalgia for his farming youth, he started walking towards the far gate which gave out onto the lane that led back to civilisation. He had no particular purpose in mind, no belief that he would find anything concrete to help restore the missing Ralph to Mire End. But he had to start somewhere. And there was something about the gate that intrigued him. He was almost at it when he realised.

The tracks. Twin tyre marks coming inside the field a short distance, as though something had been unloaded.

Nothing unusual about tracks on a farm, though. So what else was it?

He stared at the gate. It was a typical Mire End design; a rusting metal contraption that was tethered to a post with barbed wire at one end. At the other, a padlocked length of chain wrapped around another post held it upright.

It wasn't used much. If ever. With the land inside the gate a sodden morass of churned-up mud, it would make driving difficult, if not impossible. But someone had braved it. And recently, too, as the tracks hadn't dried out.

Soil oozing around his boots, Samson stepped forward and inspected the chain looped around the left post. Like everything else on the farm, it was corroding, the old padlock bleeding red water into his hand as he caught hold of it. He ran a thumb across the keyhole cover. It was stuck, seized up with years of rain and rust. There was no way this had been opened in the last few days.

He let the chain drop back into place and to his surprise, it fell against the post and then slithered to the ground, the gate yawning open at the top in response.

'What the hell?' Shining up at him, silver against the black mud, was a severed link. The chain had been cut.

Someone had been in the field. Probably without authorisation.

Intrigued, Samson pulled the gate towards him and it immediately sagged, dragging across the wet ground before sticking fast. He squeezed through the narrow opening onto the verge that ran beside the lane, brown strands of dead or dying grass brushing against his trousers.

Which way? Right, back into Horton and civilisation? Or left into the fells? Right made more sense. He was only a few steps along the road in that direction, scanning the bedraggled growth on either side of the tarmac, when his eye was caught by a glimpse of something red.

It was lying up against the stone wall, the brown leather making it difficult to spot amongst the winter vegetation. A contraption of straps and red crayon, he knew what it was straight away.

A tup harness, fastened onto the ram before releasing him into the field with the ewes. Thanks to the block of crayon that rested on the ram's chest, a farmer could tell which ewes had been serviced and, by changing the colour of the crayon periodically, when they were due to lamb.

It was standard kit for most farmers, although the one in Samson's hand had seen better days – the leather straps worn, the rivets tarnished and the pin that held the red crayon in place sheared off at one end, leaving a jagged edge.

He took out his phone. Something was amiss here. A record of the scene might be useful.

Stooping down, he photographed the spot where he'd found the harness. Then he returned to the gate to take pictures of the scored land and the field beyond. But as he twisted to get a shot of the broken chain, his boot brushed against something in the long grass at the foot of the gatepost. There was a rattle of metal on stone as whatever it was fell onto the tarmac. Samson turned, stared at the object now resting in the lane, then bent over to pick it up.

He weighed it in his palm, deep in thought. Then he retrieved the ram harness, closed the gate, and retraced his path across the field. He needed to talk to Clive Knowles. Urgently.

*

For the residents of Fellside Court, the post-aerobics coffee-and-cake session on Mondays and Wednesdays was one of the highlights of the week. Along with the communal Sunday lunch. And the occasional group jaunt down the hill to the chippy to take advantage of the early-bird special. So when Alice Shepherd entered the cosy cafe that took up a corner of the building, she wasn't surprised that it was already busy.

'Here, Alice!' The tall figure of Edith Hird, retired headmistress of Bruncliffe Primary School who still had a commanding presence and a tendency to organise, was waving her over to a crowded table by windows that looked out onto the road and the town below.

'Room for a little one,' quipped Arty as the petite figure of Alice made her way towards them.

'There'd be room for a few more if you weren't here,' retorted the frail man next to him, eliciting laughter from the group.

'Aye,' said Arty, patting his rotund belly ruefully. 'Fair to say I'm not as thin as I once was.'

'Apart from on your head!' This time Eric Bradley accompanied his comment with a laugh that was somewhere between a cough and a wheeze, rattling the oxygen cylinder next to his chair. From beneath his bald crown, the former bookmaker gave him a wounded look.

'I've already ordered your coffee,' said Edith as Alice sat down beside her. 'But I wasn't sure what cake you wanted.'

'I can recommend the scones.' Clarissa Ralph, sister of Edith, looked up from spooning strawberry jam onto the remaining half of her treat. 'They're fresh out of the oven.'

'I don't know how you two do it,' moaned Arty, gesturing at the plates before the sisters. 'You never seem to put on weight. I only have to look at that carrot cake and I'm two pounds heavier.'

'Good genes,' said Edith. 'Sister and I come from a long line of lean Hirds.'

Clarissa was nodding. 'It's true. Father was as thin as a rake. Whereas poor Mother . . .' She shook her head, musing on the lottery of nature as she bit into the scone.

'What about you, Joseph?' Arty turned to the man sitting contentedly at the end of the table, watching the banter with a smile on his gaunt face. Some ten years younger than most of the group, he looked older, more battered by life. 'Can your svelte shape be put down to genetics?'

Joseph O'Brien smiled. 'No,' he said, his soft lilt a contrast to the Yorkshire brusqueness of his friends. 'It's mostly due to excessive consumption of alcohol. Not a diet I would recommend.'

Arty's deep bellow of a laugh had the room looking round at him and, not for the first time, Joseph O'Brien – sober two years, eleven weeks and six days – gave silent thanks to the fates that had contrived to see him arrive at Fellside Court. The place and the people in it had saved his life.

'We'll take your word for it, Joseph. Think I'll stick with my curves. I know the ladies like a fuller figure.' Arty's wink was directed at fellow resident Geraldine Mortimer, who was passing the table.

'Arty Robinson, are you flirting again?' asked Geraldine, pausing to pat her sleek, platinum-blonde hair and give him a coquettish smile. 'You'll get me into trouble!'

'Chance would be a fine thing,' muttered Edith Hird, prodding her carrot cake with a fork.

'Alice!' A voice from the doorway took their attention to a young woman who had just entered the cafe. Blonde hair pulled back in a tight ponytail, Ana Stoyanova, manager of Fellside Court, surveyed the room from over high cheekbones, her skin alabaster-pale in the winter sunlight. She fixed a cool gaze on the group by the window as she made her way towards them.

Geraldine Mortimer grimaced. 'Here comes the Ice Queen.'

'Alice,' Ana said again while she was still some distance away, her clipped words betraying her Eastern European origins even if her grammar didn't. 'This is yours, I think. It was on the floor in the lounge.'

She held out a rainbow-coloured pillbox, rattling it as she did so with a disapproving tut. 'Your tablets,' she said. 'You're supposed to take them first thing in the morning.'

Alice Shepherd stared at the object in the manager's hand in confusion. 'It's not mine.'

Ana frowned. 'I think it is.'

'It can't be,' murmured Alice, struggling to remember. The box by her bedside table – had that been today? Yesterday? Last year? Her chest tightened and her lungs constricted, making her wheeze with anxiety. 'It's upstairs,' she insisted. 'Mine's upstairs, and I've taken my tablets already.'

Long white fingers ran across the inlaid stones, along the lines of colour, and came to rest on the initials engraved on the silver base. 'This is definitely yours, Alice.'

'No! It isn't.' Alice was aware of her voice shaking, felt

the tension spreading across her shoulders, into her neck. Into her bloodstream. Then a calm hand was on her trembling wrist.

'Steady on, Alice,' Arty was saying. 'No point in getting het up over this. There's probably been some mistake.'

But she could tell from the way he said it, and from the looks on her friends' faces, that they didn't believe her. Because there couldn't be any mistake. The pillbox in Ana Stoyanova's palm was too unique. It was the very same one that Elaine, Alice's geology-loving god-daughter, had given her last Christmas. Compact enough to fit in the hand, the silver box had a spectrum of colour across the lid, each day of the week designated by a different slice of semi-precious stone, with the interior segmented into seven corresponding sections.

It was beautiful. It was practical. Right now, it was terrifying.

Alice had a sudden memory of the desk at young O'Brien's when she'd emptied her bag onto it. The pillbox had been there with her other stuff. Hadn't it? Which meant . . . She reached for her handbag, frantically searching amongst her things, feeling for the hard edges, the cool of the stones.

Nothing.

'I thought . . . it was in here,' she whispered, staring into the depths of her bag.

'It probably fell out during the aerobics session,' said Ana, a smile turning the corners of her lips. 'Don't worry, Alice. No harm done. Just make sure you take your medicine.' Slender fingers picked two capsules from the section marked 'Wednesday' and left them on Alice's saucer. Then, with a sharp tip of her head, Ana turned towards the door.

'Honestly,' muttered Geraldine, as the manager left the cafe, 'the way that woman speaks to people. So rude! I don't know why they couldn't have got someone more local for the job.'

'More British, you mean?' asked Edith with a wry smile.

Geraldine pouted. 'Just because I don't approve of the woman doesn't make me a racist.'

'Technically, I suppose it would if you don't approve of her because she's from Eastern Europe,' said Clarissa, eyes round and innocent.

Her reply brought a huff from the other woman and in a sweep of expensive perfume and cashmere, Geraldine strode off.

'What?' asked Clarissa as Edith doubled up in mirth, revelling in her younger sister's artlessness. 'Did I say something wrong?'

'Not at all,' said Edith, wiping her eyes. 'Not at all, eh, Arty?'

But Arty was watching Alice reaching for her pills, a tremor in her hand. A sign of old age, he thought, like us all.

It was only as Alice looked up that he saw the fear in his friend's eyes.

'Do you recognise this?'

Clive Knowles leaned a pitchfork laden with foul straw against the doorframe and approached Samson in the yard. Behind him, a cow lowed sadly from the depths of the dark barn. 'Recognise what?' he asked.

'This.' Samson lifted his arm, the tup harness dangling from his hand.

The farmer's mouth dropped open. 'That's Ralph's. How the hell did the bugger get out of it?'

Samson ignored the question, holding out his left hand instead. 'What about this?' Lying in his palm was what looked like a miniature hand grenade, dark green with a black top, a chain looping between the two.

Clive Knowles shook his head, puzzled. 'What is it?'

Samson flipped off the cap and pressed down on the side, the farmer flinching back instinctively as a bolt of flame flared up. 'A cigarette lighter.'

'Bloody fancy for a lighter.'

'It's not yours then?'

'Don't smoke. It's bad for the health,' came the pious reply. His attention wandered back to the harness. He took it from Samson and inspected it closely. 'Aye, that's Ralph's all right,' he said, running his hands over the leather straps. 'Beats me how he slipped it off without breaking it. Where'd you find it?'

'Out on the lane. And the lighter was just beyond the gate.'

The farmer's head snapped up. 'The gate at the top of Ralph's field?'

'Yeah. Is it used much?'

'Never. Got stuck in the mud coming in through it once too often. There's bad drainage up there, so I always go in from down here.'

Thinking that the bad drainage wasn't confined to that one patch of field in Mire End Farm, Samson pointed towards the lane that ran across the top end of the property.

'Where does that take you?' he asked.

'Horton,' came the brusque reply.

Samson stifled a sigh. 'I know it goes to Horton. That's where I came from. But where does it go beyond here?'

'Nowhere.'

'It must go somewhere.'

'Aye. It goes up the hill.'

'What's up the hill?'

A frown formed on the farmer's brow. 'Nothing.'

'So the road just goes up the hill and then ends?'

'Right.'

'So no one would go past here normally?'

'What for? I just told you, there's nowt beyond Mire End.'

'What about hikers? Mountain bikers? Get anyone like that up here?'

'Oh aye, get quite a few of them buggers. All laden up with rucksacks and waterproofs.'

'So where are they heading?'

'Langstrothdale,' said the farmer, naming a valley on the other side of the hills to the east.

'So the lane does lead somewhere,' said Samson with a burst of exasperation.

'No, it doesn't. The lane ends up the hill. Then it becomes a track.'

Deciding that any attempt to deflect Clive Knowles from his literal responses was useless, Samson changed tack. 'So you haven't been in through the top gate recently then?'

'Not in more than five years. I keep it padlocked.'

'And when did you last check the padlock?'

Clive Knowles removed his cap and scratched at his

bald head. 'Must've been two weeks ago. When I put Ralph in there with the yows.'

'Everything was all right?'

'Gate was locked, if that's what you mean. Why?'

Samson held up the chain that he'd brought down with him, the broken link a stark silver against the rust. 'Because it's not now.'

'Bloody hell!' The farmer stared at the now-useless gate tether, his face flushed as he noticed the severed end. 'Someone's been in the top field?'

'Without a doubt. There are fresh tyre tracks up there.'

'You mean . . . ?'

'Ralph hasn't wandered off. He's been stolen.'

The harness slipped from Clive Knowles' hand and fell to the morass of mud at his feet. 'Someone's taken Ralph?' He blanched as the implications hit home. 'You have to find him,' he begged, grabbing hold of Samson's sleeve. 'You have to, or it'll be the ruin of this place.'

By early evening Arty had noticed that Alice Shepherd was feeling out of sorts. She seemed more befuddled than usual, struggling to complete her bingo card and mixing up the names of her friends. They were all used to it. She'd been getting more forgetful of late. It made her anxious, too. So when she declared at seven-thirty that it was time for her to retire, Arty didn't protest like he would have done normally.

He liked Alice. She was a gentle soul with a good word for everyone – even the more unpleasant residents of Fellside Court, of whom there were a few. But today he was worried about her. She seemed agitated, the incident with the pillbox at lunchtime a prime example.

'Do you want me to escort you to your room, Madam?' he asked with exaggerated gallantry, holding out an arm for her as she stood.

'Thank you,' she murmured.

'Don't be too long, Arty,' said Edith Hird. 'The next game starts soon. Goodnight, Alice.'

A chorus of 'goodnight' came from the rest of the group and Alice looked around, her gaze vague.

'Goodbye,' she said. 'And God bless you.'

'*Goodbye?*' chuckled Arty as he led her to the lift. 'You sound like Ingrid Bergman in *Casablanca*. "We'll always have Fellside Court!"'

She smiled, but he could tell she wasn't listening. When they got to her front door he kissed her gently on the cheek and wished her a good night's sleep. As the door opened, he didn't notice the rainbow-coloured pillbox on the coffee table. Even if he had, he wouldn't have thought anything of it. But he might have been surprised if he'd seen Alice open it a couple of minutes later. And he would definitely have been perturbed if he'd seen her extract two tablets from the section marked 'Wednesday' and take them with a swallow of water, admonishing herself for her forgetfulness as she did so.

4

On Thursday morning, like every other day of the week, at a time when most folk in Bruncliffe were rolling over to silence the alarm, Samson O'Brien was already up and showered, his sleeping bag stowed away, all evidence of his nocturnal sojourn erased from the back room on the top floor of his office building, and the shower cubicle and tray wiped down.

The former was to prevent Delilah Metcalfe from discovering that her tenant was making full use of his contract by sleeping illicitly on her premises; the latter was to prevent Ida Capstick, the cleaner, from killing him.

Despite being back in Bruncliffe for nearly two months, Samson had yet to find accommodation – basically because he couldn't afford it. When he'd made the decision to return to his home town, he hadn't banked on discovering the family farm sold and himself homeless. What's more, he'd impulsively spent the money that could have secured his bed and board on a six-month rental of the office downstairs, offering to pay it all up front in order to cement the deal with a landlady who hadn't wanted him around. A landlady who shared that opinion with most of the town.

While his generous payment had been enough to overcome Delilah's objections, he'd left himself without anywhere to stay. Or the means to pay for it. Which is when he'd discovered the top floor. Above the two levels of offices, this old house on a back road of Bruncliffe had a third storey with a bathroom and two spare rooms. And it was in the rear bedroom that he'd made his bed that very first night, persuading himself that it was temporary; that there was no need to tell anyone because he would find somewhere else soon.

Seven weeks later and he was still spending his days in a mesh of deceit, pretending to leave work every evening for Hellifield – a village five miles down the road where he claimed to be renting a flat – only to return to the office when Delilah had gone home to her cottage up on Crag Lane. Then he sneaked upstairs to sleep amongst the stored furniture. In Delilah's old bed. Not that he'd known it was hers. He'd discovered that nugget of information when the formidable Ida Capstick had caught him red-handed – and red-faced – wearing nothing but a sleepy expression as she walked in on him one early morning. Once the cleaning lady had overcome the shock, she'd agreed to keep quiet, on the understanding that he made an effort to find somewhere else to stay.

As the clank of the cleaner's metal bucket came up the stairs, Samson placed a mug of tea on the kitchen table, a plate of biscuits next to it. He'd assessed the strength of the tea by comparing it to the dark brown of the teapot it was poured from – lighter was not acceptable, anything darker was – and had then coloured it almost white with milk.

It was far removed from the beverage he knew as tea, but he'd learned over the last few weeks or so that there was no fighting it. There was no drinking it, either, as far as he was concerned.

'Tha's still camping out upstairs then?' Ida Capstick entered the kitchen, placed a shopping bag on the floor and threw a couple of letters on the table, before sitting down to her morning cuppa. And biscuits. The posh ones. That had been part of the deal that bought her silence.

'Morning, Ida,' said Samson with a grin, amused as always by her gruff approach to conversation. Small talk didn't exist in the Capstick household, where words were used as sparingly as money.

Samson had known Ida and her brother George all his life. Living in a cottage on a smallholding at the start of Thorpdale that they'd inherited from their parents, they had been the O'Briens' only neighbours. Some in Bruncliffe would say that was an unlucky draw, Thorpdale – the little-known dale tucked away to the north of the town – being isolated enough, without having the reticent Capsticks as the nearest human contact. Samson knew from experience, however, that while Ida and George might not bother with social conventions, they were steadfast friends.

When Kathleen O'Brien was diagnosed with the cancer that would take her from her family within six short months, Ida Capstick had stepped in. Cleaning. Cooking. Looking after young Samson when his parents were at the hospital.

And when Joseph O'Brien had started drowning his sorrows not long after his wife's death, George Capstick – funny old George, with his unique approach to life – had simply started working on the farm. No discussion with Joseph or his son. No broadcasting his good deeds to the world. He appeared when work needed doing. And then he left, usually on whichever vintage tractor he was restoring at the time.

Neither of the Capstick siblings had ever cast judgement on the catastrophe that became the O'Brien family, as Joseph sank deeper and deeper into the bottle and the farm sank deeper into dept. Neither had they shunned Bruncliffe's black sheep when he'd returned in October – although the welcome from George at Twistleton Farm had been typically unconventional, levelling a shotgun at Samson as he crossed his own threshold.

Except it wasn't his threshold any more, as George had told him. Rick Procter, Bruncliffe's most successful property developer, had bought it off a drunk Joseph O'Brien for a song, and had further added to the injury by then selling the broken man a retirement apartment in the newly built – and Procter Properties-owned – Fellside Court. An apartment that Joseph could only afford through a shared-ownership scheme, which meant he was still paying rent.

A solid farmhouse and all that land. And in return? A one-bedroomed box in the heart of town, and a lifetime of further payments. It made Samson's stomach sour to think about it. Made him feel guilty, too. Perhaps none of this would have come to pass if he'd stayed. He certainly wouldn't be skulking around in his landlady's spare rooms, making unauthorised use of the furniture she had stored up there.

'Yes,' said Samson, taking a seat opposite Ida. 'I'm still here. Haven't quite got the money together yet to move out.'

Ida tutted, taking a second biscuit as she did so. 'Tha'll never have it, either, if tha won't take paying!' She fixed him with a glare, daring him to contradict her.

But she was right. Samson had refused payment for his first Dales Detective Agency case, unwilling to benefit from an investigation that had rocked the town and left many people grieving. Since then, he'd had a steady stream of trifling assignments – a lost cat; a background check on a prospective au pair; some detailed property-search requests for the solicitor, Matthew Thistlethwaite; a couple of security risk-assessments for local businesses . . . It was just about enough to keep his head above water, but if he was going to survive for the six months he'd allocated himself in Bruncliffe, then he needed more substantial work.

Yet only yesterday he'd turned away Alice Shepherd. Ida would have a fit if she knew.

'Anyway, there's the post.' The cleaner pointed at the letters she'd dropped on the table. 'Though why tha can't just have it redirected here, I don't know.'

'It's complicated,' he said, picking up the envelopes. Complicated in that he didn't want his address broadcast, certainly not to the few threads remaining from his life in London. He wasn't sure what would follow him up the motorway to Yorkshire but he knew something would, and it probably wouldn't be friendly. For now, using the unoccupied Twistleton Farm as a dead-drop and its caretaker, George Capstick, as a go-between was the safest option.

'I've said nowt about our arrangement,' Ida continued, 'but the postman can't help but have noticed. And as he's a cousin of Mrs Pettiford in the bank, happen it won't be long before the whole town knows tha's been getting letters delivered up there.'

'It shouldn't be for much longer. Hopefully I'll have sorted everything before Easter.'

Sorted everything. Such a euphemism for the mess he was in.

'Humph.' Ida gave another of her wide range of non-lexical utterances, most of which were of the disapproving kind, and reached down to pass the large bag at her feet to Samson. 'Well, don't go making this lot last until then.'

Samson grinned and blushed at the same time. His washing. Since he was eight, he'd never had anyone do his laundry for him. It was one of the chores he'd taken on, as grieving father and son tried to establish a new routine in the O'Brien household. Now he felt a pang of embarrassment as Ida presented him with a pile of clean and ironed clothes.

'There's no need for you to do this,' he protested.

'Like I told thee before, I'll not have tha clothing dripping all over that bathroom upstairs.'

'But I can go to the launderette.'

'*Launderette*? Those gossips in there would have tha secrets out across Bruncliffe in a heartbeat.'

'At least let me pay, then,' insisted Samson, reaching for his wallet.

A ferocious shake of the head stalled his hand. 'It's Rick Procter as is paying me to do this. About time he put something back. Figure tha washing is a good place to start.' Ida's mouth twitched, the closest Samson had ever seen her come to a smile, and he raised his hands in resignation. If his old neighbour was happy to subsidise doing his laundry through her cleaning job at the property developer's Fellside Court, he knew better than to argue.

'Thank you. And have another biscuit.' He pushed the plate towards her and while she was deliberating over which one to choose, he bit the bullet. 'About your job at Fellside Court . . .'

'What about it?' Her eyes were on him, sharp, sensing this wasn't going to be an idle chat about cleaning.

'What's it like working there? I mean, what's the atmosphere like?'

She shrugged. 'I couldn't say. I get my work done and leave. Same as anywhere.'

'And the staff? Do they get on well with the residents?'

It was almost visible, the closing of her defences, like a drawbridge pulled up before his questions. 'I don't gossip, young man. Tha should know that by now.'

'It's not gossip – it's just . . .' Samson ran a hand through his hair, not quite sure what it was that had prompted him to ask Ida about Fellside Court. When Alice Shepherd had left the office the day before, he'd made the decision not to pursue her case. He simply couldn't justify charging her for his time, investigating claims which had as much substance as a will-o'-the-wisp. But he'd woken this morning with the frail pensioner on his mind.

'Alice Shepherd came to see me yesterday,' he said, knowing that his client confidentiality wouldn't be broken by the cleaner. Even so, he found himself toning down the old lady's words – murder sounding too far-fetched for first thing on a Thursday morning. 'She wants to hire me because she thinks she's in danger.'

Ida put her mug of tea on the table and stared at Samson. 'Mrs Shepherd said that?'

'Quite clearly, and several times.'

'What kind of danger?'

He shook his head and told a lie. 'She wasn't specific. But she seemed to think there's something going on at Fellside Court.'

'And tha believes her?'

'I don't know. She was confused about so many details. And it seems so absurd. I just wondered if you'd picked up on anything while you were cleaning there.'

A sharp snort greeted him. 'There's no one wandering round with an axe, if that's what tha means.' Ida picked her tea back up, contemplating the query as she drank. 'The place is well run now, and the folk in there seem happy,' she finally said. 'But I wouldn't have put Mrs Shepherd down as one of them that seek drama. If she feels worried about something, happen there might be substance to it.'

'What did you mean by well run *now*? Wasn't it before?'

Ida sniffed. 'Depends on tha standards, I suppose. All I know is tha can tell the tone of a place by how clean the management are. And that young woman who took over in October keeps her office pristine. There might be some as find her ways a bit sharp but there's allowances have to be made for foreigners.'

'She's foreign?'

'Eastern European. Not sure where.'

'Do the residents get on with her?'

Arms folding across her chest, Ida pursed her lips as

she considered him across the table. 'Tha's taking Mrs Shepherd's case?'

'I'm not sure.'

'Then I'm not sure I should say anything further. I'm not one for idle conjecturing.'

Samson sighed. He was cornered by the strict moral codes of his former neighbour. 'How about if I promise to at least go and visit Mrs Shepherd? Have a look around Fellside Court? Then would you tell me what you think?'

The arms unfolded and Ida stood, clearing the table with brisk efficiency. 'I'll tell thee what I think. I think we're all afraid of outsiders, and that does nowt but get stronger as we age.'

'You're saying they're afraid of this new woman . . . what's her name . . . ?'

'Ana Stoyanova. Not so much afraid as suspicious. Tha knows only too well what folk round here can be like. It's not all of them, mind. Just a handful. But it may be enough to have poisoned Mrs Shepherd's mind. What with the couple of deaths there's been in there of late.'

'More than usual?'

'More than usual for normal life, perhaps. Not more than usual for a place filled with old folk.'

'Nothing strange about them?'

Ida turned from stacking the dishwasher. 'No. Nothing strange. Don't think Bruncliffe could hide anything like that.'

'What about the thefts? Mrs Shepherd mentioned that some things had gone missing.'

'Aye, I heard about that. A watch and a scarf or something.' She shrugged. 'It was just before I started working there. You'd be best off asking around when you call in.' She reached for the empty bag on the floor and made her way into the hall, the clank of the bucket as she picked it up signalling the end of her interrogation.

'Thanks, Ida,' Samson said.

She paused at the foot of the stairs to the second floor and looked back at him. 'While tha's over there, tha may as well call in on tha father. Only proper a son should visit now and again.'

Then, with heavy steps of admonishment, she ascended to the floor above, leaving Samson with his second lecture on filial duties in two days. Bruncliffe and its interfering culture, he decided as he headed downstairs to his office, was definitely an acquired taste. A taste he seemed to have lost in his years down south.

'What made you change your mind?' Delilah asked on the walk up Fell Lane to Fellside Court, the swollen, dark clouds seeming to rest on the roof of the building. While the threatening weather of the day before had merely resulted in an overnight dusting of snow on the top of the fells, these clouds forecast rain. Lots of it, before the day was out. She'd been lucky to get a run in first thing.

'I needed the fresh air,' said Samson. He bent down to pat the grey shadow ambling along next to him. 'Isn't that so, Tolpuddle?'

The dog barked up at him while Delilah rolled her eyes. 'Guilty conscience, more like.'

Samson greeted the accuracy of her remark with silence and she felt a momentary twinge of contrition, knowing from bitter experience how Bruncliffe's tight-knit society excelled at inspiring feelings of shame. The returned black sheep didn't need her adding to it. She'd already noticed him hang his head as they walked past Peaks Patisserie in the marketplace earlier – her sister-in-law Lucy's cafe no doubt reminding him of Ryan.

'Are you still on for coming up to the barn this week-end?' she asked, changing the subject. The barn in question was High Laithe, a building in mid-conversion up on the fells above Bruncliffe. It was where Lucy, Ryan and their son Nathan had made their home, living in a caravan while Ryan worked on the property between tours of duty with the army. When he'd been killed in Afghanistan two years ago, work had stalled. When the caravan had been burned to the ground in early November – a victim of the cyclone of trouble that had hit the town – Lucy and Nathan had been left with nowhere to stay. So Will and Ash, the oldest and youngest of the five Metcalfe brothers, had stepped in, working up at the barn every weekend, trying to get it habitable for Christmas. Their efforts has been augmented with help from friends and from the two other Metcalfe lads, Craig and Chris, whenever they could make it back to Bruncliffe.

'Sure,' said Samson. 'If you think Will won't mind? I got the sense when I was up there last Sunday that he didn't appreciate my presence.'

It was Delilah's turn to feel the sharp edge of self-reproach, something she'd forever associate with her eldest brother, whose approval she never seemed to win. Allow-ing Samson O'Brien to rent an office from her hadn't eased the relationship between the siblings. In Will Metcalfe's eyes, Samson was the man who'd left town under a black cloud and had then, as Ryan's best friend and godfather to Nathan, neglected his obligations following Ryan's death. The Metcalfes weren't known as the forgiving type. Will was living up to that reputation, and although there'd been some thawing in the frostiness with which the two men greeted each other since the dramatic events the month before, he still wasn't in the mood to accept Samson into the family fold.

Even when Samson was trying to help.

'Sod Will!' she muttered. 'Christmas is only two weeks away, so we need all the bodies we can get up there or we'll never be ready. Besides, it's Lucy's home we're building. She gets the final say. And she told me to ask you.'

Samson laughed. 'So I can hide behind Lucy when Will's looking murderous with a nail gun in his hand?'

The image brought a grin to Delilah's face. Slender Lucy hiding the broad-shouldered Samson while the much stockier Will menaced him. 'Don't worry,' she said. 'I'll bring Tolpuddle. He'll happily guard you.'

'Then it's a deal,' said Samson.

They turned into the courtyard at the back of Fellside Court and Delilah bent down to loop Tolpuddle's lead under one of the wrought-iron chairs that decorated the paving.

'We won't be long,' she promised, a pair of amber eyes regarding her with reproach. 'Try and be a good boy.'

'Isn't he always?' asked Samson, ruffling the dog's ears.

The question was met with a wry smile. 'Depends where you rank destroying perfectly good trainers on the naughty scale. Punctured uppers and torn soles were what greeted me when I got up this morning.'

'Were they yours?'

The smile disappeared, a dark look taking its place. 'Who else would they belong to?'

Samson held up both hands in submission, grinning mischievously at having triggered the famous temper. 'Just asking.'

The grin transported Delilah right back to her childhood and school holidays spent trailing round after Ryan and Samson, the much older lads tolerant of her to a point. Until they started teasing her, provoking her until she blew up. She'd give anything to be able to go back there for a day.

She'd also give anything for the trainers in her porch to have been hers. But they weren't. They were her ex-husband's, Tolpuddle having found them stowed in a place that Delilah had overlooked when she cleared out all of Neil's stuff and moved it to the office building. He would hit the roof when he came back to collect his belongings and saw what had become of his very expensive Reeboks. *If* he ever came back . . .

But as Samson wasn't even aware that she'd been married, as far as she knew, she wasn't about to tell him and risk another lecture on the perils of youthful romance. Bad enough that she had to suffer Will's moral superiority on the topic every time her marital status came up.

She sighed, her spirits sinking like the clouds on the fells, and Samson kicked himself for taunting her. What was it about Delilah that made him revert to the behaviour of his youth?

'Come on.' He nudged her with his elbow. 'Let's get this over with and go for lunch in the Fleece. My treat.' He opened the door to the retirement complex and ushered Delilah in ahead of him. 'Who is your meeting with this morning, anyway?'

'The new manager – Ana . . .' Delilah pulled her notepad out of her bag as she entered the foyer. '. . . Stoyanova,' she said, reading from the pad.

'Not Rick Procter?'

'No. He doesn't get involved, just lets a subsidiary company run it.' She bent over to sign the visitors' book that lay on a sideboard in the hallway. 'That said,' she continued, passing her pen to Samson, 'he's asked me to meet him for a drink later, to run things past him. Typical Rick. Can't bear not to be hands-on.'

The thought of the good-looking property developer being hands-on with anything that involved Delilah triggered a flash of annoyance in Samson. He knew that most of Bruncliffe viewed the man differently – a successful entrepreneur who hadn't forgotten his roots, despite his wealth, and gave a lot back to the town. Even the purchase of Twistleton Farm was considered an act of kindness by many, taking a derelict property off old Boozy O'Brien and offering him the chance of a new life.

Something the man's own son hadn't been around to provide.

But Samson didn't trust Rick Procter and never would. Biting back a retort, he signed the visitors' book and then nodded towards the wall of glass through which they'd entered, the fells rising in the background. 'Stunning, isn't it?'

'It sure is. The residents must love it.'

'I assure you, they do.' A clipped voice made them turn

to see a young woman coming down the stairs to their right. 'Ms Metcalfe? I'm Ana Stoyanova, manager at Fellside Court. Pleased to meet you.'

The words were warm enough, even if the woman's features remained frozen, no hint of a smile on her red lips, green eyes coolly appraising the visitors. Whatever her temperament, she was beautiful, making even her uniform of fitted tunic and black trousers look chic.

'Delilah – please call me Delilah.' The two women shook hands and Ana turned to Samson.

'And Mr O'Brien. You're here to see your father?'

Samson made no attempt to hide his surprise. 'Have we met?'

She nodded. 'Briefly. The first time you visited. But I've heard a lot about you. It's good to see you visiting more often. I think people don't realise how important family contact is in old age.'

A hint of red curled up Samson's cheeks and Delilah wondered if it was triggered by the attentions of an attractive woman, or by the sting of what she'd said.

'If you've both signed in,' continued the manager, 'Ms Metcalfe, would you join me in my office? Enjoy your visit, Mr O'Brien.' Ana gestured to an open door and Delilah followed her inside, leaving Samson standing in the corridor. He was racking his brain as to how he didn't remember meeting such a remarkable woman when he heard his father calling from the far end of the hallway.

'Samson! What brings you here?' Unlike Ana Stoyanova, Joseph O'Brien was sporting a wide smile, his time-worn face alight with pleasure.

'What makes you think it isn't you?' asked Samson, as

the two men shook hands, a slight awkwardness lingering in the physical contact which had ceased to be normal decades before.

Joseph gave a gentle laugh. 'Sure, I don't mind either way. It's a joy to see you. You're just in time for a coffee, too . . .'

'Why, if it isn't the prodigal son!' exclaimed Arty Robinson, spotting the two O'Briens entering the crowded lounge. A devilish smile accompanied his words as he turned to the gathered residents. 'But what a shame, ladies. He's come fully clothed!'

A loud burst of laughter from the pensioners saved Samson from having to reply and Joseph led him over to where his group of friends was sitting.

'Take no heed of him, Samson,' said Edith Hird, casting a reproving glance at the stout figure of the bookmaker, who was still chuckling. 'He's beyond taming.'

'Yes,' said Clarissa Ralph, patting Samson's hand as he took a seat next to her. 'Arty doesn't mean any offence. He's just excited, as we all are, about the adventures you've been having.'

Not sure whether he'd classify leaping through a fire in his boxer shorts as an adventure, Samson grimaced. 'Hopefully I won't be having any more for the foreseeable future,' he said.

'Oh, but you must!' exclaimed Arty. 'What else would Bruncliffe have to talk about?'

'Your expanding waistline?' wheezed Eric Bradley, a grin visible below the thin tube connecting him to his oxygen cylinder.

'Expanding? I'll have you know . . .'

Samson let the banter wash over him, glancing at his father in the chair opposite, a contented look on the older man's face. No signs of drinking. A light in his eyes that Samson remembered from his childhood. And a flush to his cheeks that wasn't caused by alcohol.

The place was good for him, thought Samson.

The same could be said of the others as they carried on an animated conversation punctuated by laughter, comfortable in each other's company and in their surroundings.

And who wouldn't be? High-backed chairs and a few sofas – most of them occupied – were scattered around the room in small clusters; coffee tables covered in magazines and board games formed focal points; and a long wall of floor-to-ceiling windows looked out onto the courtyard. The space was well lit, tastefully decorated, and felt like home.

Alice Shepherd must have got something wrong. There was nothing malevolent about Fellside Court.

'Would you like a coffee, Mr O'Brien?'

Samson twisted in his chair to see a woman wearing a navy-blue staff tunic, dark hair swaying along dimpled cheeks, a pot of coffee in her hand. 'Yes, sorry, I don't think we've met?'

'I saw your picture in the paper – you know . . .' She smiled.

'Sorry, son. Where are my manners?' Joseph O'Brien gestured towards the woman. 'This is Vicky Hudson, our care assistant.'

'The angel of Fellside Court,' chipped in Arty with a wink. 'She keeps us all on the straight and narrow.'

'A big task, then?' Samson smiled at Vicky, who laughed.

'Oh no, they're mostly well behaved. And besides, I leave the discipline to Ana.'

'She's better suited to it,' muttered Edith Hird.

If Vicky heard, she made no comment, simply poured a coffee for Samson and placed it on the small table next to him. 'Sugar, Mr O'Brien?'

'No, thank you. And call me Samson, please.'

'Yes,' said Arty, nudging Eric. 'No need for formalities with Bruncliffe's boxer-shorts hero.'

Vicky laughed again, shaking her head at the roguish old man. 'I wasn't going to mention that,' she said.

'Why not?' said Samson with an exaggerated sigh. 'Everyone else does.'

'Well, boxer shorts or not, it's a pleasure to meet you.' She held out a hand and took his in a firm handshake. 'I hope you'll stay for the talk?'

'Talk?'

'We have talks on a Thursday morning,' said Joseph. 'Something Ana started when she took over. They get some expert in to speak about their field of interest. Last week was a retired policeman talking about rural crime. It was fascinating.'

'And today?'

'A local lass. Talking about the geology of the Dales.'

'Elaine Bullock,' said Edith Hird. 'You might remember her from school, Samson? She was a year or two below you, I think?'

'I know her.' Samson grinned, thinking about the week before when he'd seen Elaine waiting on tables in Peaks

Patisserie, looking totally harassed. Officially a lecturer in geology, she supplemented her part-time hours by working in the cafe, saving the money to pay for trips around the world. Trips to see rocks. 'I think that might be worth waiting for. If only to see her face when she spots me in the audience.'

'Talking of audience,' said Arty, looking at his watch. 'Where's Alice? She won't want to miss her god-daughter. Especially when she suggested that Elaine be invited to speak.' He pulled his mobile out of his pocket.

'Elaine Bullock is Alice Shepherd's god-daughter?' Samson asked his father, as Arty held the phone to his ear.

Joseph nodded. 'You know how it is around here. Everyone's related. Kick one of them and they all limp!'

'No answer,' said Arty.

'She's probably left her phone in her handbag, as usual,' said Edith. 'You'd best go and get her.'

'I'll go,' Clarissa offered, already getting to her feet. 'I need to get my glasses anyway.'

As she left the room, Ana Stoyanova entered, accompanied by Delilah. They were deep in conversation – Ana's face serious, Delilah taking notes. When the manager saw Samson sitting in the group at the far end of the room, she indicated for Delilah to follow her towards them.

'I hope you're going to stay for the talk, Mr O'Brien?' she said as she approached. 'I've persuaded Ms Metcalfe to join us so she can get an idea of the social activities Fellside Court provides. It would be good for you to witness it too.'

'I've already had my arm twisted,' said Samson with a grin.

Ana dipped her head slightly, no lifting of the lips in response. 'Good. Now if you will excuse me, I have some calls to make.'

'Before you go,' said Delilah, 'I need to take your photograph for the website. Shall we do it now?'

A delicate eyebrow arched up, followed by a frown. 'Is it really necessary?'

Delilah smiled. 'A friendly face is a powerful marketing tool.'

'I'd really rather not today. I'm very busy. Perhaps another time—?' The manager broke off as footsteps sounded along the corridor and Clarissa burst into the lounge. 'Why, Clarissa! Whatever—?'

'Call an ambulance!' exclaimed Clarissa, eyes wide with shock. 'It's Alice. She's collapsed.'

A crash of crockery underlined her announcement and a hush descended. Then Ana Stoyanova was rushing out of the room, Samson and Delilah close behind her.

5

They followed Ana up the stairs, all of them taking the steps two at a time. Turning right through the stairwell door, Ana led the way down the corridor, mobile phone pressed to her ear, talking to the ambulance service as she hurried towards the open door of the first flat on the left.

'You two, wait outside,' she snapped over her shoulder, before rushing through the lounge to the bedroom, where the petite shape of Alice Shepherd could be seen crumpled on the floor by the foot of the bed.

'I'm a police officer,' Samson replied, following her. 'Let me help.'

Ana was already feeling for a pulse, her phone trapped between her head and shoulder as she gently laid her fingers against the frail wrist protruding from a fleece dressing gown. 'Here,' she said, thrusting the mobile at him. 'Tell them where we are. And tell them to hurry.'

'Is she okay?' Vicky Hudson was in the doorway, her voice quavering. 'I mean—'

'Fetch the defibrillator and then call Dr Naylor. And you,' she pointed at Delilah, 'no one else is to come in here other than the paramedics.'

Delilah nodded and turned to man the door, grateful not to have to witness Alice Shepherd's indignity any further as, with practised efficiency, Ana turned the old woman onto her back, checked her airways and began to administer CPR. When the manager saw Vicky still hovering, she snarled. 'Go! Now!'

Vicky stumbled from the room and Samson – having given the emergency services all the information they needed – dropped to his knees beside Ana.

'Any pulse at all?' he asked.

She shook her head, hands moving rhythmically on the old lady's chest. 'Come on, Alice,' she muttered under her breath. 'Come on!'

In the distance came the sound of sirens, growing ever louder.

'Here, let me,' offered Samson, but Ana shook her head.

'She's my charge. My responsibility.'

'And she's my friend's godmother,' said Samson.

Ana glanced up at him, gave a brief nod, and allowed him to take her place. But Alice Shepherd refused to respond.

After what seemed like an age since Vicky Hudson had raced back into the apartment with the defibrillator, Delilah heard the ambulance pulling up outside, the crash of doors and the pound of heavy feet across paving stones. And voices. Confused voices, Arty Robinson's rising above them all, calling for calm, telling everyone to stay in the lounge. Then a voice she knew, floating up the stairwell and down the corridor. A voice full of panic.

'Delilah!' Elaine Bullock was running towards her,

dark plaits swinging, glasses slipping down her nose. 'Alice? Is she . . . ?'

'She's collapsed,' said Delilah, taking her friend's hands, feeling the tremors in the fingers. 'Samson and Ana are with her.'

Footsteps on the stairs heralded two paramedics, one male, one female, the authority of their uniforms giving a sense of relief. And fear.

'In here,' said Delilah. 'She's in here.'

'What's her name, love?' asked the woman.

'Alice Shepherd.'

'And her age?'

'Eighty-one,' replied Elaine, entering the apartment with the two paramedics. As the door closed behind them, Delilah could hear the man already talking to Alice.

She didn't hear any response.

A cold breath of air brushed across her neck, making her shiver. She thought it was shock. Then she spotted the corridor window slightly ajar, the chill December air stealing in.

It took a couple of strides to reach it. An outstretched hand to close it. She didn't look out. She was too busy worrying about what was happening behind Alice Shepherd's apartment door.

For a Weimaraner with anxiety issues, Tolpuddle had been behaving impeccably. Having tested the extent of his freedom against the weight of the chair restraining him, he'd settled down on the cold paving, his lead stretched taut. He'd whimpered a couple of times, more out of habit than genuine emotion, then had lain down reluctantly, head on paws as the skies above grew darker. His grey shape merged into the courtyard background and the growing gloom.

When the ambulance arrived, he'd watched warily as two people jumped down and hurried across the courtyard, one of them banging into a table with his hip as he passed, a chair knocked over in the impact. Uttering a muffled curse, the man raced after his colleague, not stopping to reposition the furniture. Not realising there was a dog behind it.

Tolpuddle felt it straight away. The slight tension on his collar eased. He sat up and inched further from the fallen chair, his slack lead following snake-like across the paving slabs. Then he heard a familiar voice.

Ears picking up, he walked around the corner towards the car park and was just in time to see her hand, outstretched, as she closed the window above. He trotted over directly beneath, ignoring the divisions between footpath, grass and border, and stood amongst the low bushes staring up at the glass. He barked, once. But she didn't reappear.

So he sat. Eyes on the window. Until he got bored. Then he looked around him. The wall in front of him. The bush. The puzzling stripe of colours at the back of the bush. He edged forward, pushing at the colours with his nose, a smell – alien but intriguing – coming back from them.

A clatter of noise, voices in the courtyard. Tolpuddle, sensing the impropriety of his behaviour, clasped the colourful object in his mouth and turned to slink across the path to the copse of trees at the side of the car park, where he could satisfy his curiosity in peace.

Alice Shepherd was pronounced dead by a sombre Dr Naylor. The finality of the news took the air from the room, and left Samson trying to console a stunned Elaine Bullock as the paramedics packed away their equipment. Ana Stoyanova was still kneeling on the carpet, a hand over her mouth.

'I'm sorry, Ana,' Dr Naylor said as he helped her to her feet. 'But there's nothing more we can do. I suspect she was already gone when you found her.'

Ana's jaw clenched, as though the doctor's words were a physical slap.

'And I'm also sorry,' he continued with a contrite look, 'but I'm going to have to notify the coroner.'

This was enough to make the manager's cold gaze snap onto the doctor. 'You're joking! Why on earth would you put the family through that?'

'I have to. I haven't seen Alice since last month when we increased her medication. It's more than two weeks ago, so I can't sign the death certificate.'

'But you were Alice's doctor. You know she had high blood pressure.'

The doctor gave a tired shrug in the face of the manager's annoyance. 'It's the law.'

'Will that mean a post-mortem?' Elaine Bullock's gaze was worried behind the round lenses of her glasses.

'Possibly.'

'No . . .' She glanced down at her godmother. 'Oh no . . .'

Ana shook her head in disgust, glaring at the doctor. 'This is exactly what I meant,' she snapped. 'Pointless bureaucracy!'

'It can't be helped,' the doctor said. 'And besides, only a handful of referrals are subjected to a post-mortem. There's a good chance this won't be one of them.'

'Let's hope that's the case,' retorted Ana. 'We all know Alice's death doesn't merit the coroner's attention.'

Samson, however, wasn't sure he shared the manager's opinion. Because he couldn't help remembering the conviction with which Alice Shepherd had told him she was going to be killed.

Looking at her lifeless body on the floor in front of him, he wondered if she'd been right.

'She didn't seem herself last night. I should have paid more attention.'

'Don't be ridiculous, Arty.' Edith Hird tempered the brusque words with a gentle tone. 'She was a bit confused, that's all. No more than she'd been of late.'

With the grey clouds turning to black beyond the long windows, the subdued pensioners in the lounge of Fellside Court were trying to take in the passing of their friend while, in true Bruncliffe fashion, Delilah served them cups of tea.

After Samson had emerged grim-faced from the apartment to tell her that Alice was dead, she had felt useless in the ensuing activity; Ana and Vicky had begun to contact the necessary authorities and a tearful Elaine was on the phone to Alice's family. So Delilah had come downstairs, where the sad news had already been received, and at

Joseph O'Brien's suggestion, she'd helped him settle the residents in the lounge so they could absorb the shock. But as she'd handed out hot drinks to the groups scattered around the room, her thoughts had remained with Alice Shepherd.

What had the old lady been so afraid of that she'd called in on Samson yesterday? And did those fears have anything to do with her death?

In the context of the comfortable surroundings of Fell-side Court, the idea seemed ludicrous.

'Is there any coffee left?' Samson was by her side, his features showing the strain of the morning.

'Sorry, I've just given the last one out.' Delilah pointed to the teapot. 'I can offer you a tea?' She began pouring, but he shook his head at the thick, brown liquid issuing from the spout.

'Thanks, but I'll pass.'

'Here, son. Take mine. I was only having it to be sociable.' Joseph gave Samson his cup of coffee before any protest could be made, laying a hand on his shoulder at the same time. 'I don't know what brought you here today, but it's a good thing you came.'

His father's misplaced gratitude did nothing to ease the remorse Samson was feeling. He'd come to talk to Alice. But he'd been too late. 'Cheers, Dad.' He took his coffee and followed Delilah and Joseph across the room to where Arty was sitting with Edith, Eric Bradley and Edith's sister, Clarissa.

'Was it peaceful, Samson?' asked Arty, his face forlorn as Samson took a seat. 'Did she suffer?'

'Arty!' Edith Hird frowned. 'Let the lad have a minute's break, at least.'

'Sorry. It's just . . .' Tears formed in the bookmaker's eyes and he wiped a plump hand across his cheeks. 'Damn it.'

For once, Edith didn't reprimand him for his language. Instead she leaned across and took his hand in hers.

'Alice was happy here,' said Clarissa, her light voice filling the heavy silence. 'And you were a large factor in that, Arty. That's what you need to remember.'

Arty nodded, head down, staring into his tea. 'I know – it's just yesterday . . . I should have asked her what was wrong.'

'He's right.' Eric Bradley's wheezing tones cut across Clarissa's demurrals. 'Alice was a bit more anxious than usual. That incident at lunchtime wasn't like her.'

'What incident?' asked Samson.

'It was over her pills,' said Joseph. 'Ana found Alice's pillbox and realised Alice hadn't taken her medication that morning. When Ana raised the matter, Alice became really agitated. Said she'd already taken them.' He shrugged. 'It was out of character. Alice Shepherd was never a woman prone to overreacting.'

A woman who didn't overreact. Yet, thought Delilah, twenty-four hours ago the same woman had claimed someone was trying to kill her. And now she was dead. From his creased brow, Delilah could tell that Samson was thinking along the same lines.

'Did she get on with everyone here?' he asked casually.

'Yes.' Edith's unequivocal response was qualified by a dissenting murmur from Arty.

'You don't agree?' Samson turned back to the bookmaker.

'It's a brave man that disagrees with Edith.' Arty gave a small smile and Edith patted his hand. 'But there was something bothering Alice, I'm sure of it. She's been – she *was* – more anxious than normal. She had to have her medication increased because of her high blood pressure. And then there was her visit to see you.' He lifted his head and looked straight at Samson. 'She told me she'd been, but wouldn't say why.'

'It was nothing.' Samson accompanied his reply with an easy smile and Delilah noted, somewhat warily, the proficiency with which he could fall into role. No doubt it had been a useful trait when he was undercover. Now it was serving to calm the suspicions of Arty Robinson. 'Just something about a theft,' he continued. 'She mentioned something about cufflinks?'

'Oh, that!' Arty gave a half-hearted chuckle. 'I lost a cufflink, one of a pair of gaming dice. Never did find it. But Alice was convinced it had been stolen.'

'Did you think that too?'

'No. Why on earth would someone have taken just the one? It's probably down the back of a cupboard somewhere.'

'There was my scarf as well,' added Clarissa. 'I couldn't find it. Still can't. But Alice kept saying someone had taken it.'

Edith snorted. 'As if! It was over twenty years old and as faded as my looks!' Her blunt retort brought a smile to Arty's face. 'It was just Alice. Lately she'd begun to get worked up over things. Mostly because she was starting to forget.'

'Forget what?'

'Everything, my lad. Everything. Alice knew she was beginning to lose her mind. And when that's gone, what do you have left? It's what we all fear, far more than death.'

This time it was Arty who offered comfort, squeezing Edith's hand, which was still resting in his.

'But what about your watch?' Samson asked the headmistress. 'Didn't that go missing too?'

Arty was already shaking his head. 'It was Alice who lost a watch, not Edith.'

'Alice? But she said . . .' Samson paused, remembering Alice's muddled accusations from the day before, and her heated response when he'd queried them.

'Her watch went missing and she claimed it had been stolen,' explained Edith. 'Then she found it in her handbag a few days later.'

'Luckily she hadn't told anyone,' added Clarissa. 'No one on the staff, anyway.'

'And you think this was just confusion?' Samson looked around the group.

'What else could it be?' asked Joseph.

'I don't know. Perhaps someone playing a trick on her? Maybe she didn't get on with someone?'

'This is Fellside Court,' said Clarissa, looking at him with surprise. 'Things like that don't happen here. And besides, Alice got on with everyone, didn't she?' She turned to the group for confirmation and the others nodded and expressed agreement. Except for Arty. He was staring back into his empty cup with a frown.

'Arty?' Delilah asked. 'What's troubling you?'

'Yesterday.' He glanced up at her. 'When Alice got het up about the pills.'

'What about it?'

He shook his head, his gaze dropping to the floor. 'I don't know. Maybe I'm being daft, but it looked . . . it looked as though she was scared.'

'Scared of what?' Samson kept his tone light.

But Arty simply shook his head again. 'I . . . I couldn't say. It was just a feeling.'

Before Samson could press him further, he saw Elaine Bullock approaching, her cheeks tear-stained, her nose red below her glasses. In her hand she was holding the rainbow-coloured pillbox he'd last seen on his desk.

'Elaine . . .' He stood, awkward in the face of her grief. Delilah, as always, had no such constraints. She put her arms around her friend and hugged her. Then she led her to a chair and produced a packet of tissues.

'The undertakers have just been,' mumbled Elaine, drying the fresh tears that were forming. 'So I just want to say thanks for everything, before I go.'

'I'm not sure we deserve it,' said Samson, looking contrite. 'We were too late.'

'We all were,' said Joseph. 'No one's to blame.'

'It's just a shock. Alice was so excited about me coming in to talk today, and instead . . .' Elaine's voice broke and she gestured at the pillbox in her hand. 'Ana said it would be all right for me to have this. Feels strange to be taking back a Christmas present.'

'Alice really loved it, you know,' said Clarissa. 'She could name every stone on the lid and was always telling us interesting facts about them. It was such a thoughtful gift, Elaine.'

A patter of rain fell against the long windows.

'Come on,' said Delilah, getting to her feet. 'I'll walk back into town with you before it gets really wet. You coming, Samson?'

Samson stood, knowing the time wasn't right to probe any further into the background to Alice Shepherd's death. Hopefully the coroner would order a post-mortem and Samson's unease at having made light of his client's fears could be laid to rest, along with Elaine's godmother.

Tolpuddle heard the door opening from across the car park. Despite a concerted effort, he'd been unable to find the source of the persistent rattle that came from inside his new toy. So he'd dug a shallow hole and was in the process of covering up the rainbow colours when the door opened and familiar voices interrupted his progress.

Leaving his labour unfinished, he raced across the grass, skittered around the tumbled chair and bounded over to the three figures in the courtyard, jumping up at them.

'Tolpuddle! Get down! Sorry, Elaine, I don't know what he's been doing . . .' Delilah brushed at the mud on her coat and the paw prints on Elaine's trousers, but Elaine was laughing.

'Don't apologise. He's just showing his love and after this morning, that's not a bad thing.'

'Huh!' Delilah stared at her dog, who was now sitting,

head tipped to one side, an ear cocked and his face wearing its most mournful look. 'Butter wouldn't melt,' she muttered.

'What do you expect when you leave him alone all morning? Digging the odd hole is no sin, is it, old boy?' Samson scratched behind Tolpuddle's ears and the dog's expression became ecstatic.

Delilah sighed. As if the hound needed any more encouragement to adore the new man in his life. 'Let's get a move on,' she said, turning to go as the rain became heavy, fat drops splattering on the paving.

Tolpuddle followed the three of them across the courtyard, around the corner and away from the building. He didn't spare a thought for the object that had kept him amused all morning.

Arty Robinson watched them leave through the rain-smeared windows of the lounge and wondered if he'd done the right thing. Should he have said? Even when it was a half-formed suspicion?

'Arty?' He turned to see her standing in the doorway, looking immaculate. Hair pulled neatly back into a ponytail, features controlled. Only the creases to her uniform and the darkened skin beneath her eyes betrayed her stressful morning. 'Have you got a moment?'

He nodded. To himself as much as to her, reassuring himself he'd been mistaken. Alice Shepherd had had no reason to be afraid of Ana Stoyanova.

Relieved that he hadn't confessed his misgivings to Samson, Arty turned his back on the courtyard where the rain was streaming across the paving slabs. Beyond, across the strip of grass and into the copse of trees beside the car park, Tolpuddle's toy was left below a cherry tree, half-buried, it's spectrum of coloured stones getting wet as the rain fell harder still.

6

The rain that began the day Alice Shepherd's body was discovered was unrelenting. For a full twenty-four hours it fell from leaden skies, filling the becks and streams to overflowing, pooling in the hollows of sodden fields and swelling the river that ran through the middle of Bruncliffe. By Saturday morning, the waterfall at the disused mill to the north of town was a tumbling, dun-coloured torrent, the steps of the fall negated by the volume of water flowing over them. Newly formed white lines snaked down hillsides in the distance, and springs emerged overnight from the already saturated soil. As far as Samson O'Brien could remember, it was a typical Dales December.

'Now I know why I left this place,' he muttered as Delilah drove them up out of town on streaming wet, narrow roads, windshield wipers slapping at the misted glass. 'How can anyone live in this climate?'

'Oh, stop moaning! It's not as if London is that much better.'

'You're joking?' He turned to look at her. 'It's a paradise compared to here. Don't think I've ever seen so much rain. I'm in danger of getting trench foot.'

Delilah laughed, but kept her concentration on the hill that led out of the back of Bruncliffe, a daunting incline on a road only wide enough for one car. Trying not to be too concerned about the groaning engine, she nursed her newly acquired Nissan Micra upwards.

'Christ!' muttered Samson, as the noise from under the bonnet reached an ear-splitting shriek, the load of two adults and a large dog demanding a lot on the steep terrain. 'Couldn't you have got something with a bit more oomph?'

'It's all I could afford,' snapped Delilah.

Two days she'd had the car and already she was fed up with the criticism it was provoking, particularly amongst her brothers, who were generally scornful of anything that didn't have good ground clearance and the capacity to carry at least four sheep. But with new recruits to the Dales Dating Agency hitting a bit of a lull and payments for her web-design work not due until after Christmas, even the Micra had been a stretch – a purchase that Uncle Woolly, her bank manager, would probably say was a luxury too far. But then he'd not had to run across the fells to help Samson catch a ruthless killer.

After what had happened in November, Delilah had vowed she would never be in that situation again – stranded without a vehicle when someone's life was in danger. And because something told her working alongside Samson O'Brien would always involve a bit of adventure, she'd started looking for a car.

Praying that nothing would come over the brow against her and force her to stop, she glared at the strip of tarmac through the rain-spattered windscreen.

'It was too good a deal to turn down,' she muttered.

'You mean you actually paid someone for this?' Samson grinned.

Delilah glowered at him. 'Not technically. I got it as

part-payment from Barry Dawson for setting up a website for the business. His mother died last month and it was sitting in a garage, doing nothing.'

'Plastic Fantastic Barry?' Samson asked, referring to the shop next to their office which sold items of every shape and colour, all in plastic. He flicked the dashboard contemptuously. 'What was it – out-of-date stock?'

This time she punched him, regardless of the fact she had to take a hand off the steering wheel to do so. Tolpuddle barked in excitement as Samson tried to twist out of reach, but the interior of the red Micra was too small and he felt the impact of her left jab.

'Any more comments and you can walk the rest of the way. Besides, I don't see you riding your precious motorbike in this,' she said, gesturing at the weather. The wind had picked up and as they climbed onto the open fell, she could feel the little car being tugged by the strong gusts. 'Bad enough that you had to come in from Hellifield on it this morning. You must have got drenched.'

Samson coughed and looked out of the window, unable to explain that the only soaking he'd suffered on his commute had been in the shower of the office bathroom. Hating the deception, he was grateful when the car turned off the road and onto the track leading to High Laithe, home to Lucy Metcalfe and her son Nathan. Delilah wiped the fogged-up windshield and the burned-out carcass of a static caravan came into view at the end of the lane, sitting next to a barn that was in the final stages of conversion. In front of the barn was a Land Rover Samson recognised.

'Damn it! Will's here.'

'Don't worry about it,' said Delilah, features setting into a determined line that he knew well. 'He'll be fine.'

Samson rubbed his right arm where she'd hit him and made a wry face. 'Easy for you to say. Personally, I can't afford any more run-ins with the Metcalfes today.'

They were both laughing as they got out of the car.

He watched them pull up, the pair of them just about visible through the misted-up windshield of that ridiculous car she'd bought. They emerged laughing, the dog exploding out of the cramped back seat in a riot of legs and ears to run with them for the cover of the barn.

He could tell from how she was behaving. She was making yet another mistake.

'Did you invite him?' he asked, turning to look up at the tall figure beside him.

Ash Metcalfe shook his head in despair at his older brother. Fair where Will was dark, he had the characteristics typical of the Metcalfe clan – a rangy height and an even temperament. Only Will and Delilah had inherited the shorter stature and darker hair of their maternal ancestors. The fiery nature too, of course.

'Honestly, Will,' sighed Ash, 'he's a good bloke. You just need to give him a chance.'

'He's Samson O'Brien,' said Will, turning from the door, his broad shoulders squared in annoyance. 'Or have you forgotten everything that means? Delilah's a fool for having anything to do with him.'

'He saved Lucy's life, or have you forgotten that?'

'And I'm grateful for it. But that leopard won't change his spots.'

The stress of taking on the renovation project for his sister-in-law, combined with his brother's stubbornness, finally triggered a rare outburst of temper from the usually affable Ash.

'Whatever! Quite frankly, I'll take any help I can get if it means we can finish this bloody barn by Christmas and get Lucy and Nathan moved in. So keep a civil tongue in your head and try to smile once in a while. And if you can't manage that, then bugger off!'

He stepped out into the rain to meet his sister and Samson, leaving Will staring after him.

The morning passed by in a blur of activity. Ash, his good spirits having returned, was finishing off the plumbing in the utility, whistling while he worked. As a carpenter by trade – and the only professional builder amongst them – he'd accepted the role of project manager, assigning Will the task of tiling the bathroom and setting Delilah and Lucy painting one of the bedrooms. Harry Furness, the livestock auctioneer, who was known more for his love of talking than for his love of labour, was put to work sanding the floorboards of the large lounge, the ensuing noise of the sander guaranteeing his productivity. And Samson, simply out of Ash's desire to keep the detective and Will as far apart as possible, had been given the back-breaking job of grouting the floor tiles in the kitchen. He'd acquired an eager assistant in fourteen-year-old Nathan, his godson, who had taken to following Samson around ever since the fire at the caravan when Samson had saved Lucy's life. When Elaine Bullock pulled up in the Peaks Patisserie van and walked in with a tray piled high with sandwiches, there was a collective sigh of relief and the clatter of downed tools.

'Now there's a sight for sore eyes,' said Ash with a grin, as he relieved Elaine of her burden, Tolpuddle following the transfer with interest.

'He means the food, Elaine,' said Delilah. 'Just in case you thought he'd gone soft.'

Elaine laughed. 'Don't worry. I know you Metcalfes too well. Food always comes first.'

They gathered round a makeshift table in the hall, with camping chairs providing seating, and for the first ten minutes there was no talking as the hungry workers attacked their meal.

'Crikey,' said Elaine as the mound of sandwiches rapidly dwindled, the auctioneer reaching out for his fourth. 'I didn't factor you into the equation, Harry, when I calculated how many to bring.'

'An army marches on its stomach,' retorted the auctioneer through a mouthful of food.

'Judging by the way yours was wobbling when you were using that sander, you should be fine marching for a month or more,' said Samson, eliciting laughter from the others and an affronted look from Harry.

'Watch it,' warned Delilah. 'He'll drop you from the darts team.'

Harry, captain of the Fleece's resurgent team – which owed its recent success to Samson's prowess – was already shaking his head. 'Never. He can insult me all he likes, as long as he lines up on the oche on our side.'

'Does that mean I can also pick your brain?' asked Samson.

'About what?'

'Tups. The theft of them, in particular. Have you heard of any being taken lately?'

The auctioneer's face grew serious. 'There's a fair bit of it about, unfortunately. Even with all the technology in the industry and the improved traceability, animals still get stolen.'

'But what do thieves do with them?' asked Lucy. 'I mean, they're tagged, so they can't exactly be sold at auction.'

'Black market,' said Harry. 'Unscrupulous abattoirs take them. And sometimes, if they're good specimens, they'll be used for breeding on the quiet.' He turned back to Samson. 'Why are you asking?'

'He's chasing a missing tup,' scoffed Will before Samson could reply. 'Clive Knowles has hired him to find that Swaledale he bought last backend.'

'Clive Knowles?' Harry looked sceptical. 'Then I'd take payment up front if I were you. He's known to be slow paying his bills, is Clive. I was surprised when he forked out for that tup.'

'Do you think it was stolen, then?' asked Will, his concern as a farmer overriding his reluctance to engage Samson in conversation.

'I'm not sure yet. But someone definitely visited the field in a truck around the time Ralph went missing.'

'When was this?' asked Ash.

'This week.'

Will frowned. 'Was the tup not in with the yows?'

'Yeah, he was.'

'But they took only the tup?'

Samson nodded, impressed by Will's sharpness. 'Exactly. That's what's been puzzling me. Why take only Ralph, when there was a field full of sheep?'

'I'm surprised they were able to,' continued Will. 'Get a tup in with the yows and they won't want to leave. It'd be a job to isolate him. Easier to take a load.'

'Any clues as to who might have done it?' asked Lucy.

'Like I said, it's just a theory at the moment. But I did find this.' Samson pulled the odd-looking lighter out of his pocket. 'I don't suppose anyone recognises it?'

He passed it around the group, all of them shaking their heads until it reached Harry. He turned it over in his hands, frowning, and then looked across at Will.

'Didn't Pete Ferris have one like this? I seem to recall him showing it off in the pub one night.'

'Not that I'm aware of,' said Will. 'But Mire End Farm is in his patch.'

'Patch for what?' asked Samson, struggling to place the name Harry had given. He vaguely remembered a pack of whey-faced kids at school called Ferris, who had always looked on the verge of malnutrition.

'Poaching. He followed his dad into the family business.' Will's tone was sarcastic. 'Given that he shares an IQ with the game he hunts, he'll probably follow his dad into prison, too.'

'Where would I find him?'

'Out lamping, mostly.'

'Anywhere else?' asked Samson, not relishing the idea of trying to approach someone while they were out hunting at night. That was how accidents happened.

'He has a caravan on a field over near Horton. You could try there.'

'But be careful,' warned Harry. 'He's as likely to take a shot at you as answer questions. And his dogs are vicious.'

'Talking of which,' said Elaine, starting to clear the table, 'I'd best get back to work before my boss gets vicious.'

Lucy laughed. 'Good to know my reputation is intact. But I'm a pushover compared to Ash. He's a regular slave-driver.'

'Well, in that case,' Elaine continued, 'perhaps now is a good time to ask for a few days off.'

'For Alice's funeral?' Lucy put a hand on her friend's arm. 'You know you don't have to ask. Have you got a date?'

'No, not yet. We're still waiting to hear from the coroner about the post-mortem.' Elaine pulled a face. 'We're all hoping it won't be necessary. But I need to sort out Alice's apartment. Ana, the manager, called me yesterday to find out what we were planning to do with it. She's keen to get it cleaned and on the market.'

'That seems a bit insensitive.'

Elaine shrugged. 'She's very clinical. Good at her job, though.' She turned to Samson. 'And she was full of questions about you and your police background. I'd say you've got yourself a fan there.'

Harry groaned. 'Christ, if he's not rescuing damsels in distress in his boxer shorts, he's winning them over with his drugs-busting past.'

Joining in the laughter with the others, Delilah was aware of Will's brooding stare resting on her. 'Do you want a hand cleaning out Alice's things, Elaine?' she offered, trying to deflect his attention.

Elaine shook her head. 'It won't take long. I'll put most of it in bags for the charity shop. This is what I'll remember her by.' She took Alice's pillbox, with its seven stripes of colour across the lid, out of her bag. 'Even if it's not the original.'

'How do you know it's not the original?' Samson had taken the box from her and was opening the lids, all of the compartments now empty.

'Look underneath.'

He turned it over to see a blank surface of silver. 'Nothing on it.'

'Exactly.' Elaine gave a sad smile. 'The one I gave her was engraved with her initials. Alice must have damaged it and bought a new one to replace it, without saying a word.'

'How sweet,' said Lucy. 'Just shows how much she treasured it.'

'Yes, that's what I thought when I noticed the difference. She was a very special lady.'

Samson caught Delilah's eye. A very special lady who had been afraid she was going to die. He felt the familiar stab of guilt and was relieved when Ash stood up and started ordering them back to work.

'Escape while you can, Elaine,' said Delilah as her friend took the empty tray back to the van. 'And we'll see you tonight. If my bossy brother hasn't worked us all to death by then!' She picked up her paintbrush and a stepladder and followed Lucy up the stairs, while Samson headed back into the kitchen.

'You're coming tonight, aren't you, Samson?' Nathan was already kneeling on the tiles, long legs tucked under him, a lock of thick, fair hair half covering his face as he wiped down the grout that had dried from the morning session.

Samson's knees popped as he joined his godson on the floor and he cursed Ash silently for this punishment. 'Coming where?'

'It's the Christmas lights turn-on in the marketplace this evening.' Nathan was regarding him with expectation.

Samson couldn't think of many worse ways to spend his time. Apart from grouting. He'd claimed to be busy when celebrations to mark the opening of the town's festive season had originally been scheduled for two weeks before. But a storm system from the west had brought high winds across the Dales, and the leaders of Bruncliffe had seen fit to postpone the event, rescheduling it for a fortnight's time. Tonight. And Samson had no excuses ready.

'Erm . . . what does it involve? Someone famous flipping a switch?'

Nathan pulled a face. 'Not even that. It's lame. Typical Bruncliffe. It would've have been so much better if they'd held it during the storm.'

'Are you going?'

'Yeah. I promised Mum . . .' The lad's reluctance was palpable. 'It'd be good if you were going.' He glanced sideways at Samson, looking up from beneath long eyelashes, a replica of his father.

The Christmas lights turn-on. Samson wasn't sure he was up for it. An evening spent in the company of people who still weren't that keen to have him in town and who would only want to remind him of his past. It wasn't worth it. Even if Nathan wanted him to go.

He turned to make his apologies and sensed someone watching them from the hallway. A sideways glance was enough to tell him it was Will Metcalfe – one of the many who wished Samson had never come back. And that was enough to make him change his mind.

'Sure,' he said, applying grout with exaggerated care. 'I'll come.'

The smile that spread across his godson's face made up for the possible ramifications of provoking Will Metcalfe. Besides, what else did he have for doing on a wet evening in Bruncliffe?

'Didn't think this was your cup of tea, young man.' Seth Thistlethwaite, retired geography teacher and former athletics coach, greeted Samson with a handshake and a twinkle in his eyes. 'Mixing with Bruncliffe's high society.' He cast a disdainful look at the makeshift stage in the marketplace, where various dignitaries from the town were standing to one side as a choir from the primary school sang carols.

With the rain having given way a couple of hours before, it was a chilly, damp evening. The ground was covered in puddles, the skies already dark, and a persistent wind was tugging at the strings of lights looped across the streets, buffeting the tarpaulins of the festive market stalls lined around the edge of the square. But the folk of Bruncliffe were hardy when it came to weather, and determined when it came to celebrating Christmas. Consequently, the small square was packed, the shops that surrounded the cobbled centre were brightly lit, with seasonal displays of reindeers, red-cheeked Santas and fake snow decorating their windows, and the aroma of mulled wine and hot mince pies scented the air.

'Not sure I'll ever be accepted into the inner circle,' said Samson with a smile. 'I'm just happy to see a friendly face. It's good to see you, Seth.'

Seth grunted, bushy eyebrows pulled together in a frown. He'd always defended the O'Brien boy, even back when the lad was being painted as the town's black sheep. The determination to make a success of the farm, despite the odds; the reluctance to accept the version of his father that the town wished to portray. Plus his ability on the fells, those long legs propelling Samson over the hills with ease. All of that had endeared him to Seth, a man not known for sentimentality.

For the last fourteen years, however, since Samson had fled town on a stolen motorbike following that infamous fight with his father, Seth had been championing a lost cause. Bruncliffe had condemned the boy as a reprobate, and that was that.

Then he'd come back, and within a couple of weeks the place had been abuzz with stories about him. New ones. The punch that had greeted him. The darts match he'd won. And then that extraordinary day when the rugby club had been burned down and Lucy's Metcalfe's caravan destroyed. The black sheep had saved two lives that day. More maybe, considering that he'd helped catch the killer who had been targeting Delilah Metcalfe's business.

But still the locals were wary. Seth had watched Samson

approach a few minutes before, seen the way people were torn between acceptance and rejection as he made his way across the square.

'Funny how folk hold onto the past,' he muttered. 'Even when the future can offer so much more.'

'There you are!' The men turned to see Delilah pushing her way through the crowd towards them, Tolpuddle by her side, with Nathan, Lucy and Elaine Bullock following. The three women were wearing Santa hats, Tolpuddle had a red bow on his collar and Elaine's bright-scarlet Dr Marten boots added to the festive colours. 'Nathan said you were coming, Samson,' continued Delilah, 'but we didn't believe him.'

'What? Miss the chance to see a celebrity turn on the Christmas lights? How little you know me.'

Nathan laughed at the unveiled sarcasm and Lucy threw Samson a grateful glance. Her son hadn't had much to be happy about in the last two years, but the recent improvement in his relationship with his godfather was having a positive effect.

'A chance to have some mulled wine, more like!' came the jovial tones of Harry Furness, the auctioneer elbowing his way towards the group, a tray of drinks in his steady hands. He was followed by the tall form of Ash Metcalfe, who was carrying a stack of hot rolls, the smell of pulled pork and apple sauce oozing from the wrappers and making Samson's mouth water.

'Courtesy of Lucy,' said Harry as he started handing out glasses while Ash passed around the food, Tolpuddle watching his every movement hopefully. 'Mulled wine and a hog-roast sandwich, for all your hard work.'

'Hey up!' A sharp nudge in the ribs from a grinning Elaine Bullock almost made Samson drop his roll. 'I think you might have competition for the Fair Lady of Fellside Court.' She was nodding towards two figures at the side of the stage, the handsome features of Rick Procter leaning down towards the delicate beauty of Ana Stoyanova. Both blonde, they made an arresting couple.

Perhaps sensing the attention, Ana glanced over and caught Samson's eye. She quickly averted her gaze as Rick continued talking to her. Whatever the topic, it was clandestine. Ana nodded, cast one last look at Samson and then walked away.

'Samson?' Harry passed him a glass, pulling his attention back from the manager of Fellside Court, and gave another to Seth.

'Not sure I qualify,' Seth protested. 'I haven't done anything.'

'No,' quipped Lucy. 'But you're here and Will isn't, so make the most of it!'

Seth smiled and raised his drink in toast. 'To your new home,' he said. 'May you be in it by Christmas.'

Ash groaned. 'Thanks, Seth. Not like I'm under pressure already or anything.'

'Don't worry,' said Harry, biting into his sandwich and licking his fingers. 'We'll get it done. Some of the rugby lads have agreed to come up and get painting. And the darts team have offered to pitch in, in any way they can.'

'Goodness,' Lucy said with a grateful smile. 'Thanks, Harry, for organising everything.'

Harry shrugged. 'No organising needed. They all asked to help. Ryan had a lot of friends and they won't stand by and see you and Nathan struggle. Not after what happened to you . . .' He paused. Then a smile broke over his florid features. 'Mind you, that lot'll take some feeding!'

Lucy laughed. 'If they're anything like you, they'll bankrupt me.'

'Talking of bankruptcy . . .' Seth turned to Samson and lowered his voice as the others continued chatting. Only Nathan, close by his godfather's side, was in earshot. 'I hear you've taken on a case for Clive Knowles, looking for that halfwit tup of his?'

Samson wasn't surprised at the old man being well informed. Despite his taciturn manner, Seth Thistlethwaite had an uncanny way of gathering local news, even if he rarely passed it on. 'As usual, Seth, you've heard correctly.' Samson waited for the inevitable comment that would follow. For while Seth was anything but a gossipmonger, he was always happy to deliver his judgement on whatever rumour was doing the rounds.

'Aye, well make sure you get paid up front,' said Seth, taking a sip of his wine. 'Clive Knowles' wallet doesn't see the light of day very often.'

Harry had joined them, a couple of mince pies in his hand, and was nodding his head in agreement. 'That's exactly what I said. Now there's two of us telling you, you'd best take heed.'

'Noted,' said Samson. 'And thanks for the advice.'

'Have you asked Seth about what you found up at Knowles' farm?'

Seth looked from Harry to Samson expectantly and Samson took the grenade-shaped lighter out of his pocket. 'I came across this at Mire End. Do you recognise it?'

The old man peered at the object in Samson's hand. 'That's Pete Ferris's. Seen him in the Fleece with it many a time.' He glanced up, eyes shrewd, while Nathan examined the unusual lighter with interest. 'You thinking he might have summat to do with the missing tup?'

'Not sure. For now, I'm just trying to find out who owns this. I want a word with them.'

'Well, it's Pete's all right. But I'd be right careful about how you approach him. He's not the most stable of people.'

'Yeah,' said Harry, swallowing the last mouthful of his mince pies. 'I'd take backup if I were you.'

'Backup for what?' Delilah appeared at Samson's shoulder, collecting the empty glasses onto a tray.

'He's heading up to Pete Ferris's place,' said Harry and then winced as a well-placed kick caught him in the ankle. But Samson was too late. Delilah had heard and was already turning to him.

'I'll come with you. We can bring Tolpuddle, too.' She nodded at the dog, who looked up momentarily and then resumed eating the scraps of hog-roast that had fallen to the ground.

Samson shook his head. 'No way. This doesn't involve you. And besides . . .'

'It could be dangerous?' Delilah raised an eyebrow. 'And I'm a girl?'

'No . . . yes – there's that, but . . .' Samson's stuttering petered out, to be replaced by Seth's chuckling.

'That's sorted, then,' said Delilah, taking the glass from Samson's hand. 'Besides, I was at school with Pete. I know him. You don't. We'll go Monday morning.'

Samson started to protest but Seth cut him short. 'She's right, Samson. Pete hasn't seen you in years. He won't know you walking up to his caravan, and he's more likely to take his gun to you than greet you. Whereas Delilah . . . He's always had a soft spot for her.'

Delilah smiled, a trace of pink on her cheeks. 'See,' she said to Samson. 'You need me.'

He was about to reply when the smile slipped from her lips and a scowl replaced it.

'Evening, all.' Will Metcalfe was standing behind Samson. Beside him was the golden-haired Rick Procter.

'Everyone enjoying the festivities?' asked the property developer, leaning over to place a kiss on Delilah's cheek.

'We were, until you brought Scrooge along,' muttered Delilah.

Rick laughed and ruffled her hair. 'Cheer up. The lights are about to be switched on.'

'Who's the celebrity?' asked Nathan. 'Do you know?'

'It's a secret,' said Rick, tapping the side of his nose. He turned his back on the lad and focused on Delilah, asking her about her work on the website for Fellside Court.

'Arse!' muttered Nathan under his breath. Making sure he was shielded from his Uncle Will by Samson and Seth, he held the lighter behind the property developer's backside and pressed the switch, a flash of fire shooting up and almost catching Rick's trousers. The lad jumped back, surprised by the ferocity of the flame, while Seth Thistlethwaite, never a fan of the arrogant property developer, collapsed in silent laughter.

'Behave, you two,' whispered Samson, reaching out to

take the lighter and trying hard not to smile. 'You'll get me in trouble. And I can't afford any more of that.'

A surge of applause from the crowd prevented any further mischief, and they turned to face the stage where the children's choir had finished singing. Samson didn't notice how it happened, but as everyone repositioned themselves he ended up with Will Metcalfe behind him and Rick Procter next to him. He shifted uncomfortably. While the centre of Bruncliffe was a far remove from the alleyways and deserted spaces where he'd conducted his undercover drugs operations, he felt every bit as exposed. Every bit as under threat.

A heavy weight came to rest against his legs. Tolpuddle, leaning into him as was his way. He reached down and stroked the dog's head, getting a lick on the hand in return.

At least he had one ally.

As the choir filed off into the wings, a portly middle-aged man stepped out of the ranks of local officials, microphone in hand and a chain of office propped on his broad chest.

'Our esteemed mayor,' said Ash. 'Mr Bernard Taylor.'

Samson watched the man on the stage, the intervening fourteen years since he'd last seen him having added at least a couple of stone to what had already been a well-padded frame. 'Looks like selling houses has been profitable while I was away,' he remarked wryly, glancing across the square to where what had once been a small office for Taylor's estate agents was now a double-fronted expanse of glass.

'A lot's been profitable while you were away,' said

Rick, as Bernard Taylor started to address the crowd. 'But not Twistleton Farm, I grant you.'

It was said in an undertone meant only for Samson's ears. He stiffened, his tension transmitting to Tolpuddle, who growled softly. Lowering a hand to reassure the dog, he tried to calm his own thumping pulse, while the injustice at what had happened to his home raged through him. It wasn't the time or the place to confront Rick Procter.

'Oh, look!' Lucy was pointing at the stage, where a life-size Mickey and Minnie Mouse had appeared, waving at the crowd. She waved back, eliciting a groan from her teenage son.

'Oh God,' muttered Nathan. He turned to Samson with a pained look. 'I told you it would be lame.'

'You think everything's lame,' said Delilah, laughing as she put an arm around her nephew. 'It's just an age thing. You'll get over it.'

With the mayor looking awkward between them, Mickey and Minnie took their positions centre stage next to a giant plunger, and the countdown started, a big screen flashing out the numbers, encouraging the audience to join in. Standing next to Nathan, Delilah was happily taking part, clapping her hands and teasing him until he started laughing and began calling out along with her, his face alight with pleasure.

'Forget it!' Rick Procter's words were sharp enough to penetrate the surrounding noise but were aimed at Samson alone. 'She's out of your league, O'Brien.'

'Thanks for the warning,' said Samson, keeping his voice low and his attention on Delilah.

'I've plenty more warnings for you. Stay around and you'll find out.'

It was enough to make Samson turn to face the property developer as the countdown reached its conclusion and the characters on the stage pressed down the plunger, bathing Bruncliffe in the spirit of Christmas. In contrast, Rick Procter was staring at him with undisguised hostility.

Tolpuddle stirred and Samson slipped a hand under the dog's collar. He knew what the faithful hound was capable of. He also knew what he was capable of himself.

'Time to go!' said Delilah, twisting round to smile at Samson. He forced himself to relax. 'There are fireworks up next and Tolpuddle doesn't like them, do you, boy?' She leaned down and rubbed his head, the dog panting up at her.

'I'll walk you home,' said Rick.

Delilah shrugged, casting her farewells over her shoulder. She caught Samson's eye and grinned. 'See you Monday,' she said. Then she was gone, swallowed up by the crowd, the tall figure of Rick Procter blocking any view of her.

'Arse!' muttered Samson, echoing his godson's opinion. He should have let the lad loose with the lighter.

Loud music began to pump out of the speakers at the side of the platform and a local dance troupe came running onto the stage. Samson, his mood dark and far from festive, tapped Lucy on the shoulder and said goodbye, throwing a hand up in farewell to Nathan and the others.

'You off?' asked Harry, half a gingerbread man in his grasp, the other half already consumed.

Samson nodded. 'Had enough.'

'Me too,' said the auctioneer, falling into step alongside him. 'Reckon I'll get a swift pint in the Fleece and call it a night.'

'You not staying for the fireworks, then?'

'No, I've had my fill of them this year.' Harry grinned ruefully, acknowledging the close call on Bonfire Night, when he'd nearly lost his life. 'I only came along tonight to support Rick.'

'Rick?'

'He sponsors this.' Harry gestured back at the far side of the stage and Samson noticed the banner bearing the name of Procter Properties. 'He does a lot for the town, and he's thick as thieves with the council.'

Samson grimaced. 'Thick as thieves with Delilah, too. Not sure Ryan would approve of them being together.'

His comment drew a deep laugh. 'Delilah and Rick?' Harry shook his head. 'There's nothing going on there. I'd have heard about it.'

'But . . .' Samson paused, remembering the shoes littering the back porch at the office, all of them a size that would fit Rick Procter. Had he jumped to conclusions? 'They're not an item?'

'Nope. Delilah hasn't dated anyone since her divorce.'

'Divorce?' Samson blinked. Delilah had been married?

'Christ, Samson, you didn't half hide yourself away when you left town. How can you not know all this?'

'Easily. Feel free to fill me in.'

Harry glanced over his shoulder to make sure they were out of earshot, the crowd thinner at this end of the market square. 'She married Neil Taylor,' he said. 'It didn't last long, though.'

'Neil Taylor?'

'Bernard Taylor's son. He came home after college and swept Delilah off her feet.'

Casting his mind back to school, Samson pictured a tall, spotty-faced teen in the year below him swaggering around town, arrogant on the back of his father's commercial success. A father who had gone on to become mayor. 'What happened? Why didn't it work out?'

Harry frowned. 'Bastard broke her heart. Had a couple of affairs, the last one not long after Ryan died. Will was ready to kill him if he hadn't left town.'

Samson felt a surge of respect for the oldest Metcalfe sibling.

'It was bad,' continued Harry. 'You know what it's like around here. Everyone knew everything about it. Or at least they thought they did. But Delilah is stubborn. She held her head high and took on both businesses, as well as the cottage they'd bought. It nearly destroyed her, though, financially and emotionally.'

'I had no idea.'

'No, I guess you didn't. Still, she's over it now. Not seen her as happy as she's been lately for a long time.'

Ahead, the lights of the Fleece were spilling out onto Back Street. Samson shook the auctioneer's hand. 'Thanks for bringing me up to speed.'

'Any time. But don't go telling Delilah I told you,' said Harry. 'I've no desire to find out just how powerful that right hook of hers is.'

With a laugh and reassurances of discretion, Samson made his way to the small ginnel that ran along the back of the properties opposite the pub. Picking his way down the alleyway, the black mass of the crag looming up above him on the left, he stopped outside the third gate, unlocked it and let himself into the courtyard of the office.

Well, well. Delilah – little Dee, who'd trailed around after him and Ryan like a persistent shadow – had been married and divorced, with all of her life history laid bare for the vultures of Bruncliffe to pick over. And judging by the stack of boxes and the furniture in the spare rooms at the office, she was still hanging onto the past.

Deep in thought, he passed his motorbike and made his way up the path to the back door. He had his key in his hand when his mobile began to ring.

Pulling it from his pocket, the light from the screen sliced through the dark. Unknown number. He answered it as he turned the key in the lock.

'Be careful, Detective O'Brien.' The voice was female, seductive, measured. Enough to make him pause.

'Hello? Who is this?'

'Be careful . . . Samson.' His name sounded intimate in her sultry tone. 'They are going to make you pay.'

'Hello? Hello . . . ?' Dead air rushed back to him through the phone. And the hand of the past touched his shoulder, making him shiver.

It was coming. Perhaps sooner than he'd expected.

7

'Do we need to go so fast?' On Monday morning, Samson was clutching the dashboard, the Nissan Micra taking the first bridge in Horton with the stone parapet startlingly close to the passenger window as the car whipped to the left and over the second bridge. In the rear, Tolpuddle gave a small whine of agreement.

'Sorry,' muttered Delilah, easing up off the accelerator as they followed the road out of the village, heading north for Selside and Pete Ferris's caravan. 'Bad start to the day.'

'Dare I ask?'

'Best not.' She glanced in the rear-view mirror, met the amber gaze of the dog, and felt her stomach knot.

The email had arrived the night before. Normally she wouldn't have seen it, Sunday being spent in the warm embrace of her family at Ellershaw Farm. The Sabbath had always been sacrosanct in the Metcalfe clan, not so much in terms of religion, but in that everyone gathered for a late lunch which lasted through the evening. Since the incident that had almost cost Lucy her life, the Metcalfes had been observing this tradition even more faithfully. And by mutual consent, mobile phones were banned at the table. So Delilah should have had longer before the blow fell.

But an argument with Will – a regular occurrence these

days, usually instigated by her association with the man sitting next to her in the car – combined with the novel situation of having her own transport, had seen her leave the farm mid-evening. She'd been so wound up by her oldest brother's meddling ways that she'd returned home and settled down to work, hoping the routine would help soothe her agitated mind.

How wrong she'd been. She'd heard the tone that signalled new mail, seen the name of the sender, and her heart had started to pound.

Neil. Getting in touch out of the blue. She'd presumed it was about his belongings, which were cluttering up the top floor of the office building. When they'd split – or to be more precise, when he'd left her for a student and had disappeared down to London – he'd promised he would be back to collect his stuff. So she'd boxed it all and shifted everything over to the office, even though everyone was telling her to sell it; to get her own back by making money out of his possessions.

But she wasn't like that. Yes, she was capable of punching Samson when he'd turned up after fourteen years, but that was more honest. Sneaking behind Neil's back in such a vindictive way just wasn't her.

Although that might be about to change. Because Neil's email hadn't mentioned his belongings at all. It hadn't even mentioned Delilah. In fact, the email had focused on only one topic.

Tolpuddle.

Neil was asking for custody of their dog.

Her throat clenched and tears pricked the back of her eyes. She blinked furiously. There was no way she was going to let her ex-husband take Tolpuddle, a dog he hadn't even thought twice about when he'd left town with his new flame. She would fight him tooth and nail.

'Are you sure you don't want to talk about it?' Samson was staring out of the windscreen, hands still gripping the dashboard, and Delilah realised she was speeding once more, the left bend under the railway bridge already upon her in a blur of stone.

'Yes, sorry.' She blinked again, swallowed and pushed the thought to the back of her mind. 'You know where we have to turn off?'

He allowed himself to tear his frightened gaze from the approaching road. 'We take a right at Selside,' he said, looking at the map on his phone. 'Then follow the track. The caravan should be at the end of it, according to Seth.'

Delilah nodded, her grip on the steering wheel relaxing and the car slowing to a more moderate pace, allowing Samson to appreciate the view. To their right, Pen-y-ghent was veiled in a blanket of mist, its flat peak hidden, the fields on its lower flanks sodden and sombre. The few trees they passed held bare branches up to the grey sky, and enclosing the lot was the steady march of the stone walls that defined the Dales.

Even in the cloak of winter, it was beautiful. And unique. A distant cry from his metropolitan life in London.

The car crested a small rise and rounded a bend, a row of railway cottages visible tucked into a copse of trees, the train track running next to them, parallel to the road. In less than a minute they were approaching the collection of houses that comprised the village of Selside.

'There, that's our turning.' Samson pointed at a narrow lane cutting off between two houses.

Delilah slowed up, indicated and pulled off the road, the Micra immediately bucking and bouncing through potholes filled with water. 'Hell!' she muttered, worried about her car. 'Let's hope it's not too far.'

They passed under the railway and took the right-hand fork as the track branched at a farm. More holes pock-marked the gravelled road, the car crawling along, lurching from one to the next, Delilah cursing beneath her breath.

'How much further?' she asked.

Samson pointed. 'There.'

At the end of the track, in a field containing a dilapidated barn, was a small caravan. Filthy net curtains hung at the windows, mould and dirt covered the once-white roof and a ramshackle porch leaned heavily against its side. A muddy path led up to it and a battered pickup truck was parked alongside.

'There's no way I'm driving in there,' said Delilah, pulling the car over on a patch of grass and stopping the engine. 'We'll walk the rest of the way.'

They got out, the rain that the low clouds had heralded now beginning to fall. Tolpuddle, eager despite the weather, loped ahead, expecting a run as they headed through the gateway into the field. They were halfway between the car and the caravan when a cacophony of barking split the silence.

'Damn.' Delilah called Tolpuddle back and slipped his lead onto his collar. 'We might have a welcoming party.'

The porch door swung open, drunken on its hinges, and two solid shapes came hurtling out, covering the distance towards Samson and Delilah at a rapid pace. Lurchers. Trained to kill.

'Now what?' asked Delilah, feeling the tug of resistance as Tolpuddle fought to be released.

'Don't move,' said Samson. He stepped in front of her and as the dogs closed in, reached in his pocket and tossed a handful of something into the air.

The dogs froze, assessed and leapt, sharp teeth catching the objects as they fell.

'What the—?' Delilah watched in awe as the lurchers started chewing, tails wagging.

'Dog-gestives,' said Samson with a smile, his attention fully on the two dogs. 'I didn't think Tolpuddle would mind sharing.'

Delilah laughed quietly as Samson threw another couple of biscuits to the now-contented canines. Tolpuddle whimpered, and she turned to reassure him that he too would get treats. But he wasn't watching the lurchers. He was watching the caravan. She followed his gaze and went rigid.

'I don't suppose,' she murmured, 'that you've got something in your other pocket to deal with this?'

'What?' Samson looked up from the dogs and across the field. Standing on the ramshackle porch of the caravan was a man. In his hands was a shotgun. It was trained on them.

The low-lying cloud that was covering the peak of Pen-y-ghent was mirrored in the mist that had settled over Bruncliffe, dampening the morning with fine rain. In the cafe of Fellside Court, a despondent group of residents was sitting around a table, post-aerobics cakes and coffees largely untouched.

'Has anyone called for him?' Edith Hird looked at the concerned faces of her friends, the empty chair in their midst testament to Arty Robinson's absence.

'I did. He said he didn't feel like aerobics,' replied Joseph O'Brien with a frown. 'It's just not like him.'

'Definitely not.' Edith tapped her spoon against the side of her cup and pursed her lips. 'We need to do something.'

Over the five days since Alice Shepherd's death, the normally buoyant bookmaker had become morose, his cheerful smile missing as he went about his daily life. Withdrawing further and further into himself, he'd been shunning communal activities, staying in his room and turning away all offers of comfort from those who cared for him. And as his sunny personality became eclipsed by grief, so a shadow was cast across Fellside Court, plunging its inhabitants into melancholy too. Joseph had never known the place so downcast.

Take the morning aerobics session. There'd been little laughter, despite the best efforts of the lovely Vicky trying to lift the mood. Attendance had also been down, the usual seats of Arty and Alice not the only ones left vacant. Numbers had been low for the weekly Sunday roast in the cafe the day before as well, an event that was normally fully booked.

As tangible as the mist outside the window, a muted atmosphere had settled on the retirement residence.

'How is everybody this morning?' Ana Stoyanova was standing at the end of the table, face pale against the blood-red vibrancy of the cardigan she was wearing over her uniform, a file clutched to her chest.

'Not so good,' said Clarissa with her trademark honesty. 'We're worried about Arty.'

'He didn't come down for aerobics?'

Clarissa shook her head. 'We haven't seen him properly in days. He answers his door but doesn't invite us in.'

'He's depressed,' said Edith.

Ana frowned. 'Yes, I've noticed. He is missing Alice.'

'Do we know when the funeral will be?'

The frown on Ana's forehead deepened and her lips drew into a thin line of disapproval. 'Not yet. I heard from the family that they are still waiting for the coroner to make a decision on the autopsy. So, we must wait.'

Her reply drew a sigh from Edith and further glum expressions from the others. A flicker of worry rippled across the normally impenetrable expression of the manager and she attempted a smile. 'Anyway, what are you up to today? Any plans?'

'Eric's son is visiting on Wednesday,' volunteered Joseph, trying to match Ana's efforts to lift the spirits of his friends. 'Isn't that so, Eric?'

'Oh, that's wonderful. Where does he live?' Ana turned to the frail man sitting next to the empty chair.

'Down south,' said Eric with the disdain he reserved for anything below Skipton on the map. Then he looked at Ana with renewed interest. 'You and he might have something in common.'

Ana lifted an eyebrow. 'Really? What?'

Eric coughed and took a few breaths to recover. 'Serbia,' he said.

The reaction was immediate. Ana stiffened, her face fell back into its habitual inscrutable mask and her arms tightened across the folder she was carrying.

'Sorry,' said Eric, noticing her reaction. 'Have I got it wrong? I thought you said you were from Serbia? My lad was out that way, peacekeeping in the war.'

'I'm from Bulgaria.'

'Oh, my mistake.' He smiled apologetically. 'Never was good at geography.'

'No harm done,' said Ana, her clipped tone at odds with her words. She looked at her watch and turned to go. 'Have a good day, all of you.' She walked away, back rigid, steps hurried.

'Whoops,' said Edith, eyes on the manager as she left the cafe. 'Think you might have hit a nerve there.'

'I didn't mean to.' Eric looked upset, his breathing rasping in response. 'I was only trying to make conversation.'

Clarissa patted his hand. 'Of course you were. Don't worry about it. I'm sure Ana will have forgotten all about it already.'

Her sister chuckled. 'I wouldn't be so sure,' she said. 'She's hard to fathom, that one. You might want to appoint Joseph as a bodyguard.'

Joseph raised two fists and scowled, making the group laugh.

'Then again,' continued Edith, smiling at the gaunt figure of the Irishman, 'Arty would be a better bet. There's a bit more meat on him.'

'Talking of which,' Joseph got to his feet, addressing Eric. 'How about we go and find him and see if we can't get him to join us?'

He helped Eric out of his chair and the two of them left the cafe, Eric's oxygen cylinder trailing behind him on its trolley.

'Bugger off!'

The shotgun was unwavering, both barrels pointing at the intruders as the thin figure on the porch shouted at them. Already shielding Delilah from the dogs, Samson took a step forward, wanting to protect her even more.

'I said bugger off!' the man yelled again, lowering his cheek to the stock, clearly meaning business.

'Go back to the car, Delilah,' whispered Samson over his shoulder. 'Slowly.'

'And what about you?' she asked.

'I'll go and talk to him.'

Delilah snorted. 'Like hell,' she muttered and stepped out from behind his back, the shotgun immediately focusing on her.

'I warned you—'

'Pete! It's me, Delilah Metcalfe.' She passed Tolpuddle's lead to Samson, raised both of her hands in the air and took another step towards the caravan, wary of the lurchers, which were no longer occupied with the dog treats and were watching alertly.

'For God's sake, Delilah!' hissed Samson as the man's cheek lifted off the gun and he stared across the field at her. 'Don't be an idiot.'

Ignoring him completely, she inched further forward. 'I just want to talk to you,' she continued, addressing the man on the porch. Tolpuddle whined behind her, drawing the attention of the two dogs in front. 'It won't take long.'

There was a long pause and then the gun lowered fractionally. 'Delilah Metcalfe?'

She nodded, smiling.

The barrels dropped and a bony hand waved her forward. Samson made to go too, but the raising of the gun forestalled him.

'Just Delilah – not you!' shouted Pete.

'You're joking,' muttered Samson as Delilah moved further away from him.

'It's okay,' she said. 'He won't hurt me.'

Samson was forced to watch helplessly as she walked past the lurchers and towards the caravan. A tug on his arm reminded him that he wasn't the only one who was worried. Tolpuddle was straining on his lead, anxious to be with her too.

Arty Robinson stood before the sheet of glass in the empty lounge at Fellside Court and watched the water trail down its surface.

'There you are. We missed you at aerobics, Arty.' Joseph O'Brien was in the doorway, a look of concern on his face. 'Why don't you join us in the cafe? The others are all there.'

Arty shook his head. 'I'm not good company,' he said.

Joseph paused, reluctant to intrude on his friend's desolation. He was on the verge of suggesting to Eric that they leave Arty alone, when he felt the jab of a sharp elbow in his ribs. Edith was behind him.

'Here. Take this,' she whispered, holding out a tray containing three mugs of coffee and three plates, each bearing a slice of cake. 'And don't take no for an answer.'

Joseph smiled, taking the tray from her. 'You're a good woman, Edith.'

The former headmistress brushed aside his compliment with a flick of a hand. 'Nonsense. I'm acting out of self-interest. This place isn't the same without Arty's banter. Now get in there and cheer him up.'

She shooed the two men into the room, Joseph carrying the tray and Eric pulling his trolley.

Arty turned at the clink of china and a sad smile lifted his lips temporarily as he saw his two friends entering the lounge. 'I see you've been sent on a mission,' he said.

'And our lives won't be worth living if we fail,' replied Eric, taking a seat as Joseph placed the tray on a table and distributed the coffee and cakes.

'Come on,' said Joseph, patting the empty armchair next to him. 'Don't refuse or Edith will have our guts for garters.'

'I should have known she was behind this.' Despite wanting to be left alone, Arty crossed the room and sat down, knowing they meant well. 'Thanks.' He picked up his coffee, leaving his cake untasted on the plate. 'Any news on the funeral?' he asked.

'Not yet. Ana said the family still don't know if there'll be an autopsy,' said Joseph.

Arty winced. He hated the thought of poor Alice having to endure such an indignity. It seemed so unfair, inflicting such a final humiliation on such a private lady.

But then it all seemed so unfair. Since Alice passed away he'd been unable to shake off the cloud of guilt that was hanging over him – a vague sensation that there was something he could have done, something he should have seen that might have prevented her death. With sleep eluding him, he'd spent several nights looking across at Alice's empty apartment on the other side of the courtyard, nursing a glass of whisky as the blank windows rebuked him for her absence. From the adjoining flat, he could see the regular pulsing light of Eric's night-time oxygen machine behind the thin fabric of his curtains, the rhythmic flashing a contrast to the lifeless space next door to it.

He sighed, the thick mantle of depression settling around him.

Discerning the direction of his thoughts, Eric slapped the arms of his chair and leaned forward with as much energy as his body – racked by chronic obstructive pulmonary disease after a lifetime of heavy smoking – would allow.

'There's no point moping around here thinking about it,' he wheezed. 'We ought to do something. Go on a trip somewhere.'

The enthusiasm from his frail friend brought a halting smile to Arty's face. 'It's raining.'

Eric shrugged. 'So? Where's your sense of –' a fit of coughing interrupted him, the oxygen cylinder rattling on the trolley next to him – 'adventure?'

'He's right,' said Joseph, trying to fan the faint spark of interest Arty was displaying. 'We need to get out of here. Get a change of scenery.'

Arty pointed at the window. 'But we'll get soaked.'

'Not if you go to the coast.' The three men twisted round to see Ana Stoyanova. She had her mobile in her hand, a weather app on the screen. 'It's dry over there.'

'Morecambe,' declared Eric with a grin.

Joseph was nodding. 'Fish and chips on the beach . . .'

'The amusement arcade . . .'

Arty laughed. After so many days without the sound, Joseph and Eric both jumped at the deep bellow of amusement.

'Incorrigible!' the former bookmaker declared, knowing that his friends had dangled the prospect of the seaside resort and its fruit machines in the confidence that he would be unable to resist. 'But brilliant. How do we get there?'

'I'll book you a minibus,' said Ana. 'Bruncliffe Cabs has a fourteen-seater – would that be big enough?'

Joseph looked at Eric, who shrugged and looked at Arty. The bookmaker was grinning, already on his feet. 'I reckon. Come on, lads, let's get the ladies and tell them to grab their handbags. We're going to the seaside.'

'What do you want?'

The blunt question displayed none of the affection which Seth had claimed still lingered in Pete Ferris's heart. Although the poacher had lowered his gun, his dogs had trailed Delilah back to the caravan and now sat watching her. Or guarding her. It was hard to tell.

'Just a couple of questions. We don't mean any trouble.' She smiled warmly, but the bloodshot eyes staring back at her remained hostile.

It was a while since she'd seen Pete Ferris close up. She remembered him from school, despite the poacher being several years older and hardly ever turning up to class. The thin frame, the grubby clothes, the furtive manner – they were traits the entire family had shared. In adulthood, Pete had become a peripheral figure in Bruncliffe. Sometimes she'd see him leaving the Fleece, staggering down Back Street. Or catch sight of him on the other side of the marketplace, slouching across town. He seemed to slink through life, hugging walls and slipping through doorways, as feral as the animals he hunted illegally.

Now she had the chance to assess him in detail. Skeletal face under the peak of a baseball cap, jumper hanging off the points of his shoulders, dirt-caked jeans dropping to scuffed trainers – he had the look of a starved man down on his luck. He didn't smell too fresh, either, his pitted skin grey with grime.

'Get on with it, then. Got things to do with my day.'

'Right.' Delilah looked across the field to where Samson and Tolpuddle were standing, both of them straining to see what was happening. 'We found something. It might be yours.'

Suspicion flickered across the man's face and he twitched, shoulder hitching up to his ear, the gun jerking in response. 'Found what?'

'A lighter. Samson has it.' She gestured towards the figure in the distance.

'O'Brien? Is that O'Brien?' Pete turned and stared at the man with the dog. 'I heard he was back.'

'So do you want to see the lighter? See if it's yours?' persisted Delilah.

Pete twitched again, cheeks hollowing further as he chewed on the inside of his lip. Then he gave a tip of his head, which Delilah took for consent.

'Samson,' she called, beckoning him over, trying not to worry that the shotgun had lifted partially back into position or that the lurchers were rising to their feet. Under this attention, Samson and Tolpuddle approached the porch.

'Hi,' said Samson as they stepped up to join Delilah. He sounded relaxed, unperturbed by the gun or the dogs, and Delilah wondered how much of that was due to his police training. She surreptitiously wiped her damp palms on her jeans and felt the weight of Tolpuddle leaning against her leg, reassuring her that he was there. She slowly put a hand down to his head, wary of agitating the lurchers.

'Welcome home, O'Brien,' said Pete. He gave a sharp cackle, his gaze turning sly. 'Bet you've got Rick Procter rattled.'

'Not sure I'd go that far. Does he have reason to be rattled?'

The poacher shifted uneasily. 'None of my business,' he snapped. 'What do you want to show me?'

'It's in my pocket,' Samson cautioned, sliding a hand into his jacket, careful not to make any sudden movements. The lurchers, anticipating more biscuits, shuffled closer, panting eagerly as Samson pulled out the odd-shaped lighter. 'Here,' he said, holding it out. 'Recognise it?'

Teeth gnawing at his lip, Pete glanced down at the object in Samson's palm and then nodded. 'It's mine. Where'd you get it?'

'Up at Clive Knowles' farm.'

Another spasm pulled at the poacher's shoulder and his gaze flicked beyond his visitors to the foothills of Pen-y-ghent.

'Any idea how it got up there?' asked Samson.

Pete was shaking his head before the question was even finished, attention back on his visitors. 'Someone must have taken it.'

'From where?'

'How would I know? The pub? My truck? It's never locked.'

'You didn't lose it while you were out hunting one night?'

The gun snapped up, barrels inches from Samson's face, and the lurchers started growling. 'I don't care for the nature of your questions,' said Pete. 'I think it's time you left.'

'Sure.' Samson held out an arm, gesturing Delilah ahead of him. 'Ladies first.'

Heart pounding, Delilah took Tolpuddle's lead and led him down the steps, twisting back to make sure Samson was following. He was, and was composed enough to wink at her. 'Go to the car,' he whispered.

Go to the car? Where else would she go? Aware of the gun pointing at them, she began the walk across the field. A tense shout from behind made her jump.

'You're testing my patience, O'Brien!' Pete Ferris was at the edge of the porch, shotgun trained on the detective who, instead of following Delilah, was over by the poacher's battered pickup, opening the door. 'Bugger off, and that's your last warning!'

But Samson was holding up his hands in innocence. 'I was only putting your lighter back,' he said, the truth of his words visible in the green-and-black object he was placing on the passenger seat.

It was difficult to discern if the savage growl that came from the direction of the porch was issued by owner or dogs, but it was clear that neither biscuits nor Delilah's charms would be sufficient to pacify either. Samson walked hurriedly across the field, caught up with Delilah and Tolpuddle, and the trio hastened away.

'What the hell were you up to?' spat Delilah when they reached the safety of her car, her legs trembling. 'He could have shot you.'

Samson grinned. 'I took a gamble.'

'On what?'

'I wanted a look at his truck.'

'And?'

He held out his right hand. Clasped between finger and thumb was a tuft of wiry wool. 'I pulled it out of the join between the cab and the back.'

Delilah looked up at him. 'It's a bit of fleece.'

He nodded. 'Want to bet where it came from?'

She looked back across the field to the distant figure still watching them from the porch. 'Ralph? Pete Ferris took Ralph?'

'That's what it looks like,' said Samson. 'Now we just need to prove it.'

8

Half an hour after being run off Pete Ferris's land, Samson and Delilah were walking along a bridleway in the soft falling rain in the direction of the rising mass of Pen-y-ghent, Tolpuddle trotting ahead of them. They'd left the car tucked out of sight of the poacher's caravan and had set out across the land.

'You're convinced he's involved?' asked Delilah.

Samson nodded. 'In some way or other. How else can you explain the lighter up at the farm and the wool in the back of his truck?'

'Coincidence? He poaches up that way. He could have innocently dropped his lighter, and as for the wool – it could have blown in on the wind.'

'Sure. Equally, he could have been up there stealing a tup and stupidly left a trail. I'm leaning towards the latter.'

'I still think you should give him the benefit of the doubt. Not everyone is a criminal.'

Samson snorted. 'He's a well-known poacher.'

'Okay, so he is a criminal. But not necessarily one that steals sheep. And by the way,' she asked, exasperated as she stepped over yet another puddle, her boots already caked in mud, 'where are we going?'

As if in answer to her question, they turned a corner and the river was in front of them.

'There.' Samson looked across the fast-flowing water to the land on the other side. Tucked in under Pen-y-ghent, even from this distance he could see it was badly managed. Broken stone walls, weed-infested fields. A farmhouse stood to one side, a couple of barns beyond it.

'What's so special about that?' asked Delilah.

Samson grinned down at her. 'Don't you know where we are? I thought you called yourself a local?' Not waiting for a retort, he veered right and followed the bridleway, which had narrowed into a riverside path.

Delilah frowned, taking in the landscape as she walked behind him, the mist-shrouded peak of the mountain, the brown tinge of the damp winter fields below it. She thought back over where they'd come from. They'd travelled north-west out of Bruncliffe up the dale, passing through Horton on the way. Then they'd turned east into Selside and down the track to Pete Ferris's caravan. From there, the path had taken them further east and now . . . Now they were heading in a southerly direction, back towards Horton.

'Worked it out yet?' Samson asked over his shoulder.

The smug smile on his face took her right back to childhood, the memories so vivid she could see Ryan laughing as his friend wound her up. Then she would fly at her tormentor, small fists flailing, and Ryan would have to intervene. There was no Ryan now. Nothing to stop her shoving the man in front of her into the cold waters of the river beside them.

As if sensing the direction of her thoughts, Samson stepped to the side and ushered her ahead of him with a gallant sweep of an arm.

'Not that I don't trust you,' he laughed as she stalked past him. 'So, any idea?'

She didn't have a clue, but was too ashamed to admit it. Instead she picked up her pace, trying to put distance between them while she struggled to get her bearings. When they reached a small bridge that spanned the river, she mutely followed Samson's directions and crossed over to the other side, Tolpuddle choosing to take the scenic route by going through the water.

While the dog was shaking himself dry on the bank, Delilah looked around, failing to spot any identifiable features. It was just farmland, nothing to mark it out as different apart from its poor condition. 'I give up,' she muttered, turning up her collar in an attempt to stop the rain trickling down her neck.

'And there was me thinking *I* was the offcumden.' Samson walked past her, back upstream in the direction they had come from, towards the farmhouse they'd spotted from the other side. They were approaching a stone wall when he crouched down behind it, beckoning Delilah to do likewise, Tolpuddle already by his side.

'What about now?' he whispered. He was pointing at a figure, which had just left the building and was making its way towards the furthest barn. Even from this distance, there was something about the slightly stooped shuffle that was unique.

'That's Clive Knowles!' she said, head turning sharply as she reassessed their location.

'Correct. Welcome to Mire End Farm. And that,' Samson pointed back across the river to a white oblong in a field, 'is Pete Ferris's caravan.'

'They're virtually neighbours.'

'Doesn't mean one wouldn't steal from the other.'

They waited until Clive Knowles had entered the barn and then they slipped back across the river, careful to give the lonely caravan and its gun-wielding occupant a wide berth on the way back to the car.

'This is the life!' Eric Bradley gave a contented sigh that quickly dissolved into a bout of coughing, chips spilling out of the polystyrene container on his lap.

'Take it easy,' said Joseph O'Brien, holding onto his friend's portion of fish and chips to prevent further accident, 'or this life you're so enjoying might be shorter than you expected.'

The two men, along with Arty Robinson, were sitting on a wall on the promenade looking out across Morecambe Bay to the Lake District in the distance. With the tide at its highest, the sea stretched out before them, glinting in a surprisingly warm sun. Surprising because it was December and they had left behind a dismal day in Bruncliffe.

After a frantic bustle to get everyone ready, a group of twelve pensioners had set out from Fellside Court. Thanks to the reluctance of some residents to subject their newly styled hair to the wind and brine of the coast – Monday being the day Geraldine Mortimer organised the Coiffure Club – the men almost outnumbered the women, for once. But reduced numbers hadn't dampened the excitement on the minibus at the prospect of an unexpected day out; it was an excitement which amplified as the weather improved the further west they travelled. They'd arrived in the seaside resort to blue skies, and even Arty had felt his spirits lift as they walked down to the beach, the smell of salt and seaweed washing over them. They'd strolled the length of the promenade slowly, to accommodate those who were less mobile, and had then decided it was time for fish and chips. With the breeze picking up, the majority of the group had opted to eat in, taking seats at the cafe window with a view of the bay. But, egged on by Arty, three of them had decided to brave the elements and eat outside. The combination of chips, vinegar and fresh sea air had worked wonders on Arty's disposition.

'Thanks,' he said to Joseph as Eric finally got control of his breathing. 'This was exactly what I needed.'

Joseph shrugged. 'It's Ana we should be thanking. I'm not sure we'd have organised it without her help.'

'I can't have offended her too much,' said Eric with a smile.

'Offended her?' Arty looked confused.

'It was nothing,' said Joseph. 'We were having coffee this morning and Eric was talking about his son coming up and his time over in the Balkans. In the process, he mistakenly said Ana was from Serbia.'

'She's not. She's from Bulgaria.'

'Yes,' said Eric. 'I know that now. She didn't seem too happy with my slip-up. I didn't mean to upset her.'

Arty patted him on the back. 'Given the recent history in that area, you can understand her reaction. Perhaps we should get her something as a souvenir of our day out, to make amends?'

Eric's face split into a smile. 'What a wonderful idea.'

'And then,' said Arty, grinning now, 'let's hit the fruit machines.'

The three of them laughed, revelling in how perfect this day had turned out to be.

The drive back to Bruncliffe wasn't much easier on Samson's nerves, Delilah's troubles of the morning replaced with the excitement of their recent sleuthing. Combined with a windscreen that was steaming up, the reverse trip over the double bridges of Horton village saw Samson clutching the dashboard in pretty much the same way as he had several hours earlier, the stonework of the old bridge just as hair-raisingly close to the side of the Nissan Micra.

'Do you want me to drop you at the office?'

Samson was tempted to insist that she stop the car immediately and let him out, but the rain had got heavier and the walk would be a long one. 'Fine,' he said, eyes glued to the road. 'Just get me there in one piece.'

'Sorry,' said Delilah, wiping the glass in front of her with a sleeve and reducing her speed. 'I'm buzzing from all that. The dogs, the shotgun, the evidence you found . . .' She glanced over at the frozen face of her companion, his hand still glued to the dashboard. 'How did you cope?'

'With what?'

'Life undercover. You must have faced a lot worse than Pete Ferris with a shotgun. How did you unwind afterwards?'

'You learn to compartmentalise. Detach yourself from everything else in your life.'

'So it all becomes normal?'

He thought about that. What was normal? For him, the last six years had been spent living day to day, one case to the next, constantly reinventing himself, constantly on the edge of danger. That had been normal.

Now he was in a car in the Yorkshire Dales, driving through pastoral scenes which had nothing in common with the dingy environments he'd inhabited in London. And beside him was the little sister of his best friend. Yet this felt far more surreal.

'It's all relative.'

She screwed her face up at his answer. 'Relative to what? Living on the moon?'

He gave a dry laugh. 'Yeah, sometimes it did feel like that.'

'Must have been lonely.' She glanced sideways, but he kept his face passive. 'No special person in your life, then?'

The teasing tone made him smile. 'No,' he said. 'Not in that life. It wasn't possible.'

It wasn't safe now, either. Not with what was happening to him.

'Actually, drop me in the marketplace,' he said, moving the topic on as the first of Bruncliffe's two mills came into sight. 'I'll pick up some sandwiches from Lucy's. Count it as payment for your time.'

Delilah laughed. 'Thanks, but I've got a meeting with Rick Procter. He's taking me to that new restaurant in Low Mill.' She glanced at her watch and cursed. 'Damn. I'm already late. I won't have time to change.'

Jaw clenched, Samson forced himself to look at her. Her dark hair was soaked, wet tendrils curling on her damp collar, her jeans were splotched with mud and her nose was bright red. 'Don't worry,' he said, allowing his disgruntlement free rein. 'You look perfect. Go straight there. He's not a man to be kept waiting.'

'You're right. He'll have to take me as I am,' she said, pulling up outside Peaks Patisserie. 'Could you do me a favour and look after Tolpuddle? He doesn't seem to care for Rick and I don't want to leave him in the car.'

'My pleasure.' Samson got out, dog in tow, and watched her drive off, a mixture of emotions churning his gut. He looked down at the Weimaraner, who was panting up at him. 'Don't like Rick Procter, eh, Tolpuddle?' The dog barked in agreement. 'That kind of good judgement deserves special treatment.'

Turning his back on the cafe, Samson crossed the marketplace towards Hargreaves' butcher's. They did superb pies, which he and Tolpuddle were both partial to.

'Great minds, Tolpuddle – great minds,' he muttered. And he wasn't just talking about the pies.

Lunch was in the newest addition to the Procter Properties portfolio, towards the south end of town. As Delilah pulled up outside Low Mill, she was struck by the changes. What had been scrubland now boasted a housing development that was almost completed, executive-type detached homes being built alongside more compact town houses, and all neatly arrayed around the old mill that dominated the skyline.

The mill itself was an impressive building, stone-built, three storeys high, with a tall chimney at one side. Under Rick Procter's hand, it had been converted into a mixture of flats and commercial interests, boasting a delicatessen, a designer-clothing boutique, a bespoke jeweller's and a brasserie. Not a cafe. A brasserie.

It was very upmarket for Bruncliffe. Rick seemed to think it would make money, however, and judging by the number of cars in the car park, it was busy, so who was she to know any different. But it would be a while before she could afford to visit it on a regular basis.

Delilah reached for her bag on the back seat and noticed the mud on her jeans. Damn. She wet a tissue and scrubbed at the marks, simply smearing them even further. Double damn. Twisting the rear-view mirror, she checked her appearance and promptly wished she hadn't. Her nose was bright red, her hair was a wreck . . .

She looked at the imposing entrance to the establishment in front of her. Then at the other cars around her. Mercedes. BMWs. A couple of Audis. No other Micras.

It wasn't the kind of place for someone who looked like she'd just come off the farm. She should have gone home and changed, not listened to Samson.

The trill of a mobile from the footwell below the passenger seat cut through her apprehension. Leaning over, she picked up the phone. It was Samson's. Should she answer it?

Unknown caller.

Thinking it could be him calling from the Fleece or somewhere, she flicked her thumb across the screen and held the mobile to her ear. 'Hello?'

'Samson?' A woman's voice, low and sensuous.

'I'm sorry, he's not here at the moment. Can I take a message?'

A bewitching laugh, then that purr. 'No, darling. I don't think so.' The connection was ended.

Bemused, she dropped the phone in her bag and got out of the car. When she entered the plush premises of Low Mill Brasserie, she wasn't thinking about her bedraggled state. She was thinking about the fact that Samson had lied to her. There *was* a woman in his life. A sophisticated and alluring woman.

When Rick Procter reflected on his lunch date later that evening, he would blame her distracted manner on the surroundings. He'd curse himself for overawing her with such a demonstration of his wealth and success. He would have no inkling that in fact, while she picked at her chargrilled swordfish loin with little appetite, Delilah wasn't thinking about him at all.

As Delilah sat opposite the property developer and watched him savour his roasted venison haunch, in the centre of town Samson was sitting at the office kitchen table, watching Tolpuddle devour a steak-and-kidney pie. His own pie lay neglected on his plate. Meanwhile, to the north of Bruncliffe, the Fellside Court residents who hadn't absconded to the coast were eating their lunch in an unusually quiet cafe. In the kitchen, Ida Capstick, her cleaning duties at the retirement home almost finished for the day, was having a quick cup of coffee and a sandwich with the cook, before heading back upstairs to clean two last rooms.

The corridors were silent. The lounge was empty. In the entrance hall, a partially decorated Christmas tree had been abandoned for the duration of the mealtime. The courtyard was bleak, wet leaves plastered to the paving stones, the chairs and tables dripping in the persistent rain. Rising up above them, the sheet of glass that separated the two wings of the building stared blindly out, the conditions too dull to reflect the fells. Behind it, a figure walked swiftly along the first-floor corridor and turned left at the end. It passed the empty flat, entering the one next to it. Moving quickly, it went into the bedroom. Moments later it left.

Outside the rain continued to fall.

'How was lunch?' Samson looked up from his desk as Delilah came to stand in the doorway.

She smiled widely. 'Brilliant. You should see what Rick has done with Low Mill.'

'Pretentious?'

'Tasteful. And the food . . .' She puckered her lips and kissed the air. 'Delicious. How about you two? Did Tolpuddle behave?'

'Like an angel.' A snore from the corner of the office punctuated the comment. Tolpuddle had become such a part of the detective's working day that Samson had bought a dog bed – an item the Weimaraner used liberally, dividing his time between the two offices.

'Woolly popped in,' continued Samson, using the local nickname for Norman Wollerton, Bruncliffe's only remaining bank manager. And Delilah's uncle. 'Said he was passing, but asked you to call him straight away.'

'Right, well, I'd best had. He's probably wanting ideas for Christmas presents,' she said breezily. She turned to leave and then paused. 'Oh, I almost forgot. Here. I found this in the car.' She casually placed his mobile on the desk. 'Hope you weren't panicking about losing it.'

He stared at the phone, hand automatically going to the back pocket of his jeans – which was empty. Of course it was. His mobile was on the desk in front of him. He'd been without it for the best part of two hours and hadn't even noticed. What the hell . . . ?

'Thanks,' he said. She smiled again, and then headed up the stairs to her office.

Berating himself for being so preoccupied with Delilah's lunch date, Samson pulled the phone towards him and checked the recent activity. No new emails. No new texts. A phone call . . . That was odd. An actual phone call, not a missed call.

He opened up the log. Unknown number. Just like the other night.

It seemed she'd called again, his mystery woman. But this time Delilah had answered.

To the accompaniment of Tolpuddle's sonorous breathing, he thought about that for a moment. What had the woman said? And why hadn't Delilah mentioned her call?

It didn't bode well. Perhaps she'd said something that had alerted Delilah to his impending problems? Which would explain Delilah's over-bright smile just now, her performance of normality. Or had that been to disguise the fact that the bank manager was on her back?

He slipped the phone in his pocket and tried to concentrate on the laptop in front of him. But for the rest of the afternoon the property-search requests he was conducting for his old friend Matty Thistlethwaite didn't get his full attention.

Night descends quickly in the Yorkshire Dales during winter. After a day of dismal weather and dark skies, it was almost a seamless transition, marked formally only by the Christmas lights in the marketplace coming to life. By the early hours of the morning, when the rain finally cleared away and stars appeared to rival the festive decorations, Bruncliffe was fast asleep.

Or most of it was.

In the small cottage high up on Crag Lane, Delilah Metcalfe was sitting on her sofa, a mug of hot chocolate in her hand and Tolpuddle's head resting on her lap as she stared out across the slumbering town. She'd been unable to sleep, fitful dozing replaced with full-on insomnia, concerns about her business looming large in the dark until she'd deemed it useless to lie in bed, twisting and turning under the covers. Pulling a hoodie on over her pyjamas, she'd gone downstairs, where the wood-burner was still glowing. A couple of good pokes and some fresh wood and soon flames were flickering.

The moment she'd entered the cosy lounge, Tolpuddle had stirred in his bed, opening an eye to watch her pad across to the kitchen area to make a drink. When she'd settled on the sofa, he'd roused himself, leaving his warm bed to come and sit next to her, his large head flopping onto her lap.

But if she'd thought a change of environment would calm her restless thoughts, she was mistaken. Even as she stroked the dog's soft ears, soothing him back to sleep, her mind was churning.

Uncle Woolly. Contrary to the pretext she'd invented for Samson's benefit, Bruncliffe's bank manager hadn't called in to the office to discuss Christmas shopping. He'd seen the dip in revenue for the Dales Dating Agency over the last month and wanted reassurance that Delilah was on top of things. That the six-month loan he'd reluctantly extended to her in October wasn't in jeopardy.

On top of things? What a joke. Since she'd started the dating agency two years ago, it had been a bumpy ride. Neil leaving. Cash-flow problems. And then someone killing off some of her clients. Although, perversely, business had picked up in November after the tragic events that had shocked the town. But in the run-up to Christmas, new members had been thin on the ground and several subscriptions hadn't been renewed. It was the time of year. Finding love took a bit of a back seat when there were bills to pay and presents to buy. Come January things would improve. That's what she'd told Woolly. She wasn't sure he'd believed her.

A deep sigh of contentment came from the now slumbering Weimaraner, his head heavy on her legs. Tolpuddle – yet another reason she couldn't sleep. She couldn't bear to think about what life would be like if Neil got his way and took back their dog.

His dog. That's what Neil was saying. He'd bought him. It was his name on the Kennel Club registration papers. According to her ex-husband, Delilah didn't have a leg to stand on – even though they both knew that he'd got Tolpuddle for her, when she was in the depths of depression over the death of her brother.

She sipped her hot chocolate and tried to shift her focus to brighter things. Samson sprang to mind. That image from earlier in the day of him at his desk, dark head bent over his laptop, the grey shape of Tolpuddle snoring by his side. The pair of them were becoming inseparable. Delilah smiled. But her pleasure was short-lived. The honeyed tones she'd heard on Samson's mobile came out of the night to haunt her.

It might not be long before her life was devoid of both Samson and Tolpuddle. Then she'd have nothing to distract her from the financial worries that kept her awake at night.

She leaned her head back against the sofa and closed her eyes. It wasn't an attempt to sleep. It was an attempt to stop the tears that were welling up from falling.

In Fellside Court, Eric Bradley was fast asleep. The oxygen pumping through his fragile lungs, the machine beside the bed emitting a low hum, its pulsing light keeping pace with his every breath. If he stopped breathing, an alarm sounded. If the level of oxygen being dispensed dropped for whatever reason, an alarm sounded. And in the rare case that the machine stopped working . . .

Snaking back from the oxygen concentrator, the flex crossed the carpet then ducked out of sight behind Eric's bedside cabinet, where it concluded in a plug; a plug that was normally inserted directly into a wall socket. Tonight, however, there was an intermediary. A lethal one. A chunky white rectangle with a plug socket below and a dial above, marking out the hours of the day.

At two-thirty precisely the dial turned, emitting a quiet click and cutting off the power supply to the plug. To the concentrator. To Eric's lifeline . . .

It took a few strangled breaths. Then he woke with a gasp, the mask on his face no longer providing him with the precious air he needed. He clawed it away from his nose and gulped, lungs tightening, chest heaving, aware of the concentrator's alarm sounding. He pushed aside the duvet and tried to stand, shaky on his feet, the lack of oxygen making him dizzy. Already his body was struggling. He managed a couple of steps across the room towards the beeping machine, but then he stumbled, collapsing on the floor, the noise loud enough to wake his neighbours. If he'd had neighbours.

The crash of his fall echoed in the empty apartment next door and in the residents' lounge below without a single person hearing it.

Like Delilah, Arty Robinson couldn't sleep either. It was a combination of excitement from the stolen day at the seaside and remorse. He'd allowed himself to be cajoled into the outing and was glad he had, as the fresh air and the company had done him good. The win on the fruit machines hadn't hurt either, covering the cost of the minibus for everyone.

A smile crossed his tired face as he thought about Edith Hird waving her stick around when all that money had started spilling out, a golden torrent of one-pound coins. They'd struggled to get her out of the arcade after that.

It had been a good day. But now he was home in his apartment and like every night for the last week, he'd been unable to sleep.

He'd tried. He'd taken what had become his regular nightcap, but an hour after lying down he'd still been wide awake, tormented by regret. Several hours later he'd abandoned all hope of a peaceful night and had got up and made his way to the drinks cabinet in the lounge. He'd poured a generous measure of whisky, pulled his curtains open and stood at the patio doors that led onto the balcony, looking out across the courtyard while he sipped his drink. To his right, the wall of glass stretched over to the other wing, the lights of the corridor bright against the dark, the twinkling Christmas tree on the ground floor an off-key note against the exterior gloom. Opposite, Alice's flat stared back at him. Windows bare of covering, not a flicker of life inside it.

By contrast, the flat next door to it had the curtains tightly drawn. Eric had been tired after a day gallivanting and had retired to bed earlier than normal. No doubt he was fast asleep.

Draining the last of his drink, Arty decided to have another go at getting some rest. He left the glass in the kitchen, walked back across the lounge and reached for the curtains. Arms outstretched, his gaze fell on Eric's window again. And he paused.

What was it? What was missing?

He stared out into the night, the only light coming from the corridor to his right. Then he realised. The familiar blink of green from Eric's oxygen concentrator. He couldn't see it. Screwing up his eyes, thinking it was his vision that was at fault, a product of his weariness or perhaps the alcohol, he waited another heartbeat. But the dark across the courtyard remained unpolluted.

It took another moment for the importance of that missing light to sink in. Then Arty was hurrying out of his flat, rushing down the corridor to hammer on Joseph's door.

'Wake up! Wake up!' he shouted. 'Hurry!'

He heard movement, the door was pulled open and Joseph was there, bleary-eyed. 'What's the matter?'

'It's Eric,' exclaimed Arty. 'I think his oxygen has cut out. Who has the spare key for his flat?'

'Edith does.'

Arty was already turning away, hustling down along the wall of glass to the corner apartment shared by the two sisters. The door was opening when he reached it.

'What's all the noise?' Edith, hair in curlers, was peering out at him.

'We need the key to Eric's. His oxygen machine has stopped.'

Edith moved fast, reaching into the top drawer of the sideboard in the hall as her sister appeared behind her.

'What's happening?' asked Clarissa, fingers clutching the throat of her nightdress, eyes wide with worry.

'Eric's in trouble,' said Arty, holding his hand out for the key. But Edith was already pushing past him and down the corridor, stick tapping the floor. He followed her white shape, her nightgown fluttering around her legs, aware that Joseph was behind him, that other doors had opened and residents were gathering in the hallway.

'Eric!' Edith called out as she unlocked the door. 'Eric,

it's me. Edith.' She flicked the lights on and with a worried glance at Arty, hurried inside, the pair of them heading straight for the bedroom. Neither of them heard the slight click from behind the bedside cabinet as they entered or noticed the oxygen concentrator come back to life.

They were too focused on the incapacitated form of Eric lying on the floor.

9

'Eric Bradley's in hospital!' Delilah didn't even say good morning. Just blurted out the news as she got to Samson's office door.

'What happened?'

'Complications with his breathing. One of the residents found him collapsed in the early hours and called an ambulance. He's in a bad way, apparently.'

Samson looked at his watch. It was just eight o'clock. The speed of Bruncliffe's grapevine was truly amazing.

'Mum got a call from Vicky Hudson, the care assistant, this morning,' continued Delilah, as if sensing Samson's need to know how the news had travelled. 'She was asking if Mum could go in to do an extra volunteer session. You know, to help lift spirits.'

Spirits would need lifting, thought Samson. Alice Shepherd was dead less than a week and now Eric was in hospital. He slipped his mobile in his pocket and stood up to get his helmet.

'Where are you going?'

'To see Eric.'

Delilah's eyes narrowed. 'Is this a personal or professional call?'

'Right now, I'm not sure.'

'So you think Alice might have been right? Something's going on at Fellside Court?'

'Probably not. I mean, Alice had high blood pressure and Eric has a long history of lung disease, so their respective decline in health is hardly surprising.'

'But you think there might be something in Alice's suspicions,' Delilah insisted.

'I'm keeping an open mind,' said Samson, putting on his jacket and heading for the door. He was also keeping his conscience clear. He wouldn't forgive himself if, somewhere down the line, it became known that there had been something malicious happening at the retirement complex and he'd ignored the warnings of one of the residents.

He was at the back door when he realised Delilah was following him, his spare helmet in her hand.

'Oh no,' he said, trying to herd her back into the porch. 'You're not coming with me.'

She stuck a hand on her hip, head tilting, chin rising in defiance. 'I am.'

'What about Tolpuddle?'

'He's with Nathan. The school's closed for a training day, so Nathan volunteered to take him for a long walk.'

Samson sighed as she walked past him to open the gate. He wheeled the motorbike out into the ginnel and as she got on behind him, he tried one last time.

'Don't you have a dating agency to run?' he asked.

'About that,' said Delilah, settling in behind him, hands on his waist. 'I'm still one man short for the next speed-dating event, so I was wondering if you'd—'

He kicked the bike into life and drowned out the rest of her request.

Eric Bradley didn't look good – grey-faced behind an oxygen mask, eyes closed, machines beeping by his bedside. Samson could see why the doctors were concerned. The livid bruise staining the old man's temple didn't augur well, either.

'They said it's too early to give a definite prognosis, but he's lucky to be alive.' Constable Danny Bradley, grandson of Eric and Bruncliffe's newest member of the police force, was sitting by the bed in his uniform, looking far too young for the responsibility it bestowed on him. On the other side of the unconscious pensioner was a visibly upset Arty Robinson.

'They reckon he got out of bed and fell, his mask coming off in the process,' continued Danny.

'He hasn't come round yet?' asked Samson.

'Briefly. He was groggy and confused. Couldn't remember a thing. The doctors decided it was better to sedate him for a while.'

'Who found him?' asked Delilah, taking a seat next to Arty while Samson leaned against the wall.

'I did.' Arty ran a hand over his face. 'Actually, we all did.'

'But you were the one who raised the alarm,' added Danny. 'You saved his life.'

'How did you know he'd collapsed?' asked Samson.

'I'm not sure I did know,' Arty said. 'I was looking out of my patio doors as I couldn't sleep and . . . I just thought

. . . it seemed like the light had gone out on his oxygen machine. Normally I can see it through his curtains at night, flashing away. So I roused the others, got a key to Eric's flat—' He broke off as Joseph O'Brien came in carrying a tray bearing three cups of tea.

'Morning,' said Joseph, nodding at Samson and Delilah before passing a cup each to Danny and Arty. He gave the third drink to Delilah, who started to protest, but Joseph cut her off. 'I'll go and get another couple for me and Samson. Coffee, son?'

'How well you know me, Dad. Thanks.' Samson turned his attention back to Arty. 'How come you had a key to Eric's flat?'

'Edith had it. We all leave keys with one another, in case we forget to take them with us and lock ourselves out. Memory isn't the strongest faculty amongst the residents of Fellside Court.' He gave a wry smile.

'Just as well someone did have a key,' said Danny. 'Grandad wouldn't have been discovered until morning, otherwise.'

Arty sat silently, letting the praise wash over him. He didn't feel worthy of praise. He felt guilty. First Alice. Now Eric. He took a drink of his tea, the corrosive taste burning his tongue, and became aware of the soft touch of a hand on his knee. Delilah. Her gesture brought the tears he'd been fighting to the fore and he reached for his handkerchief and blew his nose.

'Here, Samson. Coffee. At least that's what they claim it is.' Joseph O'Brien was back with two cups and a small packet of biscuits.

'Thanks.' Samson took a sip as Delilah tried to offer Joseph her chair. The older man waved her away and stood next to his son instead. 'Was there a problem with the oxygen machine, then?' Samson asked, turning back to Arty.

'I don't know.'

'But I thought you said the light was out?' said Delilah.

'I thought it was.' Arty shrugged. 'I could have sworn it was. But when we got into the apartment, the machine was working fine.'

'Yet Eric had collapsed.'

'He was on the floor by the bed. He'd ripped his mask off, stupid bugger—' He blew his nose again, eyes welling up.

'Arty put the mask back on Eric while I called the ambulance,' said Joseph O'Brien, taking up the tale and giving his friend a chance to compose himself. 'Then Edith phoned Vicky, who was on call that night. I gave Ana a call too, and it was just as well as she was there in minutes and took charge.'

Arty stuffed his handkerchief back in his pocket, eyes red-rimmed, shoulders sagging, and finished off his tea. It had been an awful wait for the paramedics – Edith kneeling beside Eric, trying to rouse him; Joseph on the phone; Clarissa standing in the doorway silently panicking, with Geraldine Mortimer and a host of other residents behind her like a pyjama-clad chorus. Then Ana had turned up. She'd dressed hastily, shirt tails sticking out from beneath her sweater, collar sticking up, and she was tying back her hair as she rushed into the room, her face still creased from her pillow.

She'd taken over. Calming them all down. Dealing with the paramedics. Getting Vicky to make tea when she turned up ten minutes later. But all the time Arty was watching her, and puzzling over two things.

How had she got there so quickly from her rental property in Hellifield, a village five miles down the road? And why wasn't she wearing a coat?

Inconsequential things. Yet they'd nagged at him as Ana dealt with the drama with her trademark calm efficiency. Nagged at him enough that he'd raised it with her as they left Eric's apartment, the ambulance gone, the residents all encouraged back to bed.

'You must have been freezing, coming out without a coat,' he'd said.

She'd stiffened, her back to Arty as she locked the door. 'I was in too much of a hurry to get one.'

'Well,' he said with a half-laugh, 'I hope none of Bruncliffe's finest were out on patrol. You'll have broken the speed limit getting here that quickly.'

She turned, her cheeks still marked with faint lines from her sleep. 'I did my best,' she said. Then she'd walked away down the corridor, that familiar icy demeanour firmly in place.

It wasn't a good feeling, this kernel of suspicion. But the look on Alice Shepherd's face when Ana had confronted her with her pillbox had haunted Arty for the last week. Should he say something? Mention it to young O'Brien, seeing as he was a detective?

'So it wasn't a problem with the oxygen machine that was to blame?' Samson was asking.

'Not that we could see,' Joseph replied. 'It was working fine. After they'd taken Eric away, we even turned it off and on again, but there was nothing wrong with it.'

'And yet the light went out earlier, Arty?'

The bookmaker's spirits flagged. Had it been out? Or had he been so tired he'd not seen it flashing away from across the courtyard? Or maybe Eric had got up to go to the bathroom and had blocked his view of it? There was also the matter of the large whisky he'd drunk just before . . .

'I don't know,' he said wearily. 'I honestly don't know.'

Delilah gave a slight shake of her head at Samson as she placed an arm round the old man's shoulders. 'It doesn't matter,' she said. 'What matters is that you found Eric and got help.'

Danny Bradley murmured his agreement and then stood to go. 'I have to get to work or Sergeant Clayton will be on my case,' he said. He paused in the doorway and then looked back at Samson. 'About that oxygen concentrator. Would you have time to have a look at it today? I don't get off my shift until late, and I'd quite like to know it wasn't the machine that was at fault.'

'Of course,' said Samson. 'It's time we were heading off too, so I'll go straight there.'

'I'll come with you,' said Joseph, putting a hand up to ward off the objection he knew was coming. 'I'll give you an excuse for going up to the first floor. I'm not sure how Ana would take it if you just wandered in on your own.'

'He's got a point,' said Delilah, a mischievous grin forming. 'Here, take my helmet, Joseph, and you can go back together.'

'No way!' said Samson, both hands up. 'I don't need any help. I'm just going to look at the concentrator. Besides, how will you get back to town?'

'I'll take her in the patrol car,' Danny offered eagerly, the young man keen to have some time alone with the famous Delilah Metcalfe. As a fellow fell-runner, he had heard all about her exploits in the sport and held her on a pedestal of considerable height.

Samson sighed. It was checkmate. 'Okay, Dad, you're with me. Danny, if you could take Delilah and Arty—'

'I'm not going back just yet.' Arty glanced at his friend in the bed and back at Samson. 'I'll stay with Eric a bit longer. Someone needs to be here when he wakes up.'

'Are you sure?'

'Yes. I'm fine. The nurses will look after me.' He tried a smile, but it was half-hearted. Then he reached into his pocket and passed a key across the bed. 'You'll need this. It's Edith's spare for Eric's flat. In all the commotion last night, I somehow ended up with it . . .'

His smile faltered and Delilah gave him a kiss on the cheek, before putting on her coat and joining Danny in the doorway.

'I'll come and collect you at midday, Arty,' offered Danny. 'My uncle and aunt should be up here by then. And thanks again. You too, Samson,' he said, shaking the detective's hand. 'I owe you for this.'

Samson smiled, thinking of all the assistance the young constable had given him over the past couple of months. 'I think it's the other way round. Glad to be able to help.'

He was also glad to have a legitimate excuse to enter Eric's apartment. Because while Delilah might have pacified Arty by telling him the sequence of events the night before didn't matter, any detective worth his salt knew that they did. And Samson wouldn't be satisfied until Eric's collapse had had a bit more investigating.

The return journey from Airedale Hospital to Bruncliffe took longer than the usual forty minutes, thanks to a slow tractor on the road out from Skipton and Samson's caution, given the age of the passenger on the back. A passenger who had tried to speed things up by continually nudging his son in the back.

When Samson had started up the Royal Enfield in the hospital car park, Joseph O'Brien had laughed with joy, cast back to his youth by the gleaming motorbike that had been so much a part of it.

'By God, but your mother and I had some fun on this old girl,' he said as he sat up behind his son.

'Not sure I need to know the details, Dad,' replied Samson, flicking down his visor and pulling out onto the road. But even he could see how the wonderful machine must have been a magical part of the romance between his parents. Riding back towards the Dales, the air washed clean by the recent rain, a low sun streaming down from a cloud-dappled sky onto the majestic fells, he had a mad desire to just keep riding. Perhaps riding back through his own youth to a point where the man behind him on the bike had been the father he barely remembered. To a point where he'd had a proper relationship with him.

He'd arrived at Fellside Court in an irritable mood.

'Thanks, son,' said Joseph as he got off, removing his helmet to reveal a beaming smile. 'That was fantastic.'

'Thank Delilah,' muttered Samson.

'I'll be sure to.' Joseph had sensed his son's shift in temper. It had to be hard for the lad, trying to rebuild connections with the father who had drunk away their past. Not sure how to overcome the innate suspicion of the neglected child, Joseph fell back on the task in hand. 'Come on then, let's get you up to Eric's flat. It's coffee time, so the corridors should be clear.'

He led the way across the courtyard, glancing into the lounge where a few residents were in the far corner watching TV, backs to the window. They entered the foyer but instead of turning towards the stairs to the left, Joseph veered right, skirting round the huge Christmas tree that had taken up residence in the entrance hall.

'Avoiding the cafe,' Joseph said by way of explanation, pointing at a second flight of stairs and a lift, which Samson hadn't noticed before. They were passing the corridor that ran down the right wing when a voice hailed them.

'Joseph! How's Eric?' An elderly lady with grey hair cut close above an impish face was approaching, leaning heavily on a walking stick.

'Rita Wilson,' muttered Joseph to his son. 'She's discreet.' He turned to the lady with a smile. 'Morning, Rita. Eric's still unconscious but he's in good hands. Sorry, but I don't know any more than that.'

'Poor Eric!' Rita shook her head. 'What an awful accident.'

'When I hear more, I'll let you know.' Joseph made to move on but then paused, tapped his finger to his nose and tilted his head in the direction of Samson. 'If anyone asks, you never saw us, okay?'

A wicked smile lit up Rita's face. 'Oh! Intrigue in Fellside Court. Is he here on official business?'

'No. But you know how funny Ana can be about visitors signing in. We're keeping under the radar.'

'Go quickly, then,' she said with a chuckle, shooing them towards the door at the foot of the stairs. 'My lips are sealed.'

They slipped away and, true to her word, Rita Wilson entered the cafe and didn't tell a soul. Apart from whispering something in Edith Hird's ear. But then Edith could be trusted.

The flat already had the feel of a deserted space, the click of the closing front door sounding hollow in the silence. Having left his father standing guard in the corridor by the wall of glass, Samson stood in Eric Bradley's hallway, aware of Alice Shepherd's empty apartment next door, of the residents' lounge below. Even if Eric had called out when he fell in the middle of the night, who would have heard him?

Musing on the mystery of the missing green light that had led Arty to raise the alarm and no doubt save Eric's life, Samson moved down the hall. The apartment was bigger than Alice's, two bedrooms as opposed to one. According to Joseph, there were only four of these more spacious residences, all placed in the corners – the three others included the one Edith and Clarissa shared above the cafe, another on the ground floor at the front occupied by a couple in their late eighties, and then there was the apartment across the courtyard on the first floor, which was reserved as a guest suite. With the astronomical prices his father had quoted, it was a wonder they'd sold any of them at all.

Pausing at an open door on his left, Samson glanced into the bathroom. Opposite was the smaller of the two bedrooms. He poked his head into both. While Danny had only asked him to check the oxygen machine, it seemed sensible to have a thorough look at the place while he was there. Not that he could be certain Eric's stay in hospital had been premeditated, but it would be a shame to miss such an opportunity should Alice Shepherd's suspicions about Fellside Court be proven well founded.

The bathroom was clean, the sparse collection of toiletries on a shelf indicative of a single male occupant. Likewise, the spare bedroom was spartan. Bed. Small wardrobe. A single bedside table with an old lamp. Neither room suggested anything untoward. Samson moved through to the open-plan lounge and kitchen.

Tucked into the corner of the property with access to two balconies, it was an impressive space, looking out onto the fells and into the courtyard below. The kitchen area was immaculate, not a splash or spot of grease to be seen on the modern units and the hob gleaming. Eric had a cleaner. Possibly Ida Capstick. Samson filed that thought.

The lounge looked more lived-in, a couple of books on the coffee table, a fleece throw draped across the sofa, a well-worn footstool in front of an armchair and, to one side, Eric's portable oxygen cylinder which he used during the day. Crossing the plush carpet, Samson gave the cylinder a quick inspection, but nothing seemed amiss.

The master bedroom, then.

If the rest of the apartment had the antiseptic feel of a show-home, Eric's bedroom bore testament to recent drama. The duvet was in a tumbled heap on the bed, the discarded oxygen mask lay on the floor by the window, and the picture on the wall near the door to the en-suite was at an angle where a shoulder had caught it in the commotion. Tucked into the furthest corner, between the window and the bed, was the oxygen machine.

Samson stood in front of it and looked out of the window. On the diagonal across the courtyard he could see Arty Robinson's balcony. He turned to the concentrator and pressed the on/off button. Nothing happened.

Following the flex that exited from the back of the machine, he crossed towards the bedside table where it disappeared. It was plugged into a socket behind the small unit. Badly plugged in. The pins weren't fully inserted.

Odd.

His father had said they'd tested the oxygen concentrator after the paramedics took Eric away, turning it off and on again. How had it worked, if it hadn't been plugged in properly?

Pushing the plug snug into the socket, he tried the machine again. This time the display lit up, a single short beep sounding as the machine hummed into action. From the mask on the floor came the gentle hiss of oxygen. And at the top of the control panel, a steady green light showed. Arty's green light. Only it wasn't flashing. Because the mask had no one breathing at the end of it.

He picked it up, held it over his face and took a breath.

And another. The oxygen was a shot of pure air, heady and delicious. Another breath. The green light flashed in time. And again. He breathed in and out for thirty seconds, the light on the machine keeping pace. As his father had said, there didn't appear to be anything wrong with it.

He removed the mask and turned off the machine.

Arty had seen the green light. Then he thought it had stopped and he raised the alarm. But when they entered the flat, Eric had been collapsed here on the floor by the window, yet the machine had been working.

Samson began pacing back and forward in front of the window, allowing his thoughts to roam. There was something here. Something that wasn't making sense.

He passed in front of the window just as she was looking up from the entrance hall. That mass of dark hair, the broad shoulders, the brooding expression. Even across the distance of the courtyard he was unmistakable. Even when she saw him for only the briefest of moments.

Problem was, he wasn't where he should be. And he hadn't signed in.

Ana Stoyanova slipped her hand into the pocket of her tunic and took out her mobile. Her call was answered on the first ring.

'He's here snooping around,' she said, still staring out of the glass wall towards Eric Bradley's apartment. 'You said to tell you.'

That was all she needed to say. She returned to her office and waited.

*

Eric. He'd been found on this side of the bed, close to the window.

Samson paused and viewed the room afresh. Eric Bradley had fallen on the side of the bed furthest from the en-suite bathroom. If Arty's theory was right, that was a logical place for Eric to be. The oxygen machine had stopped, he'd been ripped from sleep and in difficulty, so he'd got up to check what was wrong. Yet when the others had arrived, there had been nothing wrong with the concentrator.

If Arty had been mistaken and the machine hadn't stopped, then why had Eric got out of bed on this side? The bathroom was across the other side of the room.

It didn't make sense either way. Especially when the machine didn't seem to have been plugged in properly in the first place.

He looked over at the bedside table which concealed the plug. It was a heavy oak unit with a small cupboard at the bottom, a drawer above and a green marble top. Placed on the marble were a plastic beaker of water, a book and a pair of glasses. He moved closer, slight indentations in the carpet in front of the unit catching his eye. They were too faint to have been there more than a day or so, as though the bedside table had been pulled forward for a short while.

Kneeling down, he ran his fingers over the soft pile, back along the base of the unit towards the wall. Where the wooden base ended he encountered another couple of inches of flattened carpet, much deeper impressions made by furniture over a long period.

The bedside table wasn't in its normal place. It was

further away from the wall. Someone had pulled it out for a brief time and then pushed it part-way back.

But why?

'What's going on?' Edith Hird appeared out of the lift and approached Joseph where he was standing guard in the corridor. 'Rita said you were up to something.'

'Nothing's going on!' protested Joseph, internally cursing Rita Wilson.

Edith fixed him with what they called 'the look' – her head tipped forward and slightly at an angle, her fierce gaze concentrated on him.

'Okay,' he muttered. 'Samson is in Eric's flat.'

'Why?'

'Danny Bradley asked him to have a look at the oxygen concentrator.'

At the mention of the policeman, Edith's expression morphed into one of shock. 'Whatever for? Surely he doesn't suspect foul play?'

'No. I don't think so. He just wants to know if there was a problem with the machine – what with Arty saying the light was out.'

'I hope Danny isn't setting too much store by what Arty saw,' she said, concern in her voice. 'We both know the machine was working fine when we got in there. And I'm sure you noticed Arty had a distinct whiff of alcohol about him – not for the first time lately.'

To his shame, Joseph had noticed. As his friend had blurted out his fears for Eric in the early hours, Joseph had found himself concentrating on the enticing aroma of whisky that curled around Arty's words.

'True,' he said. 'But either way, it was Arty who raised the alarm.'

'And for that we must all be grateful. So I take it you brought Samson in on the quiet?'

Joseph nodded. 'I didn't think Ana would take too kindly to him sticking his nose in.'

'You did the right thing,' said Edith. 'She can be funny about—'

'Damn!' Joseph was staring through the wall of glass at the man running across the courtyard, blond hair glinting in the winter sun. Rick Procter.

'For once,' said Edith, as the sound of raised voices reached them from the hallway below, 'your use of profanity is justified, Joseph. Quick, get Samson out of there while I stall Mr Procter.'

Joseph wheeled round and hurried down the corridor. He could already hear footsteps pounding up the stairs.

Aware that he'd gathered more questions than answers in Eric's empty flat, but nothing that suggested anything other than an accident had occurred, Samson checked that he'd turned off the oxygen concentrator and made to leave. He was in the hallway when the front door flew open and his father rushed in, breathing heavily.

'Rick Procter's here. Ana, too. You need to get out. Now!'

But it was too late. From the corridor beyond the open door, they could hear Edith Hird.

'Mr Procter,' she was saying, her headmistress's tones carrying even further than usual. 'What a coincidence. I've been meaning to talk to you about—'

'Sorry, but I'm in a bit of a rush, Miss Hird. Ana and I have to—'

'Nonsense,' said Edith, the voices getting closer. 'Surely you've got a moment for your old headmistress?'

There was a pause and when he next spoke, Rick was slightly further away.

'Now what?' hissed Joseph as he eased the door closed behind him, shutting out Edith's enquiries about the progress of the housing development down at Low Mill. 'They're in the corridor. We can't get out of here without being seen.'

Samson weighed up the options. While he wasn't breaking any laws, Procter Properties had the right to say who was allowed on the premises. And he doubted his name would be on that list. At the same time, however, Danny Bradley had asked him to visit the apartment. So should he just brazen it out?

The thought of another confrontation with the arrogant property developer made his decision for him. A quick exit was called for.

'You can't get out of here, Dad. But I can.' Samson strode into the lounge and out onto the balcony that overlooked the back of the complex. Thankfully, the obsession with glass that predominated the architecture of the building didn't extend to the balcony railings. He leaned over the wooden barrier and looked down. Below was a small flower border tucked in against the wall of the communal lounge, a strip of grass beyond that and then a footpath. Of hard concrete slabs.

'Don't be daft, son.' Joseph was at his side, looking concerned. 'You'll only hurt yourself.'

But Samson was already clambering over the balustrade. 'Thanks for keeping watch, Dad,' he said with a grin. 'You'll have to think of an excuse for being in here.'

'Don't worry about that,' said Joseph. He patted his son on the arm. 'I can take care of myself. Just make sure you aim for the grass.'

Then Samson lowered himself over the edge, working his hands down two uprights until he was dangling from his outstretched arms and facing the end wall of the lounge.

'Aim for the grass,' he muttered. He let go and the ground rushed up to meet him.

'So there's plenty of availability?' asked Edith Hird, putting a hand out to detain the property developer, who was eager to get away, his smile of several minutes ago replaced with an impatient frown. 'I mean, if my niece wanted to put her name down for one of those gorgeous town houses, there wouldn't be a problem? It's just that she needs a bit of time to—'

'There won't be a problem, Miss Hird. Now I'm sorry, but you'll really have to excuse us.' He turned away, Ana Stoyanova at his heels, and headed back down the corridor towards Eric's flat.

There was nothing more she could do. She'd spent what felt like an age trying to stall them, prattling on about those new homes down by Low Mill like a scatterbrained old woman, in the hope that Joseph and his son might somehow escape from the apartment. But how on earth would they manage that, when the only exit was right past the very people they were hoping to avoid? Past the very man who was inserting a key into Eric's front door at this very minute.

Rick Procter turned the key, the door swung open and a startled Joseph O'Brien was standing on the threshold.

'Mr Procter!' Joseph had a hand to his heart. 'You frightened the bejesus out of me!'

'Sorry.' Rick Procter's smile didn't reach his eyes. 'But I have to ask what you're doing in Mr Bradley's apartment.'

Joseph looked bemused. 'Why, fetching these,' he said, holding up a pair of spectacles. 'Eric can't see further than his nose. He'll need them when he comes round.'

Rick pushed past him and into the flat, the sound of doors being opened and closed filtering down the corridor to where Edith waited, holding her breath.

'Is something wrong? Did I do something wrong?' Joseph was asking, a realistic tremor in his voice.

Ana put a hand on his arm. 'You did nothing wrong. Don't worry. It's just a security check.'

Rick Procter had reappeared in the doorway, scowling. 'He's not there,' he muttered to Ana.

She frowned. 'But I saw—'

'I said, he's not there! You must have been mistaken.' Rick stalked back up the corridor.

'Eric? Are you looking for Eric?' Joseph called out to the retreating figure. 'Sure, he's in hospital, Mr Procter. Haven't you heard?'

Edith Hird had to call on all the skills she'd acquired as a headmistress not to burst out laughing as Rick Procter strode past her and down the stairs.

10

It felt like he was in the air for a long time. In reality, it was seconds. Then the solid impact of the ground as his body hit the strip of grass and his legs slammed into the concrete.

'Oof!' Breath rushing out of his lungs, Samson rolled as he landed, aware of pain erupting in his right ankle, bruising in his right hip. But he was up and on his feet, running across to the car park through the cover of the copse of trees. The Royal Enfield started first time, purring into life and taking him away from Fellside Court.

Halfway down the road, he realised he was grinning.

What a rush! It had been like old times, adrenalin racing, that element of risk. Memories of his previous life washed over him. The stake-out at a rural airfield, waiting in the dark for a planeload of drugs to emerge out of the night. The raid on a warehouse in the early hours which uncovered millions of pounds' worth of heroin. The thrill of speeding across rough seas in a Border Force cutter to intercept a yacht stashed with almost a ton of cocaine. He missed it. To have his heart pounding and his mind in overdrive in sleepy Bruncliffe had been unexpected.

So had his father's level-headedness. He hadn't panicked when Rick Procter turned up. Not even when Samson clambered over the balcony. The old man kept surprising him. Perhaps he'd been too quick to doubt his father's sobriety.

He cut across the marketplace and turned down the ginnel that ran parallel to Back Street, pulling up outside the gate of the office building. Leaving the bike on the hardcourt in the yard, he was still smiling as he entered through the back porch, tripping over the clutter of walking shoes and trainers which he now knew belonged to Delilah's ex-husband, Neil Taylor.

Passing through the small kitchen that came with his lease – but which he never used, not having bothered to stock it when Delilah's kitchen on the first floor already had milk and coffee . . . and biscuits – he was in the hallway when he heard voices coming from his office.

Delilah. And a male voice he recognised but couldn't place.

Alert once more, Samson slowly looked round the open door to see Delilah sitting at his desk, notebook in hand. Opposite her was the skeletal shape of the poacher, Pete Ferris.

'Damn it, Ana. He wasn't there.'

In the manager's office at the front of Fellside Court, Rick Procter was trying to control his temper. Across the room from him stood Ana Stoyanova, head bowed, a faint flush of colour on her cheeks.

'I'm sorry, Mr Procter, but I was certain—'

'You were wrong. It must have been Boozy O'Brien you saw.'

'Boozy O'Brien?' she asked.

'Samson's father. It's a local nickname.' He turned to

stare out of the window and missed the ripple of distaste that disturbed the passive features of the woman standing behind the desk.

'I'm sorry to have wasted your time,' she said, the words sharp, whether through accent or intent, it was hard to say.

Wary of losing a vital asset, Rick turned back to face his employee. 'Not at all, Ana. You did right to call me, even if it was a false alarm. Samson O'Brien's not the sort of person we want wandering around Fellside Court. Do you understand?'

Ana gave a measured nod of her head, expression neutral, the exact same reaction she'd given when he'd first broached the topic of O'Brien at the Christmas lights turn-on. Perturbed at hearing the returned detective had been present when Alice Shepherd died – and sensing Ana had concerns of her own about Bruncliffe's black sheep – Rick had persuaded her that the O'Brien lad needed watching; that she should keep tabs on his visits to Fellside Court. All in the name of the residents' welfare, of course.

So far she'd proven a more than capable spy. Until today's fiasco. Rick didn't appreciate being made to look like a fool, not in front of a gaggle of pensioners. But given the things he had in the pipeline, he couldn't afford to alienate Ana Stoyanova. He needed her onside. Because what he didn't need was a suspended police detective prowling around his premises.

He leaned towards her, placing a hand on her shoulder.

'This isn't public knowledge,' he said, 'but O'Brien's currently under suspension from the police and from what I hear, he could go to prison. So don't hesitate to phone again if he comes back.'

'Even if he comes to visit his father?' A fine eyebrow was arched above Ana's cool gaze.

'You don't need to go that far,' said Rick, taking a step back as he fought a surge of irritation at her impenetrable poise. 'Use your common sense. If he seems to be acting suspiciously, then let me know.'

'As you wish, Mr Procter.'

'Thanks, Ana. I know I can rely on you.'

She walked him out of the building and across the courtyard to his Range Rover. Still thinking about Samson O'Brien, Rick Procter got in, waved goodbye and drove off. He pulled out of the car park without a final glance at the slim figure in the tunic, her blonde hair pulled back in a ponytail being whipped by the wind. He didn't see her walk across to the footpath that ran under Eric Bradley's flat. He didn't see her bend down and inspect the grass. He didn't see her trace her fingers over the imprint in the soft ground, or notice the frown of displeasure as she looked up at the balcony above.

Rick Procter also wasn't aware of Ana's brief moment of hesitation, her hand reaching for her phone. Then, letting it slip back into her pocket, she pulled her cardigan round her shoulders and with a worried expression, hurried back into the building.

Tolpuddle – back from his walk with Nathan and having a sneaky mid-morning rest, head on paws, eyes half-closed – announced Samson's presence, letting out a sharp bark before rushing over from his bed to greet him.

'Oh, Samson!' Delilah looked over to the doorway and

then gestured at the man across the desk from her. 'Pete's come to talk to us.'

Us. Samson felt a surge of laughter and frustration in equal measure. His landlady was sitting in his office, behind his desk, in his chair, interviewing his client. 'So I see. Hopefully he's left his shotgun at home?'

Pete grinned, teeth crooked and stained. 'I was only teasing you.'

'And the dogs?'

The poacher gestured over his shoulder to the street outside. 'In the truck. Probably chewing the seats.'

'As long as it's not my leg.' Samson's response triggered a laugh, one tinged with nervousness. 'How I can I help you, Pete?' He gave Delilah a pointed glance, expecting her to leave him to it. Instead she tipped her chin at the spare chair in the corner of the room and opened her notebook, pen at the ready.

Accepting the inevitable, Samson positioned the chair at the end of the desk, some distance from the gamey odour of the poacher – an odour which didn't quite mask a more cloying smell. Cannabis. Samson thought he'd caught a whiff of it up at the caravan. Here in the confines of the office, he was certain. He sat down, wincing as his right hip protested. 'In your own time,' he said.

Pete flushed, his pockmarked skin mottling, fingers toying with the lighter he'd been reunited with the day before. Without his baseball cap he seemed less menacing, his shaven head all hollows and ridges. The man needed a decent meal. And a shower. He shifted in his seat, body turned sideways to Samson.

'I lied,' he said.

'You don't say,' retorted Delilah.

Samson smothered a groan. So much for the softly-softly approach. Delilah had just committed the interrogation equivalent of springing a trap before the prey was in it.

'What do you mean, you lied?' he asked, trying to draw the poacher back out into the open.

The gaunt cheeks turned to him. 'About where I lost my lighter.'

'We know where you lost it,' said Delilah. 'Up at Mire End Farm.'

Samson shot her a look. For a woman who sold romance for a living, her interview technique was far from gentle. But then this was Bruncliffe, in the heart of Yorkshire. Things had always taken a more direct approach around here.

Pete was nodding. 'Aye, that's true. I was up there.'

'When?' asked Samson, before Delilah could barge in again.

'About a week ago.' The man's gaze sidled away to fall on the lighter gripped in his bony fingers.

'The night Ralph was taken?' demanded Delilah.

This time Samson couldn't stop a sigh escaping his lips. She was breaking every rule in the book. But Pete Ferris was nodding again.

'Yes,' he admitted, eyes still on the grenade-shaped lighter. 'I was there.'

'Where exactly?' asked Samson, putting up a hand to silence Delilah.

'Up at the top gate to the main field. I was . . .' the poacher stuttered, 'well, you know . . .'

'Poaching?' Delilah was ignoring any attempts to force her into a back-seat role. She was leaning across the desk, willing the poacher to confess all.

A bone-pointed shrug met her question. 'I can't say owt to that. Not without getting myself in trouble. But I was up there.'

'What time was it?' asked Samson as Delilah scribbled down notes.

'Gone midnight. I was just getting set up and then this van comes up from Horton way.'

'Did you get the registration number?' interjected Delilah.

Samson glared at her. She glared back at him, mouthing a single 'What?', and he wondered briefly if it was worth risking his life to ask her to make tea, getting her out of the room in the process.

'It was too dark,' continued Pete, seemingly unfazed by the staccato interview. 'I just saw it was a Transit. White, I think. It pulled up at the gate, two men got out and they went into the field.'

'With the truck?' asked Delilah.

Samson's patience snapped. 'You know what we could do with?' he said, forcing a smile at her. 'A cup of your tea.'

She turned with a smile equally sweet. 'Sorry, we're out of teabags.'

'I don't have time for tea,' muttered Pete. 'I need to head off in a minute.'

Delilah's smile turned triumphant. 'So, did they take the truck into the field?'

'Yes. They backed it in. I couldn't see much of what

happened after that, as the headlights were pointing straight at me. But I could tell what they were doing.'

'What was that?'

'Stealing a sheep.'

'Just the one?' asked Samson, deciding that if he couldn't derail Delilah's interviewing technique, he might as well adopt it.

'Seemed that way.'

'Which way did they drive off?' asked Delilah.

'Towards Horton.'

'And what did you do then?' Samson demanded.

'I went home. No point in me hanging around somewhere I might get accused of something illegal. Not in my line of work.'

'You didn't see anything else?' asked Delilah.

'That was it. Then next thing, I hear Clive Knowles' tup is missing.'

'You didn't report it to the police?' Samson asked.

Pete and Delilah both looked at him in disbelief, and he wished the ridiculous question unsaid. Of course the poacher hadn't said anything to the authorities. Silently cursing his stupidity, Samson wondered if having Delilah as co-interviewer had addled his brain.

Taking the lull in questions as a cue to leave, Pete got to his feet and pulled his baseball cap back on. 'Those dogs of mine will need seeing to,' he said. 'I've told you all I know. And if anyone asks me about this, I'll deny it.'

'Just one final question,' said Delilah as the poacher reached the door, her insistence on getting the last word raising a wry grin from Samson. 'Why are you telling us this?'

Pete stalled, halfway out of the door, eyes sliding to the peeling lino on the floor. 'Clive's lost a sheep,' he said. 'It's not right. Thought I'd try to help.' He tugged his baseball cap further down onto his head and slipped out of the back door.

Delilah flipped her notebook closed and with a smug smile, stood to leave. 'Still want that cup of tea?' she asked. She laughed and headed for the stairs, Tolpuddle trotting after her. Samson was left alone in his office and he had to acknowledge, as he reflected over the interview, that Delilah had asked the most pertinent question of all.

When Delilah arrived back in the office carrying two mugs and a plate of biscuits, Samson O'Brien didn't have the look of a man who'd just been handed a breakthrough in a case. He was still sitting in the spare chair, a pained look on his face, rubbing his right hip.

'Why now?' he asked, before she even had a chance to put the drinks on the desk.

'Because this is Bruncliffe and you can't go an entire morning without a cup of tea,' she said, passing a mug to him and then sitting back down in the chair she'd appropriated when the poacher had arrived at the back door, furtively asking to see Samson.

'No, I mean Pete Ferris. You asked him why he'd told us about what he saw. What we really need to know is why he's telling us now. Why not when we were up at the caravan yesterday?'

Delilah laughed. 'He's a poacher. His first instinct is to lie. Plus we caught him unawares. He wasn't expecting us to be able to place him at Mire End that night.'

Samson reached for his tea and she registered the flicker of an eyebrow at the milky colour and the pungent smell – his ability to drink a true Yorkshire brew diminished by his years down in London. He took a sip, flinched and immediately reached for a biscuit.

'I think it's more than just Pete's first instinct to lie,' he said. 'I'm not sure I'd trust anything that passed his lips.'

'You think he's not telling the truth about that night?'

'Not all of it, no. He was up there, that much I'd agree on. But the rest of it is a bit too convenient.'

'Like what?'

Samson frowned. 'All of it. The lack of registration number. The vague identification of the van. And he didn't mention the harness.'

'Maybe he forgot?'

'I think you'd remember seeing someone flinging a harness on the road as they roared off with a stolen sheep. At the very least you'd hear it.'

Delilah shrugged. 'You're overthinking it. Pete Ferris saw Ralph being stolen. He probably lied about how long he was up there and whether or not he caught anything. But there is no logical reason why he'd come and see us with a fabricated tale. Not in his line of business. The last thing he'd want is to be involved in anything to do with the police.'

'So you think he only came down because we found the lighter?'

'Yes. Once we found the lighter, he knew he could be connected to the scene. Perhaps even implicated in the crime. He had no choice but to come forward.'

Samson took another drink of tea and then put the mug

back on the desk and pushed it away from him, the cuppa clearly too strong for his southern-softened tastes.

'You could at least smile,' she said. 'You've been given a lead and even if you don't find Ralph, Clive Knowles can contact his insurance company and tell them he's had a ram stolen. You get paid. He gets compensated. Everyone's a winner.'

Samson grunted and leaned forward for another biscuit. Delilah noticed both the wince as he stretched and the red stain on his shirt sleeve.

'You're bleeding!' she exclaimed. 'What happened?'

A quick glance down at his arm confirmed her words. 'I fell off a balcony onto some concrete,' he said, giving her a roguish smile. 'Over at Fellside Court.'

Her eyebrows shot up. 'While you were checking out Eric's oxygen machine?'

He nodded. 'Your friend Rick turned up, and I thought it was best if I wasn't caught snooping around someone else's flat. So I made a quick getaway and did this in the process.' He indicated the blood seeping through his shirt.

Delilah bit back a retort, stung by the derision in his voice, the implication that she was more than mere friends with Rick. 'And the oxygen machine?' she asked. 'Was it working okay?'

'Fine.' He frowned and she sensed that he was keeping something from her.

'You don't think it was anything other than an accident, then?' she persisted.

'Didn't seem to be.' He stood up, ending the conversation. 'Come on. I need something to wash away the taste of that awful tea. How about we get some lunch at the Fleece?'

'Lunch? You have been down south too long,' she muttered, the term striking her as odd coming from someone from Bruncliffe. 'When did you stop calling it "dinner"?'

He grinned down at her as she followed him out of the office. 'Dinner, lunch . . . Either way, it won't be as swanky as the place your friend Rick took you to, but the company might be better.'

Mindful of his sore arm, she thumped him on the leg instead and he yelped in pain. 'Ouch! I fell on that bit, too,' he moaned as she opened the front door, Tolpuddle at her heels.

'Next time, try landing on the grass,' she retorted, before crossing the road to the pub, Samson limping along behind her. She knew, without looking round, that he was still grinning.

'How's he doing?' Danny Bradley, his constable's uniform hanging off his slight body, was standing in the doorway of the hospital ward, a middle-aged couple next to him. 'Any change?'

Arty looked up, startled out of his morbid thoughts, and shook his head. 'No change.'

The older man advanced, hand outstretched, his posture that of an army man. 'Alan,' he said. 'Eric's oldest. And this is my wife, Laura.'

They shook hands, Alan's grip firm. 'Eric's talked about you a lot,' said Arty. 'About your time in the forces.'

Alan looked towards the bed and shook his head at the

sight of the frail old man beneath the sheets. 'What was Dad doing, the daft bugger? Why did he take his mask off?'

Arty had no answer.

'Danny tells me we've you to thank for finding him in time,' continued Alan.

'It wasn't just me. The others helped raise the alarm, too.'

Laura smiled. 'You've got a good community in there. That's one of the reasons Eric chose to live at Fellside Court. He said it was like a home from home.'

Arty swallowed hard, his eyes misting up. 'Aye. We try to look out for each other.'

'Thanks, anyway,' said Alan, shaking his hand once more. 'We really appreciate all you've done.'

'Come on, Arty,' said Danny. 'It's time I took you back. You've been here all morning.'

All morning. It had passed in a stream of thoughts as his friend slept silently beside him. Thoughts about Alice. About Eric. And about Ana Stoyanova. About the inconsistencies in her behaviour. The rapid arrival. The lack of a coat. Alice Shepherd's expression when she saw her.

He should tell someone.

'You ready?' Danny was waiting by the door.

Arty nodded, even though Fellside Court was the last place he wanted to go. For the first time since he'd moved there, it didn't feel like home.

If he was really honest, it didn't feel safe any more.

11

As tarmac gave way to rough track, Samson wasn't sure that having lunch at the Fleece had been such a good idea. The excellent pheasant pie and large serving of Yorkshire curd tart were now jolting around in his stomach in a distinctly unpleasant manner, as his motorbike bucked and bumped along the lane towards Mire End Farm. He was relieved to finally pull up in the shadow of one of the dilapidated barns, chickens scattering at his arrival.

Receiving no answer to his calls in the yard, he walked around the back of the farmhouse where the only greeting he got was a desultory bark from the old sheepdog, lying on a bale of hay as before. In the field beyond, he saw the bulky shape of Clive Knowles stooped over a sheep. Picking his path through the bits of cars and farm machinery and skirting the teetering piles of abandoned tyres, Samson crossed over to the gate and entered the field. The farmer noticed him at last and straightened up, eyes narrowing as the detective approached.

'You've found the bugger?' he grunted, one hand buried in the thick fleece of the ram he had trapped between his legs.

Samson shook his head and the farmer made a noise of disgust and resumed his work, applying a half-used block of red crayon into the harness trussed around the struggling ram. Judging by the wear on the straps and the rusty rivets, it was the same harness that had been left discarded by the roadside when Ralph disappeared.

'Damn thing keeps falling out,' Clive Knowles muttered as he fiddled with the contraption, trying to hold the crayon in place with a pin that was broken and jagged.

'Need a hand?' offered Samson.

'I need you to find my bloody tup!' The outburst was followed by a curse as the farmer's thick finger snagged on the rough edge of the pin. Blood mixing with the red of the crayon, he persevered until the crayon was held in place and then released the animal.

'You've got a replacement?' asked Samson as the ram ran off, heading for a group of ewes over by the stone wall.

'Had to. Need lambs come spring, or this place will go to the wall. Not a patch on the pedigree of that Ralph, though.'

'He's doing his job,' remarked Samson, nodding towards the red splotches across the rumps of some ewes nearby.

'Aye. Can't fault him. But he's no prize-winner.' With a wipe of his hands on his overtrousers, a smear of either blood or crayon left in its wake, he started walking back towards the gate. 'Reckon you didn't come all the way out here to admire my stock,' he muttered as Samson fell into step beside him.

'No. I came to tell you I've found a witness.'

Clive Knowles stopped to face the detective. 'A witness? You mean you've proof Ralph was taken?'

'Kind of. The witness saw him being stolen, but he won't come forward to testify.'

'What did he see?'

'A Transit van pulled up over there late at night.' Samson gestured towards the gate at the top of the field. 'It was too dark to get a registration number, unfortunately.'

The farmer let out another grunt. 'Reckon that'll be the last I see of Ralph, then. Most likely been through an abattoir already.'

Samson didn't contradict him. From what Harry Furness had said about livestock theft, Clive Knowles was probably right. 'Do you want me to continue looking?'

'Not much point,' said the farmer gloomily. 'Throwing good money after bad. Might as well get a claim in and be done with it.'

'You had Ralph insured?' Samson asked with relief.

'Too bloody right I had him insured. Cost a bloody fortune. Least this ways I'll get some of it back.'

'Well, if you need me to corroborate anything for the claim . . .'

The farmer nodded. 'Reckon you'll want paying, too,' he muttered as he led the way back towards the farmhouse.

Ten minutes later, with cash in his pocket, Samson was riding away from Mire End Farm. All things considered, he thought as he guided the Royal Enfield around the worst of the potholes, the case had gone rather well. Not for poor old Ralph, obviously. But finding proof that the ram hadn't just wandered off was what Clive Knowles needed in order to place his insurance claim. What's more,

Samson's payment had been prompt, despite all Seth and Harry's warnings about Clive Knowles' parsimony.

He turned the motorbike onto the road to Horton and, in an excellent frame of mind, started back towards Bruncliffe. He was in sight of the town when it came to him.

Clive Knowles hadn't asked who the witness was.

Was it significant? In a place like London, maybe not. But here? Where everyone knew everything about the folk they lived amongst. He would have at least asked, surely?

But he hadn't. Hadn't even shown the slightest interest.

Strange. Yes, maybe. However, that didn't mean it was suspicious.

He let the thought go. Delilah was right. He was overthinking things. Right now, all he wanted to do was put his feet up and have a decent cup of tea. It had been a long day, he was covered in bruises, but at least he had money in his pocket.

He cut across the marketplace, the fairy lights bright against the growing dusk, the shop windows filled with festive cheer. And he found himself looking forward to Christmas.

'I'm sorry, Delilah . . .' The solicitor shook his head and Delilah's heart sank. 'There's nothing you can do.'

Knowing this was going to be the worst Christmas ever, she reached a hand down to the warm head that was resting on her thigh and fondled the dog's ears. 'Nothing at all?'

Matthew Thistlethwaite – Matty to his friends – frowned,

his thick eyebrows bushing together to identify him as the nephew of Seth, Delilah's former teacher and athletics coach. 'These are pretty damning,' he said.

Laid out in front of him on the glass table were the documents from the Kennel Club that had accompanied Tolpuddle to his new home. Having spent last night tormenting herself about the email from her ex-husband, Delilah had called Matty after she got back from the hospital that morning and had made an appointment to see him. When she'd walked into his office she'd been hoping for a miracle. Now she was wishing her ex-husband dead.

'Unfortunately for you,' Matty continued, pointing at the papers, 'Neil is named on the certificates, which is grounds enough for him to be awarded custody of Tolpuddle in a court, should you take things that far.'

'But that's only because he bought him as a surprise for me. Tolpuddle's my dog!' Sensing her anxiety, the hound in question lifted his head and let out a low whine. 'It's all right, boy,' she murmured, patting him until he settled once more.

Matty was watching with a pained expression. 'I really am sorry. I know how much he means to you. But in the eyes of the law . . .'

'The law is an ass!' she said.

'You'd be surprised how often I share that sentiment,' replied the solicitor with a dry smile. 'What are you going to do?'

Delilah shrugged. 'What can I do? Neil says I have until the New Year, then he's going to come and collect Tolpuddle.' Her voice caught on the dog's name and a hand went to her mouth.

How would she cope without this grey shadow that had become so much a part of her life? She'd been in a deep depression following the death of her brother Ryan, when Neil arrived home one night with a cheeky smile and a writhing bundle under his jumper.

Tolpuddle. A daft pup with long legs and a generous nature, he'd bounded into her world and brought sunshine to the dark corner where she'd been hiding. For a while he'd also helped bolster the crumbling foundations of her marriage, binding Delilah and Neil together in a shared love of this new arrival.

Then Neil had had another affair. Many weeks of bitter arguments later, he'd told her he was leaving and this time, caught up in trying to rescue their failing businesses, Delilah hadn't had the energy to persuade him to stay. He'd never mentioned the dog. Had brushed him aside as easily as he had his marriage.

Delilah and Tolpuddle had become a single-parent family, both of them bruised by the break-up. Delilah had buried herself in work to hide the pain while Tolpuddle had developed an anxiety disorder, unwilling to let Delilah out of his sight. On the rare occasion when she did have to leave him, he would take out his fears on anything to hand. Shoes became tattered. Curtains became torn. Cushions – there was usually little left of cushions when Tolpuddle became anxious.

Not that he'd had an attack recently. If you discounted the dog's obsession with footwear, his last fit of panic had been almost two months ago when she'd had to go to the bank to renegotiate her loans. She'd returned to the cottage, where she'd locked Tolpuddle in the porch, to find the innards of two cushions strewn over the floor, paw prints all over the glass and the Weimaraner's best impression of an air-raid siren greeting her as she opened the door.

It had been the same day that Samson O'Brien had arrived back in Bruncliffe. Tolpuddle hadn't had an anxiety attack in all that time . . . Delilah was contemplating this coincidence when Matty broke in on her thoughts.

'Have you told Samson?' he asked, watching her with concern. 'He might be able to help.'

She shook her head. 'Not yet. He's . . . they've become really close. I don't want to upset him if I don't have to.'

Matty smiled, but said nothing. If he thought her last remark unclear as to whether she was referring to Samson or Tolpuddle, he didn't ask for clarification.

'Thanks, Matty,' she said. She stood to go.

'I'm not sure I deserve your gratitude,' said the solicitor. 'But I know Neil didn't deserve you as a wife. Or Tolpuddle as a dog.'

Tolpuddle cocked his head to one side and regarded Matty as though concurring, while Delilah laughed. 'I don't know about the former, but the latter is definitely true. So if you come across anything that might help . . .'

'I'll do a bit of research but I think your best bet is to reason with Neil. I don't think the law can help you. In the meantime, I'd consider telling Samson if I were you.' He saw the sceptical expression on her face. 'You never know,' he said with a smile as he showed her to the door. 'He's very resourceful. He might come up with something. At the very least, you wouldn't be bearing the weight of this alone.'

'I'll think about it,' said Delilah, knowing that she had no intention whatsoever of sharing this burden with Samson O'Brien. He wasn't a man she wanted to become reliant on, for so many reasons. 'And thanks again.'

She walked down the stairs, Tolpuddle at her side, and out into the marketplace where weak sunlight was spilling onto the cobbles. She blamed the brightness for the tears that were forming in the corners of her eyes.

'How's Eric?' Rita Wilson was the third person to ask in the few minutes it had taken Arty to cross the courtyard, enter the building and head for the stairs. She put a hand on his arm, worry etched onto her face.

'It's hard to say. He's still sedated and the doctors are reluctant to give a prognosis.'

'I'm sorry to hear that. He's such a lovely, gentle man.' Then she offered help, as they all had. 'If there's anything I can do . . .'

Arty smiled. 'I'll keep you posted. And thanks.'

'No need to thank me. We all look out for each other in here. It's what we do. That's why we love living at Fellside Court.' She squeezed his arm and then moved slowly down the hall towards the cafe, her body bent over her stick.

Arty continued on to the stairs, wanting a bit of exercise after a morning spent sitting down. He climbed them at a moderate pace, feeling his heart thumping heavily before he was halfway up. That delicate heart, which he was supposed to be careful with. Two heart attacks already and they said the next one would take him.

If whatever was going on at Fellside Court didn't take him first.

He reached the first floor and passed through the door into the corridor, the wall of glass greeting him, giving him a perfect view diagonally across the courtyard to the empty flats of Eric and Alice. And of the slight figure of Ana Stoyanova at Eric's bedroom window.

She turned and he jumped to the side out of sight. It was a reflex born of fear. Had she seen him? He peered round the pillar. There was no one there.

Chest pounding, he fumbled for his keys and hurried over to his front door. Once inside, he leaned against it, taking deep breaths and willing his heartrate to ease up. He was safe in here.

A jingle of metal in the corridor outside his door made him turn, putting his eye to the spyhole. She was there. Ana. Blonde hair pulled back, uniform on. Staring at him.

His chest constricted, heart rattling, a stab of intense pain. His pills. He needed his pills. But he was transfixed, watching as the manager of Fellside Court glanced down at the ring of keys in her hand and back towards his door.

She had a key. Of course she had a key.

She took a step forward and then froze as the doors to the stairwell banged behind her.

'Ana? Elaine Bullock is on the phone. She's heard from the coroner.' Vicky Hudson, care assistant and a woman Arty had never been happier to see, came into the hallway. 'I thought you might want to speak to her?'

Ana nodded curtly and walked towards the stairs, Vicky following her. Behind the door of his flat, Arty sank to the floor.

He wasn't safe. None of them were.

His mobile rang. Edith Hird. She'd be down in the cafe wondering why he hadn't called in when he got back. He let the phone ring unanswered. He had no desire to leave his flat.

Fellside Court was no longer the happy place it had been. Not while evil roamed the corridors.

12

'You haven't forgotten about Alice's funeral?'

It was Friday morning, the weather wet against the office window with the slap of sleet. Samson glanced up from his laptop to see Delilah standing in the doorway. Her hair was plastered against her cheeks, her top was soaked and her leggings were splattered in mud. But her face was glowing with the satisfaction of a morning run. He had a twinge of envy, remembering that feeling.

'No. Have you?' he asked, gesturing towards her dishevelled appearance.

'I'm changing here. How about you?'

He looked down at his shirt and black jeans, both ironed, thanks to Ida. Having arrived in town with only a rucksack to his name, Samson had subsequently lost a pair of jeans and a good jacket to the fire at Lucy's caravan, leaving his choice of attire very limited. He looked back up at Delilah, feigning hurt.

'I'll have you know this is my best outfit. I've even polished my boots.'

She grinned. 'This is Bruncliffe,' she said. 'You'll fit right in with all the farmers.'

'What time does it start?'

'Ten. Elaine said to tell you there's a small wake in the

Fleece afterwards as well. It was the only place she could get at such short notice.'

The notice had indeed been short. Informed by the coroner on Tuesday that there would be no post-mortem on Alice Shepherd, the family had organised the funeral for the end of the same week. With Christmas approaching and Elaine leaving for a geology field trip on Saturday morning, there hadn't been much choice.

'I just hope there's a good turnout,' said Delilah. 'What with the time of year and the weather . . .' She saw the time on her watch and spun round, heading for the stairs at a jog. It was only then that Samson realised something – or someone – was missing.

'No Tolpuddle?' he called out after her.

She paused to lean over the bannister rail. 'He's up at the farm. I didn't want to leave him alone while we're out. Will's going to drop him down later.'

'Thank goodness,' laughed Samson. 'The place doesn't seem right without our hound.'

He was already refocusing on his laptop and was oblivious to the impact of his casual comment as Delilah bit her lip, wiped an annoyed hand over her eyes and jogged on up the stairs.

Our hound. Perhaps Matty Thistlethwaite was right. She should tell Samson what Neil was trying to do. It was only fair. He had developed an affection for Tolpuddle. But . . .

But she was wary of involving men in her life. And she didn't relish revealing to Samson that she'd been married by twenty-five and divorced by twenty-eight.

She entered the bathroom on the top floor, threw her

running kit on the tiles and stood under a hot shower, hoping to wash away both the mud from her exercise and the troubles from her ex-husband.

Samson didn't hear the boiler fire up in the kitchen along the hallway. Didn't hear the shower running on the third floor. He was vaguely aware of Delilah humming as she wandered about getting ready. But mostly the images in front of him held his attention.

They were of Mire End Farm.

He'd returned to the office on Tuesday afternoon following his visit to Clive Knowles, determined to close the case, move on and not overthink things. But with no pressing investigations and no clients knocking on the front door in the run-up to Christmas, he'd finished off the few bits of work he had on Wednesday. Then on Thursday he'd started on his accounts.

It hadn't taken him long to get distracted, flicking through files on his laptop rather than sorting out his finances. He'd ended up rereading his notes on the missing Ralph. And he'd been thinking about them ever since.

The wool in Pete Ferris's truck. The poacher's sudden attack of social conscience, which had led him to confess what he'd witnessed. Clive Knowles' passive acceptance of the mysterious witness. The discarded harness – why would thieves take the time to remove such a contraption in the haste of an escape?

Something wasn't right.

So despite the fact that he'd already been paid, Samson had found himself preoccupied by the case. Starting with the only evidence he had, he'd spent part of the day fruitlessly trying to track down the Transit van that Pete Ferris claimed to have seen on the night Ralph was taken.

It was useless. With no registration number, no identifying features, not even a definite colour, it was like looking for the proverbial needle. He'd even resorted to calling young Danny Bradley in his official capacity, to see if the police had news of any stolen Transits in the area. He'd drawn another blank.

Frustration mounting, Samson had woken early on Friday morning with the idea of going over his notes yet again. Not that there was much in the Mire End Farm file, but he'd found on previous cases that simply reacquainting himself with the facts sometimes brought something new to light.

Several hours on and he was staring at his computer screen and getting nowhere.

He checked the time. Ten minutes before they needed to leave for the funeral. With a sigh he scrolled back to the top of the photos he'd been looking at, all taken on his first visit to Mire End, and went through them one more time. When he heard Delilah coming down the stairs, he closed the laptop and stood up to go. She entered the room in a black trouser suit, dark hair washed and dried and framing her face, and the images of sodden fields and sheep were chased from his mind.

'Will I do?' she asked with a grin, as he started putting on his tie.

He didn't answer, mainly because she'd flicked his hands out of the way and was tying some kind of fancy knot at his neck. But also because she was his best friend's sister. And he doubted that Ryan would have appreciated exactly what he thought about how Delilah looked. Especially as they were about to attend a funeral.

The weather didn't get any better as the morning progressed. The hills at the back of Bruncliffe were smothered by low clouds hanging across the town and the sleet had become heavier, on the cusp of being proper snow and beginning to settle on the ground. By the time the church doors opened and the funeral procession filed out, it was a bleak winter's day, the slow toll of bells muffled by the damp air.

Looking out from under her umbrella at the backs of the other mourners, Delilah decided she needed a bit more joy in her life. It was her second funeral in less than two months. There had been far too much death of late.

A soft incantation of a prayer came from the priest standing at the head of the grave, interceding with God on behalf of Alice Shepherd. To his side was Elaine Bullock, dressed in respectful black apart from a vibrant scarf around her neck. She looked tired. It had been a stressful couple of weeks for the family, the indecision on the part of the coroner making it impossible for them to begin the process of moving on. What a relief it must have been to finally hear that there would be no post-mortem.

Delilah glanced to her right to see the broad-shouldered figure of Samson O'Brien, face solemn as the funeral came to a close.

How was he feeling? Did he still think Alice Shepherd might have had reason to be worried about her safety?

He'd been cagey about his visit to Eric Bradley's flat, saying nothing more than that the oxygen concentrator was working fine, a fact young Danny Bradley had been pleased to hear. He'd offered no more than that. In fact, for the past few days she'd barely seen him. He'd been out of the office on some case or other.

Not that she hadn't been busy herself. The Dales Dating Agency's fifth speed-dating event was scheduled for Monday evening. With Christmas Day falling a few days later, it was going to be a festive occasion and she'd been occupied sourcing mistletoe and holly and other Yuletide trimmings. It would be the final event of the year for her dating agency and would bring some badly needed revenue into the business. It would also be the first speed-dating night without any of her friends to support her.

After the drama following the last one, Lucy had opted out, a decision Delilah totally understood. And Harry Furness, having met the lovely Sarah Mitchell at the event in November, had also cried off from lending his backing to the Christmas edition. Elaine Bullock – apart from not being in the frame of mind for thinking about romance – wasn't going to be around as she was setting off tomorrow to run a field trip in the Lake District. As for Samson . . .

'Penny for them, sis?' Ash ducked under the rim of the umbrella as the mourners moved away from the graveside and made their way towards the church gate. Taking the umbrella from her to hold it at his height, he promptly removed all of its protective benefits from his much shorter sister.

Delilah didn't complain. What was a bit of snow anyway, in the scheme of things? 'I was thinking about love,' she said.

Ash smiled and tucked his arm through hers. 'Appropriate. Considering.'

'It was good of you to come.'

He glanced towards Elaine up ahead of them, leading her mother up the road towards the marketplace with its strings of fairy lights bright through the thickening snow. 'Thought it would be appreciated. She's had a hard couple of weeks and she's been a rock for Lucy the last month.'

Delilah squeezed his arm in affection, wishing her relationship with her oldest brother was as good. 'How's the barn getting on?'

The smile dropped from Ash's lips. 'It's one step forward, two steps back at the moment. I don't know if I'm going to get it finished in time for Christmas Day.'

'It's still almost a week away. Is there a lot left to do?'

'Nothing major. Painting. Glossing,' he said, ticking things off on his fingers. 'A little bit of grouting. There's a few light fittings that need putting up . . . Why? Are you offering to help?'

She nodded. 'I can come up tomorrow. I'm sure Samson wouldn't mind, either.'

'What wouldn't I mind?' asked the man in question, falling into step with the siblings as they crossed the marketplace, the cobbles slippery underfoot, pockets of white forming on the old stones.

'Helping up at the barn,' said Ash. 'Delilah's put your name down for some more grouting.'

Samson groaned, his knees protesting at the thought. 'Anything but grouting,' he said.

'Okay. I'll sign you up for glossing the skirting board instead,' replied Ash with a grin.

'And while you're volunteering,' said Delilah, 'I'm still one man short for Monday's Speedy Date—'

'Oh no!' Samson backed off, grimacing. 'No way. Last time it was in the line of duty.'

'But you enjoyed it,' she protested.

'I said that under duress. Ask Ash, if you're desperate.'

Ash was already shaking his head. 'No can do. I've got a Christmas party with Procter Properties that night. Thank goodness.'

'You're becoming quite the corporate man,' teased Delilah.

Her brother, as usual, failed to rise to the bait. 'You bet I am,' he said. 'I'm quite happy to hitch my waggon to that particular star. Rick has more developments in mind and I don't see why he won't put the kitchens my way, seeing as he's happy with what I'm doing down at Low Mill.'

'Guess that means the first round's on you, then,' said Delilah as they reached the Fleece. Samson held the door open and they shook the worst of the snow off themselves before entering the welcome warmth of the pub.

'Are you sure about this?' At the back of the small group of mourners heading for the Fleece, Arty Robinson was concerned.

Along with a good contingent from Fellside Court, he'd attended Alice's funeral. It had been heartening to see so many people paying their respects. Young Danny Bradley had been there, standing in for his absent grandfather. He'd passed on the good news that Eric, who had regained consciousness the day after his accident, was on the mend and due to leave hospital within a few days. The lovely care assistant, Vicky Hudson, had also turned up, struggling to hold back her tears.

Arty had been less happy to see Ana Stoyanova at the back of the church, the stark blonde of her hair and pale skin against the black of her outfit making her nickname of the Ice Queen even more apt. There'd been no sign of tears from her. She was poison – of that he was now convinced. He'd been avoiding her for the last couple of days and so when Elaine Bullock had invited some of Alice's closest friends to the Fleece, Arty had accepted. It was a fitting way to see off the old girl. And it delayed his return to Fellside Court and proximity to Ana Stoyanova.

At first, it seemed Arty would be the only resident to attend the wake. With the weather closing in and snow starting to fall, Edith, Clarissa and Rita had made the wise decision not to risk old bones on slippery cobbles and had instead opted to go home. Ana had offered to drive them across the town centre to the pub, but the women had declined, saying they were going to hold their own memorial for dear Alice in the cafe. Joseph had made to go with them but when he realised Arty was following the rest of the funeral party, he'd changed direction and caught up with the bookmaker.

Which is why, as they approached the pub, Arty was having second thoughts. 'I mean, it's not really a good idea, is it?'

Joseph smiled. 'Don't worry about me. I'll be fine.'

'Fine? You're an alcoholic and we're about to enter a drinking establishment. Of course I'm worried.'

A slight shrug of the shoulders was the only reply he got from his friend.

'You don't need to come in with me,' continued Arty. 'I'll be okay on my own.'

'Sure, I know that. But I've seen so little of you the last couple of days. It'll be grand to catch up, away from the women.' Joseph gave a roguish wink and reached for the door handle, ushering Arty inside before he could make any more protests.

Shaking the snow off his overcoat, Arty entered the pub. Behind him, Joseph took a deep breath, looked up to the heavy skies and muttered a quick prayer.

'Give me strength, Kathleen.' Then, for the first time since he was carted home from its cosy interior by George Capstick two years ago, Joseph O'Brien entered the Fleece.

Troy Murgatroyd should have been happy. His pub was thronged with people and they were drinking. His wife had laid on a buffet in the small room at the back, which meant they would all stay a while. And the weather was getting worse outside, yet another factor that would keep the customers within the four walls of his establishment.

But while his entrepreneurial spirit was satisfied, he was a misanthropist by nature and couldn't help but be annoyed by the arrival of his clients.

They were like dogs, the lot of them. Shaking off their wet clothes all over the floor, traipsing damp footprints across the carpet – these last two no exception. He glanced over at the door, a frown in place until surprise turned it upside down.

'Bugger me!' he said, overfilling the pint glass under the Black Sheep tap in shock. 'Never expected to see you in here again.'

His voice carried, making heads turn, and a gentle quiet descended. By the arch through to the second room, Samson was one of those whose attention was caught by the exclamation from the sullen landlord. He looked across to the new arrivals and cursed quietly.

'That's all we need,' he said, eyes on the figure of his father as he approached the bar.

Delilah placed a hand on his arm. 'Don't be so quick to judge him. He's here to mark the passing of a friend.'

'And then pass out on the floor,' muttered Samson. It was like being a teenager all over again. This pub. These people. That father who drank until unconscious, slumped across the bar in an incoherent mess which Samson would be responsible for getting home. 'He shouldn't be in here.'

He made to cross the floor, but Delilah pulled him back. 'Don't. Give him a chance.'

'I've spent most of my life giving him chances,' he said.

'So give him one more. For me.' She looked up at him. 'Please?'

He glanced around the room, noting the whispered conversations, the sly looks. Delilah was right. They were waiting for him to react. Waiting for yet another chapter in the O'Brien family meltdown saga.

'Hello, you two.' His father was standing next to them, a small bottle of lemonade in one hand, glass in the other. He raised the bottle in Samson's direction and smiled. 'I'm on the soft stuff, son.'

Delilah slipped her arm around Joseph and reached up to kiss him on the cheek. 'As if anyone thought any different.'

Joseph laughed but still the concern lingered on his son's face.

'Should you be in here?' Samson asked quietly.

'Probably not. But I didn't want to leave Arty.' He gestured towards the bookmaker, who was talking to Elaine Bullock, his pint of bitter already half-drunk. 'I recognise the signs of someone on the edge when I see them.'

'What's wrong with him?' asked Delilah.

'He's not been himself of late. Not since Alice died. But the last few days he's been behaving really strangely.'

'In what way?'

'He doesn't come down for any of the group sessions, for a start. And he hasn't been in the cafe for a while now. He just stays in his flat and refuses to answer the door. Or he comes into town and spends the day away from Fellside Court.' Joseph took a swig of his lemonade and winced at the sweetness, before staring at the bottle in contemplation. 'Plus he's taken to drinking. A lot. If I didn't know better,' he murmured, 'I'd say Arty is afraid of something.'

Delilah caught Samson's eye and opened her mouth to reply but Samson cut her off.

'What on earth does he have to be afraid of?' he asked.

His father looked up. 'You tell me,' he said. 'We live in a great place, surrounded by great people. None of it makes sense.'

None of it did. Unless it was all connected to Alice Shepherd's claim that Fellside Court was harbouring something malicious. Samson watched Arty return to the bar for another drink, throwing back a whisky before starting on his pint. He was tired, anyone could see that.

But he also had that haunted look which Samson had seen on undercover agents close to burnout. The constant fear. The struggle to appear normal in a situation that was tense.

Arty Robinson was under great strain.

'Have you tried talking to him?' he asked his father.

Joseph nodded. 'He clammed up, saying nothing's wrong. So when he suggested coming here . . .' The older O'Brien gave a sheepish grin. 'I happen to know all about the liberating effects of alcohol.'

'You rogue!' said Samson in admiration. 'I'll make a detective of you yet.'

Joseph raised his glass in response and wandered over to join his friend, who was finishing his second pint.

'Do you think it's connected?' asked Delilah. 'Arty's fear and Alice Shepherd's allegations?'

'Hard to say,' said Samson. 'But there does seem to be a lot of unease in Fellside Court.'

'Maybe we should take a closer look?'

There was that *we* again. 'How, exactly? And what would we be looking for?'

Delilah grinned. 'You could go undercover as an old lady. Spend a few days over there and see if anything's going on.'

He laughed, despite himself. 'If you don't mind, I'll save my old-lady outfit for when there's firm evidence of something untoward. At the moment we have nothing more than the claims of a confused elderly woman—'

'Who happened to die.'

'Old people do tend to die,' countered Samson.

'And then there's Eric . . .' Delilah continued, speculation in her eyes.

'What about him? His oxygen concentrator was working fine. He simply tripped and fell.' Samson shook his head. 'I spoke to Danny outside the church earlier and he's happy there was no malice involved. It was just an unfortunate mishap.'

'Aha! So you *are* curious. Enough to speak to Danny.'

He paused. Long enough for her to wag a finger in his face.

'See,' she said. 'You feel it in your gut. We should act on it. Have a bit of a snoop around before anything else happens.'

'Delilah,' he said patiently, 'if – and it's a big "if" – there's any investigating to be done, I'll be doing it. Not us. Not you. Not after last time. Understood?'

The door crashed open, cutting off her reply, and Will fell into the pub, cursing loudly and being pulled along by a frantic Weimaraner. A Weimaraner covered in multi-coloured blotches.

'Tolpuddle!' shouted Delilah, rushing over to greet her dog, who was now wagging his tail and barking with pleasure. She rubbed his head, careful not to mark her suit with whatever the dog was coated in. 'What happened?' she asked Will.

Her oldest brother scowled. 'Idiot dog. He nearly drove me demented all morning, whining like an air-raid siren the minute you went out of sight. The only time he calmed down was when I was replacing the marking colour on the ram and he got into the store. Had himself covered in crayon by the time I found him. Think he might have eaten some, too.'

Tolpuddle looked up at the pair of them, ears cocked,

more proud than contrite. Then he heard Samson's voice. Wheeling round, he pushed through the crowded pub, making a beeline for the detective, jostling people as he went.

'Easy, easy! I'm here,' Samson could be heard saying as he bent to stroke the dog, everyone laughing at the colours on the animal's coat.

Will wasn't laughing. He was watching man and hound with a look of distaste.

'I've never known a dog be more wrong about people,' he muttered as Tolpuddle leaned in against Samson's leg, enjoying every second of the affection being lavished on him.

Delilah shot him a black look. 'Ever thought it might be you who's wrong?' she hissed.

Will shook his head. 'Nope. That daft mutt liked your ex-husband too, remember. Look how well judged that was.'

Delilah paled. 'Jesus, Will. You never can let it go, can you?' She walked away, unwilling to let her brother see how much the last comment had hurt. Given the circumstances, any mention of Neil in connection with Tolpuddle was like a knife in an open wound.

'Are you okay?' Samson asked as she re-joined him, her dog thrusting his head into her hand, panting happily.

'Fine. Just wish I could divorce my brother.'

Samson grinned and then gestured at the splotches of colour on Tolpuddle. 'What happened?'

'He got into the crayon store up at the farm while Will was changing the colours over. You know how easily that stuff rubs off on—'

'That's it!' Samson was staring at the dog's back.

'What?' asked Delilah. But she didn't get a reply. Samson had his mobile in his hand, scrolling through photos until he reached one that made him freeze.

'It just doesn't make sense,' he muttered. Then he was striding across the pub, heading for the door.

Delilah would have followed him, sensing that he'd had some kind of breakthrough in a case and eager to know more. But she felt the heavy weight of Will's stare from the bar. So she fussed over Tolpuddle a bit more and then joined Elaine Bullock, who was talking to Lucy. There was no way her brother could complain about her keeping them company. Then again, given the state of the sibling relationship, he'd probably find a way.

He'd been taken for a fool.

Samson flicked through the photographs one more time, his conviction growing stronger as the images of Mire End Farm flashed across the screen.

An absolute idiot – that's what he'd been. And him a farmer in a previous life. How had he not noticed before?

Berating himself, he pulled up a map of the area. He needed evidence. Clear evidence. And some background information. He thought he might know where to find it. He also knew the two people who could help him. Whether or not he could persuade them to was another matter. Particularly given their family history of stubbornness.

'Time to go home, Arty.' Joseph O'Brien slipped a hand under his friend's arm and gently led him towards the door.

It was mid-afternoon. The wake had long since finished but Arty had kept insisting on another drink. Then another. Then something to eat. And the entire time Joseph was fighting the temptation to order something stronger than lemonade, the smell of alcohol seeping into his consciousness, making him salivate. Just one. He could have just one and he'd be fine.

Kathleen had saved him. The thought of her looking down, watching over him as he tried to do his best for his friend. That and the fact that he didn't want to give Bruncliffe the satisfaction of seeing him live up to the nickname of Boozy O'Brien. Not now his son was home.

'One more . . . for the road,' slurred Arty, straining to get back to the bar.

But Joseph was insistent. He didn't think his own strength would hold out much longer.

'No more, my friend. You've already had more than enough. Think what Edith will say when she sees you.'

The thought of the headmistress, face puckered in disapproval, was enough to send the bookmaker into a fit of giggles. 'Edith . . . she's a good woman . . .' Then he jerked upright, a hand reaching out to Joseph in terror. 'Look after her,' he said. 'If anything happens to me.'

'Nothing's going to happen to you,' said Joseph. 'Apart from you having a massive headache tomorrow morning. So let's get you home.'

Arty slumped back into himself, the drink taking hold, and quietly allowed Joseph to lead him out of the pub and into the cold of a winter's afternoon. The snow had relented but the ground was covered, and the pair of them slipped and slid across the marketplace and up the hill towards Fellside Court. By the time they reached the apartment building, Joseph was tiring, Arty needing a lot of support as he stumbled on alcohol-numbed legs. He was glad to see the wall of glass rearing above them as they crossed the courtyard.

'Nearly home,' he said, guiding his friend into the warmth of the entrance hall.

Arty shuddered, focusing on the familiar carpet, the photographs on the walls, and realising where he was. He shrank further into his winter coat, hand grasping tightly onto Joseph's arm.

'Quick, before she sees us,' he mumbled, almost colliding with the Christmas tree as he hurried towards the lift. He pulled Joseph in after him, muttering incoherently while he struggled to locate his keys. When the lift doors opened, he lunged across the corridor towards his flat.

'Inside, inside,' he hissed, trying to insert the key in the lock, his hands shaking so badly that Joseph had to take the key from him and open the door.

Whether Joseph had been intending to stay or not, he had no choice. Arty dragged his friend into his flat and slammed the door, breathing heavily, eyes wild.

'Did she see us?' he demanded.

'Who?'

Arty didn't answer, visibly shaking as he put an eye to the spyhole. 'She's out there. I see her. She's poison.'

Joseph put a hand on his friend's arm and Arty jumped. 'Calm down, Arty. It's just the drink talking. I should know.'

But Arty shook him off, dropped his coat on the floor and staggered across the apartment towards his bedroom.

'You don't understand,' he muttered. 'No one does. No one except Alice.'

'Alice is dead, Arty,' said Joseph gently. 'And you're drunk. Come on, get some sleep and you'll feel better in the morning.'

Arty shook his head, sitting on the edge of the bed as he tried to take off his shoes, the laces proving tricky for his fumbling fingers. 'No sleep. Too dangerous. She comes when we're asleep.'

'Here, let me,' said Joseph, ignoring the drunken paranoia. Bending down, he undid the shoes and slipped them off, eased his friend out of his jacket, removed his tie and then helped him onto the bed, covering him with the bedspread.

Already Arty's eyelids were closing, his drink-inspired terrors abating.

Joseph waited until his friend's breathing became heavy with sleep. Then he hung the discarded items of clothing over a chair and headed out into the hall, placing Arty's overcoat on a hook as he made to leave.

He paused, hand on the front door.

Arty was drunk. That much was clear. Drunk enough that he was seeing demons in the shadows.

Joseph remembered those days. He also remembered waking up in the dark all alone, his fears as large as when he'd fallen into a drunken stupor hours before.

He turned back towards the kitchen. It wouldn't hurt for him to stay a while. At least until Arty was awake again and ready to eat something maybe. God knows, enough people had done that for him when he'd been raving drunk. Time he paid back a little.

Smiling at the irony – a drunk looking after a drunk – Joseph O'Brien put the kettle on. And placed himself in danger.

Dusk fell quickly on an already dark day. The snow eased, the shadows took over, and the stillness peculiar to snowy conditions descended on Bruncliffe. Up the hill above the police station and the library, Fellside Court reflected the sombre qualities of the town around it.

Like every year in the run-up to Christmas, the retirement complex had taken on a melancholic air as its population temporarily decreased, with many residents heading off to stay with their families. So even though it was only early evening, the place was quiet. The cafe was empty; the lounge hosted a handful of people, some of them snoozing lightly in front of the television; the corridors were silent. In the cluster of six apartments overlooking the courtyard, things were no livelier. Alice Shepherd's flat was understandably vacant. Next to it, Eric Bradley's was in the dark, the old man still in hospital and then due to go to his son's for the festive season. Rita Wilson was at a WI meeting in the town, leaving her windows unlit. And the two guest suites were unoccupied. It was only Arty Robinson's flat on the first floor that showed any signs of life. And even they were muted.

In the bedroom, a soft burr of snoring drifted from under the bedcovers draped over the sleeping form of the drunken bookmaker. In the lounge, curtains drawn against the night, the TV flickered silently, the six o'clock news being broadcast unseen to the man in the armchair. Like his friend, Joseph O'Brien was fast asleep, head back, eyes closed, at home on Twistleton Farm in his dreams, his wife beside him, their infant son playing on a newly formed hay bale under a summer sky . . .

When the front door eased open, he didn't hear a thing. Was unaware of the silhouette slipping into the hall, the shimmer of blonde hair before the door closed quietly behind it. A couple of soft steps and the figure was in the archway that gave onto the open-plan living area, the television casting the space in a sickly light. Enough light to reveal the outline of the man in the armchair, his back to the hall.

Perfect. He would die in front of the TV. Wonderfully normal. No suspicion. A heart attack in a man with a history of heart disease.

Syringe in hand, death approached the unsuspecting Joseph O'Brien. It wasn't meant for him. But fate, and a kind heart, had placed him there. In the wrong place. Definitely at the wrong time.

Arty Robinson was in a deep, troubled, alcohol-infused sleep. Several decades younger, he was at the counter of his betting shop in Leeds, reliving an attempted robbery by two young lads in balaclavas and carrying baseball bats.

They'd stormed in, threatening customers, smashing glass and demanding money. Big Al had been out of the office like a shot, throwing himself at the nearest offender and pinning him to the wall with his bulk. The second lad had turned on the big man and Arty had seized his chance, leaping over the counter and lunging at his back. The lad had whipped around, sensing danger, baseball bat swinging, and instinct had taken over. Falling back on the boxing training from his youth, Arty had ducked low and then risen with an almighty punch, his fist aiming for the lad's chin.

In the dark bedroom of the here and now, limbs twitching, dreams mixing the present and the past, Arty's right arm shot out of the bedcovers and smashed into the bedside lamp, a hoarse shout accompanying it.

It saved his friend's life.

The crash came from the bedroom, overlaid by a bellow, and stilled the syringe. Someone else was in the flat. Hastily stowing the instrument of death in a pocket, the figure hurried back into the hallway, heading for the exit. But the man in the chair was stirring, roused by the noise.

'What's going on?' he murmured, his distinctive accent slurred as he surfaced to unfamiliar surroundings, confusion befuddling him for a few vital seconds. He stared at the room around him, the TV on, and saw a slice of light reflected across the screen, a silhouette caught in it.

'Who's there?' he muttered, twisting round to the dark hallway.

No one. Just the coats hanging off the hooks by the door and the sound of Arty snoring from the bedroom.

Laughing at his own jitters, Joseph O'Brien roused himself, stiff from his impromptu sleep, and padded into the kitchen.

A cup of tea. For him and Arty. It would do them the power of good. Make Arty feel alive after such a heavy session.

He filled the kettle and contemplated how wonderful his life was. Fellside Court had been the saving of him.

13

Samson O'Brien was on a mission. A charm offensive. He wasn't sure of his success, given that his target was Will Metcalfe. However, he could but try.

The morning after Alice Shepherd's funeral he eased the Royal Enfield along Back Street, the engine noise bouncing off the buildings on either side. He was soon on Hillside Lane – the road that led up onto the fells – and with the town falling behind, the shops and houses quickly yielded to fields and the dramatic rise of land that crested above Bruncliffe.

It looked beautiful any day of the year, in Samson's biased opinion. But today . . .

Today, thanks to the wintry weather of the day before, it was like something out of a fairy tale.

White fields glittered under bright sunshine. Grey stone walls were adorned with a festive topping, softening the direct lines that had been etched into the terrain centuries before. And the fellsides sloped upwards in smooth, pristine scoops of snow, unmarred by rock or soil.

The roads, thankfully, were clear, if a bit wet, making the ride to High Laithe possible.

'It's beautiful!'

The shout carried over his shoulder, the excitement audible over the engine and echoed in the tightening of the grip around his waist. He grinned. It hadn't been his idea. In fact he'd been set against it, worried about the weather and the road conditions.

But he had to admit. She'd been right. For once.

The sound of her delighted laughter carried on the breeze. With Delilah Metcalfe riding pillion, Samson could have ridden through the snowy landscape for a lot longer than the ten minutes it took to get to High Laithe. In no time at all, however, he was pulling up at the barn, Will Metcalfe's thunderous face staring out at him from the doorway.

As charm offensives went, Samson suspected he wasn't off to the best of starts.

The snow kept Rita Wilson at the window longer than normal. Having a flat in the rear corner of Fellside Court, she was blessed with a bedroom that looked out towards the hills at the back of the town. Usually she opened the curtains, admired the view, and then got on with the day. But this morning was worthy of prolonged attention. The fell was covered in a blanket of white, even the defining stone walls smothered into nothing, a winter's blue sky stretched gauze-thin over it all.

It wouldn't last long. The sun was already warm enough to begin the thaw, the trees in the copse next to the car park dripping steadily, the courtyard paving stones wet and bare.

Not quite walkable just yet, perhaps. A couple of years ago she'd have risked the short stroll into town, confident in her sturdy boots. Now she wasn't so rash. Although there wasn't a hint of ice out there. Another hour and then she could head into town.

It was the flash of colour that would prompt her to change her plans. To leave the cosy comfort of her flat and venture out into the melting morning. She spotted it out of the corner of her eye as she turned to leave the window. She paused, turned back and stared across the car park to the huddle of trees skirted in white.

Something was glinting in the sunshine.

The small binoculars she used for birdwatching were on the windowsill. She held them up and focused them, the ground blinding in its brightness as she scanned across it.

There it was. A rainbow buried in the snow.

Puzzled, she lowered the binoculars, blinked and then looked again. It was still there. But just too far away for her to make out what it was.

How odd. What could it be?

Moving into the hall, Rita buttoned up her cardigan, reached for her coat and scarf and slipped on her boots. She'd go as far as the other end of the courtyard and have a look. Just to satisfy her curiosity.

She was at the front door when she thought of her grabber. A handy gadget that her son had bought her for picking things up off the floor, it might come in useful. Not that she was intending on going further than the pavement.

Grabber in hand and leaning heavily on her stick, she left the flat and walked up the corridor towards the wall of glass.

*

'What the hell were you thinking? She could have been killed!'

Face red, finger pointing, Will Metcalfe was storming across the yard before Samson had even got off the bike. That the oldest Metcalfe sibling's concern didn't extend to Bruncliffe's black sheep hadn't escaped Samson's notice, but it wasn't something he was prepared to query right now. He did contemplate leaving his helmet on, however, not really wanting to enter the festive period with bruises. Especially when the ones he'd arrived in Bruncliffe with – the ones that had been his leaving present from three balaclava-clad men in London – had only just faded.

Judging by the anger simmering on Will's features, he was capable of being every bit as brutal as the men in balaclavas had been.

Taking a chance, Samson removed the helmet and brushed his hair back over his shoulder, glancing at Delilah as he did so. She was frozen, staring at her older brother, tension rigid across her shoulders, knuckles white where she gripped her helmet.

'Didn't you see the bloody weather?' Will continued, right in front of Samson now, head tipped back, staring up at the taller man. 'There's snow on the ground, you idiot. You can take whatever risks you want with your life, but not with hers!'

'For God's sake—'

'Sorry.' Samson cut Delilah off with a single word.

Will blinked. Leaned back slightly. Then frowned.

'You're right,' Samson continued. 'It was stupid. And I'm truly sorry.'

A grunt issued from the older Metcalfe, a hiss from the younger.

'Apology accepted,' muttered Will. He gave a sharp nod of his head and then stalked back into the barn.

'What the hell were you thinking?' railed Delilah, before her brother was even out of earshot. 'It's Will who should be doing the apologising! And you too. Talking about me as if I was a child without a mind of my own. Honestly. The pair of you are insufferable!'

Feet stomping in exactly the same footprints Will had left moments earlier, her shoulders back and spine rigid with temper, Delilah stormed across to the barn in an uncanny replica of her older brother.

Samson sighed. He couldn't win. His apology had been genuine, a sudden insight into Will's fear, which was rooted in the loss of a brother, making Samson repent his reckless action. Not that it had been reckless. The roads were safe enough. But he could appreciate Will's concerns and the causes of them.

In appeasing one Metcalfe, however, he'd angered the other. Which was a problem because if he was going to get to the bottom of the Clive Knowles case, he needed them both onside.

'Come here, you little . . .' Rita Wilson, definitely not on the pavement but boot-deep in the snow, was wrestling with the grabber.

Curiosity had got the better of her. She'd crossed the courtyard without incident, the ground merely wet underfoot, and had reached the edge of the car park that butted up to the grass. The grass that was covered in a layer of white.

It had seemed a shame to come this far and still not be able to tell what the splash of colour was that was protruding from under one of the trees. Besides, she had her stick with her. And at least she'd have a soft landing if she fell.

Beguiled by the hint of red and orange that burned against the stark background, she'd taken a step onto the snow and carefully picked her way across it.

Only trouble was, while she could distinguish the colours okay, her eyesight wasn't good enough to see what the object was. Nor could she bend down and pick it up, her days of such agility having passed. So she'd been trying to get a closer look by using her grabber. But the slick surface of the item in the ground was giving her some difficulty.

'There! Got you,' she muttered as she squeezed the trigger handle and the rubberised ends of her gadget finally gained purchase.

Leaning on her stick, she lifted the grabber carefully, pulling the rainbow out of the snow colour by colour. Red. Orange. Yellow. Green. Blue. Lilac. Purple.

She knew what it was now. Recognised the compact rectangle, the slices of semi-precious stone. It took a bit of manoeuvring to lift it up and remove it from the grabber, requiring her to release her grip on her walking stick and stand there slightly off balance, worried that she'd fall over and spoil Christmas for everyone. Then she had it securely in her hand, slipped it into her coat pocket and transferred her weight back onto her stick, her heart pattering with the effort.

Retracing her cautious footsteps, she made her way back to the safety of the tarmacked car park, a frown drawing deep lines across her forehead.

What was it doing there? So out of place. So unexpected.

Thoughts firmly on the puzzle of Alice Shepherd's pillbox, Rita Wilson failed to notice the shift in light on the first floor as a shadow moved out of sight, away from the glass wall.

She'd been seen. The object in her pocket had been seen. Her curiosity had placed her in a situation far more deadly than that caused by an unsteady boot stepping onto an icy surface.

Samson waited until lunchtime to broach the subject. The morning had been spent in a flurry of activity, Ash directing the willing labourers. Harry Furness had arrived with several members of the rugby club who were put to work carrying in a wood-burning stove and a range cooker, while Samson, to his relief, was assigned the job of painting the walls in the utility. Delilah, perhaps as punishment for the foul temper she'd not bothered to hide when she'd entered the barn, was given the thankless task of grouting the downstairs cloakroom, far away from her brother Will, who was fixing light fittings in the upstairs rooms. Unable to leave her cafe due to the seasonal demand for her mince pies and Yule logs, Lucy was absent. As was Nathan, roped in to wait on tables at Peaks Patisserie, despite preferring to work in the barn with

Samson. Also missing was Elaine Bullock, already on her way to the Lakes with a minibus of students for a field trip that had been rescheduled and shoehorned in before Christmas.

But in spite of the depleted numbers, by the time Lucy pulled up outside in the Peaks Patisserie van – Harry being first out of the door to help her unload the food for the workers – Ash was looking happy at all that had been achieved by the band of volunteers.

'Oh wow, it looks amazing,' said Lucy as she stepped inside, the newly installed wood-burner already alight and filling the lounge with cheer. Then she spotted the array of huge bodies gathering around the makeshift table and a hint of worry filled her voice. 'I think I've brought enough to feed everyone.'

'There's cheese-and-onion tart,' exclaimed Harry, pulling the plate towards himself and reaching for a knife. 'That's me sorted.'

Lucy laughed. 'Well, you know where I am if you need more. I can't stop. It's manic down there – the world and his wife wanting cinnamon coffees and mince pies. The festive season is in full swing in Bruncliffe.'

She gave Delilah a quick hug and was gone. When Samson turned back to the table, a lot of the food had gone too.

'Best sit in quick, you two,' said Ash, a half-eaten slice of turkey-and-cranberry pie in his hand. 'This lot are like locusts.'

There were two empty chairs at the table – one opposite Will at the end closest to them, the other at the far end. Before Samson even had a chance to choose, Delilah made the choice for him. She walked past her oldest brother and exiled herself with the lads from the rugby club, leaving Samson with the hot seat. Which was exactly what he wanted.

'How's the detective business going?' asked Harry from a few places further down as Samson sat. 'Any luck with finding Knowles' tup yet?'

'I've had a few developments,' said Samson enigmatically, pulling the tray of sandwiches towards him. He was aware of Will's interest, the farmer immediately alert for anything that might concern him. And the sudden disappearance of a prize tup in mating season would concern any farmer.

Letting the conversation hang in the air, Samson busied himself selecting a couple of sandwiches, took his time cutting a slice of the tart Harry had nearly demolished single-handedly, and then set about eating.

As he'd anticipated, Harry had turned back to the conversation at the far end of the table. But for Will, the suspense was more than he could bear.

'What developments?' the farmer asked gruffly, black stare on the detective.

Samson shrugged, lowering his voice so only Will could hear. 'Interesting ones.'

'Such as?'

'Questions of fertility.'

Will paused, sandwich halfway to his mouth and a rare sparkle of amusement in his eyes. 'Yours or the ram's?'

Samson grinned. 'The ram's. But you'd know more about this than me,' he said, leaning forward. 'How was Ralph performing last year?'

'Hard to say. Knowles brought the usual number of lambs to market. But there was nowt special amongst them.'

'No prize-winners?'

Will shook his head. 'Not that I heard of.'

'And they were definitely bred from Ralph?'

Another long pause from the farmer while he assessed the implication of Samson's words.

'That's what was claimed,' he said eventually, looking wary, his attention fully fixed on the detective now. 'What's this got to do with the tup going missing?'

Samson reached for his mobile and flicked to the photos he'd taken up at Mire End Farm.

'Here. Notice anything odd?' He held out the phone.

'Apart from it being a dump?' Will squinted at the screen, disapproval evident as he took in the state of the land and the livestock. 'When was this taken?'

'The day after Ralph went missing.'

The farmer's head snapped up. 'You mean these are the yows he was taken from?'

'Yep.'

'How long had he been in with them?'

'Two weeks.'

A frown creased Will's forehead. 'Doesn't Knowles use a tup harness?'

Samson nodded, impressed. He'd been right to trust his instinct. When it came to breeding sheep, Will Metcalfe was one of the best around, and the man's natural curiosity had overcome any resentment he harboured towards Bruncliffe's outcast. He'd spotted the mistake a lot faster than Samson had, too.

'What did he have in it, then?' asked Will, passing the phone back. 'Invisible ink?'

His caustic comment made Samson laugh. 'Reckon so. Either that or . . .' He glanced down at the photograph of the sheep in the field where the chain had been severed.

It was what he'd been reminded of when Tolpuddle had come bursting into the pub the day before, smeared in colours. Crayon. The dog had been covered in it after the slightest contact. That was what was supposed to happen. Yet in the photograph in Samson's hand, every sheep was white – not a mark of red on their rumps. As Will suggested, either the crayon-holder in the ram's harness had contained invisible ink or . . .

'You think the tup wasn't performing?' Will asked.

'Looks that way,' said Samson. 'Any ideas as to why that might happen?'

Will blew out his cheeks and scratched his head, shifting in his seat as though warming to the topic. 'Depends who you believe. There's been quite a lot of research into low-performance rams.'

'Is it common?'

'More so than you'd think. Some put it down to nutrition, some to stamina. But in a tup as young as this one, it shouldn't be that. It's also possible that the tup just doesn't want to perform.'

'You mean . . . ?'

'He could be gay.' Will saw Samson's look of disbelief and shrugged. 'Why not? I've read a lot of studies which suggest that as many as one in ten rams are born with a preference for their own kind.'

'And if a ram has that inclination?'

'As a farmer, you're stuffed. You've paid out for a prize tup and you're left with an animal that won't perform.' He shrugged again and gave a wry smile. 'Reckon in that situation, I might be wishing someone would steal my tup, too. Especially if I had it insured.'

Again, Samson had to admire Will's quick wits.

'You reckon that was what happened?' continued the farmer.

'It's a theory I'm working on,' said Samson. 'Thanks for letting me run it past you. But if you could keep this to yourself for now?'

Will grinned. 'My lips are sealed. But if you find the tup and Knowles puts him up for sale, I won't be bidding, no matter how low the price!'

Samson laughed, the sound hitting a lull in the lunch-time conversation, and he felt the stare from the far end of the table.

Delilah. Watching them. Her gaze like flint.

Samson sighed and helped himself to a slice of turkey-and-cranberry pie. As his relationship with one family member thawed, the other deteriorated. There was no winning with the Metcalfes. It was probably better not to even try.

A bacon butty. A mug of tea. By lunchtime Arty was feeling almost human. Almost.

There was a persistent thumping in his head and his eyes were gritty with tiredness. But at least he was alive, even if it didn't feel that great.

When the bookmaker had struggled from his drunken slumber the evening before, Joseph had been in the flat.

He'd proved his expertise in the matter of hangovers by plying Arty with water and dry toast before leaving him for the night, warning him to have something substantial in the morning.

Three rashers of bacon from Hargreaves the butcher. Two slices of Warburton's toastie. A liberal amount of HP Sauce. It had all gone down a treat and now only the headache remained from Arty's excesses.

He felt ashamed of his behaviour. Drinking that much. It was stress, he knew. But even so. A man of his years ought to know better. *Did* know better.

He pulled on his jumper and checked his appearance in the mirror in the hall. He looked haggard, his eyes peering back at him as though trying to ascertain the validity of the reflection.

He'd do. He was only going down to the cafe. To catch up with Joseph and apologise for yesterday.

Easing open his front door, he glanced out into the hallway. Clear. No one in the corridor by the glass wall, either. He hurried across to the stairs, slipping through the door and into the stairwell. His heart was pounding. It was ridiculous. Scurrying around the place, afraid for his life. He had to do something about it. Talk to someone.

After Christmas. He'd talk to Joseph after Christmas. Until then, he'd stay out of the way and keep his head down.

Reaching the last of the steps, he crossed to the door that led into the foyer. All clear. Just the route past her office to negotiate.

Palms sweaty, pulse racing, Arty Robinson stepped out into the welcoming environment of Fellside Court, feeling none of the festive cheer that the Christmas tree by the entrance was meant to evoke.

Rita had been puzzling about her discovery all morning and she'd come to the only two conclusions that seemed logical.

Either Alice Shepherd's god-daughter had callously thrown the pillbox away – which seemed unlikely, as Elaine was such a lovely girl and had been distraught at her godmother's passing – or it had been mislaid.

Although how you could mislay something over in the copse didn't make sense. And things that were mislaid didn't tend to be half-buried, when found.

It was odd. All ways round.

She stroked the smooth surface of the lid, the vivid slices of semi-precious stones none the worse for their neglect. It was hard to say how long the box had been abandoned, but the hinge was still intact and inside there were some pills, damp and discoloured, lying in their designated sections.

What to do with it? That was the other thing that had been occupying Rita all morning, her plans to walk down to town set aside in the excitement of her discovery.

It was a delicate situation. Rita didn't want to broadcast to all and sundry that she'd found Alice Shepherd's pillbox sticking up out of the snow under a tree. Not until she'd told Elaine Bullock about it, and given the young woman a chance to explain what it was doing there.

But she'd heard Arty saying at the funeral that Elaine was going away on a field trip today. And by the time she got back, Rita herself would be gone, off to her son's to spend Christmas with his family. Which would mean Elaine wouldn't be reunited with the pillbox until after New Year.

That just wouldn't do. Rita needed to give it to someone to pass on to the young woman. And she knew just the person.

Popping the box into her pocket, she headed out into the corridor and was just in time to see him crossing the hall.

'Arty!' she called.

He jumped, turning round with his hand across his heart, his skin pale and sheened in perspiration. Then he smiled. But it didn't quite reach his eyes.

'Rita,' Arty said. 'You gave me a fright.'

She had, too. He'd been so focused on sneaking past the closed office door ahead that he hadn't seen her approaching from the hallway to the left, which led to her flat. He tried to laugh off his reaction while his heart thumped in his ears.

'Sorry, but I was just coming up to see you. I wanted to give you this.' Rita Wilson reached into the pocket of her cardigan and pulled something out, her hands folded over it, shielding it from sight. 'Here. Put it away before anyone sees.'

'What is it?' he asked, holding out a hand.

She passed it to him and he felt the cold touch of metal and stone. Then he saw the colours.

'Alice's—?'

'Shush!' she hissed, finger to her lips, leaning into him. 'I found it outside under a tree.' She gestured towards the bare branches of the copse beyond the glass wall. 'Put it away, quickly.'

He did as he was told, sliding the box under his jumper. 'But I don't understand. How did it get to be out there? I thought Elaine Bullock had taken it?'

'I thought so, too. Which means either she lost it or—'

'She threw it away?' Arty was already shaking his head. 'She wouldn't do that. She thought the world of Alice.'

'Which is why I think we should keep this quiet. We need to have a word with Elaine before the rumour mill turns this into something it isn't. But as I'm heading to my son's on Tuesday . . .'

'You want me to speak to Elaine when she gets back?' Arty nodded. 'No problem. I'm sure we'll get to the bottom of it—'

'You two look very serious. Is everything okay?' Ana Stoyanova had approached them, shoes silent across the carpet. Her tone was light and a small smile graced her lips. But her gaze was intense.

Arty hunched forward over the hidden pillbox, words sticking in his parched throat. It was Rita who saved them.

'Secret Santa,' she said with a laugh. 'Arty's drawn Geraldine and was asking me for some ideas. I've told him not smelly stuff. Her tastes are a bit more expensive than our permitted budget.'

Ana smiled back. 'I think you've got sound advice there, Arty. I'd take it, if I were you. But you're cutting it fine. The Christmas party's Monday afternoon.'

Arty forced his mouth into a grin, lips dry against his teeth. 'Right,' he said. 'Best get ready for a trip into town. Thanks, Rita.'

He nodded in the general direction of the two women and then turned away towards the stairs. It took all of his willpower not to run. Not to take the stairs two at a time in the hurry to be away from *her*. And all the while he could feel that gaze on his back, burning into him while the pillbox rested cold against his stomach.

He needed a drink. And then he needed to talk to someone. Soon.

'That was a very cosy chat you were having with Will at the table.'

Applying a coat of gloss to the skirting board in the utility, Samson kept his head bent to make sure the already annoyed Delilah couldn't see the grin forming. He'd estimated that she wouldn't last the afternoon without tackling him about his tête-à-tête with her oldest brother. In actual fact she'd lasted an hour.

She stood in the doorway, arms folded across her chest, a smear of grout on her cheek. It was impossible to take her seriously. But he needed her assistance so he had to avoid antagonising her any further.

'He was helping me with a case,' Samson said, brushing smooth the last bit of gloss before standing.

'A case?' Interest had overlaid the indignation. 'What case?'

'The Clive Knowles case.'

She frowned. 'I thought you'd solved that already. Ralph was stolen.'

He put the paintbrush down on the tin and pulled out his mobile, holding it out so she could see the screen.

'Is this Mire End Farm?' she asked as he showed her the first picture, the sheep scattered around the field.

'Yep. I took all of these last Wednesday when I went out there for the first time. See anything odd?'

She zoomed in, pulling the photo left and right, eyes flicking over it. 'Ralph was in with them before he was taken?' she asked, looking up at him.

'For two weeks.'

'And you said Knowles uses a tup harness?'

She was every bit as sharp as her brother. Samson waited while she looked again and then raised an eyebrow.

'Reckon someone dodged a bullet,' she said, offering him back the phone. 'It doesn't look like Ralph was doing his job properly. But at least Knowles will get the insurance payout.'

'Quite an incentive, don't you think?'

Delilah glanced back at the phone and then up at him. 'You're not suggesting . . .'

'Why not? There's been something odd about this case since the beginning.'

'But a field of sheep that haven't been serviced is no proof of anything dishonest. Whereas you have an eyewitness stating the ram was taken, and you found evidence up there to suggest Pete Ferris was telling the truth.'

'What evidence?' he asked, encouraging her to list it.

'The harness—'

'Proves nothing. Knowles could have discarded it himself.'

'Pete's lighter,' she continued, undaunted. 'It proves he was there.'

'Exactly. That's all it establishes. For all we know, he was in on it.'

'The tyre tracks in the field . . .' she said, losing confidence as her mind worked ahead of her words.

He held out the mobile again, this time swiping to a different picture. 'These tracks?'

She leaned in, looking at the photo of the gate and the severed chain, the muddy field behind showing parallel lines extending into it. He zoomed in on the image.

'Apart from the fact that they suggest a vehicle was used to remove the ram,' he continued, 'do you notice anything else about the tracks?'

It took her a moment. Then she looked at the gate. The partially open gate, the gap only wide enough to allow Samson to squeeze through. 'It's wedged in the mud,' she said, a finger tracing the mark left behind as the gate opened. The same finger paused as the deep gouge in the mud came to an abrupt end.

Then she smiled.

'The gate hasn't been opened fully,' she said, pleased with herself.

He grinned. 'Not bad for a civvy.'

'No,' she retorted, her grin matching his. 'And it didn't take me a week and a half to figure it out.'

He didn't have a response to that. How had it taken him so long when the evidence had been staring him in the face all the time?

Ralph couldn't have been taken away in a vehicle. Not through the top gate, anyhow, as the tyre tracks in the field were perfect. Which meant that, as Delilah had pointed out, the gate hadn't been opened wide enough to allow access to a Transit van. If it had, the gouge left by the gate in the mud would have swiped across the tyre tracks, leaving a visible trace across them.

Delilah let out a low whistle. 'So Clive Knowles faked the theft?'

'It's looking that way.'

'And Pete Ferris was in on it?'

Samson nodded. 'I think so. They spirited Ralph away and left enough subtle clues to ensure that it looked like he'd been stolen.'

'The harness and the tracks.' Delilah paused. 'But what about the lighter?'

'We weren't meant to find that. I reckon Pete Ferris's part in all this was meant to be a secret. But he dropped his lighter—'

'And we were able to place him there. So after initially denying his presence, he then came forward as a witness.'

'Exactly. No doubt after a consultation with his co-conspirator. Which explains why Clive Knowles expressed no interest in knowing the identity of the witness to the so-called theft. He didn't need to ask who it was, because he already knew.'

'Wow.' Delilah was shaking her head. 'But why ask you to investigate? Why not go straight to the police?'

Samson shrugged. 'Maybe Knowles thought I'd do a better job of finding the evidence he'd planted.'

'Or maybe,' she said with a laugh, 'he expected you to do a half-arsed job and not question the evidence at all.'

'Thanks for the vote of confidence,' he muttered, making her laugh some more.

'So what now?' she asked.

'Now? Why now we have to retrieve Ralph.'

Her eyes lit up at the word *we*. 'Do you know where he is?'

'I have an idea, but I need your help,' Samson said. 'And it involves taking me for a run.'

He saw the flicker of uncertainty chase away the excitement. She wasn't keen. After all these years, she didn't want to share her running with him like she used to. He understood that. It was private for her now.

'If that's too much to ask—'

'No, it's okay,' she said. 'When do we go?'

'Tomorrow morning. Early.'

She grinned. 'It's a date.'

As she turned to leave, the solid frame of Will Metcalfe was standing in the hall behind her, the glare he was casting at Samson suggesting he'd caught the tail end of the conversation. Enough to damn the black sheep of Bruncliffe even more.

'O'Brien!' he snapped, the lunchtime bonhomie having evaporated under the fire of his temper. 'Ash wants a hand offloading the washing machine.'

Delilah cast a wink over her shoulder at Samson and left him to wonder whether there would ever be a day when he could count all of the Metcalfes on his side.

Arty had been sitting in his lounge staring at Alice Shepherd's pillbox as night claimed the skies over Bruncliffe, a glass of whisky in his hand. He was still sitting there many hours and several glasses later. Perturbed. Anxious. Frightened. And close to drunk.

What if he was right? What if Alice had been afraid? Had met her end by something other than natural causes?

Perhaps the unexpected discovery of this rainbow box was connected?

He stroked the cool surface, trailed a finger across the slices of colour. If he was right, then this could be dangerous. And important. Worth hiding somewhere better than in his apartment.

Where, though?

He looked at the closed curtains. Thought of what lay beyond them. It was perfect. No one would ever think to look there.

He staggered to his feet, pulled on his coat and fetched his trowel from the cupboard in the hall. For the second time in its existence, the rainbow pillbox was about to be buried.

14

Sunday morning. Samson tried to persuade himself there was no better way to spend it as he doubled over, hands on knees, and drew noisy gulps of air into his lungs.

'You're out of condition.' Delilah was standing next to him, something akin to pity on her face. Or disgust, maybe. Tolpuddle was beside her, looking no more impressed.

They'd met at the office at eight-thirty and Delilah had driven them over to Horton. From her lack of conversation, he'd sensed she was having misgivings about agreeing to run, but he needed her input. It was fourteen years since he'd been on the fells. With her alongside him, he wouldn't need to worry about getting lost on hillsides that were still topped with snow. He'd also wanted the company. And her local knowledge, his own having eroded after years away.

She'd pulled up in the National Park car park, making no protest when he offered to pay, and they'd set off at a gentle pace towards the pub on the corner. Turning right, away from the road, they'd taken the track that led up onto the Pennine Way, the low ground clear but soggy underfoot from the melted snow.

At first Samson had kept up, congratulating himself on maintaining his fitness while down in London, jogging regularly when his undercover work took him away from the gym. But it had soon become clear that running in the city and running in the Dales were two very different pursuits and, before long, the detective was suffering.

It started with his calves, knives of pain searing up the back of his legs at every step. Then a fierce stitch began sawing at his ribs. With his breath ragged, and his energy being sapped by the sodden land that pulled at his shoes and soaked his feet, turning round and heading back down to await the opening of the pub had been more than tempting – even for a non-drinker like himself.

Ahead of him, Delilah had pulled further and further away towards the snow-covered peaks, gliding over the hillside, legs strong, movements graceful, Tolpuddle a grey shadow beside her. They weren't suffering in the least.

If anything, they were enjoying it.

Gritting his teeth, he'd struggled after them, climbing steadily up the lower slopes of Pen-y-ghent and then veering off onto a smaller path which mercifully hugged the hillside, giving him a chance to recover on the easier gradient. Even so, when Delilah had stopped a couple of miles in, he was grateful for her compassion.

That compassion turned out to be something far more pragmatic.

'There,' she said pointing down to the dale below as Samson finally straightened up, sweat pouring down his face despite the cold temperatures. 'Mire End.'

He nodded, incapable of anything more as he stared at Clive Knowles' farm, the land and house looking less decrepit with the benefit of distance and the forgiving covering of snow that remained in dips and hollows.

'And that's the road coming out of Horton.' She

indicated the tarmacked surface between them and the farm, its path parallel with their own. He followed it north, away from Mire End and into the hills. The way in which he was sure Ralph had been taken.

'It becomes a track,' Delilah offered, seeing the direction of his gaze. 'We'll meet up with it in a bit and then bear right into Langstrothdale like you wanted. If you're able to continue, that is.'

He glared at her, knowing how much she was revelling in his discomfort. 'I'm getting my second wind,' he grumbled, bending down and pretending to tie his laces in an effort to stave off having to run again.

'Yeah, well, we've got another eight miles to do, so you might want to think about getting that second wind pretty soon or we'll still be on the hills when the rain comes.'

'There's rain forecast?' he asked, not relishing the thought of being soaked as well as shattered.

'Tomorrow afternoon,' she replied with a grin and started running, Tolpuddle already pulling away. 'So pick up the pace a bit.'

'This had better be worth it,' he muttered as he set off after them. If anyone was having misgivings now, it was him.

Joseph O'Brien was having misgivings. He'd called in on Arty in an attempt to persuade him out of his self-imposed seclusion – no one having seen him in the lounge or the cafe in the forty-eight hours since his drinking binge at Alice's funeral. But instead of coaxing the bookmaker into helping with the preparations for the Christmas party which were due to commence downstairs, the Irishman had found himself listening to ludicrous conspiracy theories. And worrying about his friend's well-being.

'She's up to something. I know it,' Arty was saying, leaning forward in his chair, his clothes creased, a two-day-old growth of stubble on his chin and a distinct smell of alcohol on his breath.

Behind him, the patio curtains were still closed despite the advanced hour, weak winter sunshine struggling to penetrate the gloom. Just off the lounge, Joseph could see the kitchenette, empty whisky bottles lined up by the sink.

'You have to believe me.'

It was hard to believe anything coming from a man looking so wild. Joseph shook his head. 'I think you're overreacting. Alice's death was due to ill health. As for Eric's collapse, he's said himself that he fell over getting out of bed.'

'Eric doesn't remember what happened,' scoffed Arty. 'He can't explain why he took his oxygen mask off. And no one can explain how the machine could have stopped and then started again.'

Joseph tried not to let his scepticism show. It took some believing all right. That Alice might have been the victim of something malicious. Eric, too. But the hardest bit to swallow was the person being blamed for all this.

Ana Stoyanova.

According to Arty, the woman was evil incarnate.

'I just can't see it,' Joseph said. 'Ana has been nothing but good to us.'

'I've seen her!' Arty gestured wildly at the closed curtains. 'Walking along that bloody corridor at all times of night when she should be at home in Hellifield. And how come she got to Eric's bedside so quickly when he collapsed? Eh? Answer me that.'

'That's hardly proof—'

'She's stalking me, too.'

This time Joseph couldn't hide his disbelief. 'Stalking you?'

'Outside my door. Loitering there.' Arty's voice shook, his fear real, even if his imaginings weren't. 'It's got so I don't sleep. Just spend the night here.' He slapped the arm of his chair, shadows of terror flickering across his face. 'Ana Stoyanova is bad news. You *have* to believe me.'

Joseph couldn't help himself. His gaze shifted to the empty bottles, the glass on the floor by the side of the chair.

Arty noticed. He seemed to shrink in his armchair, rubbing a hand across his worn features. 'It's not as bad as it looks,' he muttered. 'Just something to help me sleep.'

'Far be it from me to comment,' said Joseph gently. 'But don't you think you're working yourself into a state over nothing?'

It was all so far-fetched. In Joseph O'Brien's opinion, the manager of Fellside Court was a good woman. Sure, maybe Ana wasn't the warmest of souls. Maybe she could smile a bit more. But Joseph saw the work she did around the place.

He also heard the grumblings of the residents who weren't predisposed to offcumdens, to people from beyond the parish boundary of Bruncliffe. Being from Ireland, Joseph was accepted. Just. Being from Eastern Europe, Ana didn't really stand a chance.

Not that they were openly racist. They were simply

less tolerant of those who weren't their own. Quicker to find fault.

Joseph was saddened to think Arty was among their number.

'Besides, if you're that convinced Ana is up to something, then perhaps we ought to talk to the police?' he suggested.

Arty recoiled. 'No! I have no evidence and I don't want her to know I suspect anything. It's too dangerous. Promise me you won't go to them.'

'Okay, okay!' Joseph laid a hand on his friend's arm, felt the tremors besetting the bookmaker. 'We'll leave the police out of it. But what else can we do?'

'Samson,' said Arty. 'I want you to talk to Samson. He's the only one who can help us.'

Arty leaned against his front door, the soft tread of his friend's footsteps receding down the corridor. Joseph didn't believe a word of it. The man was a hopeless actor, his disbelief written right across that weathered face of his.

But at least he'd been persuaded to talk to Samson. To get the detective to come over to Fellside Court.

A spasm of apprehension clutched at Arty's guts. What if Samson didn't believe him, either? What would he do then?

He thought of the pillbox buried out on the balcony. He'd made a split decision not to mention it to Joseph – there was no point in placing him in danger by burdening him with the knowledge of what Rita had found. It was also one more thing his friend could have questioned, pulled apart, until Arty began to question it all himself.

But the pillbox was solid evidence. Proof of something wrong. Surely Samson would see that.

With one last look out of the spyhole, he shambled towards the bathroom. Time to clean himself up. Then, keeping his promise to Joseph, he'd leave the safety of his flat and head down to the cafe.

Another spasm gripped him at the thought.

'What took you so long?' The smile on Delilah's face was born of the exhilaration of a morning run. And of triumph.

She felt a faint stab of remorse as Samson shambled towards her, face red, chest heaving, his mud-flecked legs wobbling slightly as he came to rest.

When he'd asked her to join him on what she was sure was going to turn out to be a wild-goose chase, she'd been uneasy. Sharing her running again, after all these years. The people of Bruncliffe had only just found out she was back on the fells, and even then that was simply because she'd been placed in a situation where she could no longer hide it. The thought of having anyone – her old training partner in particular – running with her . . . It had brought back the weight of expectation that she'd walked away from years ago.

So, after their brief pause above Mire End Farm, she'd been pushing the pace, following the track northwards, the incline negligible as they hugged the contour line. Then she'd taken a sharp right, cutting back onto the Pennine Way. Back uphill and into the snow. That's when she'd really begun to test him, lengthening her stride, bounding up the fell with her heart thudding while Tolpuddle raced ahead. To her surprise, Samson had responded well.

Kind of. Not as well as the Samson of fourteen years ago would have done. He'd have left her for dead as his long legs tore up the hillside. But then she could hardly boast. Six months ago she'd have thought twice about even walking up here.

More surprising than Samson's ability to cope had been her own reaction to running with him. She'd forgotten how rewarding it was to turn to someone after a sharp climb and share a sense of achievement. She'd forgotten how good it was to have company other than Tolpuddle's. Especially someone she stood a chance of beating – her canine friend never letting her be first up a hill.

Even if it was a wild-goose chase, she was enjoying it.

'Christ!' Samson groaned, crumpled over at the waist. 'Was it always this hard?'

'It never gets easier,' Delilah said, echoing their old coach's mantra. 'Just faster.'

Samson choked on a laugh. 'Bloody Seth. The number of times he said that to me.'

'He was right. About that and a lot of other things.'

He looked up at the hint of regret in her voice. 'Danny Bradley told me you gave up running with the Harriers. How come?'

She looked away at the mention of the local running club. She wasn't about to explain to Samson O'Brien the complexities of having a social life and trying to be the best female fell runner that Bruncliffe – or even Yorkshire – had ever produced. In her late twenties, it was easy to see how she could have managed it better. At the time, barely out of her teens and caught up in her first love, when faced with running at a competitive level or a life with

Neil Taylor, giving up running had seemed like the only option. Because Neil had made it very difficult for her to have both.

'I couldn't find the time,' she said. 'You know how it is.'

His silence suggested he could guess at the truth of it – he knew how much being out on the fells had meant to her. How she'd lived for that feeling of euphoria as you crested a hill and the Dales spread out before you.

'It's beautiful up here,' he said, twisting round to take in the outlines of Ingleborough and Whernside draped in snow to the west. A soft sky hung above them, puffs of cloud breaking up the blue.

'Had you forgotten?' she asked. 'What with all that drama you had living in London?'

'No,' he said. 'Never. I just put it to one side for a while.'

'What made you come back? You still haven't said.'

It was his turn to be evasive. He shrugged. 'Felt like a change. You know how it is.'

She laughed. 'Touché. Well, you didn't ask me up here to admire the view. That's where we're heading.' She pointed to the track disappearing into a forest of conifers. 'It's all downhill, so you should be able to keep up.'

With a grin, she was off, haring down the path before he had a chance to retort. Behind her she heard Samson following, steps hesitant at first, but finding his confidence as they approached the trees where they left the snow behind. The shade grabbed them and the temperature dropped, and then they were bursting out into the sunshine in a small clearing. Below them, in a lonely field, was what they had come for.

Delilah stopped as soon as she saw it, Samson almost colliding into her, his hands on her shoulders to stop them both falling.

'There!' she said, pointing. 'Could that be . . . ?'

'Let's go and find out.' He overtook her, running down the last section of track to where it joined a tarmacked lane, heading for the field nearest to them and its lone occupant.

Christmas was coming in Fellside Court. Under the guidance of Clarissa Ralph and her band of helpers, things were taking shape in the cafe in preparation for the party the next day.

Silver and gold streamers had been strung across the room, snowmen danced on the windows and the paper chains that some of the residents had been busy making for the last week were looped along the walls. Above the door hung a brightly coloured star and a bunch of mistletoe.

'It looks fantastic!' exclaimed Joseph. 'Doesn't it, Arty?'

The bookmaker smiled, a pale imitation of his usual beam. But at least he was there. When Joseph had left him earlier, the Irishman hadn't been convinced that the promise of a visit from Samson would be enough to persuade Arty to leave his flat, such was the man's paranoia. Yet here he was.

Not that he seemed to be enjoying it. He'd jumped visibly when one of the residents popped a balloon, and his eyes were constantly shifting towards the doorway as though expecting trouble. Thankfully, Ana Stoyanova was off duty, but even knowing she wouldn't turn up, Arty was still a bag of nerves.

'Reckon we're all owed a cup of tea,' said Rita Wilson, taking a seat and rubbing her bad hip. Even though they hadn't been climbing up and down stepladders – Vicky Hudson and the caretaker getting that job – the decorating of the cafe had taken a couple of hours and had involved a lot of standing. Especially when Clarissa was so picky.

A mild-tempered woman for the majority of the year, when it came to preparing for Christmas she could be just as bossy as her sister. Everything had to be right. Consequently, everything took time.

'I'm not sure about that star,' Clarissa murmured, head on one side as she regarded the burst of colour hanging over the doorway. 'I think it might be too gaudy.'

Edith Hird raised an eyebrow and cast her eyes around the room. 'Just the star?' she muttered, Clarissa's approach to Christmas ornaments being far from subtle.

'It's fine,' said Joseph. 'Come and sit down and have a rest. Or you'll be fast asleep when Santa comes.'

Clarissa's face lit up. 'Oh, I do love the Christmas party. Especially Santa's visit. Have you got your suit all ready, Arty?'

Secret Santa. It had become a bit of a tradition, instigated by Arty a couple of years ago. All the residents drew names from a hat in early December and were tasked with buying a present for that particular person. The presents were wrapped with the name of the recipient clearly identified, given to Arty, and then distributed by Father Christmas at the party the week before Christmas Day.

The residents loved it. Especially as Father Christmas was one of their own, the rotund body and booming laugh impossible to disguise behind a red suit and a white beard. He was funny. He was full of fun. He made the party memorable.

But Arty was shaking his head. 'Sorry, Clarissa. I'm not up for it this year. You'll have to find someone else.'

'Not up for it?' Edith asked, peering at him. 'Whatever's the matter?'

'I'm not really in the festive spirit. It's been a tough couple of weeks.'

Edith patted his hand. 'Never you mind,' she said. 'It's time you had a break anyway. We'll find someone to give out the presents, won't we?' She was looking at Joseph expectantly.

'We will? I mean, we will,' said Joseph, injecting more confidence into his words as Edith stared at him.

'See, Joseph will sort it. All you have to do is come along and enjoy it. Ah, Vicky!' She smiled up at the care assistant, who had arrived at the table with a tray bearing teapot and mugs. 'Just the ticket. What would we do without you?'

As the care assistant made a cheeky reply, Joseph heard Rita mutter beside him.

'Everything okay?' he asked.

'Idiot that I am, I've forgotten my sweeteners.' She was reaching for her stick.

'Do you want me to fetch them?'

'No, it's okay. Although . . . you could come with me and get my contribution to the Secret Santa, seeing as you're in charge. It'd save me bringing it up to you later. Do you mind?'

'Not at all.' He stood and offered her his arm and she leaned gratefully on it.

'All that decorating has worn me out,' she said as they passed into the corridor. 'But I wouldn't miss it for the world. Such a shame Arty's not in good form, though.'

'Yes. He's not himself, all right.'

'Any ideas who you'll ask to replace him tomorrow?'

'Not a clue,' he replied honestly. 'And I don't exactly have a lot of time. There'll be mayhem if Santa doesn't turn up.'

'You should ask Samson,' she said.

'Samson?' He couldn't keep the surprise out of his voice.

'Why not? He's a favourite in here. Just make sure he keeps his trousers on, though, or there really will be mayhem.'

'I don't think he'd . . .'

'You won't know if you don't ask,' she said as they reached her apartment. She opened the door and passed inside, leaving Joseph full of turmoil on the threshold.

Could he ask Samson to stand in for Arty? It would mean the world to the residents. And to Joseph himself. Having his son beside him for the first Christmas meal in years. But did he have any right to place obligations on the lad?

'How odd!' Rita's exclamation brought Joseph inside the hallway and through to the open-plan living area, tastefully decorated and awash with light. She was standing by the coffee table looking puzzled, a Christmas present in her hand, a further pile neatly stacked on the glass surface.

'What's the matter?'

'Look.' She gestured at the wrapping paper, which was gaping open like a badly buttoned shirt. 'All the tape is peeling off. Serves me right for buying cheap decorative stuff!' She laughed and turned to the sideboard, reaching for a roll of plain Sellotape before turning back to the coffee table. 'Now, where's the one for the Secret Santa. I was sure I left it on the top . . . Ah, here it is.'

She pulled a present from halfway down the pile, tutting over the defective tape. Quickly cutting several new strips, she resealed the paper and handed the gift to Joseph. 'That should do it. Right, just let me get my sweeteners . . .'

While Rita moved over to the kitchen area, Joseph leaned down to study one of the presents that hadn't been resealed. He ran his fingers over the decorative tape that should have been holding the edges of the paper together. A corner was curling up slightly. Like it had been lifted by a fingernail. Glancing through the pile, he could see the same tattered corner on quite a few pieces of tape.

If it didn't sound so crazy, he'd say someone had opened some of the presents and attempted to rewrap them. But why would someone want to do that?

'Jesus!' he muttered, dismissing his burgeoning suspicion before it had a chance to form. A bit of cheap tape and he was as jittery as Arty.

'Well, have you given it some thought?' Rita was standing in front of him, ready to go.

'Sorry?'

'Samson. Why don't you ask if he'll step in for Arty?'

'Samson . . . ?' Was it such a bad idea? He glanced

down at the rewrapped present in his hand. It wouldn't hurt to have him here, one way or the other, and maybe it would help settle Arty. Plus it would be fulfilling a promise. 'You know, Rita, I think I will.'

Problem was, Joseph O'Brien wasn't sure his son would say yes.

15

'It's not him.'

'How can you be so sure?'

'I'm telling you now, it's not him. That is not a prize-winning tup.'

'For God's sake, Delilah, just check the bloody ear tag, okay? Before he breaks free and it takes another half an hour to catch him again.'

As if sensing a lowering of resistance, the ram, currently being restrained by Samson, started struggling while Delilah leaned in and tried to compare the number on the bright-yellow tag in its ear with that in the photo of Ralph on Samson's mobile.

Having left the clearing, they'd run down the track until it became a narrow tarmacked lane, fields either side, a beck running to the right and the tree-covered fellsides stretching up away from them. In the nearest field had been the reason they'd come all this way. A Swaledale tup.

Ralph. Or at least, they thought it was Ralph.

After a lot of chasing, they'd managed to herd the ram into a corner, allowing Samson the chance to grab him. But even with hands on both horns, it was taking all of his strength to hold the animal still enough to let Delilah read the ear tag. And Samson wasn't exactly dressed for the job, running shorts and bare legs not ideal attire when wrestling with a sheep.

'It's not him,' Delilah finally announced, straightening up. 'Like I said—'

'Damn!' Samson released the animal and it ran off, shaking its head, before standing some distance away to stare balefully back at them. 'You took your time!'

'You weren't holding him still enough for me to see the tag. Besides, I didn't need to look at his number. I could tell from the size of him it wasn't Ralph.'

'The size of him? You've never clapped eyes on Ralph.'

Delilah rolled her eyes. 'Thought you were a farmer once? I'm not talking height!' She pointed over to the ram, now contentedly eating hay. 'Look underneath.'

Samson looked. She was right. The ram was a poor specimen of a male. No prize-winner, for sure.

'Bloody hell,' he muttered, knowing she would be smiling that smile when he turned back to her. 'I was sure . . .'

'Ah well. At least you got a run out of it.' Her words were laced with amusement as he followed her out of the field to where a patient Tolpuddle was waiting.

It had been a long shot. A hunch he'd had that Clive Knowles wouldn't have risked transporting Ralph through Horton, where he might be seen. Which left only one direction: north on the track that ran past Mire End Farm and through into this narrow dale, which led into Langstrothdale.

As Clive Knowles had said, hardly anyone ever came this way. Even the walkers who did would most likely be following the Pennine Way, which passed the farm and then veered off around the forest of conifers rather than through it. So Samson had been confident they would find the missing ram here. Tucked away. Awaiting an off-the-record sale. Or worse.

'Sorry,' he said as he closed the gate and joined Delilah and Tolpuddle on the road. 'I dragged you all the way out here for nothing.'

'Don't speak too soon.' She was looking over his shoulder at the next field down the dale. 'Because that is as fine a Swaledale ram as you're likely to see around these parts.'

He turned just in time to catch the last few movements of a tupping, the ram moving away, the ewe's backside now daubed in blue. As were the backsides of most of the ewes in the field.

'Only thing is,' said Delilah as the ram started making moves towards another ewe, 'I thought you said Ralph didn't perform . . .'

Samson was already jogging towards the gate.

'It's him!'

'How can you be so sure?'

'I'm telling you, it's him.'

'But there are no tags,' said Delilah, standing to one side with a doubtful look.

'I don't need tags,' said Samson, a wide grin forming as he leaned over the tup.

They'd caught this ram a lot easier than the last one, the animal trotting over to them when they'd entered the field. Straight away the differences were clear. The way the ram stood. The broad, level back. The muscle under the thick fleece. And of course, the all-important undercarriage.

But as Delilah had pointed out, there were no tags in the ram's ears, only empty holes. Which meant they couldn't use the identification number to say for certain if it was Ralph or not. Samson, however, had found another means.

He ran his hands over the ram's chest once more. It was smeared in blue raddle, an oily substance rubbed directly onto the tup as an alternative to a harness and crayon at mating time. But that wasn't what Samson was interested in. Pushing his fingers through the thick fleece, he felt the abrasion. It was just under the right foreleg. A nasty lump of scarred tissue where something had been rubbing. It didn't take a genius to put two and two together—

'Hey! You two! What are you at?' A farmer was at the gate, scowling across the field at them, and at Tolpuddle tethered outside. He held a bucket in one hand, a small pot of raddle in the other.

'Bugger!' muttered Delilah as Samson let the ram loose, his hands Smurf-blue. 'Now we're in trouble.'

'I don't think so,' said Samson. He strode confidently over to the disgruntled farmer.

'What you wanting with my tup?' demanded the man, the animal in question nudging at the bucket, looking for his usual treat.

'*Your* tup?' asked Samson.

The farmer paused, put down the bucket and pushed back the cap on his head, a deep red flushing up his neck and into his cheeks. 'Not sure I know what you mean.'

Samson laughed. 'I think you do. At what point did you decide to use him?'

An appropriately sheepish look stole across the man's

face. 'Aye. Fair cop all right. But it's a crying shame to have such genes going to waste.'

'Perhaps,' said Delilah, looking from the farmer to Samson and then to the ram, 'someone would like to tell me what the hell is going on?'

'Delilah, meet Ralph,' said Samson, nodding at the ram, which had its head in the bucket, munching away.

'You were right? This is Ralph? But I thought he – you know – couldn't perform?' She looked around the field at the blue-stained ewes.

'Ha!' The farmer cackled, his eyes creasing with amusement. 'Reckon that's what old Knowles thought, too. He told me his tup needed a rest. Wanted to rent my top field for a couple of weeks so the lad could get his stamina back.'

'What happened?'

'The tup kept breaking out, is what happened. And then breaking in here with these lasses. Couldn't keep him away from them.'

'So you swapped out your own ram and let Ralph in here,' said Samson.

The farmer gave him a shrewd look. 'Any bugger would have done the same. Look at him. He's sex on legs, that boy.'

Delilah coughed and turned away, bubbles of laughter threatening to overwhelm her.

'You've seen my poor Jackson next door,' the farmer continued. 'He couldn't keep up. This lad got in here and had more ewes under him in a day than Jackson could manage all week. Didn't seem right to deprive the youngster.'

'So Ralph's not a dud,' murmured Delilah.

'A dud? Whoever told you that? This fella will go down in history.' The farmer ran an affectionate hand across the rump of the ram. 'I suppose Knowles wants him back, then? Is that why you're here?'

'Something like that,' said Samson. 'Only we don't have transport right now. Can we come back tomorrow morning for him?'

'Aye, that'd be fine. No disrespect or anything, but I'll need to check you are who you say you are, so I'll give Knowles a call—'

'I'd rather you didn't,' said Samson. 'Thing is, he's not exactly told you the truth . . .'

When the farmer heard that Clive Knowles had declared his ram missing and was even now filing an insurance claim, he was more than happy to wash his hands of the affair rather than risk getting involved in something so dubious. He agreed to an early pick-up the following day, and when Samson asked him to bring a pot of raddle with him, he didn't question it. They shook hands – Samson's still tinged in blue – and the disconsolate farmer began walking back to the distant farmhouse.

'What I don't understand,' said Delilah, already on the road with Tolpuddle, ready for the run back, 'is how Ralph has gone from dud to superstud!'

Samson laughed. 'I have a theory, but you're going to have to wait to see if I'm right. In the meantime,' he said, 'I need a favour.'

'Another one?'

'Last one, I promise. It's just, I can't take Ralph back

on the motorbike . . .' He grinned at her, one eyebrow raised in expectation.

Delilah was quick to catch on. 'You want *me* to ask Will for the Land Rover? You must be joking!'

'It's better coming from you.'

'You think? How little you know my brother,' she said. 'There's no way he'll lend it to me. And there's no way I'll give him the pleasure of saying no, by asking for it.'

'Please? If there was another way I wouldn't be asking.'

She looked away, frowning, then she smiled. It wasn't a smile that boded well for Samson. 'What's it worth?' she asked.

He knew her better than to answer glibly. 'What are you asking for?'

It was her turn to grin. 'Some participation.'

'In what?'

'Tomorrow night. The Speedy Date—'

'No!' He was shaking his head. 'No way.'

She shrugged and began jogging up the road towards the forest, negotiations over. Tolpuddle paused, looking at Samson, then he too seemed to shrug and loped off after Delilah.

'Damn it.' Samson was caught between a rock and a very hard place. 'And damn that woman.'

He ran after her.

'Delilah, wait. Let's talk about this,' he gasped, trying to catch her.

'Nothing to talk about. Unless you've changed your mind?'

'But it's not fair!' he declared, running alongside her.

'You can't seriously expect me to take part in another speed-dating session. The last one was bad enough.'

'You said you enjoyed it!'

'I lied,' he lied.

'Well, that's my offer, so take it or leave it,' she muttered, beginning to lengthen her stride as the sound of Samson's mobile cut through their debate. She didn't ease up while he answered it. Neither did Tolpuddle.

'Dad?'

'Son? Is this a good time?'

'As good as any.' Samson watched Delilah disappear into the trees.

'Thing is, son, I need a favour . . .'

Samson listened as his father aired his concerns about Arty, the bookmaker seemingly making all sorts of claims about nefarious goings-on at Fellside Court and pointing the finger at Ana Stoyanova.

'He's being irrational, I know,' continued Joseph. 'But his anxiety is contagious.' He gave a half-laugh. 'Just now I caught myself thinking someone had broken into Rita Wilson's flat, simply because a few presents had come unwrapped. It's all so absurd.'

Absurd maybe. But Samson knew that absurdities often masked crimes. And Fellside Court was appearing on his radar more than it should – first, Alice Shepherd's accusations, then the drama over Eric's collapse. Now Arty, too, was making allegations.

'What do you want me to do?' he asked.

'I want you to be Father Christmas,' said Joseph O'Brien.

'You what?'

'Father Christmas. I want you to go undercover at the Christmas party tomorrow afternoon. Have a look around while you're here, without Ana or Rick Procter suspecting a thing. It'll put Arty at ease. Me too, for that matter.'

Samson was already grinning. The conversation he'd had with Delilah after Alice Shepherd's funeral had been preying on him over the weekend. She'd been right. He *was* intrigued by the goings-on at the retirement complex. Now he had the ideal opportunity to have another look. Plus kill a second bird with the same stone. 'Does the job come with a red suit?'

'And a beard. A pillow too, for the extra padding you'd need. Is that a yes, then?'

'Yes, Dad. It is.'

The sigh of relief at the other end of the phone pulled at Samson's conscience. 'Thanks, son. I'll see you tomorrow, then.'

Samson stuffed his mobile in his pocket and started back up the track. Delilah was nowhere in sight. But Tolpuddle, that faithful hound, was waiting at the edge of the trees.

'Come on, boy,' he called as he ran towards him. 'Let's catch her.'

It took a while. And some fast running, which meant that when he did get within shouting distance as they cleared the trees and came back into the dale above Mire End Farm, Samson barely had the ability to call her name. Delilah heard him and turned, pausing, hand on hip as he came to a stop in front of her.

'Okay,' he wheezed. 'Get transport and I'm all yours.'

Her eyebrows shot up. 'Really? You'll do the Speedy Date night?'

He nodded, a lot easier than trying to speak when his lungs were so busy sucking in air.

'You star!' Delilah threw her arms around him and he grinned.

When she realised the conditions he'd imposed on his acceptance, she wouldn't be so happy.

While Delilah and Samson were finishing their Sunday-morning run, the final preparations were being made to Fellside Court for the Christmas party. By late afternoon the cafe was resplendent, the tables covered in snow-white tablecloths with red napkins, silver crackers and centrepieces of holly entwined in scarlet ribbons adding colour.

In the kitchen, the staff had been busy, getting as much ready for the meal the next day as they could. Mounds of peeled carrots and trimmed sprouts were stored in the fridge, along with three turkeys, pigs-in-blankets and lots of stuffing. As the cook hung up her apron and prepared to leave, she was confident everything had been done to make the party a success.

By early evening, tired from an eventful day and looking forward to the next one, the residents had already begun to drift towards their beds. By midnight, when across the town Samson was woken from a disturbed sleep by a brutal attack of cramp in his left calf, Fellside Court was silent.

In his room on the first floor, Arty Robinson was drifting off, propped up in his armchair facing the front door, an old golf club bought in the charity shop in town resting close to hand. A bottle of whisky even closer. He'd slipped into a dream, sharing a tender moment with his wife, who'd died years before, and was whispering sweet nothings to her with a half-smile on his restful features.

On the floor below, Rita Wilson was fast asleep too. At least she was until she heard it. Something. A bump? A crash?

It woke her completely, bringing her out of bed, shuffling into her slippers to investigate.

Next door, she thought. It had come from next door.

But next door was empty, the guest suite unoccupied for months.

Tying her dressing gown at the waist, she moved quietly down the hallway and rested an eye against the spyhole in the door.

The light in the corridor revealed nothing out of the ordinary. No movement. No one around.

She unlocked the door and gently opened it, heart starting to patter. It's the hour, she told herself; that's what was making her jumpy.

She poked her head out. And saw blonde hair bright under the lights. Ana Stoyanova. She was standing outside, keys in hand.

'Ana!'

The manager spun round. 'Rita. What are you doing up?'

'I heard something.'

Ana smiled, a tight movement of her lips. 'It was the wind,' she said. 'It's blown a chair over outside. You should get back to sleep or you'll be tired for the party tomorrow.'

Rita smiled back at her and nodded. 'You're right. Got to look my best for Santa!'

The old lady closed the door and went back to bed, glad to have such a diligent manager on hand. She was asleep before she had a chance to marvel at just how diligent the manager of Fellside Court was. After all, Ana Stoyanova wasn't even supposed to be on duty.

Outside, the clouds barely moved in the still of the night. And under the starlight, every single chair in the courtyard was upright.

16

'You have to be kidding!'

Samson stared at the Nissan Micra that was parked outside the office, Delilah standing next to it, arms folded and ready to argue.

It was Monday morning and she'd pulled up outside at eight o'clock on the dot. Not in the Land Rover, as he'd expected. But in the small hatchback, Tolpuddle already taking up quite a significant chunk of the interior.

'Where's the Land Rover?'

Delilah pouted and her chin tipped upwards. 'Not here, clearly.'

'Did Will say no?'

She glanced away, cheeks flushing. 'Not exactly.'

'You didn't even ask him?'

'You wouldn't understand,' she muttered.

'But how the hell are we going to get a sheep in that?' he asked.

'It's roomier than you think. Besides, it's this or nothing. So get in and quit making a fuss.' She strode round to the driver's side, slamming her door to punctuate her point. Faced with no alternative, Samson sat in gingerly beside her, doing his best to conceal the fact his legs were aching from the run the day before.

'I can't believe you're going to do this,' he said, as

Delilah threw a U-turn in the narrow street and headed out across the marketplace.

He was still shaking his head in disbelief as they left Bruncliffe behind and drove north towards Horton, fog closing in around them as they made their way up the dale.

'You want to put him in that?' The farmer scratched his head and looked at the Nissan Micra, while Delilah bit her lip in an attempt to keep her temper.

With a promise to overlook his involvement in a potential crime, Ralph's custodian had been persuaded to bring the wandering tup back up the track and through the trees to meet the lane from Horton that ran above Mire End Farm. As Delilah's small car bounced up the potholed tarmac, through the swirling mist had come the furtive flash of headlights. The farmer. He was sitting astride his quad bike, hat pulled low, fleece collar turned up hiding his face, and behind him in a trailer, Ralph. For Samson, against the backdrop of the dark conifers and concealed by the hill fog, the clandestine handover was like a surreal take on a drugs deal – Dales-style.

Although the car was hardly drug-lord material.

'It's all we could get, apparently,' he muttered with a glare at the Micra and then at Delilah.

She glared back at him, cursing Will at the same time. Her oldest brother had been in a foul mood when she called up at the farm the afternoon before for the traditional Sunday family get-together. Her two middle brothers had been home – Craig having come all the way up from London, and Chris over from Leeds – but even their presence hadn't alleviated Will's sour temper.

He'd heard. Someone had seen Samson and Delilah setting off on their run and, on meeting Will in the Fleece, made some joke about Delilah getting married again. Delilah wasn't sure what had irked Will more: her perceived betrayal, or the fact that he'd been so annoyed, he'd left the pub before he'd even finished his pint.

He'd pulled her aside the minute she arrived at the farm and warned her she was making a mistake. Again.

Being stubborn, she hadn't set him right. Hadn't told him there was nothing to her relationship with Samson O'Brien. That they'd simply been looking for a lost sheep. And then she hadn't had the courage to ask for the Land Rover.

But there was no way she was explaining all that to Samson. Or to the farmer, who was starting to chuckle. Yet another story would be making its way around the Dales by teatime.

'Let's just get it loaded and be done with it,' she snapped, leading Tolpuddle out of the car and then pulling the back seats flat.

'Right you are,' said the farmer with a raised eyebrow in Samson's direction. 'You're the boss.'

The two men opened the gates to the trailer, grabbed hold of Ralph and walked him over to the rear of the hatchback. Between them, they lifted him in and shut the boot. The ram stared out at them.

'There you go.' The farmer handed over a small pot of raddle to Samson. 'As you asked for. Now, I've nowt more to do with this.'

'That's great,' said Samson. 'And yes, I'll keep your part in this quiet.'

They shook hands and the farmer turned the quad and headed for home, no doubt hoping that the prize-winning tup in the back of the Micra had left more than just blue marks in the field on the other side of the conifers.

'Come on then, let's go,' said Delilah, getting in the car.

Tolpuddle and Samson looked at each other and then they both dived for the empty passenger seat. Tolpuddle won, establishing himself on the seat. He let out a sharp bark of victory, startling the ram, which bleated while Samson tried to squeeze in next to the large hound.

'Budge up,' he muttered as he managed to close the door, the handle digging into his side, his tender calf muscles threatening to cramp.

Tolpuddle licked his cheek.

'Seriously, Tolpuddle. How am I supposed to get the seat belt on? Delilah, tell your dog to move!'

Tolpuddle leaned into him, squashing Samson against the glass as Delilah pulled off.

With a rear-view mirror full of sheep, and a dog and a large man fighting over the passenger seat, she drove back down the track towards Mire End Farm, a smile tugging at her lips.

Mire End Farm didn't look any more prosperous on the Monday morning before Christmas than it had on Samson's previous visits. The mist had settled across the dale, wreathing around the forlorn barns and adding to the general air of misery that the place exuded. Chickens scuttled ahead of Delilah as she got out of the Micra, Samson almost falling onto the muddy yard as Tolpuddle pushed past him.

'Doesn't look like anyone's home,' said Delilah.

'It always looks like this.' Samson reached back into the car and pressed on the horn, a strangled burp of sound echoing between the barn walls. 'Bloody hell,' he muttered. 'Does this thing have any redeeming features?'

Despite its feeble nature, the horn did the trick, the lumbering shape of Clive Knowles appearing through the shroud of grey from behind the barns.

'What do you want?' he demanded, taking in Samson, Delilah and Tolpuddle with a surly look.

'We've brought you a Christmas present,' said Samson. He opened the boot and a loud bleat stopped the farmer in his tracks as the ram hopped down into the yard.

'Ralph?' Clive Knowles stepped forward to catch the animal, frowning, a stain of red creeping up his broad face. He stared at the ram, more in shock than elation. Then he turned to Samson. 'Where'd you find him?'

The attempt at surprise was too late. The words forced past stunned lips.

'Over the back in Langstrothdale,' said Samson, tipping his head towards the fell that rose behind them. 'He was in a field.'

The farmer's face twisted into a pretence of pleasure. 'It's good to have him back,' he muttered.

'I'm sure it is. Funny thing, though, how he escaped all the way over there and managed to lose his harness on the way.'

'They must have left him there,' said Clive, his voice strained.

'Who?'

'The buggers that stole him!'

Samson shook his head. 'I've been thinking about that. I'm not sure he was stolen after all.'

'What do you mean?' The farmer was glaring at the detective, a mixture of worry and anger on his florid features. 'Of course he was bloody taken. It was you who spotted it.'

'All I spotted was what you wanted me to see.'

'What? You're not suggesting—?'

'A harness handily abandoned by the side of the road and some tyre tracks.' Samson cut off the indignation by pointing at the pile of discarded tyres looming lopsided in the yard. 'You took the harness off Ralph, and then used one of these. Rolled it over the field to give the impression that someone had driven in to steal your tup. But you forgot to open the gate. There were no markings in the mud from where the gate would have swung across the tracks. The only way Ralph left that field was down at the bottom gate and in the back of your trailer, with Pete Ferris's help.'

'That's bloody ridiculous. Why would I want to steal my own tup?'

'The ewes,' said Delilah.

'The ewes?' Clive Knowles turned to her, desperation in his tone.

'Ralph wasn't servicing them. You'd bought a dud. So rather than lose all of your investment, you decided to have him disappear, leaving you free to claim the insurance.'

'All you needed,' said Samson with a trace of sarcasm, 'was some unsuspecting fool to verify the theft. And you chose me.'

The farmer glanced from Delilah to Samson, his blustering confidence failing. 'You can't prove it,' he said.

Samson shrugged. 'Maybe not. But I wouldn't put money on Pete Ferris keeping quiet if the police get involved.'

Shoulders slumping, Clive gave a weary sigh. 'What choice did I have? Two seasons in and that bloody beast has bankrupt me. I've shelled out all that money and for what? A fine fleece and nowt more.' He looked up at Samson, his wretched expression eliciting sympathy from someone who was well acquainted with farming debt. 'Are you going to contact the authorities?'

'What for? The insurance company hasn't paid out yet and Ralph's back where he should be.'

As if hearing his name, the ram lifted his head and began tugging at the restraining arm of the farmer.

'Much use that is,' muttered Clive.

'I don't know about that,' said Samson, taking the pot of raddle out of the car. He leaned down and smeared a liberal amount of blue across the chest of the animal, then gestured in the direction of the field beyond the barns. 'Let him loose with the ewes.'

The farmer gave a bitter laugh. 'Right. So I can watch a prize tup do bugger-all!'

'You might be surprised,' said Delilah.

With a grunt of disbelief, the farmer guided the ram across the yard, past the barns and towards the gate. Through the mist, the blurred outlines of sheep could be seen munching grass contentedly, many of them with fleeces still unmarked. The field was only steps away when Ralph started straining to get free, head up, smelling the air. And he was barely inside the gate before a cluster of ewes was crowding around him.

'Well, I'll be damned!' Clive Knowles pushed his cap back to scratch his head as he watched his prize tup do exactly what he was supposed to do, a splotch of blue soon left across a pristine white back. A broad smile broke across the farmer's face as the ram started closing in on his next partner. 'What the hell did you do to him?'

'Nothing,' said Samson. 'You did it.'

'Me? How?'

'You took the harness off him. Have you still got it?'

Clive gestured at a tangle of leather discarded by the gate. 'Bloody thing finally gave up the ghost.'

Samson picked it up. 'Look,' he said, pointing at the pin designed to hold the crayon in place, its jagged edge snagging his thumb. 'Every time Ralph lifted up onto a ewe, this cut into him.'

'No wonder the poor lad wasn't up to his responsibilities,' said Delilah.

Clive was shaking his head. 'That was it? That's what the problem was?'

'Yep,' said Samson. 'You nearly lost a seven-grand investment for the sake of a crappy harness.'

The farmer flushed. Then he thrust out a hand in the direction of the detective. 'Let me pay you a finder's fee.'

'And in return . . . ?' asked Samson, shaking the offered hand but sensing there was a catch.

'Perhaps we could keep this between ourselves?' Clive Knowles looked abashed.

'What about Pete Ferris?'

The farmer grimaced and spat. 'What about him? If it

hadn't been for that blasted lighter falling out his pocket, you'd never have known he'd been involved.'

'Probably worth our while calling in on him anyway. Let him know the game is up.'

'Aye, well, mind he doesn't set the dogs on you when you do.'

'Somehow,' said Samson with a grin, 'I think we might get a better reception than last time.'

The dogs were still there, lunging out of the misshapen porch and racing across the ground to meet them. This time they were stilled by a sharp whistle from the caravan. They set, dropping onto their haunches, eyes on Samson and Delilah, who had a firm hold of Tolpuddle's lead.

'What do you want?' shouted Pete Ferris, now out on the porch, squinting as he strained to see them. The mist had begun to lift on this side of the river, a weak sun slowly burning it off, but residual wisps still trailed above the field.

'A quick word,' said Samson.

The poacher twitched and Samson took it as an invitation. He approached the porch, Delilah and Tolpuddle behind him.

'We found Clive Knowles' tup,' he said.

Another spasm beset the thin frame of the man leaning against the caravan, his eyes large beneath the baseball cap.

'Would you like to know where?' continued Samson.

'None of my business,' muttered the poacher. He tugged on the peak of his cap and stared at his dirty trainers.

'We know all about it. The insurance scam,' said

Delilah, taking pity on the man and putting him out of his misery.

Pete Ferris jerked back, body tense. 'Don't know what you mean.'

Samson laughed. 'Sure you do. You and Clive Knowles. Quite a smart piece of work. But for your lighter . . .'

A haunted look came over the gaunt face. 'What you going to do about it?'

'Nothing,' said Samson. He gestured at the artificial tree propped up by the front door, stems frayed, a single string of lights flickering dejectedly. 'Consider our silence a Christmas present.'

The man's knees sagged with relief. 'Thank you,' he muttered, holding out a bony hand. 'I owe you.'

'I'll remember that,' said Samson, shaking hands. He turned to go, Delilah and Tolpuddle following him off the porch, the poacher and his two lurchers watching them leave with the same wariness they'd greeted them with.

'I can't help feeling they got off lightly,' said Delilah, thinking about the farmer and the poacher as she walked back across the sodden field to the car. 'After all, what they were attempting to do was a crime.'

Samson grinned and patted his jacket pocket. 'Not that lightly. Clive Knowles paid me twice, don't forget. And that will have hurt him. A lot. Besides, the claim was never settled by the insurance company, so what harm was done?'

'Apart from the sheep droppings in my car, you mean?'

'It's all part of being a rural detective,' laughed Samson. 'Like this.' He held out his right hand, still coloured blue from the raddle. 'Now if you don't mind, I've got an important appointment in town.'

'You haven't forgotten about tonight?' asked Delilah, as they got into the car. She was half-expecting him to renege, but he was shaking his head, grin still in place.

'No. I'll be there. Wild horses couldn't keep me away.'

She should have known that when Samson O'Brien was showing enthusiasm for a Speedy Date night, something was up.

'Is he here yet?'

In the lounge of Fellside Court, some nine miles and several fells away from Mire End Farm, Arty Robinson was tense. Surrounded by Christmas lights and baubles, by the residents of Fellside Court in their finery, he felt like Scrooge, a blanket of misery smothering the gaiety of those around him. But he couldn't help it.

He was afraid.

Although knowing Samson O'Brien would soon be here helped.

He glanced over to the doorway where Rita Wilson was chatting to Ana Stoyanova, the manager in a red dress, her blonde hair swept back and entwined with silver tinsel. She looked like an angel.

An angel hiding a demon's heart.

'Is he here yet?' he muttered again, leaning across to Joseph O'Brien, who was putting his phone away.

'Any minute now,' said Joseph. 'He's been up to old Knowles' farm. Seems he's found that missing tup.'

Arty's spirits rallied. He was good, this kid of Joseph's.

If anyone could get to the bottom of what was going on at the retirement complex, Samson was the man.

Then perhaps Arty would be able to get some sleep at night instead of sitting up in a chair, clutching a golf club. It was no way to live. But it was better than dying.

'Christ!' Samson surveyed himself in the mirror on his father's wardrobe door.

What had he been thinking when he'd agreed to this?

Red trousers hung loose, a couple of inches clear of his boots. A fat pillow padded out the red jacket, black buttons pulled taut across its width. A red hat topped the outfit, his hair tucked up beneath it, and a white beard covered the lower half of his face.

Santa Claus. With a blue-stained hand.

As undercover went, this was one disguise he'd never expected to don. It wasn't exactly inconspicuous. But it did give him the perfect excuse for being in Fellside Court. To get a feel for the place. And for the woman whom Arty Robinson believed was behind the catalogue of tragedy that had visited it.

He picked up the sack of presents from by the door and slipped into the corridor. It was empty, everyone in the lounge awaiting the arrival of the big man. Shifting the sack over his shoulder, he headed for the stairs. Halfway down and he could already hear the excited buzz of the gathered pensioners. Holding a hand over his fake belly, he descended the last few steps, took large strides along the corridor and entered the lounge.

'Ho-ho-ho!' he exclaimed.

'He's here!' cried Clarissa Ralph. And the room dissolved into chaos.

Arty couldn't help himself. Fear or no fear, the sight of the large Father Christmas standing in the doorway made him grin. Clarissa was squealing with delight, Edith had a wide smile on her face and Geraldine Mortimer was already flirting with the man in red.

'He's good,' he acknowledged to Joseph, and the Irishman lit up with pride as he watched his son being led to an armchair where a mince pie and a glass of sherry – non-alcoholic – awaited him.

But would he be good enough? While the rest of the room was entranced by this new addition to their yearly ritual, Arty had let his attention drift back to her.

She was standing by the door yet again. Always ready for flight, it seemed. Something shifty in the way she stayed at the edge of everything, never fully committing herself. Unlike her colleague, Vicky Hudson, who had promptly sat down on Santa's knee, sending the residents into gales of laughter.

'Arty!' Edith was calling him, beckoning him over. 'Your turn.'

With a last glance at Ana, he made his way over to the melee in the middle of the room.

'Have you been a good boy?' Father Christmas asked and Arty smiled, feeling at ease for the first time in over a week.

'Let me sit on your knee and tell you,' he said, promptly placing his bulk on the red-covered legs.

Father Christmas let out a mock howl of pain and everyone laughed.

When Arty stood up, present in hand, and extricated himself from the crowd, the doorway was empty. Ana Stoyanova was nowhere to be seen.

He felt the familiar mantle of fear descend over him once more.

17

'You'll stay for the meal?' Ana Stoyanova asked Samson, her delivery more a command than a question.

With the presents all distributed, the gaggle of old people had begun to drift out of the lounge, heading down the corridor towards the cafe, comparing gifts as they went and leaving a trail of conversation behind them. The manager of Fellside Court had appeared in the doorway in their wake.

'I'd love to,' said Samson, scratching his chin where the beard was tickling him. 'As long as I don't have to eat in this blasted thing. Thank you.'

Ana gave a small smile and shook her head. 'Thank *you*. Without your intervention, we wouldn't have had a visit from Father Christmas this year. That would have been a shame. Now if you'll excuse me, I'll go and set another place at the table.'

He watched her leave, a hand pressed to her temple, face pale.

'What do you think?' His father was next to him, his gaze fixed on the departing manager. 'Is Arty right to be worried?'

Samson turned to where the bookmaker was standing alone in a corner, staring out at the bleak courtyard, a glass of sherry in his hand, a haunted expression on his face and his eyes bright from an excess of alcohol. 'I think it's Arty we need to be worried about, not Ana. He's a wreck.'

'He's been getting worse. I don't know what to do. I thought asking you here . . .'

Samson put a hand on his father's arm. 'You did the right thing, Dad. If nothing else, at least he thinks someone's listening. In truth, there's not much more we can do. Although,' he lowered his voice, 'I wouldn't mind a quick look at Rita Wilson's flat before we go and eat. You know, just to rule out the possibility of a break-in.'

'Luckily, I know where the spare key is,' said Joseph with a grin.

He accompanied his son out of the lounge and up the stairs, telling Edith Hird, who was waiting at the door to the cafe, that Samson was just going to change. On the first floor they stopped by Joseph's apartment, giving Samson the chance to get rid of the Santa suit. As they exited the flat, Joseph took a key from a hook by the door.

'Is that Rita's?' Samson asked, remembering what Arty had said the morning they'd visited Eric in the hospital. The residents left spare keys to their homes with one another.

'Yes.'

'Who's got yours?'

'Arty.'

'And who's got Arty's?'

'Normally Eric, but Clarissa has it for now. Why?'

Samson didn't say anything. But he was thinking. Thinking that someone would only have to break into one flat in Fellside Court and they would instantly have access to the whole lot. It wasn't a secure system, even if it did give the residents peace of mind.

'Right, this way,' said Joseph, walking briskly towards the stairwell over by the lift rather than the one that led down to the cafe. 'There's less chance of us being seen.'

The stairs brought them out on the ground floor by the large Christmas tree. With the entrance hall empty, the two O'Briens hurried round the tree and turned left into the wing that housed Rita Wilson's flat, Joseph leading the way down the corridor.

'There's no one in the guest suite next door,' he murmured as they approached Rita's front door, 'and the people opposite are away with their families already. But even so, don't be too long. It doesn't feel right, breaking in like this.'

Samson took the key from him and let himself into the apartment.

It was homely. Stylish. More lived-in than his father's austere dwelling. Soft touches of curtains and cushions marked it as a woman's home. And the smell of perfume lingered, a flowery scent reminiscent of lavender and lilies.

He crossed to the coffee table and the pile of presents his father had mentioned. Flipping the first one over, he could see why his father had been intrigued. The original decorative sticky tape had been resealed with a layer of traditional Sellotape but even through this second layer, Samson could see the tattered edges of the older tape. A nail, trying to lift it? Possibly. But why?

He inspected the rest of the pile, found the same markings on the tape on quite a few of the presents.

Had someone been looking for something specific? Or had Rita simply got tired with the mundane task of wrapping and become less thorough?

Leaving the lounge, he crossed to the kitchen area, but there was nothing to suggest anyone had been in there other than Rita. The bedroom led off the hallway, the door open. He stuck his head in. Same thick-pile carpet as in Eric Bradley's place. And the same indentation by the foot of the chest of drawers.

He bent down and ran his fingers across the floor, noting the groove where the furniture had rested. Until recently. Someone had pulled the unit out from the wall and failed to put it back fully. Just like in Eric's. He peered down the gap between the drawers and the wall. Nothing. Not even dust.

A diligent cleaner, vacuuming behind the set of drawers.

Aware of the time passing, he stood up, cast a quick eye over the bathroom and then paused in the hall to inspect the frame around the front door.

No signs of forced entry. No scratches around the lock. If someone had broken in, they'd used a key. Or there hadn't been a break-in at all . . .

He left the flat, greeted by a relieved sigh from his father.

'I'm getting too old for this lark,' muttered the elder O'Brien, a hand to his heart. 'Did you find anything?'

'A few bits of tattered tape and that's about it.' Samson scratched his chin, still itchy from the false beard. 'You're right, Dad,' he said. 'Arty's paranoia is contagious.'

Joseph O'Brien shook his head in disgust. 'I wasted your time, son.'

'Better safe than sorry. Come on.' Samson set off in the direction of the cafe. 'Let's go and get some turkey before Edith Hird eats it all.'

*

Arty Robinson was nobody's fool. He'd seen Joseph and his son sneak off. Had noted that they'd taken longer to return than a mere change of clothing warranted. He was hoping it meant they were snooping around. But while feeling relieved that his fears were being taken seriously, Arty had also seen Ana Stoyanova checking her watch a few times, a frown marring her otherwise perfect forehead. She was no fool, either.

When father and son had finally appeared in the doorway of the cafe, she'd pounced, leading Samson to a chair next to hers. She'd smiled. Talked a little – more than normal anyway. That beautiful, innocent face focused on young O'Brien.

And the detective had fallen under her spell.

'More roasts, Arty?' Edith was leaning across the table, a bowl of potatoes in her hand.

He tore his attention away from Ana. 'No, thanks.'

'Have some more turkey then.'

'Thanks, but I've had enough.'

Edith looked at his plate and tutted, the sight of his unfinished meal drawing her concern. 'Not like you to be off your food, Arty Robinson. You're worrying me.'

Arty managed a smile. 'No need to worry, Edith. I'm fine. Honestly.'

She gave a sharp nod. 'If you say so.'

'Does this mean you don't want Christmas pudding, either?' asked Clarissa from the other side of her sister.

'Ah, now that is a different thing entirely,' said Arty, forcing a big grin onto his face and slapping his stomach. 'There's always room for Christmas pudding.'

Clarissa laughed, convinced by his display of good

humour. But Edith kept her stern gaze on him. Another one who wasn't easily fooled.

He gave her one last smile and then turned back to the other end of the table. Samson was talking to Rita Wilson, leaning back in his chair with a contented look on his face. But the other side of Samson was an empty place.

She'd gone again.

'Who's for Christmas pudding?' asked the cook.

A flurry of hands shot into the air amid a burst of laughter. But Arty's arms stayed by his side. His appetite, along with Ana Stoyanova, had disappeared.

'She had a migraine,' Samson said. 'She's gone home. There's nothing more to it.'

Slumped in his armchair, Arty snorted. 'Likely story. That woman is rotten to the core and no one can see it but me.'

Having retired to Arty's flat following the Christmas meal, Samson and his father had been listening to the bookmaker's condemnation of Ana Stoyanova for the last ten minutes. It was a condemnation pinned on the most fragile of evidence – a look of fear in Alice Shepherd's eyes; a sense of unease over Ana's appearance at Eric's bedside; and sightings of her in the corridors late at night.

Samson remained far from convinced, finding it difficult to cast the manager of Fellside Court in the role of villain, despite Arty's convictions.

Yes, she was reserved. Aloof even. But Ana didn't seem like the kind of woman capable of malice. Besides, what motive did she have for harming Alice Shepherd and Eric Bradley? *If* they had been harmed . . .

'But you haven't seen her doing anything inappropriate?' the detective queried.

Arty shook his head reluctantly. 'Just that blonde hair, glinting under the lights.'

'And you're sure it's her you've seen? Not someone else with blonde hair?'

'It's her!' Arty growled. 'Always her . . .'

Casting his eyes around the apartment, Samson knew who a jury would believe. The curtains were drawn tight against the afternoon light. Bottles littered the worktop in the kitchen. A stack of unwashed plates was teetering next to the sink, scraps of food congealed on them. And in the midst of it sat Arty, eyes bloodshot, skin grey, his hands shaking slightly. The man was drinking. Hard. Samson knew the signs all too well.

Unwelcome memories crowded in on him in the oppressive atmosphere, his father equally ill at ease on the couch next to him, as though he too was back in the kitchen at Twistleton Farm. Samson had a sudden longing to be out on the fells, running in the clean air with Delilah.

'You don't believe me, do you?' Arty was demanding.

'I'm sorry,' said Samson. 'But you haven't shown me any credible evidence of wrongdoing.'

Arty glanced over his shoulder towards the curtains covering the patio doors, as though contemplating something. Then he sagged back in the chair. 'I've told you enough,' he muttered.

Torn by an all-too-familiar mixture of exasperation and concern, Samson got to his feet, eager to be out of the flat. 'I think you're worrying over nothing,' he said. Then he stared at the glass on the floor by the old man's chair, his discomfort making him curt. 'And you might want to cut back on the drink. It can't be helping.'

Arty gazed up at him, eyes sad. 'This will come back to haunt you, son,' he said. Then he picked up his empty glass and pointedly walked towards the kitchenette, conversation over.

Following his father out of the apartment, Samson had a flashback to a frightened Alice Shepherd sitting in his office only a fortnight ago.

'There's nothing going on,' he murmured, as much to convince himself as his father, who'd remained silent throughout the exchange. 'Sorry, Dad,' he said finally when they reached the foyer. 'I'm not sure I was of any help.'

'You came. That in itself was a help. And don't worry about Arty. I'll keep an eye on him.'

'Someone needs to. As for Rita's flat—'

Joseph pulled an imaginary zip across his lips. 'I've no intention of mentioning my daft suspicions. Arty's imagination is wild enough without me fanning the flames.'

'Right, well, I'd best be off. Thanks for this.' Samson held up the bag containing the Santa outfit and Joseph's face split into a grin.

'Use it wisely, son.' He patted his lad on the back and watched him out through the courtyard and onto the motorbike. He waited there until the sound of the engine had faded and then he made his way back towards the stairs.

He'd call in on Arty again. Make them both a cup of tea and persuade his friend to play a game or two of cribbage. In time, Arty would emerge from this depression which had unbalanced him and affected them all. Then life would return to normal. In the meantime, Joseph would keep his word and keep an eye on him.

He headed up the stairs. He noticed nothing unusual. Because there was nothing to notice. Not yet. By the time anyone spotted it, it would be too late.

He was on his own. Keeping guard with a second-hand golf club and a glass by his side.

Arty Robinson hunkered down in his chair and prepared for another long night. Behind him, buried beneath the roots of the rose on his balcony, Alice's pillbox lay hidden.

Should he have told Samson about it?

What was the point? The detective hadn't believed a word he'd said. He'd been too busy judging him. Too bewitched by the charms of Ana Stoyanova to be capable of seeing that the pillbox was a valid piece of evidence.

The doorbell sounded, followed by the call of Joseph through the letterbox, but Arty wasn't in the mood for the Irishman's optimism. Or his sobriety. He ignored his friend. Reached for the bottle and poured himself a generous measure.

They thought he was deranged, the two O'Briens. Perhaps they were right? He took a swig of whisky, felt the burn hit his throat and dull his fraught emotions – apart from the cold slice of fear which remained lodged in his chest, as sharp as ever.

Deranged or not, he was on his own.

'Where the hell is he?'

Several hours later, when night had fallen and Bruncliffe was bathed in the glow of Christmas lights, Delilah was looking at her watch in the upstairs function room of the Coach and Horses. Situated in the centre of town, the pub was more upmarket than the Fleece – which didn't say much – and its staff were more welcoming, too. But then it wasn't hard to beat Troy Murgatroyd in the customer-services stakes. Consequently, the Coach was her venue of choice for her speed-dating events.

Tonight, it was a venue that had been transformed.

Having raced home after returning from Mire End Farm, Delilah had taken a long shower to get rid of the smell of sheep – her car, unfortunately, still carried a certain *eau d'ovine* – then she'd come to the pub and worked all afternoon decorating the room next to the upstairs bar. Her hard work had paid off. It looked amazing. Garlands of holly and ivy decorated the walls, bunches of mistletoe intertwined with scarlet ribbons hung from the ceiling, and each table held a centrepiece of a tea light floating in a wine glass filled with rose petals in water. A pile of beautifully wrapped presents were artistically arranged in the corner and the air was scented with the aroma of pine and spices. Christmas had arrived in Bruncliffe. All that was missing was Santa Claus himself. And Samson O'Brien.

The success of the entire evening rested on having an equal number of men and women. But so far, with precisely five minutes to go before the event started, she was a man down. Samson O'Brien had failed to show.

'I'll kill him,' she muttered to herself as she slipped through the doors into the crowded bar area, scanning the gathered customers for a familiar mane of dark hair.

Not a sign of him.

*

Rita Wilson was tired. It had been a long day. The excitement of the party had been as wearing as the actual event itself and now, with her case packed for the morning and her evening meal finished, she was ready for her sofa and a bit of mindless television.

But first, she wanted to go and see Arty.

He'd not been himself all day. And he had nowhere to go over Christmas, his wife long dead and his only child living in Australia. He'd be spending it in the quiet environment of Fellside Court, the majority of the residents away in homes around the area.

She felt a pang of sympathy and relief at the same time. She was so lucky. All her family were still local, her grandchildren now adults. She had no lack of places to spend the festive season. Christmas Day would be with her son and on Boxing Day her granddaughter, Hannah, was having her round. That was always fun, Hannah as wild as Rita herself had been in her youth. A woman who knew how to enjoy herself.

Rita chuckled. It was a shame Arty wasn't going with her. Hannah would snap him out of his depression.

She mulled over this kernel of an idea and the more she thought about it, the better it seemed.

She would invite her friend home with her. She reached for the phone to call her son.

Hannah Wilson was over in the corner of the upstairs bar, talking animatedly, her red hair vibrant against the green of her dress. It was hard to believe the gregarious woman was a librarian. Alongside her was Jo Whitfield, owner of the hair salon next door to the Dales Dating Agency, stout figure arrayed in a flattering black trouser suit, blonde bob immaculate. Whatever Jo was saying, Hannah was doubled over in laughter.

Similar pockets of conversation peppered the room, everyone dressed in their finest, bracelets catching the lights, perfume catching the senses. There were old faces, like Hannah's; there were also relative newcomers like Stuart Lister, the estate agent from Taylor's standing to one side on crutches, looking apprehensive. The young man's injuries had healed well after the turmoil he'd found himself caught up in following the last dating event, but still the sight of him swamped Delilah in guilt.

She'd make sure he had a good time tonight.

She'd also make sure that Samson suffered for leaving her in the lurch.

Calling the room to order with a ring of an auctioneer's bell, she stepped forward to greet the participants in the last event of the year.

'Welcome to the Dales Dating Agency Speedy Date night,' she began. 'Firstly, I have to apologise, as due to unforeseen circumstances, we are a man down this evening.' A murmur rippled around the room, some of the women looking disappointed. 'But I promise it won't spoil what will be a wonderful Christmas dating event—'

'HO-HO-HO!' boomed a voice from the doors that led to the stairs. 'Did someone mention Christmas?'

Rita hung up the phone. It was settled. Arty would be welcome to share Christmas with the Wilson family. If he wanted to, that was.

Deciding it was best to ask him in person, Rita got up,

her bad hip aching from the long day. Shuffling stiffly towards the front door, stick in her right hand, she let herself out into the corridor.

It was eerily quiet. Both flats opposite were empty, the residents having already left for the holidays. And next door to her, the guest suite was unoccupied, as always. Feeling oddly unnerved by the hushed hallway, she advanced slowly towards the bright lights of the Christmas tree at the end of the hall.

For a brief moment, she contemplated taking the lift. But thinking a bit of exercise might ease her hip, she opted for the stairs. She was halfway up and pausing to take a breather when she thought about Alice's pillbox.

If Arty was going to come with her, they'd have to leave it with someone else to give to Elaine Bullock when she got back from her field trip. Joseph probably. He wasn't going anywhere.

Brooding over the puzzling discovery of the box of rainbow colours immersed in the snow, she resumed her progress up the stairs. Above her the door to the corridor was closed. A shadow brushed across it.

Rita Wilson didn't give it a passing thought.

'Ho-ho-ho!'

Delilah turned to see Father Christmas standing in the doorway, black boots, big bushy beard, massive stomach bulging against a red coat, a sack over his shoulder.

'So, ladies,' declared Santa with a wicked grin, 'I've come to see whether you've been naughty or nice!'

Laughter split the room and a buzz of expectation rose

from the clusters of women as the mysterious Santa moved through the crowd.

Delilah was speechless. Then Santa strode over to her, grabbed her into a bear hug and planted a kiss on her cheek.

'Room for one more?' he demanded, depositing her back on the floor before making his way into the function room. The rest of Delilah's clients followed like the children of Hamelin, laughing and joking as they jostled to take their places at the tables.

It was only when Santa took the spare seat opposite a blushing blonde – the seat that should have been occupied by Samson O'Brien – that the penny dropped for Delilah. As Santa reached out to bestow a gallant kiss on the woman's hand, there was a flash of blue. Faint but sure.

Father Christmas had a hand covered in raddle.

'I'll definitely bloody kill him,' laughed Delilah as she rang the bell to signal the start of the first four minutes of a speed-dating event that couldn't be more festive if it tried.

Filled with the spirit of Christmas, Rita Wilson reached the top of the stairs. It would do Arty good, she mused. Get him away from Fellside Court for a few days. Get him into the festive mood.

Sure that her idea was a sound one, she pushed through the door into the corridor of the first floor. Ahead of her the wall of glass stretched along the hallway, letting her see across the courtyard to the dark, empty apartments of poor Alice and Eric.

At least Eric was with his family. And well on the

mend, from what Joseph had told her. Well enough to be talking about moving back into his flat in the New Year.

It would be good to have him home again. Another man around the place, in a society dominated by women.

She made her way to Arty's front door, her hip easing slightly. She'd done the right thing taking the stairs. A trip down them wouldn't hurt, either. Especially as she'd be spending a lot of the next week in an armchair while her family fussed over her. By the time Christmas was over, she'd be desperate to be back here amongst her friends and living independently. For the next week, however, she'd enjoy being looked after.

Leaning on her stick, she stood in front of Arty's apartment and rapped sharply on the door, the sound loud in the stillness of the corridor.

No answer.

She knocked again. Slightly harder this time. Then she listened, expecting to hear Arty moving to the door, the rattle of keys in the lock.

After a third attempt failed to bring him to the threshold, she gave up. He might be asleep already. He'd been looking very tired of late and she'd heard him saying he wasn't sleeping. Unwilling to disturb him, she turned away. She had time to catch him tomorrow before she left. Hannah wasn't coming for her until mid-morning.

Moving slowly down the hallway, her stick tapping out a staccato rhythm in the silence, she walked towards the stairs. She had just opened the door that led onto the stairway when the lift pinged beside her. Door held open, her weight off balance, she twisted to see who was getting out.

She didn't notice the odd sheen of light on the floor, right in front of the first step.

Two dates in and Father Christmas was proving a hit, with smiles all round, lots of laughter and not a sign of nerves. Even Stuart Lister had relaxed, currently talking to Hannah Wilson, who was behaving herself for once. Perhaps she'd sensed the fragile nature of the young man. Or taken pity on him as he hobbled over on his crutches.

All in all, it was a Dales Dating Agency event that would go down as a success.

Delilah cursed quietly, her words at odds with the smile on her lips. Bloody Samson O'Brien. She'd gone from wanting to kill him to wanting to hug him. And yet again, she would owe him.

She rang the bell in her hand and the men all stood to rotate around the tables once more, Father Christmas throwing her a roguish wink as he passed.

Kill him. That was the only option. Because if she didn't, she was in danger of falling for him. And then Will would kill her.

Feeling happier than she had in years, Delilah Metcalfe found herself looking forward to Christmas.

'Good evening!' Rita Wilson said in some surprise. 'I didn't expect you to be here.'

She'd twisted to greet the person who'd emerged from the lift, the stairway door heavy against her left arm, her stick now carrying the majority of her weight.

She smiled. Then shifted slightly, shuffling forward a

fraction to ease her discomfort, her stick now perilously close to that sheen of light on the floor.

When the hand reached out, Rita was sure it was to hold the door for her. Instead, it landed on her shoulder, violently, pushing her further off balance. She felt her stick hop across the tiles. Then it hit that sheen of light and it slid. Smoothly. Treacherously.

With nothing left to support her, Rita Wilson fell, her cries unheard in the silent corridors of Fellside Court.

18

When Delilah pushed open the back gate the following morning, Tolpuddle on her heels, she felt an unaccountable happiness at the sight of the gleaming motorbike standing on the concrete in the corner of the yard.

Good. He was in already.

In the aftermath of the Speedy Date night she hadn't had a chance to catch up with Father Christmas, the man in red making a beeline for the door the minute his last date was finished. He'd left behind a clamour of ladies wanting to know who he was and a jovial atmosphere that lasted well into the evening. Already some of the clients were asking about the next event.

She let herself in through the back porch, the dog bounding ahead and announcing their presence. From the office came the sound of Samson making his usual fuss of the hound. And from out of nowhere her happiness was submerged beneath despair.

Tolpuddle. She'd pushed it to the back of her mind for the last couple of days. Now it was starkly real. Come New Year, there was a strong chance he would no longer be here.

She paused in the hall, wiped her eyes and took a deep breath, before stepping into the office.

'What the hell were you playing at?' she demanded,

doing her best to sound ferocious. 'Turning up as Father Christmas!'

Samson looked up from where he was kneeling beside Tolpuddle, an arm draped around the dog. He blinked. His mouth opened in protest. Then he saw the gleam in her eyes and the grin that was fighting its way through her fake fury.

'Ho-ho-ho!' he said, grinning back at her. 'But the big question is, did Santa get any date requests?'

'Fifteen,' said Delilah, shaking her head, still laughing. 'Every woman in the place.'

'Not every woman,' said Samson with devilment.

Delilah's cheeks grew hot. 'It takes more than a white beard and a red suit to woo some of us,' she muttered, annoyed that she was blushing like a teenager.

Samson laughed. 'You Metcalfes always were choosy.'

Before she could retort, his mobile rang. He stood to answer it, turning slightly away from her.

'Dad?' His body tensed and when he turned back, there wasn't a trace of amusement on his shocked face. 'We'll be right there.'

He hung up and looked at Delilah. 'Rita Wilson,' he said, grabbing his jacket and heading for the door.

'What about her?' Delilah hurried after him, Tolpuddle too.

'She fell down the stairs at Fellside Court.'

'Oh my God! Is she okay?'

He paused at the back door, his features grey. 'She's in a coma,' he said. Then he turned on his heel and strode across the yard, leaving a stunned Delilah to follow.

*

'I warned you,' muttered Arty Robinson. 'I told you something was up. Now you might believe me.'

They were gathered in the lounge of Edith and Clarissa's flat – Arty and Joseph, the two sisters and, as of a few minutes ago, Samson, Delilah and Tolpuddle. The cosy room, with its floral armchairs and cushion-scattered sofa, seemed an incongruous setting for such a sombre meeting. The mellow tick of the antique school clock on the wall marked the seconds between words that were hard to come by.

It had been a night from hell. After Samson's departure following the Christmas party, Arty had remained in his flat, in the grip of a dark mood. He'd drunk more than he should have and had fallen asleep. Passed out, more like. It must have been early, as he could recall the start of the news on Channel 4 at seven, but not the sport or the weather. He woke just after ten-thirty to someone pounding on the front door, his neck cricked, his head throbbing, an empty bottle on the carpet.

It was Ana. Arty had watched her through the spyhole, her hair dishevelled, her face taut with shock. Still he hadn't opened the door. It was only when Joseph appeared in the background, the commotion bringing him out of his flat, that Arty had emerged into the corridor.

'There's been an accident,' Ana had exclaimed. 'Call an ambulance.' Then she'd disappeared through the door to the stairs.

Joseph had done as she asked while Arty had followed her. He'd pushed open the stairwell door, slipped in something and grabbed the bannister rail just in time. As he caught his breath, heart pounding from his averted fall, he'd seen Ana Stoyanova huddled over a figure on the half-landing.

She'd looked up at him, frantic. 'It's Rita.'

Sleep banished, headache forgotten, Arty had hurried down the stairs. It had been clear straight away that Rita Wilson was seriously injured.

The school clock chimed the half-hour, more of a soft burr than a pure ring. It was enough to trigger conversation.

'There's still no proof,' said Edith gently. She'd arrived on the scene minutes after Arty the night before, stoic and unflappable in the face of tragedy. 'No matter what you think.'

'Proof!' Arty shot to his feet. 'Rita is in a coma. Alice is dead. And Eric would have been, if it hadn't been for us. What more proof do you bloody need?'

Joseph put an arm on his friend, but Arty shrugged it off.

'You wouldn't listen,' he shouted. 'And I did nothing to protect her—' He halted, choked, tears on his cheeks. 'I did nothing . . .'

Edith rose and gathered him to her, the bookmaker sobbing openly. 'Shush,' she said. 'Shush. It's not your fault.'

She eased him back into his chair, the silence in the room strained with guilt.

'I'll make tea,' chirped Clarissa, eyes wet with tears. 'It's just what we need. A good cup of tea.'

Edith nodded and her sister scurried into the kitchen area, occupying herself in an attempt to overcome her distress. Delilah went to help her.

'It's no one's fault,' said Joseph as the clatter of teacups and the hum of the kettle eased the tension. 'It was just an accident.'

Arty looked up, shaking his head. 'How can you still believe that?'

'What else could it be?' asked Edith. 'Rita slipped on something that had been spilled at the top of the stairs. You said you nearly fell when you went to help Ana. It just shows that it could have happened to any of us.'

'But it didn't. It happened to Rita. And next it will happen to me.' Arty's dire prediction cast a pall over the room once more.

'Did anyone see the accident?' asked Samson.

Edith shook her head. 'Everyone had retired early after the party. We were all worn out.'

'But not Rita?'

'Rita too,' said Joseph. 'I helped her to her flat as she was in a bit of pain with her hip and couldn't wait to get off her feet. As far as I know, she was settled for the night. She said she'd see me before her granddaughter called to pick her up this morning.'

'Her granddaughter?'

'Hannah Wilson,' said Delilah from the kitchen. 'You know – she was at the event last night.'

Samson had a sudden image of the flame-haired librarian. She'd been the life and soul of the party as usual. This news would put a damper on her family's Christmas.

'What time was Hannah due to arrive?' he asked.

'About mid-morning, I think,' said Edith. 'After our usual coffee in the cafe, anyway. Rita was planning on giving out her Christmas cards when we got together this morning. Only . . .' Her hands rose to her face, shaking, the veins proud, the bones prominent. She breathed deeply, holding on to her control with a fragile grip.

'So as far as you know, Rita wasn't expecting to leave her flat before this morning?'

'Sounds about right,' said Joseph.

'In which case,' continued Samson, 'what was she doing at the top of the stairs on the first floor last night?'

Edith and Joseph looked at each other, neither having thought about this strange aspect of their friend's accident.

'I don't know . . .' Edith tailed off, while Joseph frowned.

What would have made a tired, elderly lady who had retired for the evening walk up a flight of stairs? Samson glanced at Arty, who was staring at the carpet, eyes raw from crying.

'Arty?' Samson asked. 'Do you have any idea what Rita was doing on your floor?'

The former bookmaker lifted his head and met Samson's gaze. 'No. I don't have a clue. But I know why she was attacked.'

He reached in his pocket and pulled out Alice Shepherd's pillbox, bits of dirt caught in the hinges. He placed it on the coffee table.

'Why – wherever did you get that?' exclaimed Edith. 'That's Alice's, isn't it?'

'The very same.'

'I thought Ana gave it to Elaine Bullock,' said Clarissa, who had emerged from the kitchen area with a plate of mince pies and biscuits, which Tolpuddle was eyeing hopefully. Behind her, Delilah was carrying a tray loaded with a teapot and delicate china cups.

'She did,' said Arty. 'Then Rita found it out in the copse by the car park.'

Edith stared at the pillbox and then at Arty. 'How very odd. When did she find it?'

'Three days ago.'

'She didn't say anything.'

'She wanted to keep it quiet until she'd had a chance to speak to Elaine and find out how the pillbox came to be buried out there. She thought Elaine deserved an opportunity to explain things.'

'But she told you?'

Arty nodded. 'She did more than that. She gave it to me to pass on to Elaine, as Rita knew she wouldn't be here when Elaine got back from her field trip. Turns out she was right,' he added bitterly.

'Did anyone else know that Rita had found this?' Samson picked up the rainbow-coloured box and opened each of the compartments, a small number of discoloured tablets stuck to the insides.

'No one,' said Arty. 'But anyone could have seen her out there in the snow.'

'Well, there's no denying this is all very peculiar,' said Edith, looking over the rim of her cup at the pillbox which had turned up so unexpectedly. 'However, it's hardly grounds for someone to attack poor Rita.'

'I'm telling you, it's all connected,' insisted Arty. 'And Ana Stoyanova is at the heart of it. Alice was shivering afraid of her. Remember, that afternoon before she died?

Ana was telling her to take her pills and Alice was all het up. I saw it in her eyes. She was terrified of that woman.'

'And Eric?' asked Joseph with scepticism.

'He said himself that he upset Ana just before we went to Morecambe. Something to do with her nationality.'

Arty had caught Edith's attention now, her finger pressed to her lips as she tried to remember the conversation. 'That's right,' she said. 'Eric said she was from . . . oh, where was it?'

'Serbia,' said Clarissa, who was surreptitiously feeding Tolpuddle bits of biscuit. 'And then Ana corrected him. A bit sharp, I thought. Poor Eric was in a right state.'

'Where is she from?' asked Delilah.

'Bulgaria,' said Joseph. 'Given the politics in the region, you can understand why Ana might be touchy about being associated with the wrong country.'

'Still, it was a bit over the top,' said Edith.

'But surely no one is suggesting Ana somehow attacked Eric because of that?' asked Joseph.

Arty shrugged. 'It's linked. That's all I'm saying. It's all linked to Ana. She haunts the place like a malign spirit, turning up out of the blue when Eric collapsed and then first on the scene last night.'

'Oh, for goodness' sake, Arty!' Edith said, eyebrows raised. 'That really is daft. You're starting to sound like Geraldine Mortimer.'

'Geraldine Mortimer?' Samson asked.

'She's the resident racist,' muttered Joseph. 'She lives in the flat opposite Eric's and just about tolerates me – Ireland being part of the UK, in her eyes. But she's not happy about Ana working here. And she's made her views clear.'

'Anyway,' said Edith, 'say your suspicions are correct, Arty. How do you explain what happened to Rita?'

Arty pointed at the pillbox still in Samson's hand. 'That – it has to be that. Rita found it. And now she's lying in hospital.'

'You think Ana was looking for it?' asked Delilah.

Joseph shuffled in his chair and cast a glance at his son.

'What?' asked Arty, alert to his friend's reaction.

'Nothing – at least I don't think . . .' Joseph paused, looking again at Samson, who nodded.

'Best get it all out in the open,' said Samson.

'Get what out in the open?' asked Edith.

'Dad thought Rita's flat might have been broken into.'

His statement was met with a sharp gasp from the two sisters, while Arty sagged further into his armchair.

'I wasn't sure,' said Joseph. 'I didn't want to create alarm, so I asked Samson to have a look at it yesterday.'

'And?' asked Edith, swivelling to fix her gaze on the detective.

'It's hard to say,' Samson acknowledged. 'There were no signs of forced entry and nothing had been stolen. Nothing that Rita noticed, anyway. But some of her presents looked as though they may have been tampered with.'

'As if someone was looking for something,' muttered Arty. 'Looking for that!' He pointed at the pillbox again.

'It's a vague possibility. Not enough to start throwing accusations around, though.'

'But why didn't you say something?' Edith asked Joseph.

The older O'Brien looked contrite. 'I thought it was nothing. I thought I was being paranoid.'

'Like me, you mean?' Arty said with reproach.

'It wasn't just Dad,' said Samson. 'I had a good look around and decided it wasn't worth pursuing. We still can't say for sure that it was.'

Arty shook his head. 'Believe me, it was.'

'Okay,' said Delilah, sensing the relationships in the room beginning to strain. 'Let's assume Arty is right. According to him, everything revolves around Ana. And around this.' She took the pillbox from Samson. 'If we accept Arty's theory, then Rita was attacked because of this. Why? What makes it so special?'

Arty lifted both hands. 'Search me.'

Delilah flipped the box over, her fingers brushing the remaining dirt off the bottom and onto her empty plate. She froze. Then she looked at Samson and passed him the box.

'Look,' she said.

He looked. Initials engraved into the metal. *A. S.* 'Alice Shepherd.' He glanced back at Delilah, who was staring at him. 'What about it?'

'You don't remember? When Elaine came up to the barn after Alice died?'

He glanced back at the box and then up at Delilah. 'Call Elaine,' he said. 'Now.'

Delilah pulled out her mobile and headed for the hallway.

'What is it?' asked Arty. 'What have you found?'

All of them were watching Samson, tea and mince pies forgotten.

'This isn't the box that was given to Elaine,' he said.

'Of course it is,' said Edith. 'It's Alice's pillbox. We all saw Elaine with it the day her godmother died.'

'No we didn't. We saw her with a rainbow-coloured box, but it wasn't this one. The one Elaine was given doesn't have the initials on the bottom.'

Delilah had reappeared in the doorway, putting her mobile back in her pocket.

'Well?' asked Samson.

'I've just spoken to Elaine. She's got hers with her.'

'There are two boxes?' asked Edith, confused. She stared at the object on her coffee table and then at Arty, who was frowning.

'Why would Alice have two pillboxes?' he asked. 'It's hard enough keeping track of our daily medication, without complicating things.'

'Perhaps Alice only had one.' Samson stood up and began pacing across the thick carpet. 'This was hers. The one with the initials.'

'And someone else had a second one made?' Arty was tracking the detective's movements as well as his train of thought.

Samson nodded. 'Identical in all but one aspect. They forgot to get it engraved.'

'But why would someone want a replica?' asked Clarissa.

'Her pills,' whispered Arty. 'The day she died, Ana told Alice to take her pills. And Alice was so insistent she'd already taken them . . .'

'But the box Ana had in the cafe had Alice's pills for that day still in it. Ana was right. Alice hadn't taken them,' said Clarissa.

'What if she had?' Arty's question was followed by the solemn tick of the school clock.

Samson paused. 'Yes. What if she had? What if Alice had taken her tablets, but was then presented with irrefutable proof that she hadn't?'

'Tablets in a rainbow pillbox. She couldn't argue with that,' said Delilah.

'Did she take the pills in the box Ana presented to her?' Samson asked Arty.

'Yes.' Arty swallowed. 'She took them.'

'Goodness!' Edith's hands were covering her mouth. 'You're suggesting Alice might have inadvertently taken an overdose?'

'What he's suggesting,' said Arty, his expression grim, 'is that Alice was murdered.'

Murdered.

The word dropped into the already strained atmosphere like an axe onto a chopping block. Brutal. Uncompromising. Clarissa let out a small cry, her tiny hands clasped together, Tolpuddle looking unsettled next to her.

'Could you clear the plates, Clarissa dear,' said Edith, releasing her sister from the tension.

Clarissa was quick to comply, happy to get away, even if it was only to the far corner of the room where the kitchen was. Like a guardian angel, Tolpuddle trotted after her.

'Murdered?' Joseph wasn't having it. 'That's ridiculous.'

'Is it?' Arty sat forward in his chair, looking more alert than he had for days, as though the vindication of his suspicions had rejuvenated him. 'Then come up with another explanation for all the bad fortune that's been besetting this place.'

Samson resumed his pacing. Had Alice Shepherd's death really been premeditated, like the old lady herself had predicted when she visited his office?

It would be so difficult to prove, and yet he could feel it now. That niggle which had beset him since the morning of her death. The niggle he'd failed to act upon. But how to unearth the truth?

'We'd need an autopsy to determine the true cause of Alice's death,' said Edith.

'An autopsy will take too long,' said Samson. 'They'll have to exhume Alice's body and the paperwork alone will take a while. That's if we can convince the police and the authorities that it's worth doing.'

'What about fingerprints?' asked Edith, pointing at the box.

Samson shook his head. 'Don't bank on it. Apart from the fact that we've all handled it, it was buried in snow for the best part of a day.'

'And in soil,' muttered Arty, red-faced. Seeing the questioning glances, he elaborated. 'I hid it beneath the rose on my balcony for safe-keeping when I thought someone might be after it.'

'Don't be too hard on yourself,' said Samson. 'Finding fingerprints on that box wouldn't prove anything anyway.'

'So we have nothing to go on, apart from our suspicions.' Edith sighed.

'We could change that,' said Arty. 'Go on the offensive instead of always being on the back foot.'

'What are you suggesting?' asked Joseph.

'Find out more about Ana Stoyanova. Because like I've been saying all morning, she's behind this.'

Edith looked over at Samson. 'What do you think?'

The detective shrugged. 'Ana was the one who was pressurising Alice to take her tablets. You all witnessed that. So it's a good place to start. A motive can lead to a conviction, just as much as evidence.'

'How, though? How can we find out more about her?'

'Break into her office,' said Arty without a moment's hesitation.

'No way!' Joseph shook his head in disgust. 'That would be crossing the line. We can't just invade the woman's privacy because you suspect her of something we have no grounds for.'

'I think the time for adhering to a code of conduct has passed,' said Arty. 'It's time for action. And I, for one, propose that we hire a detective to help us out.'

Edith nodded. 'Seconded. Clarissa? Are you in agreement?'

'Whatever you say, Edith,' came a voice from the kitchen.

'Joseph?' Edith turned to the older O'Brien. 'Speak up if you disagree. Because I think it's important that we're united on this.'

'I don't know,' he said. 'I don't like the idea of targeting Ana just because of a hunch. But then again, if I'm wrong . . .' He thought about Rita Wilson and the fall that had put her in hospital. About the feeling he'd had in her apartment that something was amiss. Could he have averted her accident?

'How about if we were able to rule Ana out through this?' said Edith.

Joseph nodded cautiously. 'I suppose that would make it more acceptable.'

'So we're agreed, then?' asked Edith, looking around her fellow residents. 'In that case,' she continued, addressing Samson, 'consider yourself hired – effective immediately. Find out what's going on and set our minds at rest.'

She rose and held out her hand, offering a formal binding of a contract that was unwritten. Samson stepped towards her and shook it.

'I'll do my best,' he said.

'Aye,' said Arty. 'See that you do. And quickly, before anyone else round here is targeted.'

19

With the wind howling in his face, Samson rode north out of Bruncliffe, feeling the bite of the winter morning in the absence of his usual pillion passenger. Unable to leave Tolpuddle alone without the dog getting anxious – despite the fuss Clarissa was making of the hound – Delilah had had no choice but to remain at Fellside Court until Samson returned. Much to her frustration. So it was with a chilled back and cold legs that Samson turned off the tarmac onto the rough track that led to Thorpdale.

One of the lesser-known dales, Thorpdale was no more than a dark, narrow gouge in the fells, which culminated in the steep slopes of the hills and attracted few visitors. It had very few residents, too. Ida and George Capstick lived in a small cottage at the entrance, brother and sister never having moved away from the home they were raised in. Further up, at the head of the dale, was the only other residence: a lone farmhouse, two streams running either side of it, the mass of the fells rising right behind it. Twistleton Farm. His home. Until his drunken father sold it to Rick Procter. Now it lay empty, awaiting whatever development Procter Properties had in mind.

Samson eased off the throttle to edge the motorbike around a particularly large pothole and let his eyes drift to the distant farmhouse where he'd grown up. A white rectangle against winter-brown hills, it looked remote. Unlived in. Uncared for.

With emotions as ragged as the clouds being whipped across the sky by the strengthening wind, he turned off the road into the Capsticks' yard.

To one side, with views down the dale towards Twistleton Farm, was a small, stone cottage, windows gleaming, paths swept free of leaves and two tubs of purple pansies either side of the back door. Next to it, a well-tended vegetable patch lay dormant, apart from a few cabbages and some Brussels sprouts. Strung out above the bare soil, a line of washing tugged and snapped against brightly coloured pegs.

In contrast, the yard was chaotic. Bits of machinery littered the oil-stained concrete, hens strutted amongst discarded tools, and a vintage tractor in the process of being dismantled stood before an old stone barn. The noise of the motorbike brought a figure to the arched barn doorway.

'Morning, George.' Samson turned the engine off and nodded towards the man who shuffled in the half-light, neck craning to see the bike. 'Is Ida in?'

George Capstick, eyes fixed on the gleaming scarlet-and-chrome Royal Enfield, slowly inched forward. 'Overhead valve single-cylinder four-stroke Ida's inside,' he said, pointing towards the cottage.

Well used to his former neighbour's unorthodox way with language, Samson got off the Enfield and stepped back, giving George the space to come closer.

'Four-speed right-shift long stroke,' continued George, his gaze roaming lovingly over the classic bike.

'You fixing up the old Ferguson?' asked Samson, gesturing towards the grey tractor by the barn. It had been given to the detective by a farmer over towards Hawes, in gratitude for his services after the spate of murders that had assailed Bruncliffe had been solved. Not having anywhere to keep it, Samson had passed it on to George, who already had a collection of ancient farm machinery. George had been ecstatic. His sister, Ida, less so.

'Little Grey,' said George, turning to smile at the machine. 'A beauty.'

'She's a beauty all right. I look forward to seeing her running.'

George grinned. Then he glanced at his idle hands and hurried back over to the barn to resume work on the tractor. Samson was left to pick his way through spare parts and pecking hens to the cottage.

'Ida? You home?' he called out as he opened the door and entered the kitchen.

It was a room untouched since the 1950s: free-standing wooden units, a deep porcelain sink, a table spread with an oilcloth providing the main work surface and a large dresser against the back wall. By the door into the hall, a grandfather clock marked time in deep ticks and tocks.

'I hear tha's been snooping round Fellside Court.'

Samson spun round to see Ida standing by the range, poker in hand and a stern look on her face. 'How did you—?'

'Is it true?'

He nodded.

'I'm thinking it's connected to what tha told me about Alice Shepherd.'

'It could be.'

'And now poor Rita Wilson, too?'

'I think so.'

She shook her head. 'Tha'll get thyself in trouble,' she said, already placing the kettle on a hotplate and reaching for the tea caddy off a shelf. It was Bruncliffe. She didn't need to ask if he wanted a cup of tea. 'And give that bugger Rick Procter a heart attack in the process.' She turned to put mugs on the table and he caught the trace of a smile.

'Take a seat if tha's staying,' she said, gesturing at one of the twin chairs next to the range, the upholstery faded, the wooden arms worn thin from generations of Capsticks resting their weary bones. She took the Yorkshire tea loaf that was on the dresser and cut three thick slices, smothered them in butter and then poured the tea which had been stewing on the range.

A dark mahogany stream fell into the mugs and Samson's stomach recoiled. A good slosh of milk followed and the mug was placed on the windowsill next to his chair, a plate of cake thrust in his hand.

'George, tea,' she called out of the back door. Then she sat at the table, pulled her mug towards her and turned to Samson with an expectant look.

'Tha's not one for social visits,' she said, pointedly.

'No,' he said. He'd taken a gamble on Ida being at the house, banking on the fact that her work was already winding down for Christmas. Now that he was here though, he wasn't comfortable with what he was about to ask of her. But the discovery that someone had made a duplicate of Alice Shepherd's pillbox meant he had no choice. 'It's about Fellside Court.'

'I thought it might be.' She offered no openings; no opportunity for him to broach the subject tactfully.

'The residents have hired me,' he began. 'To investigate.'

She sat there, her gaze fixed on his face, unreadable as ever.

'Thing is,' he continued, 'they think something is going on.'

'Like Alice Shepherd did?'

'Yes. They don't believe all these incidents have been accidental.'

Her lips compressed into a straight line and she tipped her head in a brief nod. Concurring or contradicting, it was impossible to tell. 'And what's that to do with me?'

'I need to ask you some questions. It's about Eric Bradley's flat.'

'Thought tha'd had a good look round it last week,' she retorted.

He laughed. 'I did. That's why I need to talk to you. Do you clean for Eric?'

'Now and then.'

'Is it part of your contract?'

'Not really. My contract is for the communal areas, but the residents can ask for cleaning services if they want. Mr Bradley's one of them that does.'

'When was the last time you cleaned for him?'

'The afternoon before he took ill.'

'Last Monday?'

'That'd be right.'

'Is that when you usually clean his flat?'

She shook her head. 'Normally it's first thing, but I was

running late that day as the lounge was in a bit of a state, so I didn't get up to Mr Bradley's until after lunch. Why? Is this connected to his collapse?'

'Could be. I'm just doing a bit of checking up.' Samson broke off to take a bite of tea loaf, starting as the combination of moist fruit and a hint of mixed spice triggered memories. He glanced at Ida in surprise.

'Aye,' she said, face softening. 'Tha mother gave me that recipe. She used to win prizes at the show with this loaf.' She shook her head, still lamenting the loss of her young neighbour all those years ago. 'Such a shame.'

Throat thickening, Samson took a swig of tea and for the first time since his return to Bruncliffe, he was glad of the harsh flavour as it cut through the nostalgia and made him cough.

Ida laughed, a brash bark of sound. 'Tha's not toughened up yet, then, lad?'

'Not yet,' he said. 'Reckon it'll take a while.'

'A couple of years at least,' she said.

He nodded, not wanting to tell her that he wouldn't be around that long. He'd be back in London before his taste buds had been damaged forever by the local brew. Feeling another wave of sadness at the thought, he took refuge in the questions he'd come to ask.

'So did you notice anything unusual in Eric's flat?' he continued.

'Like what?' Ida's arms folded across her chest and he sensed the barriers coming down.

'Something out of place? Something there that wasn't normally there?'

She stared out of the window for a moment, thinking,

lips pursed. 'Nothing. I wiped the kitchen down, cleaned the bathroom and ran the vacuum over the carpets.'

'In the master bedroom, too?'

He got a look of derision in return for querying her thoroughness. 'Of course,' she said.

'Was everything as it should be in there?'

'Apart from a bit of sloshed water where the bedside table had been pulled out—' She paused, sensing his sudden interest. 'Tha's wanting to know about that?'

He nodded.

'It was nowt but a bit of spilled water from the glass he has next to his bed. Must've happened when that timer were fitted.'

Samson felt the familiar tingle of excitement at encountering something significant. Because he sensed that what Ida was telling him was significant. 'What timer?' he asked.

'The one plugged in behind the bedside table. The unit had to be pulled out to get to the plug. That's when the water spilled, I reckon.' She gave a sharp nod as if to say he wasn't the only one with powers of detection.

'This timer,' asked Samson, his mind racing. 'Had you seen it before?'

'Not as I can remember. But then I don't make a habit of prying. It was just that I mopped up the water and noticed how far out the unit was from the wall. I went to push it back in and couldn't. That's when I saw the timer. A plastic thing, about so big.' She spanned her fingers to give an idea of the dimensions.

'Was anything plugged into it?'

'Aye. Mr Bradley's oxygen machine.'

That snaking flex winding across the bedroom floor and disappearing behind the bedside unit. The flex that ended in a plug which hadn't been fully inserted into the socket when Samson had visited the flat. According to Ida, the afternoon before Eric Bradley's collapse that very same flex had been connected to a timer. A timer which had miraculously disappeared when Samson arrived on the scene a few hours later, leaving nothing behind but a telltale splash of water and some indentations in the carpet.

Was it possible Eric had plugged his oxygen concentrator into a timer? And then removed it?

'He couldn't have shifted it.' Ida cut through his thoughts, her eyes narrowed. 'It that's what tha's thinking, I'm telling thee now, Mr Bradley couldn't have moved that unit. It weighs a ton.'

She was right. The elderly man was frail, weakened by years of lung problems. He had trouble wheeling his small oxygen canister after him. There was no way he could move the marble-topped bedside table.

'So you're saying someone else put the timer there?'

Ida nodded. 'There's no other explanation. As to why they did it, tha needs to ask them.'

Samson had a horrible feeling he knew why they did it. Only trouble was, he didn't know who 'they' were.

He finished his cake in silence. She could tell he was on the trail of something. An air of distraction had fallen over him when she'd mentioned the timer, like a good hound on the scent of a hare.

Could there be a connection between all those accidents? Something rotten in Fellside Court? Ida shook off the notion as quickly as it came. She was too pragmatic for drama and too old to believe in wives' tales. Whatever it was, Samson would no doubt get to the bottom of it.

'I asked you before about Ana Stoyanova,' said Samson. 'Remember?'

'Of course. I'm not senile.' She waited. Let him fill the silence, already sensing where all this was heading.

'What would you say if I told you some people believe she might be behind the accidents that keep happening over there?'

'That they needs their heads looking at,' she snapped.

'But you accept something is going on?'

'Aye. Reckon there might be. Three incidents in a fortnight is high by anyone's standards. Doesn't mean it's Ana's fault, though.'

He looked at her, those blue eyes just like his mother's, seeing right through a person. 'I need your help,' he said. 'I want to prove Ana isn't involved. To eliminate her from the enquiry.'

'What's that to do with me?' she asked, pretending she didn't know.

'I need access to her office. If you don't want to help, I understand,' he continued. 'I know it's asking a lot.'

She folded her arms across her chest, trying to decide what was best. 'Tha's looking for proof that she's innocent?' she demanded.

'Yes.'

'And there's a chance tha might put a stop to whatever's going on?'

'Yes.'

She stood and crossed to the dresser, pulled open the

right-hand drawer and lifted out a bunch of keys. 'Here,' she said, taking one from the ring and passing it to him. 'Though I'm not convinced it's the wisest thing I've ever done.'

'One other thing,' he said. He gestured to the key ring and told her his plan . . .

'I'll try not to get you in trouble,' he said a short while later, as he stood to go.

She snorted. 'Like that would worry me. Procter can keep his job if it comes to that. No, lad, it's the morality of the thing that bothers me. Ana's a good woman. I don't like the thought of going behind her back.' She followed him to the door. 'Tell George his tea's gone cold. That blasted tractor.' She shot Samson a dark look and he laughed, head thrown back, that hair and those eyes – he really was so like his mother.

'Thanks, Ida,' he said, shaking her hand. 'For everything.' Then he crossed the yard to talk to George.

Ida Capstick watched her brother come out of the barn in that sideways shuffle of his. She saw him smile at young Samson, easier in the man's presence than in that of any other stranger. Old Mr O'Brien had had that way with George, too. When he was sober. He'd always treated his neighbour as an equal, despite George's different take on life. Same with Mrs O'Brien. She'd been an angel and George had adored her. He used to take her veg from the garden when she was pregnant with Samson and had been beside himself when she'd let him hold the newborn baby. Not many would have trusted George with that.

They were good people. And it was wrong what had

happened to them. The cancer. The alcohol. Then Rick Procter stealing the farm like that.

Samson threw her a final wave, then he kick-started the bike and with George laughing delightedly at the deep throb of the engine, he pulled off, turning not towards Bruncliffe, but in the direction of Twistleton Farm.

George came over to her. 'Tha tea's cold,' she said.

He nodded. Blinked slowly. 'He's gone home. He asked me if he could.'

'Aye, thought he might want to. Tha's not going to tell Mr Procter?'

'No!' The answer came with a violent shake of the head. 'I'm on my tea break. Not at work.'

Ida smiled and patted her brother on the back. His logic couldn't be faulted. He'd been retained by Rick Procter to keep an eye on Twistleton Farm, the property developer keen to prevent anyone trespassing. In return, George got paid cash. Cash which they stashed in the middle drawer of the dresser, along with her earnings from Procter-owned Fellside Court. Because the Capsticks knew Rick Procter for what he was; they'd seen what he did to their neighbour. And they feared he might one day come for their home, too. Ida was determined they would have a nest egg to help fight him off when that day arrived.

In the meantime, what Rick didn't know wouldn't hurt him.

Standing in the winter sunshine, brother and sister watched the scarlet motorbike fade into the distant dale.

Samson pulled up outside the farmhouse, not entirely sure why he was there. It was only going to hurt.

Leaving his helmet on the bike, he walked to the porch and tried the handle. Locked. Just as well. He'd been upset at what he'd seen when he'd arrived back in October – the mould in the kitchen, the smell of damp throughout. It would only be worse now, two months on with no one looking after it.

Thoughts drifting to the past, he crossed to the row of outbuildings. The woodshed. Hours he'd spent in there splitting wood, George Capstick having taught him how to swing an axe one winter's day while his father was passed out on the sofa. He stuck his head inside. A few logs, lots of cobwebs.

Next to it was the old stable, which had never housed a horse in his time. His mother had talked of him getting one when he was ten. She'd been dead a while when that landmark passed and he'd been too busy trying to hold the remnants of the O'Brien family together to remember her promise. He pushed open the top half of the door. A few broken bales of hay lay in a corner, dusty and dry. A bucket, upturned with a hole in the bottom, along with some old tools. Nothing that struck a chord.

The last of the buildings was the big barn. His father had always joked that when their family expanded, they would move out of the house and into the barn and have more room. The young Samson had eagerly awaited these events – both the arrival of baby brothers and sisters and the excitement of living in the large stone structure with its high arched doors. As the years passed, his father had stopped joking about it. Then his mother had died and Samson had known neither would ever happen.

As he approached the barn, he noticed that the doors

had been replaced. Two solid wooden barriers now blocked the entrance, a shiny new padlock and thick chain further securing the building.

It was incongruous. Such security, out here in the middle of nowhere. The only explanation was that Procter had tools and equipment in there.

Feeling lost and alienated in what had been his home, Samson walked back to the motorbike. It was time to go. He didn't want to risk getting George in trouble by being here if Rick paid an unexpected visit to his development project.

He sat astride the bike, stared at the farmhouse and wondered again if there was anything he could do to get it back. Then he laughed, the sound echoing around the empty yard. Fourteen years ago he couldn't wait to get shot of the place. Now here he was, getting sentimental about it.

He slammed the visor down on his helmet and turned the bike back onto the track.

Tackling Rick Procter over Twistleton Farm would have to wait. Right now, Samson had other things to think about. Like who had plugged Eric Bradley's oxygen concentrator into a timer.

Thinking about Alice Shepherd and her insistence that something was wrong at Fellside Court, Samson rode back into town. He'd been a fool not to realise she'd been right.

'A timer?' Joseph shook his head. 'I didn't notice one. Did you, Arty?'

'No,' said the bookmaker. While the others looked like they hadn't stirred from Edith's lounge since Samson left for Thorpdale – the coffee table cluttered with cups and empty plates – Arty Robinson had put the time to good use. Shaven, dressed in clean clothes and with his eyes clear of the alcohol that had fogged them for so long, he was like a new man. 'But then,' he continued, 'we were hardly in a state to be noticing what was plugged in where. We were only concerned about Eric.'

'So it could have been there when you entered the flat?' asked Samson.

'It must have been,' said Arty. 'That would explain why I noticed the oxygen machine had gone out from my balcony, yet it was working when we got into Eric's.'

'You mean someone set the timer to turn off the oxygen in the middle of the night, but was cunning enough to have it set to come back on again?' Delilah looked shocked.

'Precisely,' said Samson.

'So when Eric was discovered,' she continued, 'no one would suspect the cause of his collapse.'

'Goodness!' Edith exclaimed. 'That's wicked. Who would do such a thing?'

'That's what I'm hoping to find out,' said Samson. 'We now have reason to believe that Alice, Eric and Rita were targeted. Alice's medication was tampered with, Eric's oxygen machine was deliberately turned off, and Rita was made to fall down the stairs.'

'We're accepting that someone made sure that step was slippery, then?' asked Edith.

'In light of the rest of it, yes, I think that's a fair assumption to make.'

'So you really do think the residents of this place are in danger?'

He paused, not wanting to frighten the two women. Edith raised her chin and stared at him.

'Don't lie, Samson. We need to know the truth.'

'Yes,' he said, and Clarissa sank back in her chair, a hand reaching down to Tolpuddle's head, seeking comfort. 'But I will make sure no one else is harmed.'

'How?' demanded Arty. 'What can you do that will make us safe?'

Samson reached into his pocket and drew out the two keys he'd secured from Ida Capstick. He held one of them up. 'Firstly, I'm going to search Ana's office as we agreed.'

'When?'

'Tonight.'

'And what about that one?' asked Joseph, pointing at the second key.

'This,' said Samson, holding it up, 'is the other part of my plan. I'm going to stake out the building.'

'Where from?' asked Arty.

'Next door to you,' said Samson. 'This is the key for the guest suite.'

The air of relief was palpable. Arty was nodding his head in support, the two sisters were looking less pale and Joseph was patting his son on the back.

Delilah was also looking enthusiastic. 'A stake-out! The three of us. Me, you and Tolpuddle. It's a brilliant idea.'

'Oh no, not you two—' Samson was cut short by Clarissa Ralph.

'Tolpuddle, too? Oh, wonderful. I'll sleep better knowing this gorgeous dog is in the vicinity.'

Delilah grinned at Samson. 'That's that, then. I'll nip

home and fetch my pyjamas and my toothbrush. What time are we starting?'

Samson sighed. Somehow this investigation wasn't going quite how he'd planned it.

20

By ten o'clock that evening, Fellside Court was quiet. Standing to one side at the unlit window of the guest suite on the first floor, Samson peered round the curtains at the dark expanse opposite. The flats belonging to Eric and Alice were devoid of life. And while the residents' lounge still had a couple of table lamps glowing softly, it was empty. Directly below him, no light spilled out into the courtyard, the second guest suite and Rita Wilson's flat both being vacant.

In contrast, linking the two shadowy wings, the wall of glass shone brightly. The corridors of both floors were well illuminated, the twinkling fairy lights on the Christmas tree in the foyer adding colour.

'Bugger,' muttered Samson, staring down at his objective. How to get down there without being seen, when it was lit up like Blackpool in the autumn?

It would be risky. He'd have to take the chance that the staff were all gone and the residents in bed, or away for the Christmas holidays.

'What time are we setting off?'

Delilah was behind him in the darkened room. She was dressed from head to toe in black, a black scarf looped around the lower half of her face and a black woolly hat pulled down over her hair and forehead.

When she'd met him at the office earlier that evening it

wasn't just her outfit that had suggested she was taking this stake-out seriously. She'd also come equipped with a sleeping bag, washbag, towel, a shopping bag full of food – both for them and for Tolpuddle – a change of clothes and a small rucksack full of goodness knows what.

'It's a stake-out, not a sleepover,' he'd said.

She'd glowered at him. 'I'm well aware of that. But you'll thank me for this in the small hours when you get hungry.'

He'd glanced down at Tolpuddle, the dog regarding him back with a raised eyebrow. 'You've even taken the collar off the dog?'

'The buckle,' she explained. 'It would catch the light and give him away.'

Samson had known then that it was going to be a long assignment.

They'd returned to Fellside Court just before teatime under the guise of joining Joseph for a meal, Delilah having the sense to add a bright-red coat to her outfit to make her look less like a rogue ninja. They'd signed the visitors' book and two hours later, when it was dark, they'd signed out and left the building through the courtyard. They'd turned left onto the path that looped round to the front, but as they approached the end of the north-facing wing, Samson had paused by the fire exit.

He knocked. Three quiet taps, Delilah and Tolpuddle shifting restlessly next to him.

The door had opened and Edith Hird had ushered them quickly inside into the stairwell.

'All clear,' she whispered, gesturing for them to go up the stairs. 'Arty's waiting for you.'

Sure enough, when the three of them reached the first floor, Arty was standing chatting to Joseph in the hallway, looking casual. Without even breaking off his conversation, he'd opened the door into the corridor and Samson, with his two accomplices, had hurried across the brightly lit area and down past Arty's flat. Within seconds they were safely inside the guest suite.

That had been an hour ago. The intervening sixty minutes had been spent with Delilah sorting out the bedding arrangements – her and Tolpuddle in the main bedroom, Samson on the couch – and then making a flask of tea. Once the essential details were arranged satisfactorily, she'd settled in a chair facing the patio doors, watching. And asking the same question at frequent intervals.

'I said, when are we setting off?' she repeated.

'I heard you the first time,' Samson muttered. He stepped away from the window and checked the time. 'Five minutes. And there's no "we" about it. You two are staying here.'

Tolpuddle sighed, head heavy on his paws, and Delilah nodded. 'Thought you'd say that. Give me your phone.'

'Why?'

'You need backup,' she said, holding out her hand.

He passed over his mobile and she reached for her rucksack, pulling out a set of wireless earphones.

'Put these on,' she said as she concentrated on his phone. With a few swipes of her fingers she was done. 'There. All sorted.'

She passed him back his mobile, the screen showing video footage. It was the foyer downstairs.

'How . . . ?' he asked as he slipped the earpieces in. The soft sound of silence being recorded filtered through.

'I used a pinhole camera and linked it to your mobile. You have audio and visuals of the immediate area outside Ana's office door. If anyone approaches while you're in there, you'll get a couple of minutes' warning.'

He grinned, impressed. 'Where's the camera?'

She grinned back. 'Inside a Christmas decoration. I hung it on the tree when we were signing the guest register. And this,' she continued, pulling a small device out of her bag, 'is another camera. I'll set it up here in the window to give you a wider view of outside.'

The image on Samson's screen split into two, the empty foyer now joined by the equally empty courtyard.

'What about the front?' he asked.

'It's taken care of.' As she spoke, a third view appeared on his phone showing the path to the main entrance.

'Dad?'

She nodded. 'A camera in his window. The audio is turned on in all three cameras, so you'll be able to hear what's happening but you won't be able to reply.'

'Got it,' he said as a loud cough sounded in his ear. His father. He stared at the phone and then at Delilah, astonished not for the first time at the technical abilities of the woman who'd been a gawky teen when he'd left fourteen years ago. 'Where did you get all this?'

'At a tech fair last summer.' She shrugged. 'It was all about security in the world of technology. I came away with some freebies and thought they would come in useful.'

He nodded towards the rucksack. 'What else have you got in there?'

'Thought you'd never ask.' She reached into it again and came out with a memory stick. 'Here. Pop this in the computer as soon as you get into the office.'

'Won't there be a password?'

Delilah laughed as she dropped the USB drive into his hand. 'I hope so, otherwise I've done all this for nothing. I've loaded it with software that will bypass the normal boot-up, so when you're asked for the password, you can enter whatever you like. This will do the rest.'

'It'll copy all the files? Emails included?'

'Yes. And then close down the computer. All while you're having a good look around at everything else.'

'What about the password? Won't Ana know someone's changed it?'

'Nope. As long as you don't pull the USB drive out before it's finished, the computer will be exactly the same as it was before you tampered with it.'

Samson shook his head in awe. 'I'm not sure if you're a genius or a devil.'

She smiled up at him, eyes twinkling in the gloom of the darkened room. 'A bit of both, I'd say.'

'Right,' he said, somewhat abruptly. 'Let's get this show on the road.' He strode across the lounge and into the hall.

'Good luck,' said Delilah from the window.

Samson didn't reply. He was too busy trying to remember when he'd last felt the urge to kiss someone he was on a stake-out with.

Never. Until now. And it was a Metcalfe at that. He must be suicidal.

He slipped into the empty corridor, happy to be out of

a situation that was far more dangerous than the one he was about to enter.

The office door closed softly behind him and he paused in the dark. Opposite, the window was covered by closed venetian blinds, allowing him to risk his torch. He switched it on and the room came into focus.

Observe. Assess. No rash movements. Take the time to work out an exit strategy.

It wasn't the biggest of spaces. A desk, with a computer screen atop and chairs positioned in front and behind, was set perpendicular to the window. Tucked under the windowsill between the desk and the right-hand wall was a printer on a unit of drawers.

Down the other side of the room, a grey filing cabinet sat in the far corner. Next to it, an antique bookcase stretched across the wall. And to his left, two club chairs were situated around a small coffee table.

Apart from the bookcase with its scrollwork and heavy mahogany shelving, the furniture all looked like it came out of IKEA. Practical. Simple. Functional. A brightly coloured rug covered the floor by the coffee table, the only splash of colour in the otherwise neutral tones.

None of it told him anything about the woman he was investigating. It was as featureless as the lady herself, hidden behind her mask of efficiency.

Memory key in hand, Samson sat at the desk and turned on the computer. As Delilah had promised, within less than a minute he had access, a small flashing light on the USB drive indicating it was downloading. Everything.

Switching off the computer monitor as a precaution, he

left the gadgetry to do its work but remained sitting in the chair, turning his attention to the desk. It was tidy. Impeccably so. A tray of paperwork to one side, a telephone and a small lamp on the other. Nothing else on display. No photos on the surface. No tacky souvenirs. No reminders of home and the family Ana must have left behind.

He twisted round to look at the shelves on the wall.

A spider plant, looking healthy. A couple of reference books. Some ring binders. An open packet of printer paper and several boxes of envelopes of different sizes.

No dust. But that would be more due to Ida Capstick than Ana.

Flicking a quick glance at the camera footage on his mobile, he saw nothing to concern him, the courtyard empty, the hallway beyond the office door devoid of life.

Time to have a look in the filing cabinet.

Being undercover was boring.

That was the conclusion Delilah had come to after ten minutes of sitting in the dark, staring out of the window while Tolpuddle snored softly behind her.

Boring and sleep-inducing. Already she was fighting the downwards pull of her heavy eyelids, her yawns becoming wider and longer. She was going to nod off at her post if she wasn't careful.

Food. That's what she needed. Food and caffeine.

Reaching for the shopping bag, she grabbed the flask she'd made earlier, pouring the tea in the gloom of the flat. Resting the cup on the windowsill, she reached back into the bag and got a packet of biscuits. Hobnobs.

She opened the packet, dipped one in her tea and bit into it. Better. Much better.

A soft nudge at her elbow told her she had company. The previously dormant dog, woken by the rustle of a biscuit packet, which he could hear even in the deepest sleep, was now staring at her with doleful eyes. Pleading for her to spare him a bite.

'You've got your own,' she whispered, taking a couple of Dog-gestives out of the bag. She passed one to the grateful hound and left the other on the windowsill. Next to the cup of tea.

It wasn't to prove the wisest of moves.

The bottom drawer of the filing cabinet yielded nothing out of the ordinary. Invoices, marketing material, archived accounts – the endless paperwork essential to run a place like Fellside Court. The drawers above, however, gave Samson pause for thought.

He came across the personnel files first. Ida Capstick had a slim folder; the staff that ran the cafe, likewise. He had a brief look at all of them but nothing stood out. Vicky Hudson's file was more substantial, records of the training she'd undertaken as a care assistant and copies of her certificates – Level 1 and Level 2 in Social Care and currently working towards Level 3. She'd been at Fellside Court since it opened three years before.

Ana Stoyanova's file was even thicker, though not as easy to understand. There was a handful of certificates, one possibly from a university, and a reference with an attached translation eulogising the young woman's skills and capabilities – all in the Cyrillic alphabet.

At least her CV was in English, listing Ana's studies at university in Sofia and revealing that she was a qualified nurse. A fact that surprised Samson. Surely she was over-qualified for her role at Fellside Court? Having spent six years working in Sofia after university, she'd moved to Manchester for a year, followed by six months in Leeds, all in the healthcare sector, before arriving in Bruncliffe in October.

She moved around a lot.

The final items in the file provided proof of Ana's English proficiency – results of exams taken years ago before she came to Britain. Interestingly, there were no employment references from her positions outside Bulgaria. He took photos of the certificates and the CV, closed the file and put it back.

The top drawer held information on the residents. Current and deceased.

Samson lifted out Alice Shepherd's file. Inside was a list of her prescribed medication, updated not long before she died. She'd been on Propranolol for high blood pressure. It meant nothing to the detective. But the fact that her dosage had been increased could be significant.

If Alice had been taking more each day as a matter of course, wouldn't that have made it easier for someone to push her dosage over the edge by persuading her that she hadn't taken her medicine?

He took more photos and replaced the file before turning his attention to the bookcase.

The shelves weren't exactly overflowing with light reading: *The Sociology of Healthcare*; *Good Practice with Vulnerable Adults*; *Promoting Health in Old Age*; *Drug*

Calculations for Nurses; *A Guide to Healthy Ageing*; *Keeping Active in Retirement*.

Samson paused and backed up . . . *Drug Calculations for Nurses*.

He pulled it off the shelf. It was well read, the pages marked in places with a neat hand – the same neat hand that had written Ana's name on the flyleaf.

She had a manual on calculating drug doses. Presumably that meant she knew how to medicate. Which would mean she also knew how to over-medicate. But then that would apply to anyone with basic medical training, let alone a qualified nurse.

He took a photo of the cover and the inside page anyway, before slipping the book back into place.

Only the drawers by the desk to go. So far he hadn't found anything conclusive that could point the finger of blame at the manager of Fellside Court.

Samson felt curiously relieved. He was secretly hoping his gut instinct was right: that Ana Stoyanova had nothing to do with what was going on in the retirement complex she was tasked with running.

A quick check of the cameras covering the outside showed nothing to alert him, so he moved behind the desk and opened the top drawer of the unit under the printer.

Tolpuddle was frustrated. He'd been given a biscuit. Which he'd eaten already. Now he was being expected to sit quietly while another biscuit was poised tantalisingly on the windowsill. It was there. Right in front of him. Smelling divine.

He stared at it and then at Delilah, but she was staring

out of the window, her concentration taken by something else.

He nudged her. A distracted hand fumbled backwards, finding his head. He allowed her to pet him. But he kept his focus on the biscuit.

'Good boy,' she whispered.

She spoke too soon. For Tolpuddle had got fed up of waiting. He stretched his front paws up onto the window-sill, grabbed the biscuit in his mouth and knocked over the cup of tea next to it.

The commotion that ensued went largely over his head. He was too busy eating his biscuit.

'Tolpuddle!' The frantic hiss was loud in Samson's ear, making him whip round in the empty office, forgetting for an instant where the sound was coming from.

'Bloody hell, Delilah,' he muttered, heartrate calming as he resumed his search and silence returned to his ear-piece.

He didn't check the phone. He figured that if Delilah was awake enough to be reprimanding the dog, she was awake enough to keep watch.

'Damn it!'

Delilah was frantically mopping at the dripping tea, Tolpuddle watching her warily.

He'd stepped up to get the Dog-gestive that she'd stupidly left within his reach and had sent her drink flying. All over the windowsill. All over the carpet.

She stood on the towel she'd brought with her, praying

it soaked up the liquid without staining. How would they explain that one?

She risked shining her torch on the cream carpet. It wasn't too bad. They might get away with it. Wiping up a trickle on the wall beneath the window, she dropped the damp towel back into her bag.

'It's my fault,' she said, ruffling the dog's ears. 'I forgot it was there, and you only did what was natural.'

He panted up at her, hot doggy biscuit-breath.

'No harm done, eh?'

She couldn't have been more wrong. For the camera sitting on the windowsill was soaked.

As Delilah fussed over the dog, her head bent down, she missed the shadow crossing the courtyard. The damaged camera, no longer transmitting images or audio, missed it too.

21

Samson had finally come across something of interest.

In the bottom drawer of the unit under the printer were some letters, held together by a red ribbon. He opened a couple, shining his torch across the paper. He couldn't understand them. But the handwriting style was universal. They'd been penned by a child.

A young child, judging by the erratic lettering, the sloping words, the drawings. A stick figure in a triangle dress decorated one of them, her hair yellow, a huge smile on her face, a stick-fingered hand held tightly by a boy next to her as they stood under a bright sun.

Mama. The word scrawled under the drawing needed no translation.

Ana had a child.

He photographed the letters before folding them back into their envelopes, noting that they'd been addressed to Fellside Court, not Ana's home. He checked the rest of the pile. They were all the same, and all were missing a return address. He took a few more photos and then retied the red ribbon around the envelopes.

It was only as he went to replace the letters that he realised there was something else in the drawer. Where his torch had shown what he'd thought was a black base, his fingers brushed against felt. And hard edges. The back of a picture frame.

He pulled it out and moved the light across it. Ana holding a young boy. The boy from the drawing? She was laughing, his blond head next to hers, his features as fine as hers. The glass covering the photograph showed smudges where fingers had picked it up countless times.

Why did she have it stashed away in the drawer?

Strange.

Even more curious, the reverse of the frame was bulging against the clips that held it in place. Something had been secreted inside it.

With his attention held by the object in his hand, Samson failed to glance at his phone on the desk. Failed to see the disturbing image it was projecting.

It was Tolpuddle who alerted Delilah to the danger. She'd been making a fuss of him, bent down below the level of the window, when he cocked his head, ears twitching.

'What is it?' She looked from the dog to the courtyard outside and froze.

Someone was bending down by the doors into the foyer, picking up a set of keys they'd dropped.

'Samson!' she hissed into the microphone. 'There's someone coming.'

She glanced at the screen on her mobile. Saw the blank space where her camera should be transmitting. And saw a gleam of blond hair outside the courtyard doors, captured by the fake bauble on the Christmas tree. The doors opened and the handsome features of Rick Procter were staring straight at the camera.

'It's Rick, Samson,' she hissed, her words going no further than the room she was in, thanks to the tea-sodden equipment. 'Rick's here. Abort now!'

But it was too late. She knew that. Samson would never manage to get out of there.

She was already crossing the room and heading for the door.

Two of the clips on the photo frame opened easily, swivelling on their hinges. But the other two were proving difficult. Using his penknife, Samson tried to lever them aside, but they wouldn't budge.

He poked the blade under the backing instead, feeling it hit against whatever was in there. Could he prise it out? Working carefully, he slid the blade backwards and forwards, the hidden item being manoeuvred closer to the opening. A brown envelope. As he edged it out, his fingers grabbing onto a corner, he heard a noise.

Outside in the corridor.

He glanced at his mobile. A shot of the front, looking serene. An oblong of black where the camera above the courtyard had failed. And a clear shot of Rick Procter's face as he crossed the foyer towards the office door.

Pulling the envelope free and slipping it in his jacket pocket, Samson placed the photo frame back under the letters, closed the drawer and tried to think of a plausible excuse for being in Ana Stoyanova's office. Because there was no way he could get out of there in time.

He heard the doorknob rattle and prepared to bluff his way out of it.

*

He was at the office door, his hand on the doorknob, key in the lock.

'Rick!' she called out, slapping a smile across her panicked features as she walked towards him.

Rick Procter turned sharply, frowning. Then he stepped back from the door.

'Delilah?' A reciprocal smile tipped his lips, but the frown remained. 'What are you doing here so late?'

He was taking in the red coat, the scarf thrown over her shoulder. She made a show of checking her watch as she approached, struggling to get her breathing under control after that sprint out of the flat and down the stairs.

Look natural. Act natural.

'I lost track of the time,' she said with a grin, eyes dancing up at him. 'Luckily for me. I wouldn't have had the pleasure of bumping into you otherwise.'

He laughed, bending down to kiss her cheek, his hand lingering on her back. 'Who were you visiting?'

'Actually, I came on work.' She turned to gesture at the Christmas tree resplendent in the corner, and discreetly stepped out of his hold. 'I wanted a shot of this beauty for the website. Nothing says "home" like a welcoming Christmas tree.'

It was his turn to look at his watch. 'You came here at ten-thirty to take photos?'

She grinned and held up her hands in surrender. 'You've caught me out. I arrived at seven, but then Edith and Clarissa persuaded me up to theirs for a nightcap. I couldn't get away.'

He laughed again, this time the frown disappearing.

'Sounds like hell. Being locked in a small space with those two old birds.'

She forced a complicit look. 'I was glad to escape. So, what about you? You're not working this late too, are you?'

A casual wave of his hand provided no definite answer. 'Christmas,' he said. 'Keeps me busy. Which reminds me, we need to get together for a drink over the holidays. How does that sound?'

'Like an excellent plan,' she said, letting a bright smile light her words. 'No time like the present.'

He grimaced, looking genuinely upset. 'I can't. I've got things to do. Soon, though, I promise,' he said. 'I'll text you where and when.'

'I'll be waiting,' she said. Then there was nothing else for her to do but leave. No reasonable excuse for her keeping him away from that door. Or what lay on the other side of it. 'I'll leave you to get on,' she said, aiming her words at the camera and praying that Samson had had enough time to escape. Although how that was possible with Rick in the corridor . . .

She walked towards the courtyard door, allowing the property developer to open it for her.

'Goodnight,' he said, brushing his lips across her cheek.

'Goodnight,' she said, managing to keep the panic out of her voice.

She heard the click of the lock sounding behind her and steeled herself not to turn round. Or to start running.

Delilah. She gave him the time he needed.

With her conversation with Rick playing in his ear,

Samson crossed the room and raised the blind a fraction, revealing the handle on the bottom rail of the window. The key was in it. He turned it and pushed, the window yawning open from the hinge at the top. Outside, a couple of shrubs grew up against the wall, reaching as high as the windowsill. Beyond that, the well-tended front lawn and Fell Lane, lit up by street lamps.

He'd be seen if he tried to cross the grass. He'd have to hide in the bushes.

Praying no one was out walking a dog, he lifted the blind with his hand, dipped under it and swung his right leg out. His toes could just reach the ground, the front lawns dropping away down the hill. Shifting his weight onto the leg that was now outside, he drew up his other leg and pulled it through the opening.

As his left foot hit the soil, he staggered backwards, the slope throwing him off balance, and his hand let go of the blind. It slapped back into place, sounding like a rifle shot.

He ducked below the windowsill. But there was no reaction, the door into the office staying shut.

He pushed the window closed and crouched down behind the bushes, the greenery prickling his skin, the cold cutting through his jacket and jeans. Disgruntled at having to fall out of yet another window to avoid Rick Procter, his mood wasn't improved when through his earpiece he heard the property developer asking Delilah out for a drink. He pulled out his mobile and studied the screen.

She was flirting with him. Eyes teasing, a smile dancing on her lips. It was a very convincing act. If it was an act.

Rick Procter was definitely buying it, showing her out

of the courtyard door, his hand on the small of her back. Then he leaned down and kissed her and a dark shaft of jealousy pierced Samson. He watched Delilah leave, out of earshot and out of sight, while Rick stood in the open doorway, his back to the foyer until she was gone. When he turned, the hidden camera caught the smile on his face.

It was feral. Samson hoped to God that Delilah knew what she was playing at.

He saw the property developer walk past the Christmas tree, put his key in the door and open the office. Then he disappeared off-screen, leaving Samson looking at the empty foyer and trying not to let his irrational annoyance at Delilah – the woman who had just saved his bacon – affect the operation he was supposed to be carrying out.

It was at that moment that he remembered the USB drive inserted in the computer.

Had she done enough? Delilah walked along the side of the building as slowly as possible, waiting to hear the shout of discovery. But nothing came. She edged to the front corner and peered round – Fell Lane was quiet, the police station brightly lit down the bottom of the road.

A dog barked somewhere in the town and she jumped. Tolpuddle. She needed to get back to him. She'd thrown a couple of Dog-gestives on the floor to keep him occupied when she hurried out of the guest suite, but he'd have demolished them by now. And then he'd realise that she wasn't there. Nor was Samson. Which would be enough to start him wailing. If that happened, the game was up, even if Samson had managed to conceal himself from Rick Procter.

Sending a quick text to Joseph O'Brien, she moved back to the fire exit and resisted the urge to hammer on the door.

She needed to get inside. Now.

It was only when the last crumb of biscuit had been licked up that Tolpuddle noticed the empty silence of the flat.

He walked through to the hallway, sniffed the floor, turned and headed back into the lounge. She wasn't there. She was gone.

Anxiety building, the dog padded across to the window, stretched onto his hind legs and looked out. There! She was below him, at the door of the courtyard.

He let out a small whine. Raised a paw to scratch at the window, hoping she'd notice. But she didn't. She walked beneath him, her red coat vibrant in the light spilling out from the wall of glass.

Then she turned the corner out of sight.

Tolpuddle waited, front paws on the windowsill. How many minutes? He didn't know. He sniffed the damaged microphone, which held an aroma of tea. He found a couple of biscuit crumbs up against the window frame. Then he started to fret.

She wasn't there.

He rubbed his nose against the cold of the glass and panic swelled inside him.

Samson was trying not to panic.

Squatting underneath the office window, the sharp edges of branches digging into him, he was telling himself it was too late to worry. Either Rick would discover the USB drive or he wouldn't. It was out of Samson's hands.

The light came on in the room behind, filtering round the edges of the closed blind and through the distortion in the slats where the window handle remained out of position. He might not be able to do anything about the memory stick, but at least he could watch what was happening.

Twisting around in the confined space, he squirmed upwards, raising his head slowly until his eyes were level with the warp in the blind.

He couldn't see much, the gap affording a restricted view. Down to his left, the red light blinking on the USB drive was visible as it worked away. Directly opposite, he could see Rick Procter. The property developer was moving away from the door, approaching the desk.

Another couple of steps and he'd be close enough to spot that the computer was on. That someone was copying all of its files.

Samson held his breath as the figure in the office came nearer the window. Then stopped.

Rick Procter had moved to Samson's right, towards the filing cabinet in the corner and out of sight.

'What happened?' whispered Joseph as Delilah squeezed through the fire exit and into the stairwell.

But she was already running up the stairs, the key to the guest suite in her hand.

'Can't explain now,' she hissed. 'I've got to get to Tolpuddle before he blows our cover.'

She was through the door on the first floor before Joseph had even got to the turn on the stairs.

*

The relief was short-lived. In the corner of Samson's limited vision, Rick Procter had reappeared and was coming back towards the desk. He walked round it and reached up to the shelves behind with his left hand, his right arm tucked in against his body, holding something.

If he turned a fraction towards the window, he would see the USB drive.

Samson couldn't look away, following the motion of the property developer's hand as it stretched out and took a large brown envelope from one of the boxes. Then Rick began to turn towards the desk. Began to turn towards the computer and the flashing red light of the USB drive.

Delilah hurried down the corridor, trying to be stealthy and fast, praying that she would be in time. She heard Arty's front door open as she went past but she didn't pause.

'Good boy, good boy,' she was muttering as she put the key in the lock and began to turn it.

It was like triggering a burglar alarm.

The door opened and a long, loud siren of distress came wailing out of the lounge, echoing down the corridor and through the building.

She swiftly closed the door after her, but the damage had been done.

It came from somewhere in the building. A howl of anguish, high-pitched and hair-raising.

Rick Procter flinched at the sound, twisting back round to face the door, whatever he'd been carrying spilling out of his grasp and falling to the floor on the far side of the desk.

He froze. Alert. Waiting to hear if it happened again.

After a few seconds he moved hastily around the desk and began gathering up the items he'd dropped.

The property developer was fast. But not fast enough. Through the gap in the blind, Samson saw what was on the carpet.

Rick Procter was picking up bundles of cash and stuffing them in the envelope.

What was Bruncliffe's self-made man doing with that much money? In cash? And why was he storing it at Fellside Court?

Rick turned off the lights and let himself out of the office, Samson watching the camera feed on his mobile as the property developer left through the courtyard. He was walking fast, head down, behaving as furtively as Samson himself. As if he shouldn't have been at Fellside Court that night, either.

Samson waited until Rick's Range Rover had driven past and down towards town before hauling himself back into the unlit office. With his mind still on the property developer's odd behaviour, he retrieved the USB key, closed down the computer and was at the door when he remembered. The envelope in his jacket pocket.

He pulled it out. A brown envelope, blank, the flap unsealed. He tipped the contents onto the desk and in the harsh light of the torch, the truth of what had been hidden behind the photograph stared up at Samson.

The evidence against Ana Stoyanova had just become damning.

22

'I'm so sorry!' whispered a contrite Delilah as she opened the door of the guest suite to Samson and let him into the dark of the hallway, the light from her mobile the only illumination. 'Tolpuddle didn't mean it. He couldn't help it—'

Samson put a finger to her lips. 'It's okay.' He grinned and held up the USB drive. 'Mission accomplished. And Tolpuddle was more a help than a hindrance. He put the wind up Rick Procter with that howl.'

The accomplice in question padded over to Samson and allowed his ears to be fondled and his head rubbed.

'Well,' hissed a voice from the gloom of the living room. 'Did you find anything?'

Samson looked at Delilah and she shrugged. 'They were all woken up by Tolpuddle's distress call. I didn't have the heart to send them back to bed.'

He stepped into the lounge to see four dark figures crouched around the coffee table, a weak torch on the floor between them casting an eerie glow across their elderly faces.

'We couldn't sleep,' explained Clarissa, wrapped in a fluffy dressing gown, cosy slippers on her feet.

'No one could sleep with the noise that dog made!' said Edith, likewise clad in her night attire.

Pyjamas poking out from under a jumper, Arty was sitting next to her, eyes alert despite the hour. And opposite him was Samson's father, his grey hair covered by a woollen hat, his slight figure swamped by a fleece bathrobe.

They were the most unlikely group of undercover operatives Samson had ever worked with.

'So,' asked Arty, 'what did you find?'

Samson tossed two passports onto the coffee table. One Bulgarian. The other Serbian. 'There's definitely something clandestine about the lovely Ana Stoyanova.'

'So she has dual nationality,' said Joseph, as they stared at the passports. 'Lots of people do. It doesn't make her a murderer.'

'Fair point, Dad. But have a look inside.'

Joseph did as Samson suggested, Arty leaning over his shoulder as he opened the Bulgarian passport, a younger Ana in the photograph.

'Anastasiya Stoyanova,' he read out. 'Place of birth, Sofia.' Then he opened the Serbian one. 'Ana Stoya—' He paused. 'Stoyano*vic*?'

'What else?' asked Samson.

His father looked at the Serbian passport again. 'Place of birth, *Belgrade*?'

'And the date of birth,' said Arty. 'The same year, but two months apart!'

Samson nodded. 'According to these, Ana was born in two different places at two different times. You can have dual nationality. But you can't have dual identities.'

'Maybe it's not hers?' said Clarissa, pointing at the Serbian passport. 'Maybe she's keeping it safe for a friend?'

Arty held it out so she could see the photograph. 'That's Ana,' he said. 'No doubt about it.'

'Or Anastasiya,' said Edith. 'We don't know which one is her real name. Or the real her.'

'But we do know which one she is using in order to be here.' Samson showed them the photos he'd taken in the office on his mobile. 'She's documented everything as Anastasiya Stoyanova. University qualifications, nursing qualifications, language certificates. As far as the UK authorities are concerned, the manager of Fellside Court is Bulgarian.'

'Yet she has a Serbian passport . . .' Arty shook his head.

'There's something else,' said Samson. 'She has a son.'

'A son?' Delilah looked up from her laptop, where she was busy uploading the files from Ana's computer. 'Odd that she never mentioned it. None of you knew?'

'No,' said Edith. 'Strange, isn't it? And she's never slipped up when talking to us about our families.'

'Strange?' Arty snorted. 'I'll say. She's clearly a brilliant actress. Makes you wonder what else she's hiding.'

'While I agree the passports are puzzling,' said Joseph, arms crossed over his chest, 'if Ana wants to keep her private life to herself, then that's her choice.'

'But you have to agree it's bizarre.' Edith had flicked to Samson's photos of the child's letter and the envelope it came in. 'Clearly she adores him. Yet she never talks about him.'

'And those letters are addressed here, not to her home,' pointed out Samson. 'Which is unusual. Where is her home, by the way?'

Edith frowned. 'You don't know?'

'No. Should I?'

'Well, seeing as you're practically neighbours, I thought you might have seen her out and about.'

'She lives in Hellifield,' offered Arty, sensing Samson's confusion. 'Like you.'

'Oh.' Samson nodded while frantically trying to think of a way to change the conversation before he was caught out in the lie he'd been perpetuating since the night of his arrival. The night he decided to sleep in Delilah's spare room. 'Oh, right, Hellifield . . .'

'So which is the real Ana?' continued Edith, oblivious to his unease. 'Is she Bulgarian or Serbian?'

'And,' muttered Arty, with a question that turned Samson's blood cold, 'what happened to whoever the other person is?'

Samson picked up the passports, Ana's blank expression stared up at him. Which was her? It was hard to say, the photographs taken eight years ago and with the lack of regard for flattering the subject that was common to all passports. They both depicted a young woman with pale skin and blonde hair who bore a strong resemblance to Ana Stoyanova.

'I think she's Serbian,' said Clarissa. She was hunched over Samson's mobile, peering at a photograph of an envelope that had contained one of Ana's son's letters.

'Here, try this,' said Arty, showing her how to enlarge the image with her fingers. 'Is that better?'

'Much better,' she beamed at him. She zoomed in even more. 'Look!' she said, holding the mobile up for everyone to see.

Two stamps, each bearing the image of a woman in what looked like military uniform against a background of war, filled the screen.

'What about them?' asked Edith.

'They're the stamps off that programme. Remember? The one about British women in the First World War?' She pointed at one of the women. 'This is Flora Sandes. She was the only British woman to bear arms in that conflict. And she was from Yorkshire. She somehow managed to get herself enrolled in the Serbian army—'

'Clarissa, it's hardly the time for a history lesson,' said Edith firmly.

'I'm not giving a history lesson,' said Clarissa with a rare outburst of indignation. 'I'm trying to help! These stamps are Serbian. Ana's son lives in Serbia. Wouldn't that suggest she is Serbian?'

'Not only that,' added Delilah, finally looking up from her laptop where she'd been going through Ana's email account. 'The majority of Ana's personal emails are from Serbia. Mostly from her mother, by the look of it.'

'So Ana is most likely Serbian,' mused Samson. 'And lying about her nationality.'

'And goodness knows what else,' muttered Arty. 'It doesn't bode well.'

'I can't believe she's from Serbia,' said Edith. Then she gasped, recalling a conversation in the cafe not that long ago. 'Goodness, poor old Eric!'

The others looked at her, comprehension dawning.

'No wonder Ana reacted so badly when he mistakenly said she was from Serbia,' continued Edith. 'She must have thought he'd rumbled her.'

'And then she tried to kill him.' Arty sat back in his chair, arms folded across his chest.

Joseph was shaking his head. 'You're seriously suggesting that Ana whatever-her-name-is has been killing people because she's trying to hide the fact she's from Serbia?'

'Yes, I am. Who was it who arranged our trip to Morecambe? Ana, that's who. She made sure we were handily out of the way, giving her the chance to fit that timer in Eric's flat.'

'That's ridiculous. Do all of you think this?'

Clarissa looked at Edith, who gestured at the passports. 'There's something going on, Joseph. Ana is lying about who she is. It doesn't speak of an honest person.'

'A killer, though?' He turned to Delilah and Samson. 'What about you two?'

Delilah pointed at the laptop. 'It'll take me an age to translate these emails but from the few I've seen, Ana is definitely hiding something. Whether that makes her a murderer, I couldn't say.'

'And you, son? You don't believe this nonsense, do you?'

To his own surprise, Samson found himself shaking his head, the glimmer of trust he had in Ana Stoyanova still not extinguished. 'Not all of it. While Ana is not the person we thought she was, it's too soon to start jumping to conclusions. What we need is more evidence.'

'How do you propose to get that?' asked Arty with scepticism.

Samson turned to him and smiled. 'By using you as bait, Arty. If you're game?'

*

'You're mad!' said Edith. 'This is too dangerous. You could be killed.'

Arty grinned. 'Didn't know you cared, Edith.'

She glared at him. 'Stop being so foolish, Arty Robinson. This is serious. And as for you,' she turned her fierce gaze on Samson, 'you should know better than to put a pensioner in harm's way.'

Transported back to primary school by the retired headmistress's wrath, Samson found himself momentarily tongue-tied. Delilah stepped into the breach.

'What else can we do, Edith?' she asked. 'We're all agreed that Ana is hiding something. But that's not enough to pin what happened to Alice and the others on her. At least this way we'll have a chance of triggering a reaction, rather than waiting for the next person to be targeted.'

'And Arty is to be the lure?' The tremor in Edith's words belied her anger.

'It'll be fine,' said Samson, finding his voice. 'Really, Edith. I'll be there the entire time. No one will come anywhere near Arty without me knowing.'

'We'll be there too,' said Delilah, nodding at Tolpuddle who was half-asleep while Clarissa rubbed his head. 'There's no need to worry.'

Edith stared at Arty. He was grinning and looking like his old self for the first time in weeks. Then she turned to Joseph. 'Can't you change their minds? Make them see how insane this is?'

The older O'Brien raised his hands. 'I don't see how. Everyone seems to think Ana is the devil incarnate. Perhaps this will finally clear her name?'

It wasn't the comfort Edith was seeking. She drew her

shoulders together and straightened her back, fixing Samson with her blue eyes. 'Well,' she said, 'if you are going to insist on this foolish venture, perhaps you'd better explain exactly how it's going to work. But I'm warning you, young man, if anything happens to Arty, I will be holding you responsible.'

Samson nodded, taking her warning with the seriousness it deserved. Then he cleared his throat and began to outline his plan.

'Do you think it will work?'

In the bleak hours of early morning, Delilah was standing in the doorway to the guest-suite lounge, her outline a mere shadow in the dark apartment. She padded over to where Samson was sitting, her feet bare, pyjamas and tousled hair making her look like the teenager he remembered. Apart from those curves.

He turned swiftly back to the window, resuming his watch. 'What are you doing up? You've got another two hours before you need to relieve me.'

'I couldn't sleep,' she murmured. 'I'm worried. About your plan. Do you think it will work?'

'I hope so. We don't have any other option.'

'And Arty? What if Edith's right and something happens to him?'

'I won't let it.' He tried to sound more confident than he felt. Because the reality was that in any operation there was always the chance something would go wrong. When the participants were laypeople – not to mention pensioners, a tempestuous young woman and a dog with anxiety issues – those odds increased.

Delilah nodded as though reassured. She perched on the edge of the chair he was sitting in, her thigh warm against his arm. 'I don't know how you did it for all those years.'

'Work undercover?' he asked.

'Yes. Hiding away all the time. Pretending to be someone you aren't. It's on a par with what Ana is doing. How did you cope?'

He tried to concentrate on her question and not on the fact that his arm was on fire. Or that she looked adorable in her sleepy state.

'You get used to it,' he said, thinking about the nights he'd spent on the streets courting danger. The days he'd spent hanging out in seedy bars and troubled neighbourhoods, blending in with those around him until he forgot who he was himself.

He *had* got used to it. But he'd also quickly got unused to it, his life in London already seeming an eternity ago. No contact with his father. No friends. And no Delilah.

A soft weight landed on his left foot, accompanied by a sigh as the sleeping dog turned over. No Tolpuddle, either.

If the call came tomorrow and he got the all-clear to return to his old job, would he do it? Could he do it?

'Well, at least you don't have to go around pretending any more,' said Delilah, smiling down at him, her features undefined in the gloom. 'You're amongst people who know exactly who you are.'

He smiled back at her, feeling every bit as duplicitous as Ana Stoyanova. For there were things about him that he was hoping Bruncliffe would never discover. 'You should get some more sleep,' he said. 'I'll be fine here.'

'Are you sure?' She yawned and stretched, her arms above her head, her pyjama top pulled tight across her chest. 'You don't want me to keep you company?'

He forced himself to stare out of the window at the sleeping building. 'No,' he said. 'I've got Tolpuddle for that.'

Hearing his name, the dog stirred in his slumber.

'Traitor,' muttered Delilah with another smile. 'He was supposed to sleep with me.'

Samson bit back a retort and forced himself to consult the screen on his mobile, the cameras showing nothing new.

'I'll see you in a couple of hours. Make sure you wake me,' said Delilah, standing up. Then she dipped down and kissed his cheek. 'Goodnight.'

He waited for the bedroom door to close before he released the breath he'd been holding. Coffee. He needed coffee. And a cold shower. Anything to get his mind back on the job and away from the woman in the next room.

Tolpuddle sighed again and Samson reached down to stroke him.

'Some help you are,' he said. Then he recoiled, hand to his nose. 'Damn it, Tolpuddle!'

The strong odour of recycled beer wafted up from the floor. It was enough to make Samson forget all about Delilah's charms. He stood up and edged away from the smell, to the far side of the window. Which is how he saw it.

Behind the wall of glass, a flash of blonde hair coming down the corridor on the first floor. Ana Stoyanova.

Creeping around the building in the middle of the night. How had she got in without them knowing? And why was she there?

Moving swiftly across the flat, Samson cracked opened the front door just in time to see the door to the stairs swing softly closed. He inched across the corridor, checked the stairway was clear, and followed her down, keeping an eye on the video feed from the camera in the Christmas tree as he went.

When he reached the ground floor he peered out of the glass panel in the door at the bottom of the stairs. The corridor was empty. Ana hadn't passed the camera outside her office or gone out into the courtyard. Yet she was nowhere to be seen.

Ana Stoyanova had disappeared.

Concerned that he might be underestimating his target, he slipped back upstairs and into the apartment, wide awake and worried.

Perhaps Delilah was right to have concerns. After all, in a few hours they would be putting Arty's life at stake.

23

After a night on watch with a few snatched hours of sleep, Samson wasn't in the brightest of moods as Christmas Eve dawned. It didn't help that he'd been torn from a dream featuring Delilah lying next to him on a beach, back to the reality of being on the sofa with Tolpuddle lying on his legs – Tolpuddle, who was only slightly less odorous than the night before.

'Seriously,' Samson muttered as he stuffed his sleeping bag into a small rucksack, 'you need to stop feeding that dog beer.'

'It was Clarissa,' said Delilah with a smile, looking far better than she had a right to after a stake-out. 'And good morning, by the way.'

Samson grunted. 'If you say so. I take it nothing happened while I slept?'

'Quiet as a mouse. If Ana is up to something, she behaved herself last night.'

Samson just nodded. When they'd swapped shifts two hours ago he hadn't mentioned seeing the blonde-haired manager prowling the corridor. Or that she'd disappeared on him. For some reason he still felt the urge to give Ana Stoyanova the benefit of the doubt. He only hoped it wouldn't backfire on him.

He hadn't mentioned Rick Procter's activities, either.

Those bundles of cash the property developer had been ferreting away in an envelope. Something told Samson to file that away for now. Until he could find out more about it.

'Anyway,' continued Delilah. 'Get a move on – your dad's just texted to say he's got bacon frying and the sausages are in the oven. We're to head over when we're ready.'

Christmas Eve fry-up. Samson couldn't remember when he'd last had one. Probably the December after Mum died. Dad had been trying to cling to the traditions they'd established in their brief time as a family and had done his best, despite the drink already having a hold on him. By the following Christmas Eve, and for all subsequent ones until Samson left home, Joseph O'Brien had never been out of bed in time for breakfast. Or if he had, it was simply because he was slumped at the kitchen table in an alcoholic stupor, not having made it upstairs the night before. Samson wasn't sure that counted.

'A fry-up,' muttered Samson, his bad humour darkening with the memories. 'Just like old times.'

They packed up their stuff, leaving the flat as they'd found it – apart from a slight whiff of stale hops – and sneaked along the corridor past Arty's flat to the open door of an apartment round the corner, opposite the wall of glass.

Joseph O'Brien was waiting for them, apron on and spatula in hand. 'How do you like your eggs?' he asked with a smile.

'Any way at all,' said Delilah, kissing his cheek. 'I'm starving! All this detective work is making me hungry.'

'And you, son? Sunny side up still?'

'Whatever,' muttered Samson. Because when he saw Delilah leaning in to greet his father, it reminded him of the night before. She'd been flirting with Rick Procter and she'd agreed to go on a date with him.

With his desire to eat already dulled by the thought that a man's life was about to be put in danger, suddenly Samson O'Brien had no appetite at all.

Arty joined them for breakfast, the four of them squeezed around Joseph's small dining table consuming fried eggs, smoky bacon and thick local sausages while they held a council of war. Tolpuddle lay on the floor monitoring every transfer of food from plate to mouth with endless optimism.

'Wait until mid-afternoon, Arty, and then make your move,' Samson said as he mopped up the last of the yolk with a crust of bread, his fickle appetite having reappeared the minute the fry-up was placed in front of him. 'Any sooner and it gives us longer to have to monitor her.'

'Which will make it more risky?' asked Joseph, looking worried.

'More difficult,' countered Samson in an attempt to allay their fears.

Arty laughed, a sound that hadn't been heard too much inside the walls of Fellside Court of late. 'Don't worry, I'll do exactly as you said. I've no intention of being a hero.'

'And me?' asked Joseph. 'What do you want me to do?'

'Act natural. Just do whatever you'd normally do on Christmas Eve,' said Samson.

Joseph gave him a wry look. 'You mean sit here on my

own and try not to think about everyone opening bottles of booze?'

Delilah put her hand over his. 'I never thought,' she said. 'This has to be the hardest time of the year for you.'

'Christmas Eve, Christmas Day and New Year. Those are the worst days to get through. Which never makes sense to me, as us alcoholics don't exactly need a special day to get drunk. Still, dying for a drink is better than dying because of one.' Joseph glanced at Samson, but the lad's face was inscrutable.

'Is there anything else we need to do?' asked Delilah, sensing the unwelcome memories crowding the already cramped table.

'Arty and Dad have to go into town and get the wreath,' said Samson. 'And then you need to make your special adaptations to it.'

She smiled. 'With pleasure.'

'What about Edith and Clarissa?' Joseph tipped his head in the direction of the sisters' flat at the far end of the corridor. 'They'll want to be involved.'

Samson shook his head. 'Let's keep them out of this. The fewer people involved in the action, the better. Ana will be less likely to smell a rat.'

'And Edith will be less likely to get upset,' said Arty with affection.

'So that's it, then. We're ready to go?' Delilah asked, beginning to clear the dishes.

'As long as Arty is still willing to go ahead with it.' Samson looked at the rotund man in the chair opposite.

'Willing and eager,' said Arty, his face solemn. 'It's the

least I could do for Alice and the others. And I might finally get a good night's sleep at the end of it.'

'In that case, let's get going.' Samson made to leave the table, but his father's hand on his arm held him back.

'Take care, son. Of Arty and of yourself.'

Caught unawares by his father's affection, Samson was reduced to a perfunctory nod in response.

'You too, Joseph,' said Delilah, hugging the older man with an ease Samson envied. 'If the temptation gets too much tonight, text me and I'll call round.'

Joseph laughed off her concern. 'I'll be fine. I'll have my hot milk as usual and be off to sleep in no time. I won't even wake up when Father Christmas comes creeping in.'

'Just as well,' said Samson. 'Delilah might not be around to help anyway. She's expecting Rick Procter to take her out on a hot date any time soon.'

'Rick?' Joseph swung round to look at her in surprise. 'I didn't think he was your type.'

'It's a long story,' Delilah said, casting an arch look at Samson. 'I was helping out a friend and got roped into it. I'd forgotten all about it. Good job your son reminded me.'

Wanting to kick himself for being so immature, Samson followed Arty and Delilah out of the flat. He wasn't in the best frame of mind for launching a covert operation. He certainly wasn't in the mood for Christmas.

Arty did exactly as he was told. He wandered down into town with Joseph, making a beeline for the festive market like a man who'd decided it was time to celebrate the season. He bought some snow-frosted gingerbread men for Edith and Clarissa, a beautiful wreath of holly and ivy from the man selling Christmas trees and, when Joseph was dallying over a selection of handmade fudge and chocolates, Arty impulsively purchased a rocking reindeer that danced to 'Jingle Bell Rock'. Joseph would love it.

The gingerbread men he put in his pocket. The wreath and the reindeer went in his blue Co-op bag. At precisely ten forty-five, the two men entered Peaks Patisserie. It was crowded and so it was perfectly normal that Delilah Metcalfe, who was already at a table, waved them over to join her.

They talked for a few minutes, Delilah asking them their plans for the following day. Then, as Lucy came over to take an order from the new arrivals, Delilah got up to leave. She wished the old men a happy Christmas, gave her sister-in-law a quick hug, picked up her bags and left, collecting the waiting Tolpuddle from outside the door as she went.

No one thought twice about the blue carrier bag she had with her. It was the one she'd walked in with half an hour ago.

She forced herself to walk naturally through the marketplace and down Back Street to the office. As she reached the front door, a voice beckoned her from the Fleece opposite. The low growl from Tolpuddle told her who it was before she'd even turned to see.

'Delilah? You're not working today, are you?' Rick Procter was standing in the doorway, pint in hand. 'Come and join me for that drink you promised.'

'Sorry, I can't right now.' She pulled what she hoped was a realistically disappointed face, while Tolpuddle continued to rumble deep in his throat. 'I've got a few things that need doing. Later maybe.'

He smiled, his blond hair and handsome features making him look more like a model than a builder. 'I'll hold you to that.' He raised his pint and disappeared back into the pub, leaving her and the dog to enter the office in relief. She raced upstairs and pulled the wreath out of the Co-op bag and onto her desk. It was only then she noticed the other item in there.

A toy reindeer dressed in a Santa outfit. She sat it on the desk and pushed the small button in its back, the strains of 'Jingle Bell Rock' ringing out and making her laugh as the reindeer started rocking. From his bed in the corner, Tolpuddle regarded it with a curious air.

'Two for the price of one,' murmured Delilah, as she got down to work. It hadn't been in the plan, but it was a brilliant idea.

'Act naturally, for goodness' sake,' hissed Arty as Joseph shifted in his chair and looked around the cafe for the umpteenth time. 'You'll give the game away.'

'I can't,' muttered Joseph. 'I'm so tense. How the hell did Samson do this for a living?'

Arty took a drink of coffee. He was being careful to only take small sips, partly to prolong the drink until Delilah came back, but also because if he had more than one cup he'd need the toilet. Which wasn't in the plan.

'Arty! Joseph! Fancy meeting you two here.'

Arty knew the voice. Would know it anywhere. Edith Hird and her sister Clarissa were making their way across the cafe, looking every bit as furtive as Joseph.

'What are you doing here?' he muttered as they took the spare seats.

Edith smiled at him, eyes bright with excitement. 'What – did you think we'd stay home and miss all the fun?' She gestured Lucy Metcalfe over. 'Two coffees, please, Lucy. Oh, what about you boys? Will you have another?'

Joseph looked at Arty, who shrugged. 'Might as well,' he said, deciding it was okay to deviate from the plan after all. 'And some of those mince pies too, Lucy.'

'And a couple of slices of Yule log,' added Clarissa with a cheeky smile.

Arty laughed, beginning to relax into this detective lark. If they were going to be undercover, they might as well enjoy it.

It was done. And both cameras worked at the required distance.

Mobile in hand, Delilah left the kitchen, two different images of a snoozing Weimaraner on the screen in front of her and the gentle sound of dog-snores issuing from the speaker.

'Come on, Lazy,' she said as she entered the office, Tolpuddle still in his bed under the watchful eye of the Christmas wreath and the Santa reindeer. 'We've got a rendezvous to get to.'

It was only as she picked up the wreath to put it back in the Co-op bag that Delilah noticed her hands shaking. Excitement, fizzing around her system like a double shot of caffeine.

'Act natural,' she muttered to herself as she put the reindeer in with the wreath. 'He said to act natural.'

Over in the corner the dog stretched, yawned and got to his feet to join her. As far as undercover operations went, Tolpuddle was taking it all in his stride.

'Here she comes!' whispered Clarissa, leaning in over the table with urgency.

'For heaven's sake,' hissed her sister. 'Calm down or you'll give the game away.'

'Hello again!' Delilah was approaching, a smile on her face, shopping bag in her hand. She leaned down to talk to Arty and placed the bag on the floor. Next to an identical one that was already there. 'I forgot to mention,' she said, addressing the two men, 'I was speaking to Mum last night and she said that if you pair have nowhere to go for Christmas dinner tomorrow, you're more than welcome to join us. Samson, too.'

'Oh,' Arty stumbled. 'That's . . .'

'Most kind,' said Joseph, patting Delilah on the arm. 'Tell Peggy we accept. And I'll persuade Samson to come as well.'

Delilah beamed down at him.

'What a generous offer,' said Edith, nodding with approval. 'We'll feel better when we're tucking into turkey with our family, knowing this pair are having a good time. Won't we, Clarissa?'

'Oh yes. Much better.'

'Good. That's sorted then. I'll text to let you know what time I'm coming for you,' said Delilah. She picked up the blue Co-op bag nearest to the table, wished the sisters a merry Christmas and left, a bemused Arty staring after her.

'That wasn't in the script,' he muttered at Joseph.

'No,' said the Irishman, watching Delilah untying Tolpuddle's lead outside. 'But I've a feeling it was genuine.'

'Delilah!' Lucy Metcalfe was descending the steps of her cafe, apron covered in flour, black smudges of fatigue on her face. She waited until she was alongside her sister-in-law before speaking again. 'What's going on?' she asked quietly.

Delilah turned wide eyes to face her. 'Nothing.'

'Don't lie. You're rubbish at it. Those four old folk are huddled over the table in there drinking too much coffee and twitching every time the door opens. And you're in the middle of it. So what's going on?'

'I can't say.'

'Is it something to do with Samson's work?'

'Possibly. I honestly can't tell you any more than that.'

Lucy stared at her, a frown on her pale face. 'Just remember what happened last time, okay? Be careful.'

'I will. I promise,' said Delilah, feeling awful for adding to her sister-in-law's stress at a time when she was flat out with work.

'Oh, and another thing,' added Lucy, with a mischievous smile. 'I couldn't help but overhear your generous gesture. Does Peggy know you're bringing Arty, Joseph and Samson to Christmas dinner at Ellershaw?'

Delilah grimaced. 'Not exactly.'

'And Will?' The silence that greeted her question made Lucy laugh. 'Thought not. I can't wait for tomorrow,' she said.

With a quick kiss on the cheek, Lucy rushed back into the busy cafe. Delilah and Tolpuddle headed back to the office, Tolpuddle thinking about the warm bed waiting for him; Delilah thinking about how badly things could go awry when she decided to act natural.

Ana was the first to comment on the wreath on Arty's door.

He'd hung it up as soon as they got back from town, Joseph and the sisters watching him with the solemnity reserved for a funeral, knowing the circle of greenery was more than just a nod to the season; thanks to its hidden camera pointing down the corridor, it was Arty's amulet against evil.

With the euphoria of their cafe trip wearing off and their stomachs still full of mince pies and Yule log, the four of them had decided to skip lunch and instead had retired to the residents' lounge for a quiet afternoon. And to put the next part of the plan into action.

In the pre-Christmas exodus, the lounge was almost empty. On the sofa nearest the door, two women were knitting, the small suitcases next to their feet suggesting they were expecting family to arrive any moment. In the far corner, the immaculately styled Geraldine Mortimer was sitting in an armchair, chatting to a friend. The women all looked up as the group entered, Geraldine flashing a smile in Arty's direction before she resumed her conversation.

'I thought she was going to London for Christmas?' Joseph whispered.

Edith shook her head, a rare expression of sympathy

on her face as she regarded the unfortunate Geraldine. 'Her son was supposed to be picking her up on Monday after the party, but he cancelled at the last minute.'

'That's harsh,' said Arty. 'She must be upset.'

'Hard to tell,' muttered Edith. 'She just keeps saying that the responsibilities of a high-flying barrister understandably take precedence over Christmas with her.'

'We could invite her to spend it with us,' said Clarissa, looking earnestly at her sister.

Edith gave a sharp laugh. 'It might be the season of goodwill, but I still don't have enough to endure a day with that woman!'

'Game of crib?' Joseph asked Arty, pulling a packet of cards out of his pocket and taking a seat, as Edith and Clarissa went over to talk to the women who were knitting. Soon engrossed in a good game of cribbage, Arty almost forgot why he was there. Until Ana Stoyanova walked in.

'Arty,' she said, approaching with a smile, her hair swept back into a ponytail, her cheeks sharp under her flawless skin. She was beautiful. But rotten to the core. 'I see you have embraced Christmas at last. What a lovely wreath.'

He forced a smile in response, aware that his heart was pattering dangerously. 'Joseph talked me into it.'

Ana turned to the Irishman. 'Good for you,' she said. 'Arty needed cheering up.'

'I think we all do, after the last few weeks,' said Joseph.

A slight tick pulsed at the base of Ana's jaw and she glanced down. 'Yes,' she murmured. 'It's not been the best of times.'

'Any word on how Rita's doing?' asked Arty.

'She's still unconscious.' Ana shook her head sadly. 'So awful for the family.'

'Talking of family,' said Arty, 'will you be in touch with home tomorrow?'

'If I get time.' The reply was polite but curt, a trace of pink stealing across Ana's pallor.

'You should make time,' persisted Arty pointedly. 'Nothing like family at Christmas.'

'And you two?' she asked. 'Where will you spend it?'

'We've been invited to the Metcalfes' farm,' said Joseph, intervening in an attempt to deflect Arty's barbs. 'A very generous offer on their part.'

Ana nodded, her smile returning. 'Very generous. Well, have a lovely time.'

She was turning to go when Arty called her back. He stood up, making it clear that what he was about to say he didn't want anyone else to hear.

'I came across something odd,' he said, trying to keep his voice steady. 'Actually, it was Rita who came across it, buried outside in the copse by the car park, and she gave it to me.'

'What is it?' Ana was leaning in, concentrating on him.

He put his hand in his cardigan pocket and pulled out Alice Shepherd's pillbox.

It was as if he'd slapped her. She jerked back, mouth open, and stared at the rainbow colours in his hand.

'Where did you say you got it?'

'Buried in the snow outside. Rita found it a couple of days before she had her accident. I just wondered what to do with it.'

Ana was still staring at the box, but she made no move to take it. 'I thought Elaine Bullock had it.'

'That's the really strange thing. I thought so, too. So I called her and she said she's got one. Exactly like this.'

'So this . . .' Ana looked from the box to Arty, her forehead creased. 'This isn't the one Elaine took?'

'No.'

'There's two of them?'

Arty nodded. 'Like I said, it's odd, isn't it?'

'Very odd.' Then she held her hand out, her green eyes fixed on him. 'Would you like me to look after it until we get to the bottom of this?'

'No,' he said, putting the pillbox back in his pocket and setting himself firmly inside the trap. 'I'll hang onto it, if you don't mind. But I just thought I'd mention it. See if you knew any more about it.'

'Good idea,' she said, letting her hand fall back to her side. 'And perhaps keep this between us for now?'

He nodded, his heartrate at a level his doctor would not approve of.

'If you're sure you don't want me to take it—'

'Ana! I've had a brainwave!' Vicky Hudson was in the doorway. 'A small drinks party tonight after supper. What do you think, everyone? For those of us still here?'

Ana had a smile on her lips when she turned to greet her colleague, but not before Arty had witnessed the flash of irritation that had preceded it. 'What a wonderful idea. I just wonder if it would be appropriate, though, given the circumstances.'

'I think Rita would have been the first to sign up for it,' said Edith. 'If that's what you mean?'

'Edith's right,' said Joseph. 'Rita loves a party.'

'And a chance to get dressed up,' added Clarissa. 'Oh, do we need to get dressed up?'

'If you want to,' laughed Vicky. She turned to her boss. 'So, is that a yes?'

'I suppose it is,' said Ana. She turned back to Arty. 'I hope we'll have the pleasure of your company?' she murmured.

'I wouldn't miss it for the world.'

With a final tight smile, Ana Stoyanova left the lounge, and Arty couldn't help but feel the snare he'd created closing in around him.

24

As dusk fell over Bruncliffe, the marketplace long since emptied of stalls, the cafe closed, blinds pulled down over all the shop fronts, the town had an air of expectation about it. It was the night before Christmas, after all.

Up the hill past the police station, a similar sense of anticipation pervaded Fellside Court, despite its quiet corridors and darkened windows. For, in the lounge, the remaining residents were gathering for their pre-Christmas drinks.

'How do I look?' asked Arty, standing before Delilah in his hallway and pulling nervously at his sweater.

'Handsome,' said Delilah.

'Like a juicy morsel of bait?' The former bookmaker's voice shook slightly.

'We've got your back, Arty,' said Samson from the balcony doors. He was peering round the curtains to watch the brightly lit room down below, where Vicky and Ana were handing out glasses to people as they entered. 'She won't make a move until everyone has gone to bed.'

'*If* she makes a move,' said Joseph. 'Innocent until proven guilty, remember.'

Arty snorted. 'Sorry old friend, but Ana's guilty. You should have seen her face when I showed her the pillbox.'

'For your sake, I hope I'm right and you're wrong.' Joseph patted him on the shoulder. 'Come on then. Let's go put you on show and see if we can't spring this trap.'

Samson, Delilah and Tolpuddle followed them out and slipped into the guest suite next door, while Joseph and Arty headed for the stairs.

'Will he be all right?' Delilah asked as she pulled up the video feed on her computer. Added to the camera in Joseph's window over the front entrance and the one in the Christmas bauble in the foyer, which covered the courtyard door, she had two more views: the corridor outside Arty's flat, from his wreath; and a floor-level shot of inside his hallway and the door to his bedroom, from the bonus camera in the reindeer.

'How can he not be?' said Samson, pointing at the images on her screen. 'No one can get in Fellside Court without us seeing. And no one can get near Arty without us knowing. We've got it covered.'

Delilah wished she shared his confidence. Her stomach was a knot of tension and she was as restless as a caged tiger. Just like when she was a child, she was eager for Christmas Eve to be over. Only this time she wasn't concerned about opening presents. She was concerned about keeping Arty Robinson alive.

Cameras, cameras everywhere. But not where they needed to be.

In the kitchen of Fellside Court a tray of mugs was resting on the stainless-steel worktop. In the bottom of the mugs, cocoa powder. A door slipped open, a shadow slid across the floor and a hand hovered over the tray, a small sachet in its grasp. With a practised flick, the sachet was emptied and its fine, white powder quickly mixed in, until the brown of the cocoa concealed it.

None of it was caught on camera.

'I don't think I've ever felt more alive,' murmured Arty as he stood in the lounge listening to the high-spirited chatter of the dozen or so residents.

'Make sure we keep it that way,' replied Joseph, tension visible in the tightness of his jaw and his fidgeting fingers. He'd been keeping a discreet eye on Ana Stoyanova, who was standing to one side, surveying the room with those beautiful green eyes, and the whole situation was making him nervous as hell. The thought that they might be placing Arty in jeopardy . . .

He swallowed. Watching everyone around him happily drinking alcohol wasn't helping. He had a thirst on him like he hadn't felt in two years.

He looked at his watch. An hour had passed since they'd arrived at the soirée, an event that had so far been as innocuous as the mineral water in his hand. Amongst the last to turn up, they'd reached the lounge as Geraldine Mortimer was hurrying along the corridor, Arty holding the door open for her.

'All the fashionable people arrive late,' she'd laughed, her blonde hair shimmering in the light, a long black dress clinging to her curves. She'd slipped her arm through Arty's and steered him towards the tray of drinks Vicky Hudson was holding. Poor Arty. He'd had to endure Geraldine gushing about her talented son, who'd just called to say he'd moved heaven and earth and was coming to pick her up after all, first thing in the morning. It had taken Joseph fifteen minutes to prise Arty away.

Since then, the two men had spent the time making small talk. At least Arty had. Joseph was finding it difficult to string two words together, his nerves stretched taut.

'Another canapé, you pair?' Vicky held out a plate, curls of smoked salmon on something Edith had said were called blinis. Whatever they were, they tasted good. Arty declined, patting his waist with a grin, but Joseph took a couple, hoping they would deaden the urge to drink.

'There she goes,' murmured Arty as Vicky moved out of earshot. He was looking towards the door; Ana Stoyanova was leaving the room.

Joseph's guts churned. He placed half an uneaten blini on a nearby plate. How had Samson done this for a living? The boy must be made of stern stuff.

'Still alive, then,' whispered Edith as she joined the two men, elegant in her long black skirt and silver top. She winked at Arty and he laughed, the sound rare enough in the last few weeks to cause some people to look his way. 'I don't know about you two, but Clarissa and I are ready to retire. All this excitement has exhausted us. So I'll see you both in the morning.'

She leaned over and, in an unusual display of affection, kissed Arty on the cheek. 'Stay safe,' she whispered.

'I intend to,' he said, capturing her hand and kissing it in return.

She nodded sharply, bestowed a peck on Joseph's cheek and walked away.

'One for the road, anyone?' Ana Stoyanova had re-appeared in the doorway, a tray of mugs in her hand. 'Hot chocolate with a kick,' she said as the residents crowded around her.

'How much of a kick?' asked Clarissa, abandoning her plans to go to bed and reaching for a mug.

'It's my grandmother's recipe, made with plum brandy from home,' said Ana, her face more animated than Joseph had ever seen it.

'Which home would that be?' muttered Arty under his breath as the two of them joined the group.

'Arty? Would you like one?' Ana held the tray out, only two mugs – one white, one red – left on it.

Joseph noticed the hesitation. Then Arty was reaching out to take the white mug.

'Why not?' he asked with a grin. 'It's Christmas.'

Joseph watched him raise the hot chocolate to his lips and drink, the smell of the brandy floating on the air, seducing the Irishman and making his throat clench with desire.

'Joseph?' Ana was holding out the red mug. 'It's for you. No alcohol.'

'Thanks,' he said. He took the hot chocolate and made himself drink it, when all he wanted to do was run away from the intoxicating lure of his nemesis.

'That,' said Arty, smacking his lips in appreciation, 'was the best hot chocolate ever.'

Ana smiled. 'Thank you. I think you haven't slept for a long time? Hopefully you will sleep well now. Goodnight.'

She walked away and the blood drained from Arty's face.

'He's home,' said Delilah from the floor of the kitchen in the unlit guest suite. She was huddled over her laptop, the screen set as dark as possible and twisted away from the window to contain the light it emitted. Tolpuddle was sprawled on the lino beside her, fast asleep.

'Everything okay?' Samson was over by the darkened window, watching the last of the residents leave the lounge, Ana and Vicky clearing up behind them.

'Yes. He gave a thumbs up to the wreath and he's just in the hall.' She watched as a pair of shoes walked past the reindeer camera, heading for the lounge. A faint sound of a TV came through the wall.

'So he's in and settled. Now the fun starts.'

'Glad you're finding this funny,' came a mutter from the kitchen. 'I've never felt so terrified.'

Samson didn't reply. Truth be told, he'd never felt less like laughing. In all the operations he'd run during his time undercover, he'd only ever had his own life on the line. Tonight he was risking that of a friend.

He was every bit as nervous as Delilah.

That white powder, so skilfully mixed into chocolate, was beginning to have an effect. Already he was feeling mellow, his limbs relaxing, his body slumped in his chair in the dark lounge. He hadn't managed to get as far as a light. And now he couldn't have got up if he had to. Not even if his life was in danger.

He focused on the television, the pictures a blur, the sound distorted. If he'd been capable of coherent thought, he'd have known he was drunk. Or something close to it.

Within an hour, he was unconscious.

'Anything?'

'Nothing. Not a peep since we saw her leave.'

'No one approaching the front door?'

'Nope. And before you ask, the camera in your dad's window is working fine.'

'How about the one in the foyer? Anything unusual?'

'Nothing.'

It was an hour and a half since Ana and Vicky had left Fellside Court, using the back door into the courtyard. Almost midnight. And nothing had happened.

Samson paced impatiently across the small lounge. 'Come on, Ana. It's time to make a move.'

'Perhaps we've got it all wrong?'

'You mean she's innocent?'

'It's possible.'

He returned to the window to stare at the wall of glass, thinking of the flash of blonde hair he'd seen the night before. She was up to something, Ana Stoyanova. But what?

It was easy. A key in the kitchen door. Through the kitchen, out into the cafe and then into the hallway. A right turn and the stairs were there. Even if the camera on the Christmas tree had been trained down the hallway instead of on the courtyard door, it probably wouldn't have caught any movement at that distance.

Up the stairs and there it was. The corridor and the wall of glass.

It was easy.

'Anything?'

'For God's sake, Samson,' hissed Delilah. 'Shut up. I'll tell you if I see anything.'

He glanced back out of the window, the sharp edge of tension fraying his nerves. It was the worst bit of an operation. The most exciting, too.

Outside the wind had picked up, tugging at the tables and chairs in the courtyard, blustering against the glass. He returned his attention to the brightly lit corridor spanning the two wings just in time to see her.

'She's here!' he snapped. That blonde hair spilling out from under a baseball cap, face in shadow under the peak. She was keeping close to the back wall. Coming their way. 'Can you see her yet?'

'No,' Delilah said. 'Not yet.'

'She's gone from my line of sight. She must be close to the door now?'

'Nothing.' Delilah clicked on the camera in the wreath, enlarging the picture to full screen.

'Anything?'

'No.'

Samson strode over to the laptop, checking it over her shoulder. The tranquillity of the corridor outside Arty's flat reflected back at him.

'I don't get it,' he muttered, anxious.

'Perhaps we ought to check on him anyway?' urged Delilah.

Samson shook his head. 'No. We have to catch her in the act. Otherwise, we have nothing.'

'But Arty . . . ?' Delilah clicked the mouse, returning the screen to a view of all the video feed. She was just in time to see a pair of shoes walk past the reindeer camera.

A pair of women's shoes.

*

Inside. Down the hallway. Past the toy reindeer lying on the floor. Then creeping forward towards the bedroom. Hand held down by the side and in it, a syringe.

There would be no saving him.

'She's in there!' shouted Delilah, leaping up off the floor, laptop in hand, the dog stirring.

'How the hell—?' Samson was already running for the door.

'I don't know how, but she's in there. Quick!'

They burst out into the corridor, no attempt at discretion, Samson already fitting the spare key into the lock. Turning it. Racing inside.

'What on earth—?' Arty was standing in the hallway in his pyjamas, a hand held to his chest, the other wielding a golf club. Eyes wide with fright, he stared at them. 'Are you trying to give me a heart attack?'

'Where is she?' demanded Samson. 'Ana was in here.'

Arty shook his head. 'No. There's no one here – only you two.'

But Delilah was pointing at her laptop. 'She's here. Look!'

The women's shoes were back in shot. Walking across the hallway. Arty's hallway.

Delilah glanced down at the floor. Then up at Arty. 'Where is it?'

'What?'

'The reindeer. I put a camera in the reindeer. Where is it?'

'The reindeer? I gave it to Joseph—'

'Christ!' Delilah wheeled round. 'Your dad, Samson. She's in with your dad!'

He was asleep, as she'd known he would be. Slumped over in his armchair. A hefty dose of Rohypnol in his hot chocolate and he'd lost all use of his limbs. And now he was about to get a hefty dose of death.

Ethanol injected into his system. It would look like he'd succumbed to that Christmas melancholy that seized so many alcoholics. Spiced up with another dose of Rohypnol, and no one would be any the wiser. Respiratory depression. Followed by eternal rest.

She reached into her jacket and pulled out a bottle. Whisky. Unscrewing the cap, she crossed the lounge and tilted his head back.

'Good boy,' she said, as his mouth opened obligingly. She tipped up the bottle, pleased to see him swallow. It would make his demise more authentic.

Then she raised the syringe.

'Dad!' Panic searing through him, Samson tore out of the flat. 'Call the police, Arty,' he shouted as he ran down the corridor.

And there she was. Ana Stoyanova, opening his dad's front door. Blonde hair tied up in a ponytail.

She didn't even look round. Just ran inside.

He charged after her, through the doorway, along the hall. Beyond, in the dark lounge, he could just make out two figures struggling. He didn't take time to think. He lunged, bringing both of them crashing to the ground.

In the confusion of limbs, Samson landed badly, the

full weight of a body falling on him, smashing his hip into the floor. He wrenched himself free, his shoulder screaming in pain, and a shoe lashed out, catching him full in the face. Unable to see more than shadows, he rolled over, away from the kicking feet, trying to work out which one was her. But it was impossible to tell. So he grabbed hold of the person nearest to him. It was all he could do in the dark.

'Let me go!' Ana screamed, giving an identity to the writhing figure trying to pull out of his grasp, nails raking at his hand. 'Let me go!'

Relief washed over him. He had her. Ana. He'd caught her. He tightened his grip.

The other figure was up and running, a shifting silhouette heading for the door.

Then the light came on. A harsh blaze of illumination that made him blink. And there was Delilah in the doorway. Ana on the floor. His father – he could see his father slumped in his chair. And trapped between them all, another person.

Vicky Hudson, blonde wig askew and a savage expression on her face.

'Just try it,' said Delilah, the closed laptop in her hand being wielded like a baseball bat, Tolpuddle next to her, teeth bared. 'Nothing would give me greater pleasure.'

25

By one o'clock in the morning – Christmas morning – Fellside Court was returning to normal. The last police car had driven away, the disturbed residents had been reassured that all was well and ushered back to bed, and Joseph O'Brien had been taken to hospital for a check-up.

Most of the apartments had returned to the unlit state they'd been in before the commotion had roused everyone. The apartment that housed Edith Hird and her sister, Clarissa Ralph, wasn't one of them.

Nearly every light in the place was on and burning bright, as though to ward off the evil that had come so close to claiming another one of their friends.

'I can't believe it,' exclaimed Edith. She had a dressing gown pulled tightly over her nightdress and a cup of cocoa in her hands, yet she was shivering. The shock of nearly losing Joseph had really hit her badly.

'None of us can,' said Arty, reaching out to put an arm round her. Rather than shrug it off, the retired headmistress leaned into his embrace. 'She seemed like such a nice young woman.'

'You knew?' Samson turned to Ana, who was sitting with them, a hand resting on Tolpuddle's head.

She grimaced. 'I suspected. Not that it was Vicky. But that something was going on.'

'So you were keeping watch?'

'As much as I could. Which in the end, placed me in danger too, I suppose. In danger of being wrongly accused.' She turned to Arty. 'Thanks for believing in me.'

Arty blushed at the irony. He was still trying to get his head around the events of the last hour. He'd arrived in the doorway of Joseph's flat to see a strange tableau: Samson and Ana Stoyanova lying on the floor, the detective's hand grasping Ana's arm; Joseph unconscious in his chair; and Delilah standing in front of Vicky Hudson brandishing a laptop, Tolpuddle by her side.

'The police are on their way,' he'd stammered, confused as to what was going on; confused as to why the care assistant was there. His words had broken the impasse, Vicky jerking the blonde wig from her head and pointing a finger at Ana.

'She was trying to kill Joseph!' she'd declared defiantly. 'But for me, she would have succeeded.'

Arty sensed Samson's hesitation, unsure of what he'd witnessed. Delilah, too, seemed uncertain, casting an anxious glance at the detective. Then Ana Stoyanova had wrenched her arm free and got to her feet. Samson had jumped up, ready to detain her again, but she'd stepped back from him. Stepped towards the comatose figure of Joseph O'Brien, her green gaze on Samson the entire time.

'Stop her!' Vicky had shouted. 'She's deranged.'

But Ana simply reached out and eased Joseph back against the headrest, her long fingers pushing back his cuff to check his pulse.

'Is an ambulance on its way, too?' she'd asked, glancing over at Arty.

He'd nodded.

Sensing her hold on the situation slipping, Vicky had become more emphatic. 'You have to believe me,' she was insisting. 'That woman needs locking up. I have proof.'

Arty hadn't needed any more proof than was already right in front of him. Ana Stoyanova was tenderly brushing the hair back on Joseph's forehead, an expression of concern on her normally impassive face.

'Proof?' he'd growled, turning on Vicky Hudson. 'How about this for proof?' Using his pyjama sleeve to hold it, he'd pulled Alice Shepherd's pillbox from the pocket of his dressing gown. 'Perhaps you can explain why – apart from Alice's – yours are the only other fingerprints all over this?'

The transformation had been dramatic. Like a cornered rat, Vicky had turned malicious, aiming a stream of vitriol at Ana, blaming her for taking the job that should have been hers. Even blaming the foreigner for necessitating the horrific attacks on the residents of Fellside Court. She'd still been ranting as the police took her away in handcuffs, condemning herself with her malevolence.

'I have to admit,' said Delilah, taking a sip of her cocoa and giving Ana a sheepish look. 'I wasn't sure what to think. For a split second there as the light went on, it was hard to tell who was doing what.'

Samson nodded. 'Yes. Vicky certainly muddied the waters for a few minutes. Confronting her with the pillbox and lying about her fingerprints was a stroke of genius.'

Arty grinned. 'I saw Columbo do the same once. Thought it was worth a try.'

'It certainly was,' said Ana. 'But what made you so sure I was the innocent one? Was that Columbo, too?'

'No,' he muttered, uneasy at being hailed as her defender after all he'd accused her of. 'That was thanks to King Solomon.'

Ana looked puzzled, but Edith was smiling at the bookmaker, nodding her head approvingly.

'I remembered a story from the Bible,' he explained, 'about two women both claiming a baby as their own.'

'A Sunday-school classic,' continued Edith. 'Both were adamant that the baby was their son, so King Solomon told his servant to cut the baby in half in order to settle the dispute.'

'And the woman who immediately offered to give up the baby, rather than have it killed, was identified as the genuine mother,' concluded Samson, recalling his own mother telling him the story many years ago. 'You saw Ana tending to Dad, while Vicky was only concerned with saving her own skin.'

Arty nodded. 'I knew then which one was the real carer. Which one wasn't capable of hurting the people she was charged with looking after.'

'But why?' whispered Clarissa, eyes round from the excitement of the evening. 'Why would Vicky do such awful things?'

'Jealousy,' said Samson. 'She applied for the job as manager here and was passed over in favour of Ana. Full of resentment – especially as Ana was foreign, to boot –

she set out to undermine her. To begin with, she stole things—'

'My headscarf!'

'Yes, and Arty's cufflink.'

'So Alice was right? Her watch really was stolen?' asked Arty.

'I'm ashamed to say that Alice was right about everything,' said Samson. 'Someone really was trying to kill her. And I did nothing to help.'

'None of us did,' said Delilah. 'It sounded so far-fetched.'

'But why put Alice's watch back, then?' asked Edith.

Samson shrugged. 'Vicky was trying to create an uneasy atmosphere. One of suspicion. She was planning to frame Ana for the thefts – an easy target as it turned out, given that the new manager wasn't a local—'

'And wasn't overly friendly,' admitted Ana, with a wry smile.

'But then Vicky's plan escalated into something more lethal. Alice had begun telling people something was going on at Fellside Court. She'd also mentioned that she was thinking of coming to see me. While Vicky wanted to whip up unrest – enough to get Ana sacked – she didn't want the police involved. Or a private detective.'

'So she started messing with Alice's medication?' asked Arty.

'Yes. Alice's dosage had recently been increased. Plus she was getting more confused with age. She was vulnerable and Vicky saw the perfect way to exploit that.'

'And I helped her.' Ana bit her lip, tears in her eyes. 'It was Vicky who gave me the pillbox that day. She said she'd found it on the floor after the aerobics session, and even pointed out that the pills were still inside. I forced Alice to take that extra medication.'

'You're a nurse,' said Samson. 'You know that one extra dose wouldn't have killed her. Until the authorities have carried out a post-mortem – which I'm afraid is unavoidable now, given the circumstances – we can't say how much Alice was over the limit. But I would imagine she was coerced into taking her tablets a lot more than just twice that day – and possibly the day before, too.'

'All thanks to a second pillbox.' Arty shook his head in despair at the simplicity of such a heinous act. 'Poor Alice. She's not even going to be allowed to rest in peace.'

'What about Eric?' asked Clarissa. 'Did Vicky admit trying to kill him, too?'

'Yes,' said Samson. 'She saw the unrest Alice's death had caused and decided to capitalise on it. Eric's illness made him fair game.'

'But thankfully she made a mistake,' said Ana. 'She thought turning off his oxygen supply would be enough. If she'd increased it instead, Eric wouldn't be at home with his family today.'

'Christ!' muttered Arty. 'Eric had a narrow escape.'

'You too,' said Delilah. 'If it hadn't been for Joseph . . .'

Clarissa turned to stare at Arty. 'Vicky tried to kill you?'

'Apparently,' said Arty, with more nonchalance than he felt. It had chilled him to the bone to realise how close to death he'd come, the care assistant bitterly lamenting her missed opportunity as she was taken away by the police. 'But for Joseph staying over the night after Alice's funeral, I probably wouldn't be here.'

'No doubt Vicky would have made it look like heart failure and no one would have questioned it,' added Samson.

Edith shuddered. 'It doesn't bear thinking about. I reckon we all had a narrow escape. Except poor Alice. And Rita . . . Here's hoping poor Rita pulls through.'

'If only she hadn't found that bloody pillbox,' Arty muttered.

He didn't need to ask if that had been the reason for the attack on Rita. He'd heard it with his own ears. The care assistant had seen her uncover the box in the snow – the second box that Vicky had taken from Alice's apartment the morning the old lady died. Planning on retrieving it later, Vicky had dropped it out of the hallway window into the shrubs below. In the commotion that followed, however, she'd not had a chance to go and get it straight away, and when she did get time, the pillbox was no longer there.

She'd accused Rita of stealing it. Of being about to blackmail her. She'd claimed she had no option but to kill her.

Arty felt sick thinking about it.

'What puzzles me is how the pillbox came to be buried in the copse in the first place,' said Samson. 'Who moved it?'

Heads shook around the table. 'Beats me,' said Arty. 'We were all too stunned by the news about Alice to be running around making holes in the ground.'

'Perhaps it was an animal?' suggested Clarissa. 'A squirrel, maybe?'

'It'd have to be a squirrel on steroids,' said Arty. 'It'd take a strong jaw to carry that thing all the way across the courtyard.'

It was the mention of the courtyard. Delilah had a sudden memory of the day of Alice Shepherd's death. Of a chair knocked over. Of muddy paws on her coat. Of a certain animal loping towards them from beneath the trees. An animal that had a penchant for burying things . . .

'A strong jaw,' she hissed, turning to look at Tolpuddle.

Hearing the tone she used when he'd tattered her shoes or bitten a cushion in half, the dog tipped his head sideways, raised an eyebrow and let out a noise between a whimper and a whinny.

'Tolpuddle?' Samson was looking at the dog too, comprehension dawning. 'Oh my God, it was Tolpuddle! He moved the pillbox.'

'And placed Rita in danger,' murmured Delilah, feeling awful.

But Arty was leaning over to rumple the worried dog's ears, the hound instantly repaying him with affection. 'There is another way of looking at it,' he said. 'If Tolpuddle hadn't buried that pillbox, Vicky would still be getting away with her crimes.'

'And Ana would be getting the blame,' said Samson.

'Are you sure she was trying to frame me?' asked Ana.

'Definitely. She knew that some of the residents weren't comfortable with a foreigner in charge. She wanted to take advantage of that, so she started wearing the blonde wig, walking the corridors at night. Doing enough to provoke fear and suspicion, bringing your role as manager into question.'

'And if anyone had carried out a post-mortem on Alice and discovered she'd taken an overdose, everyone had witnessed Ana forcing her to take her medication,' exclaimed Delilah.

'The same goes for the timer on Eric's oxygen machine,' said Edith. 'It was Ana who organised our trip to Morecambe, leaving the field clear for the timer to be fitted. If anyone suspected Eric's collapse was anything but natural, then the finger pointed at Ana.'

'It was a brilliant plan,' agreed Samson. 'Ana was always going to get the blame.'

Arty looked mortified. 'It nearly succeeded,' he said. 'I'm sorry, Ana, for having ever doubted you.'

Ana smiled, a proper smile. 'No need to apologise. Vicky fooled us all.'

'Not you,' Delilah said. 'You saved Joseph's life.'

The syringe. They'd found it under the armchair. And the bottle of whisky and the Rohypnol which had been intended to aid Joseph O'Brien on his way. When Ana had tried to rouse him, it was clear he'd been drugged. She'd also smelt the whisky on his breath, but that wasn't something she'd shared with the others. Wasn't something she planned on sharing, either. She was good at keeping secrets.

'Any later and Dad would have been killed.' Samson ran a hand over his face, shaken by the prospect. 'I can never thank you enough.'

'Actually,' said Ana. 'I think you can. I think all of you

can.' She looked around the table at the two sisters, Arty, Samson and Delilah. 'I think you might know more about me than you're letting on.'

Edith cleared her throat. 'Well, we did come across a bit of information—'

'You're from Serbia,' blurted Arty. 'You lied to us.'

Samson reached into his pocket and placed the two passports on the table.

Ana blushed, a deep pink that seeped from her throat up over her cheeks. Her hands rose to cover her face. 'I'm sorry. I did it for my son.'

'You're here illegally?' asked Edith gently.

'Yes. I didn't have the required points to get a visa as a Serbian. So I borrowed my cousin's passport.'

'Anastasiya Stoyanova. She's your cousin?' Samson flicked to the photo of the young woman whose identity had been borrowed. 'You look so alike.'

Ana nodded. 'We're like twins. Everyone says so. We're both nurses, too. But Anastasiya was born in Bulgaria. Now they are in the EU, she has the right to work in the UK without a visa. As a Serbian, I don't. So my aunt suggested I use Anastasiya's passport.' She dipped her head, ashamed. 'It was easy. No one ever suspected. But living a lie has been terrible.'

'Is that why you moved on from the other jobs in Manchester and Leeds?'

'Yes. I didn't try to work as a nurse. I thought there would be too much scrutiny of my background. So I applied for care work in retirement complexes, like this one. But I got too friendly with the residents in Manchester and slipped up.' She pulled a face. 'I had to leave in a hurry.

Then in Leeds, I got nervous. There were other Bulgarians working for the same agency. They were curious about me. When I saw the job here advertised, it seemed perfect. In the countryside. Probably no one from Bulgaria or Serbia. I applied and when I got the position, I promised myself I wouldn't get involved emotionally. I would keep myself apart and not risk being discovered.'

'It's harder than it seems, isn't it?' said Samson.

Ana smiled. 'Impossible. The best part of my job is the people I care for. It's been awful not allowing myself to interact with them properly.'

Arty leaned over and patted Ana's arm. 'Your secret is safe with us,' he said.

But she was shaking her head. 'No, I'm not asking you to lie for me. There's been enough lying. I decided last week to go home. I handed in my resignation two days ago.'

'You're leaving us?' asked Clarissa.

'Yes. It's ironic. If Vicky had waited, she could have had this job without resorting to such awful crimes.'

'You don't have to do this,' protested Arty. 'We won't say a word.'

'Thanks, Arty. But it's not just about the lying. It's my son, too. I miss him. I need to go home. And who knows, maybe I can come back in the future . . .' She smiled, her eyes filled with devilment. 'Hungary is offering passports to the descendants of the Austro-Hungarian Empire and my family are eligible. So I might come back as a Hungarian.'

Arty laughed. 'We'd be happy to have you here,' he said, a sentiment Edith and her sister endorsed with vigorous nods of the head.

'Now, if you will excuse me, it's time to go to bed.' Ana stood. 'Samson, if you would walk me to my car?'

'Of course,' he said getting to his feet.

Ana bid the group goodnight and followed him out into the corridor. When they reached the ground floor, she paused by the Christmas tree, a hand on his arm.

'I haven't been completely honest,' she said with a small smile.

'About where you're living?' Samson smiled back at her and tipped his head towards the guest suite next door to Rita Wilson's empty flat.

She laughed. 'How did you guess?'

'Arty said something about you arriving on the scene really quickly the night Eric was taken ill, considering you're supposed to live in Hellifield. I never thought anything of it until tonight. You appeared out of nowhere. Our cameras didn't pick you up. And you've been prowling the corridors at all hours. Plus you get your son's letters delivered here and you keep your passport in the office.'

'You really are a good detective,' she said, impressed. 'No wonder Rick Procter is wary of you.'

Samson scowled at the man's name. 'He's right to be.'

Ana nodded. 'Yes. But be careful, Samson. He is not a man to cross. There is something . . .' She struggled for the word. 'Something of the devil about him.'

'Thanks for the warning,' he said. He leaned in and kissed her on the cheek. 'And thanks for saving my father's life.'

'His is a life worth saving,' she said. 'No matter what his history is.' She turned to go and then paused, a cheeky smile cast over her shoulder. 'Oh, and by the way,' she said, with a wink, 'I hear you're supposed to be living in Hellifield, too? Just like me.'

Then Ana Stoyano*vic* walked down the corridor and let herself into the guest suite, leaving Samson thinking about his past. And his future.

26

For Christmas Day at two o'clock in the afternoon, Bruncliffe was unusually busy. Couples, dog-walkers and families were sauntering around the town, lingering to chat in the marketplace, making the most of the mild weather. Making the most of this perfect excuse to hear more about the news that had been rocking the town since the early hours of the morning.

Up on Crag Hill at the back of the town hall, Samson O'Brien was standing outside the brightly lit Spar – the only shop open that day – tapping his foot. With very little sleep in his system following the dramatic events at Fellside Court, and with little enthusiasm for what lay ahead, he wasn't at his most patient.

'Come on, Dad,' he muttered. 'Hurry up.'

'Happy Christmas, Samson!' A uniformed Constable Danny Bradley was walking up the hill towards him, hand already outstretched, a smile on his face. 'I hear you had an eventful evening.'

'That's one way of putting it. You on duty?'

'Just about to start. You're the talk of the station,' Danny said. 'Sarge doesn't know whether to curse you or praise you.'

Samson laughed. Sergeant Clayton wasn't the most dynamic of policemen, and while he was no doubt basking in the reflected glory of having caught a dangerous criminal, he would be grousing at the amount of work the arrest would generate. Today of all days.'

'Sorry,' Samson said. 'It wasn't my plan to ruin anyone's Christmas.'

'Just the opposite,' replied Danny, turning serious. 'You prevented that woman from causing any more hurt. This is a day I won't mind working if it helps put her away.'

'How's it looking? In terms of evidence?'

Danny grinned. 'Good. We found a timer at her flat like the one Ida Capstick saw. If we can get Grandad's DNA off that, it'll take some explaining. The blonde wig has proven a goldmine, too. Fibres off it at all the attack scenes and even in Arty's flat. But the best news is we have a witness. Rita Wilson has regained consciousness and is ready to talk. I'm heading over to the hospital to take a statement.'

'That is good news,' said Samson with relief. 'They wouldn't let us see her when we picked Dad up this morning. I would never have forgiven myself if she hadn't pulled through.'

'Don't go shouldering the blame,' said Danny, with a maturity that belied his youth. 'None of us suspected what was happening over there, and you put a stop to it in the end.' He nodded towards the Spar where Joseph O'Brien was standing at the till, waiting to pay. 'Your dad had a lucky escape.'

'A bit too close for comfort,' said Samson grimly. 'But for Ana Stoyanova—' He broke off as his father emerged from the shop, struck again by the depth of feeling that remained, despite the past. 'At last,' he grumbled, his look of affection at odds with his tone as Joseph approached. 'Thought you were going to be in there all day. Delilah will be waiting for us.'

Joseph smiled, clutching a box of chocolates to his chest, his pallor telling the tale of the evening before. 'We can't turn up for dinner without something as a gift,' he said. 'Happy Christmas, Danny.'

'Same to you, Mr O'Brien. Good to see you out of hospital.'

'They couldn't wait to get shot of him,' muttered Samson. 'He was flirting with all the nurses.'

'Ignore him,' said Joseph to the policeman. 'He's just jealous that he doesn't have my natural charm. How's Eric doing?'

'Good, considering,' said Danny. 'We had to break the news about Vicky Hudson to him, which has shaken him up a bit. I think it was easier for him to blame himself for his accident than accept that he was a victim. Still, he's talking about moving back to his flat in the New Year, so it hasn't put him off being independent.'

'Give him our best. And tell him we're looking forward to him coming home.'

'Will do. Have a lovely day, both of you.'

'Oh, we will,' said Joseph. 'We most certainly will.'

Twenty minutes later, and Samson wasn't sharing his father's conviction about the day ahead. Already running late when they met up with Delilah, Arty and Tolpuddle under the Christmas tree in the marketplace, it had taken an age to get going. It seemed everyone was out for a walk in Bruncliffe that Christmas morning. And everyone wanted to talk about the happenings at Fellside Court.

Samson had let Arty take the stage, pleased to see the bookmaker back on form as he regaled his audience with the dramatic unmasking of Vicky Hudson. The news of Rita's recovery had been warmly received and no one seemed in a hurry to move on. Apart from Delilah, who had become more and more agitated, checking the time repeatedly on her mobile, her jaw clenched.

She was tense. It had been apparent in her driving on the trip back from the hospital, Samson closing his eyes on more than one occasion as they hurtled along the narrow, wall-lined roads. And her mood wasn't helping Samson any.

Christmas with the Metcalfes. While the offer had been a generous one, it wasn't something he felt prepared for, not after the way Will had been treating him for the past few months. He'd already been wondering why he'd been crazy enough to accept. Now Delilah was showing signs of nerves, which meant she wasn't sure about it either.

Samson was on the verge of concocting an excuse to back out when Delilah finally managed to extract Arty and Joseph from the crowd of well-wishers and steer them towards the office, where she'd parked the car. But then Arty spotted the two-door hatchback and her mood went from bad to worse.

'You can't be serious,' he said, as Delilah opened the Micra. 'We're never all going to fit in that.'

Delilah glowered. 'It's either this or walk.'

'Touchy subject,' murmured Samson as he manoeuvred

his bulk into the back seat, Tolpuddle insisting on following him. It left very little room for Arty.

'Move up, you two,' moaned the bookmaker as he wedged himself in. 'And what the hell is that smell?'

'Prize ram,' said Samson, trying not to cough.

'Are you sure you don't want the front seat, son?' asked Joseph, peering in the back at the three squashed shapes.

'I'm certain,' muttered Samson. 'I've had enough of the front seat for one day.'

Joseph got in and Delilah had just started the engine when there was a rapping at the passenger window. Mrs Hargreaves, the butcher's wife. In her arms was an extremely large plastic bag.

'Happy Christmas, everyone,' she said, stepping back slightly as Joseph opened the window and released the ovine odour. 'I heard you were going up to Ellershaw for your meal. Thought you might like to take this. A little something for the table.'

She squeezed the present through the window, the smell of cooked ham pervading the car and mingling with the scent of sheep.

'Thank you,' said Samson, aware of how painful this Christmas must be for her and her husband, following the death of their son only a couple of months ago.

But she was frowning at the car. And the occupants – four adults, a large dog and a huge ham. 'Are you sure that thing will make it up the hill?' she asked. 'Because I don't think—'

'Thanks for the ham, Mrs Hargreaves,' Delilah muttered, before putting her foot on the accelerator and pulling away from the kerb. 'And as for the rest of you,' she said, voice glacial as they drove out of Bruncliffe and towards the fells, 'next one to complain about the transport gets to walk home. That includes you, Tolpuddle.'

The dog wasn't listening. He was too busy concentrating on the delicious smells seeping out of the parcel on Samson's lap. And Samson was too busy worrying about sharing Christmas with the Metcalfes.

Delilah had never felt so nervous about Christmas. A mere twelve hours after she'd finally got to bed following the events at Fellside Court, she was pulling up outside the farmhouse and bracing herself for the biggest row her family had ever known.

'And you're certain this is okay with everyone?' Samson was asking, clinging to the ham as he extricated himself from the back seat of the Micra, trying to wipe the worst of the dog drool off his jacket. Tolpuddle and Arty spilled out of the car after him. 'I mean, three extra mouths to feed on Christmas Day. It's very generous. Not to mention that your oldest brother hates my guts.'

'Calm down, son,' said Joseph. 'Delilah wouldn't have asked us if she hadn't checked with her family first.'

Delilah took a deep breath, panic pushing against her chest at the thought of the Christmas dinner she had invited them all to the day before.

The Christmas dinner invitation that her mother, Peggy, knew nothing about.

The back door opened and Will strode out, Peggy Metcalfe a footstep behind him. Delilah felt her courage fail. This was going to be a disaster.

'Mr O'Brien!' Will was crossing the yard, face serious. Then his hand was stretching out and he was grasping Joseph in a firm handshake. 'Welcome. We're glad you could join us. You too, Mr Robinson. And you, Samson.'

Delilah managed to keep her jaw from dropping, aware of Samson's surprised expression beside her.

'Me too?' Samson had the audacity to ask, as Peggy Metcalfe ushered the older men towards the farmhouse.

Will shot him a look with something that could be described as a smile. 'You too. Rumour has it you cured Clive Knowles' tup of infertility. A farmer would be daft to turn a man with those powers away from his table.'

Samson laughed and slapped Will on the back as a stunned Delilah followed them into the kitchen. Her mother was waiting for her inside the door.

'I'm sorry, Mum,' she whispered. 'I didn't warn you.'

Peggy smiled. 'Lucy told us what you'd done. What a lovely idea, Delilah. Sharing our Christmas dinner with Joseph and Arty is the least we could do after all they've been through.' She drew her daughter into a hug. 'I'm so proud of you. We all are.'

Delilah pulled back, tears threatening to overwhelm her. 'I'll set the table,' she muttered, wiping her eyes on her sleeve and moving across to help Nathan put out the cutlery.

The room was full of people. Will was pouring drinks for the guests. His wife, Alison, was chatting to Delilah's father. Lucy and Ash were over by the oven, talking about the last touches that needed doing to the barn, while preparing the turkey for carving. Delilah's middle brothers,

Craig and Chris, were playing cards with Will's two young children. And Samson . . .

Where was Samson?

He was outside. His mobile phone was pressed to his ear, his back to the window, the ever-faithful Tolpuddle at his heels.

Work? On Christmas Day? Or was it *her*? The mysterious woman with the seductive voice.

A pang of loneliness pierced Delilah's good humour. In the upheaval of the last few days, her concern about the future had been pushed aside. The sight of Samson and Tolpuddle together brought it all rushing back, the prospect of the year to come bleak in the knowledge that she could lose both of them.

Then Samson turned, the call ended and for a brief instant Delilah saw the fear on his face. Stark. Real.

It lasted seconds. Then he was crossing the yard and coming through the back door, a big smile as he joined them, the perfect guest.

Delilah realised she didn't know Samson O'Brien at all. Which was a bit of a worry. Because she also realised that he had completely stolen her heart.

Acknowledgements

In a book bearing the title *Date with Malice*, I'm happy to report that my requests for assistance have been met with nothing but benevolence. I owe the following a pint of Black Sheep in The Fleece:

Firstly, a huge thanks to those who answered my tentative medical questions – both human and animal. None of them shied away from talking murder! To Grace Marshall, doctor-in-training, for fielding queries about COPD with a knowledge that bodes well for the future; Alison Slinn, old friend and brilliant resource, who not only responded to my queries but went even further to offer up other potential scenarios – love your curiosity, Alison!; Catherine Speakman of North West Equine Vets who gave me the okay to have Tolpuddle running again and also regales me with fascinating horse facts while out on our bikes.

Thanks are also due to Kevin Jack, my go-to forensic expert – you're a star, Mr Jack! And to Janet Huck, farmer and neighbour, who didn't bat an eyelid at being blindsided with random questions about tups. Jane Marshall has provided her ever-wonderful support and local colour as well as much needed cups of tea. And my family . . . as always, an amazing source of encouragement and the first people to see my work in the raw.

I also had assistance from some brilliant professionals in

the publishing world. At Pan Macmillan, a special thanks and a sad goodbye to Catherine, an editor who set the bar high – New York is bloomin' lucky to have you! Thanks also to the team who worked with her, including Natalie, Mandy and Fraser – it's a joy working with editors who know their stuff! This book is sharper because of you. Alice also deserves a mention for promoting the series with such enthusiasm – and for being so good at her job. There's a warm welcome too for Victoria, who has taken on the Dales Detective and the world of Bruncliffe in a seamless transition. Finally, as always, I have to acknowledge Oli and all he does to keep me on track.

That's about it. Except for Mark – still here after seven books and all the mayhem writing brings. You deserve a medal. Hopefully you'll settle for that pint of Black Sheep!

DATE WITH DEATH

Murder's no cup of tea . . .

Samson O'Brien has been dismissed from the police force, and returns to his home town of Bruncliffe in the Yorkshire Dales to set up the Dales Detective Agency while he fights to clear his name. However, the people of Bruncliffe aren't so welcoming to a man they see as trouble.

Delilah Metcalfe, meanwhile, is struggling to keep her business, the Dales Dating Agency, afloat – as well as trying to control her wayward Weimaraner dog, Tolpuddle. Then when Samson gets his first case, investigating the supposed suicide of a local man, things take an unexpected turn, and soon he is discovering a trail of deaths that lead back to the door of Delilah's agency.

With suspicion hanging over someone they both care for, the two feuding neighbours soon realise that they need to work together to solve the mystery of the dating deaths. But this is easier said than done . . .

Date with Death, the first in the Dales Detective series, is out now

DATE WITH MYSTERY

The Dales Detective Agency's latest assignment appears to be an open-and-shut case. Hired by solicitor Matty Thistlethwaite, Samson O'Brien is tasked with finding a copy of a death certificate for a young woman who passed away over twenty years ago. But things in Bruncliffe are rarely straightforward. Particularly when Matty insists that Delilah Metcalfe, with her wealth of local knowledge, works alongside Samson on this sensitive investigation.

Beset by financial concerns, Delilah is eager to help. At the very least, the case will take her mind off the custody battle for her precious Weimaraner, Tolpuddle, as well as the looming threat of the bank foreclosing on her struggling Dales Dating Agency.

As Samson and Delilah combine forces yet again, before long they are embroiled in untangling a mystery that has lain at the heart of the town for decades. A mystery that some would prefer remained buried.

Date with Mystery, the third in the Dales Detective series, is coming 2018